# CABBAGETOWN

## THE CLASSIC NOVEL OF THE DEPRESSION IN CANADA

# HUGH GARNER

**McGraw-Hill Ryerson**

Toronto  Montréal  Boston  Burr Ridge, IL  Dubuque, IA  Madison, WI
New York  San Francisco  St. Louis  Bangkok  Bogotá  Caracas  Kuala Lumpur
Lisbon  London  Madrid  Mexico City  Milan  New Delhi  Santiago  Seoul
Singapore  Sydney  Taipei

McGraw-Hill
Ryerson Limited

*A Subsidiary of The **McGraw·Hill** Companies*

Copyright 1950 by Hugh Garner
Copyright © 1968 by Hugh Garner

ISBN: 0-07-091552-0

1234567890 TCP 098765432
Printed and bound in Canada.

**National Library of Canada Cataloguing in Publication**

Garner, Hugh, 1913-1979
Cabbagetown: the classic novel of the depression in Canada / by Hugh Garner.

ISBN 0-07-091552-0

I. Title.

PS8513.A7C32 2002          C813'.54          C2002-902455-2
PR9199.3.G3C32 2002

Publisher: **Joan Homewood**
Editorial Co-ordinator: **Catherine Leek**
Production Co-ordinator: **Sandra Deak**
Electronic Page Design and Composition: **Dianna Little**
Cover Design: **Dianna Little**

*To Alice, Barbara, Carla, Lana and Carrie —*
*the wife, daughter, daughter-in-law and*
*granddaughters in my life.*

# Author's Preface
# to the 1968 Edition

Toronto's Cabbagetown remains only a memory to those of us who lived in it when it was a slum. Less than half a mile long and even narrower from north to south, it was situated in the east-central part of the city, its boundaries being Parliament Street on the west, Gerrard Street on the north, the Don River on the east and Queen Street on the south. The slum area south of Queen Street was once called Corktown and was inhabited by Irish Catholic immigrants. To the west of Parliament Street was and is Moss Park, a neighbourhood now the temporary home or lighting place of a more transient type of slum-dweller. This neighbourhood is sometimes referred to as Cabbagetown, as is the area north of Gerrard Street, but this is an error.

This continent's slums have been the living quarters of many immigrant and ethnic poor: Negro, Mexican, Jew, Indian, Italian, Irish, Central European and Puerto Rican. The French Canadians have their Saint-Henri in Montreal and Saint-Sauveur in Quebec. Cabbagetown, before 1940, was the home of the social majority, white Protestant English and Scots. It was a sociological phenomenon, the largest Anglo-Saxon slum in North America.

Following World War II most of Cabbagetown was bull-dozed to the ground, and its remaining inhabitants moved into the Regent Park projects, which are government-built-and-controlled apartment blocks, maisonettes and row housing, erected where the slum streets, lanes and alleys had once stood.

Contrary to uninformed and malicious public opinion at the time, there were no substantiated instances of rehabilitated slum-dwellers storing their coal in their new unaccustomed-to bathtubs; stove coal had disappeared along with the Cabbagetown big black kitchen stoves. The new housing was a godsend to the ex-Cabbagetowners, a relief to the police force and a welcome change to the district fire-fighters. The social agencies now had fewer calls, and the charities fewer local recipients. The new generations of Cabbagetowners had money and jobs, which most of those who came before them had not.

Strangely, one thing didn't change. At the beginning, the new houses and apartments continued to favour the lace curtain over the ubiquitous window drape, and it was one of the last neighbour-hoods in the city to change. Another habit that lingered on was that of many of its women, who went around all day with their hair in curlers, sometimes covered with a scarf. These were umbilical ties with the Cabbagetown that had gone.

But perhaps Ken Tilling would have said, "Talking like that borders on the sentimental, and nobody should get eulogistic over a slum."

*Hugh Garner, 1968*

# Contents

# BOOK ONE

# GENESIS

## MARCH 1929—JUNE 1932

"Goodbye, Tilling, and good luck," said the principal, Mr. J. K. Cornish, proffering his hand. "Today is the big day in your life. You are going out into society—into business—into the business world, and from now on it is up to you. I hope you will retain pleasant memories of your association with us here, and that you will—er—curb your, shall we say spirits?" He smiled wanly. Then concluded hurriedly, "Goodbye, my boy!"

When Ken Tilling reached the corner below the school he turned and gazed for a short instant at the quasi-Gothic technical high school he was leaving for the last time. He took his hand from his right trouser pocket and almost without conscious effort raised it thumb to nose and wiggled his fingers disdainfully. This ritual completed, he hurried down the street, his shoes slurping in the soft slush.

The day was cold, with the penetrating dampness of a Toronto March day. The dirty snow on the streets had taken on the wet consistency of watered porridge, held to its solution by the contrary efforts of the warming sun and the freezing wind. Despite the season the boy was wearing a pair of thin unpressed gray flannel "bags" and a worn cotton-and-wool windbreaker. On his feet were a pair of shoes quite serviceable in dry weather but inappropriate for a long walk through the wet slush.

He was thinking of many things this morning: of what old Cornish had said about the curbing of his spirit, of the school, of the kind of job he was likely to find. He remembered his pride three years before when he had first entered the high school, happy to leave the crowded neighbourhood public school to become a student at the big Tech, among the pupils from all over the east end of the city. He had believed somehow that the school would release him from his shabby district and even shabbier home and make him a belonging part of its cleanliness and comradeship and happier life. It had not done this. The failure was not so much that of the school, or of his fellow students, as it was his own. The contrasts between his life inside and outside its association were too great to be bridged so easily.

Almost immediately he had run head-on into social consciousness and snobbery. The socio-economic divisions erected in a class of forty boys, and in the school as a whole, were of fine complexity but nevertheless clearly marked. He was bitter at his after-school delivery job keeping him from sports and dramatics, and of having to refuse party invitations because of his shabby clothes. He had remained an outsider from the cliques revolving around athletics, the school magazine, the auditorium stage, the possession of a Model T Ford—

But now all this was past. Tomorrow he would get a job, and the money he earned would give him equality with those among whom he had not been equal before. Getting a job was an easy step in the early months of 1929. Business and employment were climbing to unprecedented heights. Columns of help-wanted ads beckoned to anyone able and willing to work. The store windows were full of the retail manifestations of prosperity: bright yellow square-toed shoes to be worn at Easter, new gray suits, the cumbersome polished shells containing the new wonder of radio. Everywhere were new clothes, iceless refrigerators, Rudy Vallee records, banjo-ukeleles, bridge lamps, imported English prams, homebrewing supplies, the new Model A Ford, Amos 'n Andy's pictures, sporty-looking Chevrolets.

The boy halted and weighed himself on a free-weigh scale in front of a herbalist's shop. The needle climbed reluctantly and stopped at 109 pounds. The rise was slow, but he was gaining.

He jumped from the scale and pressed his nose against the herbalist's window, glad to be sheltered for a moment from the biting wind. In a stout wire cage a somnambulant Gila lizard tried half-heartedly to free itself from its prison. Arranged on serried rows of plates were small piles of dull-colored herbs. In the corner of the window stood a lithograph of a sexless human body, with small    elevators carrying food down the shaft of its esophagus to the waiting machinery of a bilious looking stomach.

The sight of the imprisoned lizard reminded him of his new-found freedom, and he watched it until his sorrow for the poor creature was overwhelmed by the returning awareness of his own escape. He smiled to himself at the knowledge that his long years of schooling were at an end.

He left the herbalist's window and strode along against the wind, warming himself with happy memories of earlier years. His running out from the movie house on Saturday afternoons, pretending he was the hero of the Western saga he had seen. Rushing down the street holding a pair of imaginary reins while beating at his rump with his other hand, shouting, "I'm Art Acord!" or Harry Carey or Hoot Gibson. The other members of his gang would be galloping beside him, also shouting or arguing, as they rode their cayuses with a wild exuberance which transported them from the mean streets to the arroyos and mesas of the fabled West.

Becoming tired of walking in the slush and cold he waited until a bread wagon passed, drawn by a trotting horse. He bounded from the sidewalk and seated himself on the back step, out of sight of the driver. Hooking his arms through the uprights from the step he watched the long rows of stores slip by.

When his conveyance turned off from the direction he was going he jumped off and began walking again. In signs, posters and on billboards, everywhere he looked was the beckoning finger of opportunity. LEARN BRICKLAYING. *Men Wanted.* WHAT MAKES YOU THINK YOU CAN'T SELL? *Mr. Roy Kirk of Philadelphia reports:* "In my first week selling the

Dirt Lifter vacuum cleaner I cleaned up $175.00—in my spare time!" *Every day in every way I am getting better and better! Fit yourself for the expanding vistas ahead*—LET I.C.S. SHOW YOU HOW! *Pellmanism.* TRADE IT IN! *Be A Radio Technician.* MONEY FOR THOSE WHO WANT TO EARN IT. *Don't just keep up with, but get ahead of the Joneses!*

He met a boy from his class who had left school the month before. The boy asked him, "How's old Cornish these days? Is he still as goofy as ever?"

"Yeah," answered Ken. "He gave me a speech about how I was going into the business world, and crap like that."

"Did you just quit school today?" asked the boy as they hurried along.

"Yeah. I got away at last. I'm sixteen today."

"Where you going to work?"

"I dunno yet."

"Why don't you come down to the telegraph office, they need messengers, I'm on nights now. I make about fifteen dollars a week," the boy said. "It's not a bad job."

"You need a bike though," said Ken. "I haven't got one."

"That's nothing, you can get one easy, on time."

"I'll think it over."

"Well, I have to go in here and get some meat pies for dinner," said the boy. "So-long."

Ken turned south from the long shopping street, cut through a big public park, crossed a footbridge over the Don River, and climbed the hill from the natural amphitheatre into Cabbagetown. The houses were smaller now, and dingier. Some windows held ROOM TO LET signs, and in one dazzlingly white-lace-curtained window was a crudely lettered sign reading, CURTAINS WASHED AND STRETCHED. The scattered neighbourhood stores were also smaller, with careless window displays. Shoe repair shops, dirty little grocery stores, broken biscuits, Salvation Army salvage store, taffy apples, tinsmith's supplies, used clothing; second-hand, third-rate, the purveyors to the poor—

He was now in familiar territory. This was his neighbourhood, dotted with the homes of his neighbours and friends. The street names greeted him with long-known familiarity—Sackville, Parliament, Taylor, Oak, Sumach, Sydenham—old names given to them at their christening when the area was a suburb of a much younger city. Now that they too were old they wore their aristocratic-cum-sylvan names like a harridan with flowers on her hat—jaunty, past caring, but clinging to something that was part of what might have been.

A few houses on almost every street were as verminous and tumbledown as any in the city, but next door or across the street was the same type of house, clean and in good repair, reflecting the decency or pride of its occupants, or reflecting the fact that the tenant was buying it. In 1929 most Cabbagetowners rented their houses, from the ingrained habit of generations or because they refused to tie themselves down forever in the district. This was a neighbourhood almost without tenements, and the streets were lined with single-family houses, many of whose upper stories accommodated a second family.

The citizens of Cabbagetown believed in God, the Royal Family, the Conservative Party and private enterprise. They were suspicious and a little condescending towards all heathen religions, higher education, "foreigners" and social reformers. They were generally unskilled working people, among whom were scattered, like raisins in a ten-cent cake, representatives of the State—such as postmen, civic employees, streetcar conductors and even a policeman or two.

As Ken hurried south towards his own street he became conscious of the increase in sound. There were more children shouting and crying, more traffic on the narrow streets, more raucous pedlars, and above all this the constant noise of the factories, the whir of machinery, the clang of metal on metal, the increased noise of streetcars on their older roadbeds.

The smells were also different. Coal smoke, chemicals, horse manure, wet mattresses, old wallpaper and dirty snow. As he passed the open windows of a mill he caught the smell of hot metal curling from the lathes. But the prevailing smell was one of decay, of old wet plaster and rotting wooden steps, the smell of a landlord's carelessness and neglect.

He turned off Sumach Street into a narrow alley whose broken street sign read, TIMOTHY PLACE. Beyond the sign was a short strip of broken pavement on each side of which stood facing blocks of narrow undivided red brick houses, their only signs of separateness being their vari-painted wooden doors and individual "parlour" windows.

Above each single lower window was a smaller replica of itself opening into the front bedroom. The undivided rows of houses were cut by thin interior walls into five separate dwellings, making a total of ten houses on Timothy Place. From each front door a small flight of rickety wooden steps ran down to the sidewalk; next to each set of steps was a grimy cellar window. These windows had once contained glass panes but now, with two or three exceptions, they were boarded up with wood or cardboard. The short street ended against a high unpainted wooden fence, behind which could be seen the upper floors of a printing-ink factory.

Ken crossed the street to the south side and along the broken sidewalk to the third wooden door. A lopsided figure 5 which he had cut out in tinsmithing class whispered its number. He opened the door and entered the house.

The house was cold, and he shivered as he took off his windbreaker and hung it on a nail behind the front door. From the dirty linoleum of the hallway he picked up a letter. On the envelope was the name of a credit clothing firm and it was addressed to his mother, Mrs. Mabel Tilling. He carried it into the small middle room.

He called out, "Ma!" but there was no answer, so he shoved his way past the big old sideboard into the kitchen. After he shook the fire he moved a dry half-loaf of bread and an empty milk bottle to the back of the table and with a damp cloth wiped off the crumbs, tea spots and ketchup stains. Then he rinsed out a cup under the sink's one tap and dried it on a dishtowel made from an old sugar sack. When the fire was red he poured some coke onto it from a pail beneath the stove.

Returning to the middle room he looked into the sideboard cupboard for something to eat. A plate held four sausages congealed in their grease, and he carried them along with the butter dish into the kitchen. When the kettle boiled he made his tea. Placing a slice of buttered bread on a plate, he poured the sausages and grease over it and sat down hungrily to eat his dinner.

When he finished his skimpy meal he went into the front room and picked up some schoolbooks from the top of the bare dresser and began turning over their pages. On the flyleaf of the second book he picked up was his name in large awkward letters, *Kenneth Tilling, 1926* and, rather uselessly he thought, underneath it were the words, *If my name you wish to see, turn to page 103.* He turned the pages as ordered and smiled as he read, *If my name you miss, turn to sixty-six.* It doesn't even rhyme, he thought, laughing at his thirteen-year-old folly. Turning back to page sixty-six he was rewarded with the cryptic admonition, *If my name is lacking, dip it in shoe blacking,* as if he had wearied of the game almost as soon as he had started it.

That was the way he had always been. Get an idea, let it race away with him, plunge into it with both feet, be almost mad with the joy of it—but then stop before it was finished and go on to something else.

Picking up his physics and chemistry notebook he turned the looseleaf pages slowly, proud of their cleanliness and neatness. A question at the top of a page asked him, Has air weight? Who cares, he asked himself, staring down at the shaky drawing of a pair of chemical balances and a blown-up balloon. He threw the books aside and lay down on the couch, revelling in his new freedom from such inanities.

During the afternoon he kept the fire going and swept the main debris from the kitchen floor. He read some stories in a coverless copy of a detective magazine, searching for ones with a sexual content but, as always, disappointed at the scarcity of actual sexual behaviour. The house warmed up towards supper time, and he pulled the green blinds on the downstairs windows and turned on the light in the kitchen. He heard the front door open and the sound of the evening paper being dropped into the hall. He hurried to pick it up and carried it back to the kitchen, opening it at the comics. After reading every comic he leafed through the rest of the paper, giving only a perfuntory glance at the sport pages, and finally found what he was looking for, the HELP WANTED—MALE columns of the classified ads. He began reading one of them from the top.

*Boy wanted for bicycle delivery. Boy to learn Hoffman pressing. Boys with bicycles for chain groceteria. Boy or young man with senior matriculation for insurance office. Boy interested in photography. Capable boy for light factory work* . . . His eye ran down the column until he found what he was searching for. *Do you want a future with our firm? Bright intelligent boy wanted for wholesale merchandising corporation; small salary to start but promotion assured; excellent opportunity for right boy with ambition, no others need apply.* He tore the ad out and placed it in his pocket. He had ambition, he was bright. This was the job for him.

When he heard his mother enter the front door he pushed the kettle on to a stove lid over the fire and went to see what she had brought for supper.

"Hello, Ken, are you home? My goodness it's getting cold out. I'll bet we have more snow before morning. I see Mrs. Wells is out of the hospital. I'm glad you kept the stove going." All this in a flat monotone as she placed her string shopping bag on the table and took off her coat.

"Is there any mail?" she asked, puffing as she warmed her hands over the stove.

"Only this," her son answered, showing her the letter he had picked up in the hall.

"Humph!" she snorted as she read the name on the envelope. "I've a good mind to let them wait." Then turning to him she said, "Look in that bag there, there's some macaroni and a can of peas. Put them on the stove."

After reading the creditor's letter she tore it into small pieces and threw them into the coal bucket. Then she moved her heavy bulk around the kitchen, placing the supper things on the table. From under the brown knot of her hair a few stray wisps fell around her ears, and she tucked them up with her fingers.

With the spring Cabbagetown came outdoors again, and the streets were alive in the evenings with the noise of children. The little girls began their skipping, afraid as yet to do Double Dutches or Salt, Vinegar, Peppers, content to start again with the old single slow-moving ropes.

On Myrtle Street a man placed four heavy pine stakes around his hankie-sized lawn and pulled taut a piece of light wire to keep the children off the new-sown grass. On Upland Street four boys were playing bicycle polo, their crude mallets aimed at an indiarubber ball, and threatening with every swing to tangle themselves in their opponents' wheel spokes. In the public schoolyard a softball game was in progress before a noisy juvenile audience, while a few men leaned on the wire fence and watched the game. Two young men in shirtsleeves were peering under the hood of an old car. One of them had a long screwdriver in his hand and he was arguing and making gestures as he pointed with it at the engine.

In Timothy Place Mrs. Wells, who lived at No. 7, was holding forth to an audience of two other women about the price of foodstuffs, potatoes in particular. "How them buggers expects us to live with them kind of prices, I don't know. A few years ago you could have got three pecks for that money." One of the women turned and chased her little girl into the house before Mrs. Wells really got started on her blasphemous tirade. The other woman, small, tired looking, and wearing a long black skirt and buttoned boots, was nodding as she tried unsuccessfully to get a word in.

Some little boys were threatening to jump into the girls' skipping rope, and the girls were screeching and attempting without success to grab them and push them away. The Gaffey's simple-minded son sat on his front steps, smiling vacantly at the children. His clothes were clean and neatly pressed, and his thin blue-veined hands clutched at his knees as if with sudden pain or effort, while his over-sized head rolled on his shoulders.

At the corner a group of boys and older youths lolled against an empty store-front, smoking cigarettes and testing their new-found strength against each other—the bigger boys grabbing the younger ones and twisting their arms to make them cry "Uncle!" or trying to trip one another to the sidewalk. A fruit pedlar getting rid of the last of his stock came slowly up the street, noticed the gang of boys, and mounted his wagon and drove by as quickly as his old horse could take him.

In No. 5 Timothy Place Ken Tilling bathed himself carefully in the washtub in his mother's upstairs bedroom. He had been busy since supper, shining his shoes, ironing his brown necktie and fixing a hole in the heel of a sock.

After his bath, as he carried the dirty water from the tub to the toilet, he was thinking ahead to the evening's party. He bad been invited by Billy Addington, a boy who worked with him. The party was to be held at the house of a girl named Myrla Patson who lived a few blocks away on Butt street. He was always nervous about going to parties, ashamed of his clothes and wondering whether the mend in the heel of his sock would show. He was afraid too of being left unnoticed in a corner, or that the others would leave him out of the fun. Though these fears had never been warranted, he could never shake them.

Since starting work at McDonald's Wholesale Grocers earlier in the spring he had managed out of the dollar he kept from his six-dollar salary to buy some underwear and two new ties. These meagre purchases made him feel a little more able to go out and mix with young people other than those who lived in Timothy Place.

He was ready an hour before Billy Addington had promised to call, and be spent most of the time peering into the mirror, straightening his tie and surveying his black hair which he brushed flat and parted in the middle following the latest "sheik" mode. In the dim light from the window he smiled at his reflection, noticing with immodest pride his good white front teeth. He stuck out his chin and held a silent conversation with his image, which smiled back at him and looked quizzical, surprised or angry in return.

When Billy finally knocked on the front door he gave his tie a final straightening and hurried to answer it. Together they walked down the street, passing carefully around a game of hopscotch, in the direction of the corner.

Billy Addington was a thin boy, taller than Ken, but about the same age. He lived not far away, and they had been classmates in public school. He had been working at McDonald's Wholesale since the previous fall.

The gang of boys were still standing around the empty store. When they spied the two resplendent youths they gave out with derisive whoops. "Catch me, Clarence! Take my hand, Algernon! Where's the suits going with the boys?" The two intrepid party-goers ignored their taunts and hurried up the street, their faces red, ashamed to be caught dressed-up on a weekday night.

When they reached Butt Street they went a short distance along it and hurried up the walk of a small detached house. A middle-aged woman answered their knock and invited them in.

"This is Ken Tilling, Mrs. Patson," said Billy, shoving Ken forward.

"Hello," said the woman. "It's early yet, but some of the others are in the front room." She smiled as she looked at Ken, and her Scots accent sounded pleasant to his ear.

The two boys moved from the small hallway into the dining

room, and glanced into the parlour where three or four girls and one boy were sitting on the sofa and on matching chairs.

"Go on in and find yourselves somewhere to sit," Mrs. Patson said, pushing the boys forward. They found seats, Billy on the piano bench and Ken on a wooden kitchen chair in a corner. Billy knew the other fellow, and he introduced him to Ken as Gordon something-or-other. Gordon then introduced the boys quickly to the girls in the room.

After the introductions the girls sat in silence, straightening their starched cotton party dresses, their eyes flitting self-consciously around the room as they avoided each other's glances. When the three boys began talking about King Street United Church's baseball team, the girls, not to be outdone, passed polite comments among themselves about the house and the girl whose party it was.

On the wall opposite to where Ken was sitting was a hand-painted photograph of a couple in their wedding clothes, the groom standing behind the bride, clutching her shoulder with a possessive hand. To the picture's left hung an intricate scroll-like piece of fretwork, while to its right was a framed marriage certificate with an arch-of-roses motif and the names of the principals and participants written in flowing calligraphy.

Ken looked the girls over. With one exception they were fifteen or sixteen years old, small and thin with the mean, pinched look of the undernourished poor. The one exception was an older girl in her late teens, whose overweight figure was topped by a round mean face that bore the pallor of illness. All the girls wore clean cheap dresses and cotton or lisle stockings that did not quite fit their ankles above their pathetic little shoes.

When more young people arrived they were greeted by their friends as they came in, and took up places around the fringes of the two rooms. The boys were unnaturally quiet and whispered among themselves, while the girls laughed too much and left in pairs to go upstairs to the bathroom. Mrs. Patson hurried around getting chairs for the new arrivals and chasing her smaller children back into the kitchen. Ken noticed that most of the guests had brought small paper-wrapped presents, and he fingered the sixty cents in his pocket guiltily and asked Billy why he hadn't mentioned bringing a birthday present.

"Aw ya don't need to, they won't know the difference," Billy assured him.

It failed to reassure Ken, who stuck his empty hands into his pants pockets out of sight.

A boy moved Billy from the piano bench and sat down, playing "Walking My Baby Back Home." He had an easy assurance which was not common in Cabbagetown among boys his age and he played beautifully. Ken stared in fascination as his clean strong hands brushed the yellowing keys.

The young people now crowded around the piano, the girls singing and some of the boys circling their shoulders with their arms as they pressed into the group. When the piano stopped those standing around it turned their heads to the doorway. Ken looked over and saw a pretty girl about his own age enter the room.

One of the other girls presented her as Myrla Patson to those who did not know her, and she circled the room smiling and shaking their hands. Most handed her the gifts they had brought, which she juggled in the crook of her arm, thanking them for their "Many happy returns of the day, Myrla." The boy began playing the piano again, this time "All Alone by the Telephone," as the young hostess and most of the girls moved into the small dining room. From the knot of girls clustered around the heavy dining-room table came little gasps of delight as each present was opened.

Ken lost sight of Myrla then, but he retained the sight of her as she had looked at him and smiled. He was convinced he had never seen a more beautiful girl. She had long jet-black hair surrounding a pert little face whose small perfect features and tiny bloodless ears were destined to remain in his memory for ever. The only flaw in her beauty was her small thin mouth that, even then, he realized might become bitter and shrewish with age. But what did he care? He couldn't keep himself from staring at her when she finally came out of the huddle at the table. He wanted so much to speak to her, but didn't know how, having to fight both his timidity and the feeling of his own insignificance.

After the presents had been put away they played such parlour games as Forfeits and Spin-The-Bottle. The crowd became noisier as the young people lost their shyness in the laughter and the fun. Someone said, "Let's play Postman!" and others took up the shout. Ken's shyness and feeling of inferiority suddenly made him vociferous and he began shouting, "Postman, Postman, who says Postman?" Soon everybody wanted to play, and Ken ran around whispering their number into the players' ears.

His own number was called sometime later, and he entered the hallway, closing the dining room door behind him. The sickly-looking fat girl he had noticed when he and Billy had arrived was waiting against the vestibule door. She was older than he was, and she took him in her arms expertly, tongue-kissing him long and hungrily. It was the first time he had "French kissed," and he opened his mouth too wide. His partner pressed up on his chin with her hand, at the same time pressing her heavy legs tight against his own. When they finished she smiled at him and gave his hand a conspiratorial squeeze before asking him what number he wanted.

He had remembered the number he had given Myrla and gave it to the girl, who passed it on to the doorkeeper. In a moment or two Myrla came into the hallway, smiling at him as she closed the door behind her. He took her gently into his arms and pressed his closed lips against hers. The smell of her face, her hair, the starched cleanliness of her clothes and the feel of her small breasts against his skinny chest made him forget everything but the moment. Her arm tightened around his neck and her lips parted beneath his. As he felt her probing tongue on his teeth he swallowed a sigh and dug his hand into her back. The party noises from the dining room and parlour became a humming in his ears.

Finally she pushed him away from her, her eyes lowered to the floor. He stumbled to the door and as he opened it looked back at her, the light from the dining room shining on her face. Her lips were turned down in a grimace of either disappointment or pity, but immediately she smiled at him, and he groped his way to an empty chair.

He was in love. Let the pedants scoff and call it "puppy love." Let everyone deride him and warn him and say, "I told you so," years later when it had become a metal taste on the tongue. Let them feel a condescending pity for a sixteen-year-old boy who kissed a pretty girl at a party and fell in love with her. Such loves are not always the lasting loves, but they are the great ones when you are young and silly and new to the game. And the one you love is beautiful and wonderful and without guile or evil. Then years later when you see your first love again and cannot recall why you ever loved her, perhaps it is not because you never did but because you loved her too well.

The game of Postman came to an end, and the girls passed around sandwiches and cups of tea. The party now broke up into small huddles scattered through the two rooms.

Ken found himself sitting beside the piano player, whose name he had learned was Theodore East. He was a year younger than Ken, but was in third form at a commercial high school, where he was specializing in accounting and bookkeeping. He was leaving school when he was sixteen.

"You sure can play the piano," said Ken with admiration.

"I don't do bad I guess. I've been taking lessons since I was eight years old." Ken noticed that his voice was low and his speech more careful than most of the neighbourhood boys' was.

"Do you live around here?" Ken asked.

"Yes. Over on Myrtle Street. We're going to move soon though;

my father wants to sell the house. I wish we'd move soon, this district gets worse every year. And now the foreigners are moving in."

They mentioned different fellows and girls they both knew, but soon Theodore carried his cup and saucer into the kitchen. Some of the girls paired off with boys on the sofa and chairs, and two girls danced together very soberly, humming their own accompaniment.

Ken strolled into the kitchen and filled a glass with water at the sink. Theodore was standing near the big coal stove talking to Mr. Patson. This innocent little tableau angered Ken for some reason, as if he resented Theodore's easy familiarity with Myrla's father. He felt, unreasonably, that the boy was an interloper who was trying to come between Myrla and himself. How the East boy could talk so unabashedly to Myrla's father, or to any other member of her family as far as that went, both puzzled him and filled him with envy.

When he left the kitchen he searched for the girl while pretending a vital interest in the two girls dancing in the middle of the floor. Myrla was not anywhere in the downstairs part of the house. A stab of jealousy caught at his belly when he pictured her out on the front porch or upstairs with another young man. He leaned against the wall in pretended nonchalance watching the dancers.

Before the party ended Myrla entered the dining room from the hallway and walked into the parlour. Ken kept his face on the dancers but followed her every move from the corner of his eye. From then on he avoided any face-to-face meeting, but instead sulked, feeling slighted, jealous, hurt and sometimes perversely happy in his pointed ignoring of her.

Myrla disappeared into the hallway to bid goodnight to those who were leaving. Billy Addington came over to Ken and said, "Come on, Ken, let's go."

"Holy smoke, don't be in such a hurry. There's still people here."

Soon however most of the others had left, so Ken and Billy said their goodnights to Mr. and Mrs. Patson in the kitchen and went into the hallway. Myrla opened the front door for them and bid them a smiling goodnight. Ken tried to say something which would stop her forgetting him, but whatever it was it stuck in his throat and he became confused and stuttering.

"Never mind your goodbyes then," Myrla said to him, an amused look on her face. "We'll see each other again."

"Sure, sure, oh you bet!" he mumbled, almost running down the front walk to catch up to Billy.

The girl stood for a minute at the open door, watching the boys until they turned out of the street. Then wearing a puzzled frown she shut the door and went inside the house.

After her guests were gone Myrla Patson sat in the kitchen and along with her father and mother ate the sandwiches left over from the party.

George Patson sat quietly in a chair against the table and listened to his wife and daughter discussing the party and the guests. Now and again he reached across to the rapidly diminishing plate of salmon sandwiches and took one, looking it over first before biting into it, chewing slowly.

He was a slightly built Scotsman about forty years of age. Before the war he and his young wife Bertha had emigrated to Canada from a small Lowlands town. Neither of them knew exactly what had drawn them to Canada, but both remembered the colourful posters depicting its wonders and enticements. They had first intended going out to Saskatchewan to homestead, but their first baby had been born to Bertha in the Immigration Building in Quebec City. The young woman had finished her confinement in a Salvation Army home there, and by the time she and the baby were released George, spurred by some glowing tales he had heard, and rather apprehensive of the far-away prairies, had made up his mind to settle in Toronto.

Bertha named her baby girl Myrla after a woman who had befriended her on the ship coming over. George had found a job on their arrival in Toronto, and bit by bit they had gathered together new and second-hand furniture pieces to replace the trunks and orange crates that had served them, along with a mattress on the floor, following their arrival. During the war George worked in a munitions plant, and in 1919 had settled down into the job he still held in a silverware company.

"Where did Olive get that blue dress I wonder?" Bertha asked. Then answering herself she said, "I'll bet it's one of her sister Blanche's cut down."

"No it's not, Ma. She bought it down at Eaton's last week," answered her daughter. "Georgina got one too, only it was beige."

"The boy that played the piano was nice—he had nice manners," said Bertha, choosing a sandwich between noisy sips of her tea. "His father works for the telephone company, and he says they're going to move soon to the Danforth. A job with the telephone company's a good paying job," she continued, glancing at George. "And what's more, it's steady," she finished, getting in her dig.

"Is that meant for me?" asked her husband, gesturing with a half-eaten sandwich. "So what if it's steady? Don't I provide for you, have you ever gone hungry?" He stared from one to the other belligerently. "Steady jobs, that's all I ever hear around here. Maybe you'd like me to quit the one I've got now, then you'd be happy?"

Bertha, not to be put down by his sophistry, picked up her cup and spoke across its rim, "If you thought as much about a steady job as you do of your painting—painting?—'daubings' my mother called them—you'd get a job where you wouldn't be laid off all the time. But no, you'd sooner go up the Don Valley and paint pictures, and me left with cold suppers—"

"Ma—Dad! For goodness sakes shut up about that stuff! Every night it's the same thing, and I'm getting sick of it," Myrla said.

"You keep out of this, Miss or—" began George.

"Leave her alone, after all it's her birthday," said her mother.

There was a silence broken only by the chink of cups in saucers. Then a voice cried out from upstairs, "Ma, can I have a drink of water?"

"No! Go to sleep, Donnie, or I'll come up and lay a strap across your bottom!" shouted Bertha, looking towards the hall stairway. George got up from the table, filled a tumbler with water at the sink and left the kitchen.

"Georgina looks nice with her hair cut," Bertha said, dismissing her departed husband and the former argument from the conversation.

"She had it done downtown," answered her daughter. "There's a new barber shop and beauty parlour for women opened on Yonge street. Margaret, that's the new girl I was telling you about at work, has hers done there too. They say it's better than going into a barber's full of men, even if they do put up a curtain in front of the chair."

"You should have your hair cut for the summer," Bertha went on. "You know how you suffered last year. But don't ever let me hear of you going to Leeko's barber shop, young lady; he gets fresh with all the girls. Mrs. Sundstrum says he tried to get familiar with her."

"Oh, Ma, not Mrs. Sundstrum! My God, she must be forty!" Myrla exclaimed, laughing at the thought.

"Forty? Forty isn't old, my girl. Wait till you're forty, you'll think you're in the prime of life."

"I'll never see forty," said Myrla unconcernedly. "I'm to live a short fast happy life."

"That's what they all say when they're as young as you," said Bertha. She got up and turned down the damper on the coal range and tried all the taps on the gas stove. "Don't worry you'll marry some young man and have three or four kids. God knows you won't have it so hard as I did, what with all the electrical things they've got today. But when you do get married make sure your husband has a good steady job. Marry one that works for the city or the street railway or something."

Myrla took off her stockings and hung them over the back of a chair, then practised a high kick.

"Watch the clothesline!" her mother warned.

"Those gloves are nice that Tom Moffat gave me, ain't they?"

"It's a funny time of year to give gloves," her mother answered.

"They'll be good next winter anyway," Myrla said. "Let's see, I got four pairs of stockings—no, five—and a necklace, and the gloves, and the purse from you and Dad—I guess that's all. I wish it was my birthday every day."

"What did the Addington boy bring you?" asked Bertha.

"Nothing I guess. I didn't expect anything from him; I hardly know him."

"Who was the other boy he brought with him, the short one? He's a fly one. Somehow I don't trust him."

"Who, Ken Tilling? I never seen him before, but I think he's cute. Betty told me in the toilet that his mother's always drunk."

"Cute!" exclaimed Bertha fixing on the word. "He's cute all right. I don't care about his mother; there's lots of them drunk around here, and the Lord knows you can't blame the young 'uns for their parents." Then coming back to her favourite theme she asked, "Has he got a job?"

"How do I know? I told you I never seen him before."

"You get a boy friend from across the Don river somewheres. Don't you go wasting yourself on any of the boys around here," said Bertha.

"Jeez, Ma, I'm not going around with him! I just said I thought he was cute. And anyways, across the river's not much; they're just as poor as we are." Myrla stretched her arms above her head. "I'm going to bed. We're beginning stock-taking tomorrow."

"Don't be as hard to get up as you were this morning then," said her mother. "Are you going to leave your stockings there?"

Myrla picked up her stockings and shoes and went upstairs.

Bertha sighed and began piling the dishes in the sink. Myrla was older now, and she was afraid. At times she wished her daughter was still a baby. Another year or so and she'd begin going and coming as she pleased. Bertha's fondest hope was that she'd get married young and settle down, as she herself had done, before life could twist and hurt her. At times she saw things in her daughter's eyes that should not be seen in the eyes of a sixteen-year-old girl. She sighed again and poured some soap flakes over the pile of dirty dishes.

During the summer Mrs. Plummer, the widow who lived across the street from the Tillings, had a goitre removed and when she came home from the hospital her enforced quietude had filled her now empty throat with so much to say that she held court for three-days-running on her front stoop. Her eager female audience learned almost everything about pre- and post-operative procedure, especially regarding charity patients. The hospital food (possibly half again as plentiful and at least twice as nutritious as what she ate at home) was chewed, digested or regurgitated by Mrs. Plummer and her sympathetic cohorts until a casual listener would have been led to believe she'd have been better off put out to pasture.

The internes, whom Mrs. Plummer called the "boy butchers," were let in for a special form of abuse. Had some of these eager, ambitious, hard-working young men heard Mrs. Plummer's criticisms they might have been filled with shame at their choice of profession.

"You know," said Mrs. Plummer, warming up to her current subject, "one of these boys tried to strip me off one day. I said to him, 'No you don't, young man, I'll see the head doctor first. I was examined twice already, all over, and I'm not going to let you see me naked now.'"

"I know what they're like," spoke up Mrs. Gaffey. "Give 'em an inch an'—" The horrible consequences were apparent to the small knot of ladies. "They think that because you're on the City that they can treat you like cattle. Now take my Leonard there (pointing to her simple-minded son sitting on their front steps) they wanted me to put him in a institution. 'Institution is it!' I said. 'Not while I'm alive you won't. I'll keep him at home where he belongs. Except for having to change his pants sometimes, he's no bother to me!" As she finished she glanced towards her son. The boy caught her eye, and with his oversized head rolling on his shoulders he smiled his vacant smile. Mrs. Gaffey smiled back at him, and in her smile was all the love and tenderness in her life.

Mrs. Plummer went on with the latest version of her narrative. "When I come to in my bed in the recovery room there was this snip of a nurse—no more'n eighteen I guess—slappin' my face. I says to her, 'Listen here, you—'" Mrs. Gaffey, Mrs. Wells and the others nodded their heads, keeping time with the cadence of Mrs. Plummer's monologue.

Ken Tilling worked all summer at McDonald's Wholesale Grocers. He and Billy Addington stacked tall piles of canned corn and peaches, wooden boxes of English biscuits, gallon cans of olive oil, steel-strapped cases of canned corn beef and excelsior-packed boxes of vanilla extract into pyramids and rectangles on the floor of the warehouse. At times the lifting was heavy for the small, thin, undeveloped boys, but they prided themselves on their geometric precision and secretly admired their hardening biceps. When they took the frequent inventories they scrambled over the piles and ran along the rows of shelves with the agility of squirrels. Three or four times a day they sneaked into the dirty little lavatory with its stained tin sink and paper-littered floor, there to smoke a forbidden cigarette, getting a rebellious thrill from striking their matches on the NO SMOKING sign.

While eating their noontime sandwiches on the shipping platform some of the older men made dirty remarks to each other for the benefit of the boys. At times one of them would ask the boys if they'd lost their cherry yet or did they still play with themselves. One of the men, a pimply young man named Carding, never tired of regaling them with stories of the prostitutes he picked up on Jarvis Street, going into scatalogical detail about his highly imaginative cohabitations.

He would say, "That's what you kids need, some big fat mama.

There's lots of them around just looking for young guys like you. They like to get 'em young and break 'em in. That's if you're still virgins though, eh?" giving them a bawdy wink.

These sessions filled the boys' heads with awakening thoughts of sex. Ken would find himself daydreaming of making love to a girl or woman as he wheeled a cart piled high with cases from the stockroom to the shipping platforms. These daydreams, formed of erroneous and quite imaginary physiological visions of nude women, both excited him and freed him from the deadly monotony of the job.

Though he indulged in such sexual fantasies with nearly every girl he knew, neighbour women, and even spinster schoolteachers he had known, he refused to think of Myrla Patson in this way. To him she was still too lovely and inviolate to associate with these things. He had not seen her since her party, but the memory of her was with him constantly. He tried to form a picture of her as she had looked when she said goodnight to him at her front doorway but her face remained a shapeless blank in which, try as he might, he could never assemble her features.

One afternoon as he was unpacking bottles of bleach in a corner of the stockroom he turned to find the boss, Mr. McDonald himself, standing close by watching him. Ken gave him a startled smile.

"What's your name?" McDonald asked.

"Tilling, sir," Ken answered, pausing in his work.

"Go on," said McDonald, indicating with a wave of his hand that he expected no work stoppage during the conversation. "You look like a bright boy. We need bright boys here. Maybe there'll be a job in the front office soon if you play the game. You want to get along in the firm, don't you?"

"Yes, sir," Ken answered.

"Well, I want you to sort of keep an eye on things around here, d'you understand? Let me know if things don't go right. See what I mean?"

"Yes, sir, I'll let you know if anything goes wrong," Ken said.

"Have you seen anybody taking stuff out of here?" asked McDonald "Carding or Davidson or anybody?"

"No, sir, I haven't," answered Ken truthfully.

"Well there's stuff going out of here, and we've got to catch the thief that's responsible. Don't forget that you're a part of this firm as well as me. We believe in rewarding our loyal employees. Don't get the idea that you'll be acting like a sneak if you let me know what you see around here. I don't like sneaks, but I do like loyal men in the firm, see?"

"Yes, sir."

"And another thing. If you see anybody smoking in the toilet or taking too long in there, let me know. I'm counting on you to help me, and if you show your loyalty we'll see about putting you in the front office, understand?"

"Yes, sir."

McDonald turned on his heel and waddled from the stockroom.

As soon as he could, Ken told Billy Addington what the boss had said.

"Let him go to hell!" Billy exclaimed with disgust. "A stool pigeon! Holy Jeez!"

"We'd better stop smoking in the can," said Ken.

They warned the others, and for a couple of days nobody smoked in the lavatory. The pilfering must have stopped too, at least Ken heard no more of it-from McDonald.

**4**

$M$yrla Patson dropped off the street-
car and walked quickly towards the corner of Butt Street, her high
heels beating out a tattoo on the broken sidewalk. She had a date to
go canoeing that evening at Centre Island with a young man from
work, and she was hurrying so she could get ready and straighten up
the house before he called. She was usually ready well ahead of time
for her dates, for she did not like her escorts to have to wait too long
in the house, where they could have time to criticize the shabby furniture or fall into conversation with her father. George Patson would
entertain them with shoptalk about the silversmith plant, while she
had been trying to build up the lie among her fellow workers that he
was a commercial artist.

At the same time Myrla was approaching her house Ken Tilling
was stepping down from a streetcar on Queen Street. Though it was
months since he had seen the girl she still filled his waking thoughts.
On occasion he had ridden up and down Butt Street on a borrowed
bicycle trying to catch a glimpse of her, and on two occasions had
even transferred quite unnecessarily, to the streetcar line she took,
but his efforts to meet her had been unrewarded. Once he had
thought he caught a glimpse of her in a downtown crowd, and his
heart had bumped sickeningly against his ribs. He had not tried to
follow her, for what excuse would he have had but that he was
desperately in love with her. He knew that if he even met her face to
face he would mumble a muttered greeting, flee, then regret for a
week the folly of not saying more.

Tonight was the evening of the Timothy Place Annual Street Dance and Bazaar, and Ken was buoyed up with the hope that Myrla would be there. For the past two years Timothy Place had copied more opulent city streets with its annual street dance, under an amateur but wildly enthusiastic committee led by Mrs. Plummer and Mrs. Gaffey. Together with Billy Addington Ken hurried outside after supper and gave the committee a hand in hanging out the decorations and setting up the few small booths along the sidewalks. Followed by a group of noisy excited children Ken helped Mrs. Gaffey string long streamers of nondescript secondhand bunting along the facades of the houses, and tack up above each door a large but totally out-of-season Christmas bell. Climbing like a pair of steeplejacks he and Billy tied coloured paper over the globes of the street lights to give the dancing space a warm intimate illumination, then helped some of the girls erect their wood-framed booths along the sidewalks.

Ken asked Elizabeth Plummer what she was going to sell from her garish paper-covered booth.

"Lemonade and women's dresses," she told him.

"What a combination," he said, shaking his head. "Why sell dresses at a bazaar?"

"Well, Mama's been buying them all year at rummage sales, and we've got to get rid of them some way. You know how she is; she goes to all the church sales and buys them because they're cheap. Then she finds half of them don't fit her anyways, and even if they did she don't wear nothing but black. I think it's crazy trying to sell them like this but she told me I had to or I couldn't get to sell my lemonade. After things get going I'm going to shove them under the counter out of sight."

Before the dancers arrived the street was taken over by hordes of grubby youngsters who ran around playing tag and threatening to knock down the flimsy stalls or pull down the bunting. Mrs. Gaffey was in a sweat what with trying to keep them away from the booths while guarding her son Leonard from their pokes and taunts.

Before darkness fell the older people began sauntering up the sidewalks from Myrtle Street, and the orchestra arranged itself at the far end of the pavement under the high board factory fence. There the musicians would be strategically placed acoustically while also being afforded protection from the dancers and from any brawls that might erupt on the dance floor.

The orchestra consisted of a set of much-battered drums, a piano-accordion, Billy Addington's brother-in-law with his fiddle, and a young man named Sweeney with the cornet he played on more solemn occasions as a member of the Parliament Street Salvation Army Citadel Band.

Billy Addington spread powdered chalk over the bituminous pavement from a cornflakes box, while a volunteer gang of youthful helpers slid and shuffled around on it until a white chalky mist rose to the rooftops.

Mr. Gregory from No. 9, as self-appointed master of ceremonies, opened the affair with a flowery speech of welcome. He had spent much time and effort in its composition, and it dealt at great length with the spirit of neighbourliness, civic virtue, and a prolix history of Cabbagetown as seen through the eyes of Patrick Gregory, city water works employee and chaplain of the Mountains O' Mourne district Orange Lodge. He had successfully advanced oratorically through his introductory remarks, given fulsome praise to the city council, incumbent aldermen, and other, to him quite important, civic functionaries. He went on, drunk with the unaccustomed attention and his own verbosity, "—and right down where the tannery is today stood McMonigle's Hotel. Many a night I stood and talked to old John McMonigle, and a finer man never drew breath in this nor no other part of our fair city. He used to say to me, 'Patrick me boy you'll—' "

Old John McMonigle's prophetic words were drowned out by what could be politely referred to as a Cabbagetown cheer made by the pursing of a pair of vulgar lips. The crowd burst into laughter and began moving impatiently, while the master of ceremonies hurriedly concluded his remarks and, red-faced, motioned to the orchestra to play.

Ken found Billy trying to beat the powdered chalk from his Sunday suit. "Let's pick up a couple of girls and dance," he said.

"What now! Let's wait till it's dark, then they won't know whether we can dance or not. I'm not going out there yet; look at my pants. After this somebody else can spread that chalk."

"I don't see why they use that stuff anyway," Ken said. "Last year and the year before they used resin."

"That was because old man Gaffey was working at the paint factory and used to bring it home in his lunch pail. This year Mrs. Porter had her kids steal it from the summer school."

They walked around in the large crowd of people that packed the narrow street. Ken kept his eyes open for a sight of Myrla Patson but she was nowhere to be seen. They stopped before a small counter behind which Mrs. Plummer was busy fishing boiling corn-on-the-cob from a large wash boiler and handing it over to the customers. "Easy on the butter, sir, thank you," she would say when a customer became too liberal as he brushed on the melted butter.

After dark the cleared space on which the dancers shuffled was packed with a writhing human carpet which valiantly tried to follow the erratic beat of the orchestra. During two numbers the band had been forced to forego its rhythm section when a child had stolen the drummer's sticks. When the child had been caught, cuffed and the sticks returned, the band had played in unison, more or less, though the accordion player was given to soaring arpeggios that made him lose the race to every clef. Once a dancing couple swept the sheet music from Sweeney's stand, and he lowered his asthmatic cornet and gave vent to some very un-Salvation-Army language.

Mrs. Wells was esconced in her teacup-reading "tent," a piece of tarpaulin suspended from her front window sill to two upright poles against the sidewalk. Serving as the front wall to this establishment was a large colorful sign announcing that Madame Tamerlane was present within to foretell the future in the dregs of twenty-five cent cups of tea, besides "telling all that the cards reveal for a dime." She was bothered somewhat by the children who peeked under the tent flaps and giggled at the unlikely metamorphosis of Mrs. Wells into Madame Tamerlane. Between unprofessional cries to her husband to bring more tea and thin-lipped cajolery and threats aimed at the children, she became a very harried-looking seer as the evening wore on.

Eventually Ken and Billy found dancing partners and ventured on to the floor.

"Do you live around here?" Ken asked his partner as they bumped and shuffled along under the pressure of the tight-pressed mob.

"No, I'm just visiting my girl friend," she answered, as if ashamed to admit any closer ties with the neighbourhood. He was sure she was just trying to put on the dog, and dismissed her as he stared into the crowd hoping to catch a glimpse of Myrla Patson. He hoped his eyes would meet hers so he could pretend an indifference which would show her what a wonderful time he was having without her.

When he and his partner reached a corner near the orchestra the girl asked him, "Do you Charleston?"

"Oh, that's old stuff," he answered. "I used to Charleston and Black Bottom a couple of years ago," hoping this would be the end of the matter.

"I just *love* to Charleston," she insisted, pulling him into the cleared corner and beginning to gyrate to the music. Ken tried to follow her, his legs wobbling in what he hoped was a fair imitation of hers.

He became so immersed in his efforts that he forgot to look where he was going. Suddenly a large hand gave him a shove, and he looked up into the leering face of a youth who had let go of his partner and was smirking at him as if spoiling for a fight.

"What's the idea?" Ken asked, summoning all his bravado.

"Who wants to know?" asked the other, making a lunge at Ken. Ken, expecting this, stepped aside, letting the other youth's rush carry him into the dancing crowd. Before the challenger could gather himself for a second rush he was seized and pummelled by those, male and female, into whom his lunge had carried him, and the war was on.

The dance came to an end as if the dancers had been deep-frozen, then the young men broke away from their partners and began striking out, the girls retreating to the sidewalks with small shrill screams.

"It's the River Rats!" Billy shouted into Ken's ear as he hurried up to his side. They began punching at every strange face that appeared in the mob. Ken was filled with a giggling exultation, and he began throwing wild haymakers in all directions until somebody slammed a fist into his ear, knocking him to the ground. From then on he offered only a token participation, aiming protective kicks from a position on the chalky pavement.

As the individual fights broke up, a fist-swinging phalanx of the River Rats gang cleared one end of the dance floor, and as the ebb of the mob passed him Ken picked himself up. He laughed as he watched the drummer trying to clear his traps from the field of battle, only to be brought down on the front steps of No. 10 with an ear-splitting cacophony of clashing cymbal and rattling drum.

Sweeney, the Salvation Army trumpeter, isolated from his friends, was laying about him with his cornet, but was gradually pushed by sheer weight of opponents against the high board fence at the end of the street.

Two of the combatants fell against Madame Tamerlane's tent and brought it crashing down around the heads of its occupants. There was an elephantine maelstrom under its folds, which parted to reveal Mrs. Wells, who headed into the fray. Despite her flashing anger she resembled a pale-faced Aunt Jemima, as with awry kerchief and swishing skirts she lay into any and all males who happened within her reach.

Mrs. Plummer brandished a long fork across her counter as she unsuccessfully defended her place of business against the heaving, pummelling knots of battlers. When the Timothy Place group and its allies finally sorted themselves out they, supported by the might of right and having the game on their home grounds, made short shrift of the River Rats, who one by one were disentangled from the crowd and forced to flee.

When comparative calm had again settled over Timothy Place the broken booths were re-erected and the festivities once more got under way. The young male veterans of the fracas licked their wounds and exchanged self-satisfied grins as their girl partners emerged from their places of refuge. Mrs. Plummer hurriedly began peddling her cold and bedraggled corn-on-the-cob, and a sweating Madame Tamerlane resumed her outward calm and sombre mien. If her prophecies were more pessimistic than before, and the drummer's beat was off and tinny, these minor deviations could be blamed on conditions out of their control.

Three uniformed policemen arrived from the Dundas and Parliament Streets station, one of them on a bicycle, and they stood watching the dancers and listening with varying degrees of credence to the voluntary explanations of the crowd. Mr. Gregory, his position as festivities chairman to uphold, pushed himself up to one of the giant police constables and, steadying himself with a grip upon the policeman's tunic, gave him his bacchanalian version of the fight. His artificially inspired vehemence overrode his prudence, and he was led away to the accompaniment of scattered boos and cheers from the opponents of civic pride and virtue.

"I guess we showed the River Rats they can't get away with that kind of stuff anywhere but River Street," Ken said to Billy, as they helped Mrs. Plummer carry some of her things into her house.

"It was a good fight for a while," Billy answered. "Did you see me give Red Corcoran one in the snout?"

"No. I was too busy trying to get out from under everybody's feet."

"Yeah. What happened to you anyways?"

"I was taking a swing at a big guy in front of me when somebody clouted me with a bat or a two-by-four on the side of the head. I went down and couldn't get up again for the crowd."

"A two-by-four?" asked the skeptical Billy. "Where would anybody get a two-by-four in the middle of a dance floor?"

"Well it felt like one anyways."

Later as he tried to get to sleep he wondered why Myrla Patson had not been at the dance. He was disappointed at not seeing her, and angry that her nonappearance had denied him the pleasure of showing her his complete indifference.

**5**

One evening in October the newspapers printed extra editions reporting a stockmarket crash. Of all the city's neighbourhoods Cabbagetown probably took the news most quietly. In the wealthier districts, and even in the middle-class neighbourhoods, the citizens were either shocked or sloughed off the news as merely a temporary halt to the inevitable spiralling of the economy. In the Bay Street financial district crowds filled the evening streets, clustering in front of the newspaper offices waiting for the latest bulletins. In residential neighbourhoods families sat down in their living rooms and laughed at Amos 'n Andy or listened with mounting impatience as the bulletins from New York and other financial centres cried havoc and interrupted the A & P Gypsies.

Cabbagetown went on its serene way, not caring whether the stockmarket crashed or didn't, such things being as far away and as alien to Cabbagetown as an aeroplane crash in Peru. With millions of dollars worth of investors' paper profits blowing away on the autumn breeze Cabbagetown knew that *its* hard-earned wealth was safe. Come Friday night or Saturday noon the same familiar pay envelopes would be carried out to the shipping platform by the foreman or handed through the timekeeper's wicket as usual. Whether some stock-market plungers lost their fortunes or whether a particular stock was worth this or that was of no particular interest. As a matter of fact most Cabbagetowners felt rather smug about the whole thing.

Ken Tilling quit work at five-thirty as usual on that Thursday evening. On the Queen Street streetcar a man sitting in front of him was saying to a friend, "It was bound to come. These panics happen every few years. If some of the suckers had had enough sense to get out when the going was good they wouldn't be crying today. After the war was the same thing. When the market's fallen far enough to let the real big boys rake in their profits it'll start up again, and everybody with an extra dime or two will plunge right back in."

The man's friend nodded his head. "It's sure cleaning some of them out though. Did you notice old Thorndyke's face when he came through the office after lunch. He looked like death on the hoof."

"Yeah, he sure did," answered the first man. "But Thorndyke's not as hard hit as some. Look at this fellow in the paper here, shot himself and his wife and kid. They say they're jumping off buildings all over the States."

"That's the trouble, they don't realize that the country—both the States and here—is basically sound. Don't worry, the panic'll clean the air of a lot of deadwood. That's what business wants, to get rid of a lot of nickel investors and give the big guy a chance to put business back on its feet."

"I guess we can be glad we're in insurance and not stocks and bonds."

"You said it, Aif."

Ken had no doubts that what the men had said was right. In a few days the hullabaloo would die down and things would not have changed at all for the little people who had nothing to invest. Mr. Stanley Keats down at the wholesale had been running around all day shouting, "I knew it! I knew it!" and asking the other employees to admit that the panic was just what he had been predicting for years. Nobody cared what Keats had been predicting. Ken thought he was half crazy anyway, always trying to stir up trouble among the workers at McDonald's Wholesale by talking about trade unions and stuff like that. Not that anybody paid any attention to him.

Shortly after Ken began working at McDonald's the old man had sidled up to him in the stockroom one day and had asked him how much he was being paid.

Ken answered him, "Six dollars a week."

The old man stared intently into his face and said, "Did you know that young Tommy—that's the boy who had your job before—was getting twelve a week for the same job?"

"That's none of my business," Ken had told him. "I was hired at six dollars a week, and if I wasn't satisfied with it I'd leave the job. Anyway I'll be making twelve myself maybe next year."

"Do you know what'll happen to you then?" the man asked, peering over his shoulder to make sure nobody else was listening. "You'll be laid off yourself and another kid'll be hired for six."

Ken asked some of the other youths if what old Keats had told him was true. Most of them thought Keats was crazy. Billy Addington told him that the boy Tommy had been fired for smoking in the toilet.

"That's where everybody smokes," Ken said.

"Sure but not if Mr. McDonald comes in," Billy said.

From then on Ken tried to keep out of Keats' way. There were other things that Keats had said that had alienated him from the boy, such as his derogatory remarks about the Royal Family. Old Keats was a real nut all right.

When Ken arrived home he found his mother sitting at the kitchen table reading one of the evening papers.

"Did you see this about these poor people losing all their money," she asked him.

He nodded.

"Look at this man that shot his wife and baby. They seem to have been a nice couple too. The people where I worked today are worried; they got stocks and bonds too. Mrs. Marshall—that's the woman today—she was phoning her husband all afternoon asking him about the market, and how this was, and that. The poor soul couldn't hardly eat her lunch. When I was leaving tonight she gave me my two dollars and said, 'Here, Mrs. Tilling, maybe next week I'll be down doing *your* floors!' I laughed at her but she was pretty serious. Anyways she gave me this stuff that she'd made for supper." She pointed to some opened sheets of newspaper on the table on top of which was lying part of a cold roast chicken and some crushed slices of apple pie.

While the market crash was a disaster to many, and presaged a disaster to many many millions more, to the Tillings it meant that they sat down to a feast of roast chicken on a day other than Christmas, and what is more, in the middle of the week.

The panic wasn't over as soon as the optimists predicted, and over the next few months its results began filtering down through business and industry, and even into Cabbagetown itself. Business said it had to retrench, and it began to cut its staffs relentlessly, and cut the pay checks of those who were retained in their jobs. The optimists changed their predictions, now claiming that the crash was a seasonable slump brought about by mysterious manipulations of some unknowns on the stock market. By spring things would be humming again.

The fun and horseplay around McDonald's Wholesale Grocers had gone, replaced by a frightened quietness and an almost servile application to their jobs by those remaining on the payroll. Wages had been slashed, almost gleefully it seemed to the employees, by McDonald, who had also laid off many of his other workers. Strangely, to Ken, whose six dollars had been cut by sixty cents a week, Stanley Keats had been kept on but at a pittance, and this former agitator now went about his job silently and morosely, mumbling under his breath.

One Monday morning as Ken was taking his usual inventory of the spice and condiment shelves he was surprised to find that some of the shelves were half empty. Because of the value of some of these items the company was very fussy about the correctness of the weekly count and the balancing of the tally cards. Ken reported the half-empty shelves to Carding, and together they rechecked the cards and made out a list of the missing items. Carding took the list to the front office.

In a few minutes he returned, accompanied by old McDonald himself. The boss swore loud and heavily at the evidence of the theft.

Looking around for somebody to take out his anger on McDonald spied Ken and shouted at him, "What the hell is the idea of not taking better care of your stock! Is this what I pay you for, to let the goddamn stuff disappear under your eyes! Now, tell me who took it?"

Nobody spoke.

"I've a good mind to have all of you pinched! This is what I get for keeping you on the payroll when I shoulda laid you all off. You're all nothing but a bunch of no-good bums anyway. Somebody'll do some time in the pen for this, you mark my words, all of you!"

"The stuff was all there on Saturday," Ken said.

"You shut your mouth till I ask you to open it!" McDonald screamed. "You're probably in it as much as anybody."

"If I was in it do you think I'd have reported it?" asked Ken.

McDonald glared at the boy, undecided whether to pick him up and shake him or not. Instead, his face working as with some secret nasty joke, he turned on his heel and strode from the stockroom.

"You shouldn't have talked back to him, Tilling," said Carding. "He's only looking for an excuse to fire somebody."

"He can't blame me for something I didn't do. He called every one of us a no-good bum too. We don't need to take that off him." He turned his head as he felt the hot angry tears welling up behind his eyes.

"You'll learn, Ken, that sometimes you've gotta take these things," Carding said. "Especially when you're married with some kids to support."

"I ain't got no kids," answered Ken. "And even if I had I wouldn't take that kind of stuff. Jeez, I'd like to—I don't know what I'd like to do to that big fat bastard." Shaking with anger and frustration he went back to work, trying to fight off his self-recriminations.

During the next few days he learned that the thief had been Stanley Keats. Keats crept up beside him one afternoon and whispered, "I heard McDonald blaming you the other morning for that stuff that's missing. Don't let him scare ya. He don't know who did it, see. Nobody knows but the one that did it." He winked at Ken. "When they don't pay you enough to live on, there's nothing else for the working class to do but get their pay anyway they can, eh?" He gave Ken another conspiratorial wink and ambled off along the aisle.

On Friday afternoon one of the office clerks brought the pay envelopes into the warehouse. As their names were called the employees came forward and signed for their envelope. Ken stood at the rear of the group until the others had received their pay. Then as the clerk turned to leave he shouted, "Hey, where's *my* envelope?"

"You'd better go see," said the clerk. "Those were the only envelopes I made up for the warehouse."

With feelings of anger and fear Ken hurried through the doorway to the front office. Two stenographers who were putting on their hats gave him startled glances as he pushed by their desks and reached the open door to McDonald's private office. McDonald sat at his desk reading the evening paper.

The man glanced at the boy framed in the doorway, then turned to his reading again.

Ken stood there, trying to stop his shivering. He heard the typists leave the office, and a silence settle over the place. It was broken only by the rustling of the paper in McDonald's hands.

After a long wait the boy said, "Mr. McDonald."

The man lowered his newspaper, took a cigar from his pocket and bit the end from it. After pulling a waste basket towards him with his foot he took the cigar tip from his lips with a thumb and finger and threw it into the basket. Then he opened a drawer of his desk, pulled out a large box of kitchen matches and lighted his cigar. Only after taking several self-satisfied puffs did he deign to notice Ken.

"What do *you* want?" he asked.

"I was wondering about my pay envelope, sir."

"What about your pay envelope?" asked McDonald, shifting his bulk in the chair and staring insolently across the desk at the boy.

"I didn't get any this week. I guess there's been a mistake."

"What makes you think there's a mistake?" asked the man sharply.

"Well," said Ken, attempting a smile, "I usually get one every week."

"What do you think you get a pay envelope for, eh?" asked McDonald. "You get one for doing a good week's work. For being a loyal member of the firm. You don't get one for not tending to your job, or for lying to me when I ask you a question—"

"I didn't lie to you," Ken said.

"Or for being impertinent to your betters either." The man sat back and blew a cloud of smoke at the ceiling.

Ken had difficulty holding his tongue, but his only thought now was to get his money and leave McDonald's Wholesale forever.

"I should hand you over to the police," McDonald said. "And I might just do that unless you get out of this office immediately. Now get the hell out of here and stay out! And if I ever catch you around here again I'll have you arrested." He leaned forward and pointed a pudgy hand at the boy.

"You've got to pay me!" Ken cried. "I've worked all week here and you owe me a week's pay!"

"I owe you nothing at all. You're damned lucky you're not in jail with the rest of your jailbird friends. Now get out!"

Ken forgot the shivering in his legs and spurred on now by the sick emptiness in his stomach he walked across the floor to where the man was leering at him across the cluttered desk. "Listen here, I never stole anything, and you know it. You can't have me arrested for nothing. You've got to pay me my money!"

McDonald pushed back his chair and stood up, towering over the boy. "Are you threatening me, you goddamn little guttersnipe? You'll get no money from me at all. Now get out of my office and out of the building!"

"I won't!" shouted Ken, a sick sense of loss forcing out the words. "If you wanted to fire me why didn't you do it on Monday morning, instead of waiting till now. You're just trying to get out of paying me my wages."

"Are you calling me a crook?" McDonald asked. "I've got proof that you stole those spices."

"No you haven't, 'cause I didn't do it," Ken said. "I'm not afraid of you; have me pinched if you think I did."

"I'll do just that if you don't get out." McDonald picked up a piece of paper from his desk and pushed it into Ken's face. "Read that!"

Ken couldn't believe it as he read the few typewritten lines. They stated that Ken Tilling had been seen pilfering stock on several occasions in the past, and had been heard to make threats against Mr. James McDonald. It was signed, "Thomas Carding."

Ken was stunned. That Carding could have allowed McDonald to coerce him into such a thing! During the time he had worked at the Wholesale he had never stolen much more than a prune! He didn't notice McDonald tear the piece of paper from his hand, and the man's words reached his ears in far off waves. ". . . some of the employees are loyal to the firm . . . had been given the chance to do the right thing but didn't take it . . . lucky to get away with it so easy . . . "

How could Carding say such things about him? Could one man lie like that about another just to keep a piddling little job with McDonald?

"Please, Mr. McDonald, this thing isn't true," he pleaded.

"I don't know why Mr. Carding did this to me. I never stole

nothing. I need my wages too; it's all the money me and my mother's got coming in."

"You should have thought about that before. I don't want to listen to any more whining. Now get out!"

Ken was nauseated at having tried to beg for the money, and with Carding's actions. But why hadn't McDonald had him arrested! It was suddenly obvious that even McDonald didn't believe the charge. He had forced Carding to make the statement just to get even with Ken for answering back, and to gratify his small mean urge for revenge.

The boy's head cleared and he glanced at the photographs on the wall behind McDonald's head. One showed the small fleet of trucks lined up at the loading platforms and the second one showed the employees at the firm's annual picnic. Seated in the front row of the picnickers was the heavy benevolent form of James McDonald, framed by his coterie of loyal employees.

Ken could hold himself no longer. "You dirty big bastard!" he shouted, reaching for the heavy onyx inkwell on the desk. The man was too quick for him however, and the boy felt his hand crushed in McDonald's thick damp paw as he was wrenched off his feet.

McDonald yelled, then sidled around the desk and threw the boy to the floor. He held Ken's crying swearing, writhing form until a couple of male employees entered the office, attracted by the noise.

They hauled the boy to his feet, hustled him through the outer office, and shoved him down the steps to the street door. Depositing him on the sidewalk they locked the door behind them and stood inside it, motioning to Ken to get away from in front of the building.

Ken beat his hands against the glass door and yelled for McDonald to come outside. A small crowd gathered to stare at the angry sobbing boy. When he heard their laughter, and feeling alone and helpless, he pushed through them and hurried along the street in the direction of the streetcar stop.

Much to Bertha Patson's surprise her husband George had been kept on at the silversmiths, but had been reduced to a piecework filing job on the finishing table. It was a bad Christmas for plated cutlery and silver figurines. George's wages were dropping all the time, and once he came home and threw down a pay envelope containing twelve dollars and thirty cents. Somehow Bertha made do, cutting down on her household expenses in various ways, such as buying cheap meat in the cut-rate butcher shops along Queen Street. She prayed that Myrla would keep her job.

Myrla had now been keeping steady company for three months with a young machinist in the plant where she worked. He was the answer to Bertha's prayers for a son-in-law, but she hoped they wouldn't marry until times got better again or her husband found another job. George was so edgy these days she was almost afraid to speak to him sometimes. After coming home from work he would sit by himself in the front room looking at the newspaper. Once or twice she had peeked in on him and found that he wasn't reading but staring straight through the paper at nothing at all.

Myrla's boy friend called for her one evening in his car, and they went for a drive. It was early in the spring and the traffic was light as they cut out towards the eastern suburbs. Myrla snuggled up beside him in the seat, listening to the hum of the tires on the wet pavement.

"Where are we going, Herb?" she asked him.

"Oh, nowhere in particular, maybe out the Kingston Road a piece. Don't you want to go for a ride?"

"Sure I do. I was just wondering that's all."

Herb had been acting very possessive towards her lately. He was prone to little jealousies, which even her speaking to another fellow at the plant could arouse. Though he hadn't said anything about it yet, she sensed that he intended to ask her to marry him. This both pleased her and made her uncomfortable, for she wasn't quite sure whether she wanted to marry him or not.

They left the lights of the city behind and shot out along the highway. After a few miles they turned off down a dark sideroad.

"My God it's dark down here," said Myrla. "I hope you know where you're going."

"Sure I do," Herb answered. "This road runs into another up here that takes you back to the city through Scarborough Junction."

She stole a glance at him. She had accepted his invitation to go out with her at first merely because he was tall and good-looking, and some of the other girls had their eye on him. Since then going out with him had become a habit, and they both took it for granted that he was her steady boy friend. Besides he was one of the few young men she knew who owned a car.

Herb turned the car into a narrow track beneath some still-bare trees and brought it to a halt, switching off the engine and the lights. For a moment or two everything was black, until their eyes grew accustomed to the gray night outside the car.

"Want a cigarette?" Herb asked, holding a package out to Myrla. She took a cigarette.

She watched him strike a match under the dashboard, and noticed that he seemed to be agitated about something. Guessing what it was, she felt herself stiffening to meet it.

They smoked for some time in silence.

Finally Myrla asked, "What are we doing out here?"

Herb answered, "I've got something to ask you," slipping his arm around her shoulders and taking a long nervous pull at his cigarette.

She didn't answer, but stared ahead through the windshield.

"Listen, Myrla, you know what I think about you. You're the most beautiful girl I've ever seen. I was wondering if we couldn't get married. Not just now maybe, but later in the spring?" He was trembling and his voice was almost shrill.

She stared straight ahead, the butt of her cigarette almost burning her fingers.

"I know I may not be so hot, but I've got a good job and a few dollars saved up. I'll make you a good husband, I know that. What do you say?" He tried to force her around to face him, his hand pressing on her shoulder.

She was surprised, not at his proposal but at his desperate eagerness. Knowing she had to say either yes or no she kept quiet.

"Myrla—Myrla, please answer me! Do you like me at all? Don't I mean anything to you?"

She answered, her voice flat and noncommittal, "Sure I like you, Herb. I wouldn't go out with you if I didn't."

"I know that but I mean—well, more than that. Do you like me enough to want to marry me?" he almost shouted. He leaned forward and tried to stare into her eyes in the darkness.

"No, Herb," she said, surprised at her own words. "I don't want to get married to nobody. Jeez, I'm only seventeen you know!" She faced him now, trying to smile and make him see how it was.

"What does your age matter? You can get married with your father's consent. God, Myrla, if you only knew how crazy I am about you! You *are* the most beautiful girl I've ever seen."

His eager protestations somehow embarrassed her, and she answered, trying not to laugh, "You said that before." She rolled down the car's window and threw her cigarette butt out onto the ground.

He leaned on the wheel, silent now.

"Are you mad, Herb?" she asked, taking his arm.

"No," he answered but did not turn to face her.

"Sure you're mad. Jeez, you can't expect a girl to say yes right away, can you?"

He didn't answer.

"Let's go back to town," she said.

He swung around then and pulling her face up to his kissed her hard on the mouth. He had made up his mind to find out where he stood that night. Frequently he had felt that she was playing him along, and he had tried at times, in his stumbling way, to probe her feelings for him, to find whether she was really uninterested in him or not. Her beauty had won him completely, and he was not sure whether it was love he felt for her or just an urge to get behind the façade of her beauty and find out once and for all what lay behind her pretty face.

When he spoke again his voice was hopeful. "Why don't you give me your answer tonight, Myrla?"

"I have given you it. I don't want to get married yet."

"Why not? Why go on living down there in Cabbagetown and working at Frosst's when you don't have to? Rents have fallen all over town since the crash. We could get an apartment or flat somewhere; maybe even up on St. Clair Avenue."

"No."

"Please, Myrla!" He banged his fist on the wheel, and the horn gave a raucous toot. Myrla jumped.

"I'm sorry," he said. Then after another silence he asked, "Is there anybody else?"

She said nothing.

"Is there?" he asked again, forcing out the words.

Myrla scanned a list of the boys she had been out with. "No," she answered. "No, there's nobody else."

With a feeling of relief Herb took her in his arms and rubbed his face against her fur collar. Then he lifted her chin and they kissed, just as they had always done. After a while he suggested getting into the back of the car, and she crawled over the back of the seat while he stepped out of the car and got into the car again. The back seat was cold, and Myrla shivered.

Herb took her in his arms again and said, "Myrla, let's get married."

"Holy jeez, are you starting that again!" she exclaimed, pushing him away. Then she smiled and pulled him to her, kissing him.

They half lay on the seat, gripping and kissing each other, her head supported on his arm. With his other hand he unbuttoned her coat.

"No, Herb, don't!" she said as he tried to cup her breast in his hand.

Her beauty, her perfume, her physical nearness, the isolation of the parking spot, pushed aside the niceties of courtship and replaced them with something more immediate and urgent. If he couldn't have her one way he'd have her another. He pressed on, his breath quick and heavy against her cheek as she tried to turn her face away.

"Please, Myrla!" he pleaded, as they squirmed around on the slippery seat.

"No! Don't, Herb, don't!" she cried, as his hand was shoved down the neck of her dress.

When he found her mouth again he pressed himself against her, trying to French kiss. She shook her head, pulling her mouth from his, and cried, "Don't, Herbert, please! You'll tear my dress! I'm not like you think I am, honest. I've never gone this far with a fella before." Then her voice rising on a desperate note, "Jeez, leave me alone!"

They pulled apart, and a trembling Herbert sank back against the cushions. His nose was still filled with the smell of her hair, his mouth sweet from its contact with hers, the smoothness of her body still there in his hand. He was sure she felt as he did, but was letting her modesty and fear hold her back.

She had withdrawn to her corner of the seat, and he was unable to discover whether she was crying or not. When he asked her, she shook her head but kept her face in her hands. Tenderly he pulled her to him again, kissed her chastely, and asked her to forgive him. She returned his kisses. Now she was more desirable than ever and his hand began wandering again over her trembling body. He lifted the hem of her dress and placed his hand on her thigh.

"No, Herb!" she cried as he persisted. "No, I said!" Her voice was sharper now, and frightened. She tried to get away from him and slipped from the seat, her clothing sliding up her back.

"Can't—you—hear—me—Herbert—I—said—NO!"

"Oh you beautiful little bitch!" he cried, trying to pull her back to the seat. Now his maleness was at stake; having failed to get her consent to his marriage proposal another failure would be unendurable.

"Jeez, you're mean! Don't!"

They fought each other now, using all their strength, in a silence punctuated only by their loud breathing and the squeaking of the car springs.

Myrla cried out at the top of her voice, "Oh God, can't anybody help me!"

One of her garters broke as she kicked out at his legs. One of her hands clutched at his wrist but with the other she slapped his face, feeling the crack against his cheek. He suddenly let go of her and slid back along the seat.

She was sobbing now, trying to straighten her clothes. He grabbed her by the hair and slapped her twice, hard, across the mouth. One of her teeth tore her lower lip, and she covered her head with her arms and lowered it to her lap.

Herb sat back in the seat, his anger and frustration washing over him. "Tease me would you, you dirty little Cabbagetown whore! Get the hell out of the car!"

She fumbled for a handkerchief in her bag, and pressed it to her lip.

"Get out of the car I said!" he screamed at her.

"I won't get out," she answered in a low voice. "Not away out here anyways." Turning on the roof light she took a small mirror from her purse and looked at her bleeding lip.

Without a word Herb climbed into the driver's seat, backed the car around with a squeaking of wheels, and headed back to the highway.

Myrla sat tense and alone on the back seat, dabbing her lip with her handkerchief, wondering if there was something wrong with her. Sooner or later something like this happened with every young man who took her out. There had been times, one of them earlier that evening, when she had almost felt like going the limit. But fear or something had always stopped her before she allowed herself to go too far. Ever since she was fifteen she had fought off boys, who had then called her dirty names. She didn't know what it was, but she couldn't help herself. Still, it didn't mean that one of them could slap her like Herb had done. Maybe things would have been better if she'd been born ugly. No, that was silly. Him asking her to marry him at first, and then acting like that! Maybe she should have accepted him and gotten his ring. No. From this minute on she was finished going out with fellows.

They didn't speak again until they reached the end of the street-car line at the city limits. Then Herb stopped the car and turned around in his seat. "It's too bad things turned out like this," he said, his anger taking the edge off his apology.

Myrla stepped down to the sidewalk. She turned then and spit at him through her swollen lips. "Don't ever speak to me again, you son-of-a-bitch!" she said. "And don't forget that the first one to get me'll be a man!" She hurried to where a streetcar was standing at the loop.

Herb watched her go, surprised at the suddenness of their breakup, unable to comprehend what had happened in such a short space of time, wondering what had changed him from a young man plighting his troth one minute to a rough slavering rapist the next. His thoughts were unable to line the events in proper sequence, and he still could not grasp what had happened between them. As the streetcar pulled away he felt a sinking inside, feeling he had lost something both ephemeral and lasting, something he would never find again.

But that was crazy. As he drove off he swore either to or at himself before shaking his head in masculine bewilderment.

During Ken Tilling's lengthening periods of unemployment his mornings were taken up by regular attendance at the National Employment Bureau on lower Church street. Along with the other regulars he would pass on through the outer office of the Boys' Department, with its high, shabby varnished counter, and into an inner room with bare green-painted walls, lined with initial-carved wooden benches. Here the regulars held clublike court every morning, laughing, telling dirty jokes or criticizing bosses, and scribbling bawdy verse on the pukey green paint. Two euchre games went on continuously for months. On occasion the old skinny clerk would poke his head around the door-frame and, peering myopically through the cigarette smoke, would ask for two boys to deliver handbills, or squeak, "Can anybody here run a sewing machine on mattresses?" Few of the regulars ever found work except for the odd handbill delivery job, and all shared the opinion that the old clerk phoned his friends when a good job came up. After months of regular attendance Ken had received nothing from the employment office but a store of adolescent dirty stories and an expert's skill at euchre.

During the afternoons, if the weather was bad, he would lounge around the house, providing his mother was not at home drunk. When the weather was good he would wander up to Riverdale Zoo, down to the St. Lawrence market, or along the harbour. He tried once or twice to get a job on a lake freighter, but had no discharge book and was too short and skinny to be hired. He had to satisfy himself watching the hustle and bustle of loading or unloading and staring forlornly as the red-and-white painted ships slipped their moorings and sailed off to such places as Sandusky, Port Arthur or Montreal.

He became an avid reader of books, and exchanged them several times a week at the public library across the Don River on Gerrard Street. His choice of reading material was as erratic and catholic as his temperament, but in fiction he searched for literature, no matter how poor, which helped to satisfy his erotic hunger. Books which contained chapters ending with a man and woman presumably having coitus among a line of dots or in the blank bottom of a page were meat for his pruriency.

He might never have read fiction at all but for this, but due to his having to read a great deal of starched cleanliness in order to reach the not so clean, he gradually developed a love for good books.

One summer evening as he was returning home from the library he met Theodore East on Gerrard Street. He had seen Theodore several times since the night of Myrla Patson's party more than a year before, but the most they had done was exchange greetings.

"Hello, Ken," said Theodore, stopping him. "How's the boy?"

"Not bad," Ken answered.

"Are you working?"

"No. Not since before Christmas."

"Holy smoke, that's too bad!" Theodore exclaimed. "A gentleman of leisure eh?"

Ken resented his patronizing tone. "Yeah."

"I see you've been to the library. What are you reading, Zane Grey?"

"No. Not Zane Grey, or Max Brand either," Ken replied angrily. "I leave those things for punks like you to read. If you must know, it's a book called *Tono Bungay* by somebody you've probably never heard of, H. G. Wells."

"Gee whiz, you don't have to get sore at an innocent little question like that," Theodore said. "Lots of fellows read Zane Grey. That's nothing to worry about."

"Well I didn't like the way you asked it. Just because you live around here people think you're putting on the dog if you read anything but *True Detective* magazine or Zane Grey or something like that. I like reading and I wouldn't read junk even if they made me."

"Nobody's telling you what to read," said Theodore, startled by the other's vehemence.

"Well, I didn't like the way you asked it," Ken repeated.

"Where are you going now?" Theodore asked, as if to change the subject. "Come up to Parliament Street and have a hamburger. We've never really got to know each other yet."

"No thanks, not tonight."

"Come on," Theodore insisted, grabbing Ken by the arm. "I'm working now, and I'd really like to talk to you."

As they walked west along Gerrard Ken said, "I see you still live around here?"

"Yes, damn it. Since the stock crash we can't sell our house so I guess we'll live there the rest of our lives. Mother wanted Dad to sell, but that's impossible now. Dad doesn't care very much—he was born down around here—but mother has been after him to move now for a long time."

"Where are you working?" Ken asked.

"I'm in the office down at Thomas and Listowel's; you know, the boxboard factory down on Keating Street. I got the job offered to me before I left school in June. I won a couple of prizes in shorthand and typing, and the company spoke for me. It's not a bad job; the future looks pretty good if things don't get any worse."

Ken wondered why he felt inferior in Theodore's presence. The other boy, despite living in Cabbagetown, seemed to carry an aura of inherent good breeding. It was as noticeable to Ken as the appearance of a boy's hair who came from a well-to-do family. Ken thought he could always spot a rich boy by his hair; soft, neat and so very clean.

"Maybe I'll hear of a job and let you know," Theodore went on. "Sometimes, even these days, there's the odd job around."

"Thanks," said Ken. "If you hear of any let me know." He began to warm up to the other, thinking that perhaps his slight dislike had only been caused by envy.

Theodore said, "I've often thought of you since meeting you at the party. There's something about you I couldn't forget. You know how it is; you have a bunch of fellows and girls in a room and that's all they are, but one or two will stand out and you remember them."

They walked in silence for some time.

"Do you wish you'd have stayed in school?" Theodore asked.

"In a way," Ken answered. "But that was impossible. With things as they are I don't know that it makes much difference."

"It does make a difference. Take me for instance. I'm a year younger than you, but I've got a job because I happened to go to the right school at the right time. You went to collegiate didn't you?"

"No, I went to tech."

"I thought you'd gone to collegiate. Anyway it doesn't matter. Do you think you learned anything in high school?"

Ken was silent for a moment, a montage of the drafting room, the chemistry labs, and Miss Hurst the pretty geography teacher flashing through his thoughts. He saw himself standing before the class reciting an oral composition. "I guess I learned a few things," he answered. "I learned to improve my reading and writing, and learned that I didn't like poetry. I know that the surface tension of water will allow a needle to float—"

Theodore laughed. "Your physics teacher should hear that one."

"I learned that Hobart is in Tasmania, and that George IV followed George III." And suddenly solemn, "I also learned that I felt out of place among the other kids."

Theodore stopped and looked at Ken with a puzzled expression. "How do you mean?"

"Well—it's hard to put into words," Ken said. "Nobody really acted snobbish to me, but I was out of a lot of things.

Lots of the other fellows came from poor families but none of them lived as I do down on Timothy Place. Most of them came from working-class families, but at least their families were *working*. My father has been away for ten years and my mother has to go out cleaning and washing for other people. We're not poor, we're poverty stricken—"

"I know," Theodore interrupted, "but—"

"No you don't know," Ken cut in. "Nobody knows who has never been this way that there is more difference between being poverty stricken and being poor than there is between being poor and being rich. The other fellows used to eat in the school cafeteria for about seventeen cents a meal at lunch time—you know how they run them, four cents for soup and so on. Well, only twice in three years could I afford to eat there. The rest of the time I took a couple of sandwiches wrapped in newspaper, and sometimes only bread and butter. Once in a while I had a nickel for a bottle of milk or pop, but most of the time I didn't even have that."

Theodore said, "I know, it must have been tough. But you weren't the only kid in school like that."

"No, I wasn't the only one, but there weren't so damned many of us either. They sold school crests to put on our gym suits, and for months I couldn't afford one of them. I got a job delivering for a fruit store after school and then I bought a crest. My clothes weren't good enough to go to the parties so I refused the invitations and finally I was never invited. I won a prize at the school's annual exhibition for my drafting portfolio, but because I couldn't afford the seven or eight dollars for a set of drafting instruments I couldn't specialize in drafting, so I took something else that didn't interest me at all. Those are some of the things I mean when I say I couldn't get along up there."

"Wouldn't the teachers have helped you out; maybe helped you get a set of drafting instruments?" asked Theodore.

"They might have done, but I wouldn't ask. The worst thing about being poor—worse than just doing without things—is having to be obligated to people. Everything a poor person receives is charity, even his pay."

They didn't speak for some time, pushing their way through the Parliament Street crowds. In the restaurant they took seats in one of the varnished plywood booths, and Theodore, rather expansively and with a studied show of worldliness, ordered coffee and doughnuts.

Before the man came back with their orders Theodore said, "You must read quite a lot."

"Yes, quite a lot. I pretty near read a book a day."

"That's what I should do, but what with school and now my job and piano lessons, I can't seem to settle down to read. Have you read *A Maid and a Million Men?*"

Ken shook his head.

"You should read it. I got it from a drugstore library. I had to hide it though around the house, and read it in bed. Boy, is it hot! All about a dame overseas in the war. Have you read any hot books?"

"Sure, lots of them," answered Ken. "You should read *Louis Beretti.*"

"They sure got some hot numbers in the Owl Drugstore. There's one there that's banned. The clerk wouldn't give it to me when I asked for it, and they charge ten cents a day to read it. It's called *Lady Chatterton's*—no, *Lady Chatterley's Lover.*"

When the man put down their coffee and doughnuts Theodore handed him a dollar bill with such a flourish that Ken expected him to ask for two cigars.

"How are you coming along with the piano?" Ken asked, from between bites of doughnut.

"I'm getting there," the other answered. "My teacher wants me to go on to the Royal Conservatory of Music. I may go too, but it costs a lot of money, and unless I plan to make music my career I might as well stop now. I can play good enough for my own enjoyment."

"Don't you like to play—I mean, isn't it sort of an urge in a musician?"

"In a way, yes. When I first began taking lessons I didn't like it. The other kids called me a sissy, and Tich Armstrong down our street threw my music into a pile of horse manure one day. But gradually I learned to enjoy music, and as I became a better pianist it began to take a hold on me. Music, and playing the piano, is second nature to me now, but I know I'll never really be any good. Through music I've met some fine people, and in the end it might open the way later to something better than this." He waved his arm as if dismissing everything for miles around.

Ken stifled a smile.

Theodore asked him if he'd been to Myrla Patson's house since the party.

The preposterous idea that he would ever be invited back to Myrla's house seemed a fantastic one to Ken. He answered, "No I haven't, why?"

"Oh nothing. I just wondered if you knew her very well? She's a hot number. I met her down at the Sunnyside Boardwalk a while ago, with her boy friend."

Ken's heart seemed to miss a beat. He had to hear more, even if it hurt. "Who—who's her boy friend?" he asked.

"Holy smoke, don't tell me you're worried!" Theodore exclaimed.

"No," Ken laughed, his laughter belying his feelings. "I just wondered that's all."

"I never saw the guy before. He was a tall guy around twenty-two or three. A pretty nice-looking guy."

Ken was thinking, I haven't seen her for months, and I was actually hoping to forget her, but now just because somebody says they met her I get that sick feeling for her all over again. Maybe I'll never be able to get her out of my mind.

Theodore was talking about a movie he had seen at a neighbourhood movie house, and about something that had broken down in the middle of the film, so that the audience began stamping its feet—Ken was nodding his head as if listening, but Theodore East's words were just a buzz from across the table. He was picturing Myrla at Sunnyside with her tall good-looking boy friend, looking up at him and smiling her knowing smile. She was hugging his arm, and later they would have a hamburger and pop before driving up into High Park—

"Ken, what's the matter with you?" Theodore asked.

"Nothing. I was dreaming I guess. What was it you were saying about the picture show?"

"You're worried about something," Theodore said. "Don't tell me you're thinking of Myrla Patson? If I'd known, I wouldn't have said anything about seeing her. Don't worry about her; she's gone out with nearly everybody."

"Who the hell's worrying about *her*," Ken protested.

"Maybe we'd better go," Theodore said, gulping the last of his coffee. "There's some people looking for an empty table."

They left the small lunchroom and walked down the streets that were still warm from the afternoon sun, through the Parliament Street crowds and past the families sitting on their verandas and front steps. Streetcars hurried along Gerrard Street, and the neighbourhood was alive with its noises of a summer evening. A group of children played Hide-And-Seek with a lampost as Home, and carried on a slight breeze was the momentary sounds of a bugle band from downtown. To the northwest could be seen intermittent flashes of lightning as a summer storm bore down on the warm and dusty city.

They parted at the corner of Myrtle Street.

"I'll see you around, Ken," Theodore promised. "Let's go down to the beach some Sunday."

"I wouldn't mind," Ken said.

"Okay, I'll call for you. What's your number on Timothy Place?"

"Never mind calling for me, I'll come up to your house," said Ken.

"Whatever you want. My number's sixty-three, near the end of the street," Theodore answered. "Good night, and thanks for the conversation."

On his way down to Timothy Place Ken remembered he hadn't thanked Theodore for the coffee and doughnuts, and he wondered what Theodore thought when he'd told him not to call for him. How could he tell anybody that he was ashamed of his shabby house and of a mother who was drunk now more than she was sober.

# 7

In the fall of 1930 Ken got his first job from the National Employment Office, delivering telephone books for the Bell Telephone Company, which farmed out the contract to a door-to-door advertising agency. The pay was twenty-five-cents an hour, and the job was supposed to go to married men with children. Ken waited outside the ad agency from four o'clock in the morning and convinced the man who did the hiring that he and his mother needed the money to stave off starvation, which was not far from the truth.

He found that he liked the work and that he was fast and accurate on the job. Having taken no lunch and not having any money to buy one he was almost starved by the time he arrived home in the evening, but on subsequent days he carried a small lunch to the job.

One morning after Ken had left for work Mabel Tilling washed up the few breakfast things in a bowl on the kitchen table and wiped the breadcrumbs up. She heard the front door opening and the heavy tread of Mrs. Plummer coming along the short hallway and across the middle room.

"My goodness it's warm in here, Mrs. Tilling," said Mrs. Plummer as she entered the room. She pretended to fan herself with her hand.

"Ain't it?" answered Mabel. "You know I'm glad summer's gone. You can't hardly breathe in here in the summer. Next year I'd like to get a job cooking up in Muskoka. A woman over on Myrtle Street goes up there every summer an' cooks at a girls' camp. It's good money too, thirty-five dollars a month."

"Where's Kenneth today?"

"He's working this week delivering telephone books," Mabel answered. "It's a good job, but he works long hours. Yesterday he didn't get home till eight o'clock. Still, they pay him twenty-five cents an hour."

"It's not much, but what can you do these days?" asked Mrs. Plummer. "Yesterday I was down at the pickin's all mornin' an' only got two bags of coke. They was them small bags too, not the big two-bushel ones. There's so many people down there these days you can't hardly get a place."

"Was there anybody else from around here?" asked Mabel.

"Only Mrs. Wells. Her and her husband was down there at six o'clock in the mornin'. That's the best time to go of course, they dump out the slag from the furnaces then an' you have first choice. Of course the coke is pretty hot sometimes an' you burn your hands pickin' it."

"I guess even the coke picking's getting pretty slim," said Mabel.

"They say it's better across the Don. There's a big dump of slag behind the gasworks at the foot of Booth Avenue, but it's so far to go from here. My wagon's not so good no more neither. My arms was nearly broke pullin' it yesterday."

Mabel clucked in sympathy as she smoothed one of her stockings.

"You goin' out?" Mrs. Plummer asked.

"No, not yet," Mabel answered, standing up and surveying her legs.

"I'm goin' up to visit my sister-in-law," said the other. "She's the one I was tellin' you had a miscarriage last month."

"How is she now?" Mabel asked, combing her hair before the small broken piece of mirror over the sink.

"Oh, so-so. You know how them things is. Anyways it's a nice day to walk up there. I can go up through Allan Gardens and see the plants an' flowers in that big glass place they got. They say there's a tree there with bananas on it."

"Is there!" exclaimed Mabel, her mouth around a hairpin. "Fancy that!"

"Sure, they can grow anythin' in that building. They got lots a heat; all it needs is heat," Mrs. Plummer said, fanning herself at the mention of the word.

"I've never been in that place in Allan Gardens," said Mabel. "When we lived on Rivington before the war we had a lovely garden. I just love flowers."

For a moment she stopped fixing her hair and looked back into nostalgic time. She could see once again the large unfenced backyard and her father in the evening tying up the creepers along the wall of the woodshed. There was the smell of the trees and the nearby fields, and the voices of her mother and sisters talking together in the kitchen.

"I like flowers too," Mrs. Plummer said. "You should get Ken to dig up the yard and plant a couple of packets of flower seeds."

"Not him. He wouldn't do anything like that. He's too busy running out," Mabel said.

"Well, I got to be goin', Mrs. Tilling."

"I hope your sister-in-law's better," Mabel said, thinking of other things.

"Yes, poor soul." Then, brightening up. "By Gawd, Mrs. Tilling, you look like a chicken." Mrs. Plummer ran her eyes over Mabel, who was wearing her best dress. "Your boy friend comin'?"

"Roy said he'd be along later," Mabel said.

After Mrs. Plummer had gone Mabel sat down on a kitchen chair and let her memories, brought back by the talk of flowers, take her home again. She remembered carrying her schoolbooks in a strap made from one of her father's old belts; of being a bridesmaid at her sister Edith's wedding; of the rustle of her long stylish skirts as she climbed into Effiot Sansome's buggy the Sunday he drove her down to Belleville. She had often wondered how different her life would have been as Mrs. Sansome. But then she had met "Little Bob" Tilling, who had been called that to avoid confusion with his father, a huge man who had always been known as "Big Bob."

The Tillings had been farmers. After their marriage she had persuaded Bob to move to the city, and for four years while he was overseas during the war she had lived in this house alone with her baby Kenneth. When Bob came home he was changed; something had happened to him during those years that she could not understand. Soon after coming back in 1919 he had disappeared, and she had not seen him since. Years ago she heard he was working on a farm near Milwaukee, but that was all, and she didn't know if it was true or not. He was gone, and gone with him over the years were any feelings she had ever had for him. Sometimes she hardly remembered what he looked like, except when she saw him momentarily in the quick smile of her son.

After the short time with her husband came the long years in which she had supported herself and her child by various jobs, each a little worse than the one before. Her efforts to remain genteel had been eroded under the onslaught of a thousand little denigrating waves, each one mild but their multiplication deadly over the years. Gradually she had given up, not even knowing it herself, so that she had become careless and slovenly, forgetting the earlier promises she had made to herself.

As a result of her gradual slipping into the lethargy of poverty, Ken had been thrown more and more into the streets, which had been allowed to shape him. At first she had tried to halt or neutralize this with things she wanted him to believe, but all her efforts were parried by the boy's stubbornness.

She sensed he was ashamed of her and ashamed of the life she had made for him. This knowledge had not angered her, for she was glad that he did not take poverty as his due, and she knew that some day he would struggle to break away from it. It was important to her that some day he should.

She rose from her chair with a sigh and went into the front room, where she picked up an old magazine she had brought home with her from one of her customer's houses. She opened it and gazed at the lurid pictures, feeling a bond between herself and the abandoned women pictured in the illustrations. They too had made sacrifices for what the stories called love. She began reading, pausing every time she thought she heard Roy's footsteps in the street. Once she got up and went into the kitchen and put some fresh coal on the stove, hating its heat and its bulk and especially the dirt and bother it caused her.

Roy arrived carrying a dirty bottle of bootleg whisky which he had bought in the west-of-downtown neighbourhood called The Ward. They drank it slowly, choking at first as its fiery fumes seared their throats. Later, as its fire turned to a warmth that filled their limbs they began to talk animatedly of the simple things that formed their lives.

Mabel mentioned Mrs. Plummer's visit, and of how hard it was, with her son in prison, for her to get along.

"Bergiotti didn't want to let me have another bottle," Roy said. "I owe him for two now."

"He's got a nerve. He knows you'll pay him when you get your cheque."

"He's scared. Says he needs the money, the cops is watching him."

"Never mind what he says, he's got plenty. My God, he's never been pinched yet, has he?"

Roy poured himself a drink and held it up to the light.

"I wouldn't go there any more if that's the way he's going to act. You can get just as good stuff at Lawrence's," Mabel said indignantly.

"I saw some pigs' feet in a butcher's window down the street," said Roy. "It's a long time since I ate pigs' feet." He continued staring at the liquid in his glass.

He was such an inoffensive little man was Roy. When she was drunk Mabel felt a tenderness towards him. "When Ken comes home we can send him down to the butcher's for some," she said.

"I should have gone with Horten today," Roy said.

"Where to?"

"Out pollacking. He made four dollars yesterday. The people up on Bloor save him their papers and stuff. He's talking about buying a truck somewheres. There's money in junk you know."

Mabel laughed. The thought of Roy out with his crony Horten, pushing their two-wheeled wagon and searching garbage cans for old paper and salable junk tickled her. It was a long way from Rivington to this, she thought.

"What do you want to go out pollacking for?" she asked him. "You can scrape by on your pension, can't you?"

"There's nobody can live on the money they give you. They promised us everything when we was over there but now they don't care a damn. If we'd a known what was comin' things would a turned out different, let me tell you—"

Roy usually had little to say about the war, but the memory of it brought a quick excitement to his eyes, reminding him of a time when he had been elevated from his obscurity to take part in a world-wide thing.

By the time the bottle was half empty Roy was loud-voiced about the plight of the veterans. "Have they done anythink?" he asked. "Has any of 'em, 'specially that son of a bitch R. B. Bennett, done anythink?"

Mabel shook her head slowly, the effects of the alcohol making her movements slow and heavy.

"What did they promise us, eh?"

"Oh shut up, you old fool!" she said giggling.

"I won't shut up. They promised us everythink, an' what've they done? I'll tell you—nothink!"

"Pour yourself a drink and shut up."

"They'll have to soon though. They'll have to soon."

"I know," Mabel said. "Pour yourself a drink, Roy."

"You listen to me," said Roy, pouring some whisky into his glass and onto the table.

"I won't. Don't forget the pigs' feet."

"To hell with the pigs' feet!"

"I just remembered Ken won't be home till after supper. I'll go down and get some. Have you got enough money?" asked Mabel.

"I've got enough, don't worry. I've got enough. I'm going to give you the right change too. The last time Ken went to the store he stole the change," Roy said with drunken belligerence.

"He did not!"

"Yes he did. I wasn't that drunk."

"Don't you accuse him of being a thief!"

"Well, somebody stole it anyways," Roy said, retreating before her anger.

"If you don't want to buy any, forget it."

"I'll buy some, but I'll buy 'em my own way. I don't need nobody to tell me how to spend my money."

"Then get out of here!" Mabel cried.

"All right, if that's the way you feel about it. But nobody's going to steal my money."

"It wasn't the kid; he didn't steal it."

"Then who did?" Roy asked quickly.

"I did," Mabel answered, challenging him.

"*You* did!"

"Yes," said Mabel, lifting a soiled handkerchief to her face and pretending to cry.

"Well, you've got a bloody nerve!"

"I know, I know, but we needed it to eat," Mabel said from behind her handkerchief.

"You should've asked. By God, to steal a man's money an' then tell him about it."

"I'm sorry, Roy."

"Oh shut up. It don't matter."

"No, not after you've made a song of it."

"I thought the kid stole it," Roy said.

"He wouldn't!" Mabel said, coming out from behind the hanky.

"You can't tell about kids. Most kids'il steal anythink."

"Not Ken!" Mabel shouted, getting angry again.

"He ain't no different from any of the others."

"Yes he is, he's different from them all. He's too smart to steal. Some day he's going to be a lot different from you and me."

"Let's hope so."

"He's going to get on. You should see the books he reads, and he's only seventeen."

"Readin' don't do you no good," said Roy. "Make him go to night school where they'll learn him to be a machinist. A machinist is a good job."

"He'll be better than that. Anyway there's plenty of machinists out of work today."

"These times can't last forever. They'll be takin' them back on soon, you wait an' see. As soon as we get rid a R. B. Bennett an' bring Mackenzie King back. There wasn't no hard times under Mackenzie King. The Conservatives was never no good for the workin' man."

"You're a liar!" Mabel screamed at him. "Let's give Bennett a chance. After all he ain't been in long enough yet."

Mabel's family had been Conservative for generations, and like most of the Cabbagetowners she was still a rabid Conservative, as well as a monarchist, an antiforeigner, a passive anti-Catholic, and more British than the people of the British Isles.

"Ken isn't going to work in a factory all his life," she went on.

"What's wrong with that?" asked Roy with drunken puzzlement.

"He says he doesn't want to."

"*He* says! A kid like that don't know what he wants."

"Yes he does. He's going to be something bigger than the rest of us around here."

"It'd be better if he learned a trade," said Roy, unconvinced.

"Where would it get him these days, tell me that?"

After Roy left during the afternoon, Mabel lay down on the couch in the front room and slept for a couple of hours. When she woke up she peeled some carrots and a small turnip and placed them in a pan on the stove. From the cupboard in the middle room she took a small parcel wrapped in grease-stained paper, took a length of oxtail from it, and dropped it in with the vegetables. Later on she would thicken the "stew" with flour. Then she returned to the couch and lay down.

Ken was out of work for months after the job delivering telephone books ended, except for two days at Christmas selling trees. He had stood half frozen in front of Joe Pergoli's Fruit and Vegetable Market on Parliament Street trying to interest the hurrying crowds of Christmas shoppers in the scruffy-looking Christmas trees. He managed to sell ten of them, and for this he received a dollar bill from Joe.

When Mabel was sober she watched Ken moving listlessly around the house, usually staying slovenly and unwashed until after supper. At times she felt a rush of maternal pity for her son as she watched him falling apart under his forced idleness and its attendant hopelessness.

One day as she watched him roll one cigarette after another while sitting before the stove reading a book she said to him, "You know, Ken, you're smoking too much."

Without looking up from his book he barked, "What of it!"

"I don't like to watch you killing yourself like that," she said.

"Never mind me killing myself. Holy Jeez, as though that's anything! Don't worry as soon as this package is empty I'll have to stop." He made a fresh cigarette, licking the paper expertly.

Mabel went into the middle room, took a dime from her purse, and dropped it in the pocket of the light topcoat he wore all winter.

There were times when Ken didn't feel frustrated from being out of work. Unemployment and hopelessness, like a long-suffered pain, can be almost a feeling of normalcy.

The worst part of their poverty, to Ken, was his weekly visits to the House of Industry, an old grey stone downtown building used as a food-distributing agency by the city's Welfare Department. The building had long been used by the city to house elderly indigents, and was known to its patrons by the tramp's colloquialism for hospital, "pogey." Before the Depression was over this word would be used as a synonym for city relief and public welfare.

At the House of Industry long lines of men and women first had their employment cards stamped and then shuffled along beside a series of bare wooden counters where the week's groceries were placed in individual bags by other reliefees who were working their weekly stint. Some of the men were refused their groceries until they completed a few hours' work, chopping logs or sluicing down the floor. Public assistance was still looked upon as charity, and those who asked for it had to atone for their mendicancy by honest toil.

One afternoon as Ken slowly shuffled towards the counter a fidgety little man just ahead of him turned and said, "It's a bloody shame this is, making me an' you and the likes of that poor woman in front of you come down here for this handful of junk. I'll bet half of it's thrown away anyways. What they need here is to give it to you by cheque like they do in the States or Montreal or Vancouver. It's a bloody circus, that's what it is. There's nobody that meets you on the street don't know you're comin' from here."

Ken nodded.

"Look at some of these people carryin' club-bags and paper to wrap their stuff up in. They don't fool nobody. I seen a man last week walk back two car stops along Dundas before he got in a street car goin' the other way, just so's people wouldn't know he'd been here. He had his rations in a suitcase too. It's gettin' so everybody that carries a suitcase on the street gets the name 'Pogey Stiff.'"

The little man laughed, and Ken joined with him. There were several smiles from others in the line.

The man warmed up to his audience and went on, "Take me now. I've got six kids at home, an' me and the missus makes eight. When we first went on relief the kids used to like the peanut butter, but you ought to see 'em now. They couldn't eat any more of it if they was starvin'. And beans! I'm going to buy my kids a pea-shooter apiece to get rid of some of 'em. I guess I've got a ton of dried beans in the cupboard." He laughed again and several of the crowd joined in.

A woman farther down the queue turned around and asked, "What do you do with the rolled oats?" This caused more laughter. A man answered, "Burn 'em in your stove, lady. They burn good." "No, don't," warned the little man in front of Ken. "I tried that but they plugged up the stove-pipes." Several people in the queue, and in the one next to it, began to laugh. The men who were filling the bags looked up and a policeman walked over to see what was causing the unfamiliar laughter.

Ken was handed the Tilling's weekly ration of bread and milk tickets, and an order for coke. Then he was given his rationed packages of beans, rolled oats, potatoes and other staples of the relief diet and finally, as an unlooked-for treat, a small cardboard container of apple butter in lieu of the usual peanut concoction.

He waited for his packages to be placed in a large paper bag by a man across the counter, and watched several other people shoving their supplies into old army kitbags or suitcases. The bolder ones walked out to the street with their stigmata held out for all the city to see.

It wasn't only Cabbagetown and the West-End slums that were represented in the relief lines now. It seemed that the Depression, as it was beginning to be called, was, like a war or revolution, a leveller of the population.

During the evenings Ken and his friends lounged around the corners under the streetlights bumming "the makin's" from each other and making remarks about passing girls. During the warm weather some of them mounted their own or borrowed bicycles and rode in a group through downtown to The Ward to try to pick up the little Italian and Jewish girls to take for rides on the bars of their bikes.

When the gangs of young fellows in The Ward proved too tough they rode down to Cherry Beach or Simcoe Beach, along the East-End lakefront, to flirt with and pick up the girls.

Many of the girls willingly went for bike rides down behind the gas works or along the deserted factory streets, and when the gang remustered later they would brag and lie about their largely imaginative conquests. Nothing much happened on these nocturnal forays except a little kissing and what was to become known as petting but the adventure of the game and its possibilities drew them almost every night.

During the cold weather, when both standing on the corner and riding bicycles were given up, one way of passing the evening was to sneak into the Corinth Theatre to see the movie. This was done by opening a door to a coal chute with a table knife. The gang would slide down the chute to the basement and sneak up some stairs to the rear of the darkened stage. Then one by one they would slip through a curtained doorway and on hands and knees crawl into the seats, mixing with the paying customers. The gang made up for the management's lack of door receipts by their hearty laughing and clapping and other manifestations of approval.

One winter's evening, as some of the gang were walking home from the skating rink in Riverdale Park, a member of the gang named Bob McIsaacs asked, "Do you guys want to make some money?"

The other three showed their interest.

"I know how we can make plenty," McIsaacs said.

"How?" asked Ken.

"Well I know a guy—I ain't mentioning no names—that runs a junk yard, see? He wants me to get him all the copper wire I can and he'll pay plenty for it."

"What you gonna do, strip it off the lamp poles?" asked Billy Addington.

"Yeah," asked Les Winters. "Where you gonna get it?"

"I know where to get it, don't worry," answered Bob. "If you guys want to come in with me we'll split the dough four ways."

Ken said, "I'll go in with you, McIsaacs." The other two nodded.

"Okay," said Bob. "I'll meet you guys tomorrow night and take you to the place where we can get it."

"Where is it?" asked a skeptical Billy Addington.

"I'm not going to tell you guys tonight. Wait till tomorrow."

The following night they hung around a Queen Street pool-room, watching some older men shooting a game of snooker for quarters, until McIsaacs arrived, after ten o'clock. He took them down to a lonely neighbourhood of factories, builders' supply yards and freight sheds along the lower Don River. The place was deserted except for the watchmen inside the factories and warehouses and the drivers and passengers of a few cars heading across the river from downtown.

They cut along lanes and alleys until they came to a high board fence topped with barbed wire surrounding the piled-up yard of a salvage company.

"This is the place," Bob said. "The wire's just over the fence."

"For chrissakes, are we going to pinch it off of the guy you told us about!" Les Winters asked.

"Don't be so dumb," Bob said. "This ain't his yard."

Ken wanted to laugh. It was like sitting in church or school and choking with an uncontrollable urge to giggle, the urge acting like a tickle in the throat.

"Jeez, I'm not goin' over that fence," said Billy. "Look at that barbed wire."

"Somebody's gotta go over," Bob said. "How about you and me, Tilling."

Ken looked at the high fence. "I guess so," he said.

He wanted to laugh. It seemed so unreal. Here they were going to rob somebody, and if they were caught they'd go to jail, and it didn't seem that important at all. It was no different than breaking into the coal chute at the Corinth. He realized for the first time how a criminal must feel starting on a job. There was really nothing to it at all.

Bob said, "Okay then, you guys, me an' Tilling goes over, and you, Winters, stay on top of the fence. We'll hand you the wire and you hand it down to Billy." He swung around and stared at Ken. "Jeez, Tilling, what are you doin', laughin'? Don't make no noise 'cause there's a watchman in the office."

"There's no watchdog is there?" Ken asked.

"No."

Ken and Bob climbed on Les Winters' shoulders and got over the barbed wire, letting themselves down into the yard on three horizontal two-by-fours nailed along the inside of the fence. Bob touched Ken's arm and they crouched behind a big rusty boiler. Ken felt his heart pounding in his temples as the fence now stood between himself and escape. When Bob whispered, "That's it over there," and pointed to a pile of dark coils on the ground, Ken knew that he was nervous too. There was dirty snow on the ground and it was very dark.

They ran to the coils of wire, keeping low, their eyes on the building down the yard. Bob struggled for a moment with a heavy coil of the wire before hanging it on his shoulder and carrying it to the fence. Ken followed his example, but as he stumbled along he had the panicky feeling that the watchman was taking aim to shoot him in the back. He almost dropped the wire, but McIsaacs whispered, "Come on, Tilling, don't get scared. There's nobody can hear us." They lifted both coils up to Winters, who lowered them down into the lane to Billy.

After three more trips Ken and McIsaacs climbed back over the fence again and joined the other two. "Put a coil on each shoulder," said Bob, picking up a pair of them. The others did the same, and they trudged down the lane, across a couple of empty streets, and finally came to another high fence surrounding a second junk yard.

McIsaacs knocked at the wooden gate, then again, harder this time. Footsteps crossed the yard and a voice asked, "Who is it?"

"It's me, McIsaacs," Bob answered.

A key rattled against a heavy padlock, the heavy gate swung away from them, and a man let them into the yard.

After locking the gate again the man said, "Come with me." They followed him across the yard and into a low shed illuminated by a naked bulb hanging from the ceiling. Around the walls was an assortment of automobile engines, iron pipe, boxes of lead shavings, and a hodge-podge of all kinds of metal junk. The man took a crowbar and lifted a hinged door in the floor, pointing down the hole. The boys dropped their coils of wire into the hole, then rubbed their shoulders and smiled, relieved that the job was over. The man, a sad little middle-aged Jew, pulled an old metal bathtub and a pile of old sacks over the trapdoor and looked the boys over carefully.

"This is Mister—" Bob began, but the little man stopped him.

"No names please. It's better that the boys they don't know no names, eh, boys? I don't know your names, you don't know my name, eh?"

Ken said, "Let's have the money and get outa here."

"I'll pay you boys, I'll pay you, don't be in a hurry," said the man. He opened a change purse and pulled out two ten-dollar bills, handing them to Bob McIsaacs.

Bob said, "Kee-rist, this ain't enough! Them coils musta weighed fifty pounds apiece."

"No, no," said the man, grinning at the others. "They don't weigh thirty pounds. Believe me, I'm in the business an'—"

"Like hell they don't!" Billy Addington said, walking towards him.

"Now, boys, listen, I'll give you five dollars more because we're friends, but believe me I won't make that much myself out of the deal."

"Oh, shit!" shouted Los Winters. "Give us the money and let's go."

The man handed Bob a five-dollar bill and they followed him out of the shed and through the yard. When they reached the gate he said, "Let me know when you got more goods to sell." He opened the gate and gave them a grin and a little nod.

Later on in a small Bulgarian restaurant on King Street they had a sandwich and coffee apiece in order to change the five-dollar bill. Bob Mclsaacs gave one of the tens to Ken to split with Billy, and kept the other to share with Winters.

On the way home Ken changed the tenspot at the cashier's cage of a Queen Street movie house and gave Billy his half.

It had been so easy. Billy said they should do it every night, and Ken laughingly agreed.

When he arrived home though Ken noticed that his hands were shaking. He took his six dollars from his pocket and stared at it in disbelief. It was the most money he had handled in months, and more money than he had ever earned so quickly before.

That winter the four boys made a few more forays into junk yards south of Cabbagetown to steal copper wire, lead pipe and fancy plumbing fittings, which they sold to the little man Mclsaacs knew. Most of their amateur thefts earned them only a couple of dollars apiece, but it was the only cash any of them earned at all.

Mabel Tilling asked her son where the money was coming from, and he told her he found an evening's work now and again as a relief usher in a downtown movie theatre. With the few dollars he made from the thefts he bought himself a pair of secondhand shoes and a secondhand suit.

One bitterly cold night, when the few bags of relief department coke had run out and a drunken Mabel was trying to chop up a kitchen chair for fuel, Ken left the house and borrowed a two-wheel push wagon from Mr. Wells next door. When he reached the railroad yards down near the river he filled the wagon with good anthracite coal, throwing it from a gondola car on a siding. When he reached home again he dumped it through the front cellar window.

The salvage yards were getting too dangerous now for the gang to attempt any more jobs. The watchmen had been put on the alert and the police cars cruised the neighbourhood more than they had done before. Goldy, the fence who had bought their stuff, said to them one evening as they sat around in his shed, "You know, boys, I could use some more lead pipe and a few toilet fixtures."

"Sure, and we can get a bullet in the back from a watchman," Ken said.

McIsaacs chimed in. "The other yards is too hot, Goldy. We gotta lay off for a while."

"Don't go getting yourself in trouble," Goldy said. "I just thought maybe you were smart and wanted another chance to make some money."

"We ain't that smart," said Les Winters.

"Have you boys thought of the houses?" Goldy asked, looking from one to the other.

"Yeah, the big house," Bob answered. Les Winters began to laugh. "Shut up, Winters," McIsaacs said.

"Listen, boys, I have a customer for a bathroom set. Three pieces, you know, toilet, bath and wash basin. I'd pay fifty dollars for a new one if I could get it. Maybe you boys could help me out."

"We'd never be able to carry a bathtub down here. Don't be goofy," said Les. He looked at Bob for confirmation; be was afraid of McIsaacs.

"I thought you boys could get a truck," shrugged Goldy. "Of course if you don't need the money—"

"We need it all right," Ken said. "But hell we're not going to steal a truck too!"

"Maybe you could borrow one," Goldy said. He took a package of tailor-mades from his pocket, lit a cigarette, but did not offer them around.

"Maybe we could get a guy that owns a truck," Bob said, thinking.

"I know a guy," Billy Addington cut in. "I could ast him tomorrow."

"Where's these houses?" Ken asked.

"You get the truck and I'll find out for you," Goldy replied.

A few evenings later the gang headed for a group of houses that were being built in Forest Hill, Ken, McIsaacs and Winters riding in the back of a two-ton truck while Billy Addington rode in the cab with a friend of his named Battersby. They had decided to cut the fifty dollars from Goldy five ways, Battersby getting ten, which was as much as he made some weeks in the cartage business.

Arriving at the address Goldy had given them they parked the truck at the curb and Ken walked across the lot to one of the half-constructed houses, joined in a moment by Bob Mclsaacs. They stood together in the muddy lot and looked over the house, which was one of four being built. The front door had not yet been hung, and only a plank nailed across the doorway barred their entry. The street lights here in the half-suburban Forest Hill Village were few and far apart, and it was quite dark. Lights shone in a few windows across the street, far away across deep lawns, but the nearest occupied house on the same side as the new ones was across a wide vacant lot.

The two boys swung under the nailed plank and entered the hall-way of the house, looking around them in the light from a match that Mclsaacs lighted. Lined against a wall were the bathroom fittings, in wooden crates lined with excelsior pads. Bob returned to the doorway and called softly to Les and Billy. When the others arrived the four of them grabbed a corner each of the bathtub crate, slid it under the front door plank and carried it across the snow and mud to the truck. They returned to the house for the other two pieces. Ken and Bob wrestled the heavy wash basin crate through the door and across the ground to the truck.

"Hurry up, you guys!" Battersby cautioned, hurrying back to where the boys were busy shoving the crate over the tailboard. "I saw a guy come out of a house up the street with a dog. He looked at us for a minute then went back in."

Ken and Bob pushed the crate into the truck and ran back to the house to help Les and Billy with the toilet bowl and water tank. Les and Ken cursed as they struggled with the awkward case that held the toilet bowl. Then the four boys stopped and listened. Mclsaacs dropped his end of the tank case and ran to the doorway, to be joined by Ken. The small taillight of Battersby's truck was disappearing up the street, while from the other direction, but still two blocks away, came the headlights of a car.

"It's the cops!" Ken yelled, pushing Les Winters aside and heading for the back of the house. Billy Addington fell over a crate and hopped around holding his shin, then ran through the front door. The others stumbled around panic-stricken through the unfamiliar house.

Ken tripped into an unfinished section of hardwood flooring but finally found the side door and fell through it to the ground. He stared around him wildly, looking for a hiding place, and finally found one behind a pile of lumber. He heard the car come to a stop in the street, the sound of running feet, then the car pulled away again. He scrunched himself lower behind the lumber.

Things were quiet for a moment or two then a deep male voice cried, "Here's one here!" There was the sound of another pair of running feet then silence again. Ken's heart was beating so fast he felt sure the policemen could hear it.

A bright light appeared along the top of the lumber, came around the end of the pile, and shone into Ken's staring eyes. From behind the flashlight a deep voice said, "Get up, you son of a bitch!" Ken stood up, blinking in the blinding light. "Come on out here and don't try nothing funny," the voice said again. Ken, shielding his eyes with his arm, approached the light and a heavy hand grabbed the collar of his windbreaker and he was marched back into the house.

In a corner stood the other three boys, Bob trying to look tough and defiant, Les Winters sniffling and wiping his eyes on his sleeve, and Billy looking white and scared. Two policemen were keeping their flashlights on the boys. Ken was pushed over to join them.

After a couple of minutes during which nothing was said by anybody they heard the car come back, and a fourth policeman came into the house. They were given a cursory search and then herded out to the police car. The drive to the police station was a short one, not more than a block away, around a corner from the street they were arrested on. This explained the four policemen, Ken thought, quietly cursing Goldy for sending them there.

After being grilled separately at the station they were booked on theft and attempted theft charges, and placed in the police station cells. The following morning they appeared before a magistrate, were remanded for a week, and sent in a crowded patrol wagon to the Don Jail. Though Ken was quite familiar with the outside of the jail, having played around it as a child in Riverdale Park, and once having stared at it through the window of his ward in the Isolation Hospital during a six-week stay there with scarlet fever, the inside of the place was not what he had imagined at all. To him it was a depressing place of bars within bars and doors within doors, and the jail slum made him even long for a plate of welfare beans.

The four boys lounged around their corridor or read, played cards or just shot the bull. Billy Addington's father sent him a little money and with it Billy bought them each a package of tobacco. Ken was surprised to see so many men he had been acquainted with outside.

Bob McIsaacs told the others, "This rap'll be easy to beat. They can't prove we stole nothing. What we'll do is say that we was just hanging around an empty house. Hell, anybody's allowed to do that."

A serious young Jewish lawyer named Rapaport was appointed to defend them, and he advised them all to plead guilty and throw themselves on the mercy of the court. McIsaacs wanted to ask for a judge and jury trial, but when he talked it over with the others, and they realized they'd have to stay in the Don until the next assizes came up, the others talked him out of it.

They decided not to mention Goldy, as this would only implicate them in the thefts from the scrapyards. Billy was the only one who knew Battersby, and he said he wouldn't squeal on him. Mr. Rapaport told them that the bathtub and wash basin had been recovered; apparently Battersby had thrown them from his truck.

One morning after breakfast Billy Addington asked Ken what he was going to do when he got out.

"Going to do? I guess I'll do the same as I did before."

"I meant are you gonna swipe more stuff?"

"No, I'm finished with that stuff. The only man I ever want to rob is old McDonald down at the grocery wholesale. Jeez, if I could only get a chance to do it I'd back a truck up to his place and steal every damn bit of stuff he's got."

"I guess I'm not working for him no more either," Billy said without regret. "He'll never take me back there now."

"That shouldn't worry you."

"Do you ever feel funny about havin' stole stuff like we did?"

"No."

"I mean do you feel scared sometimes that—well like it was a sin?"

"Hell no! Do you?"

"Sometimes I do."

"Not me. That dirty bastard McDonald blamed me for somethin' I didn't do, an' the guy that stole his stuff is still working there. If that's the way things are I don't see any reason why anybody should try to be good. He stole a week's pay from me and what did the cops do when I reported him? They told me to forget it because he could have me pinched if he wanted to. My mother reported him to the Neighbourhood Workers, and they told her to forget it. All those outfits work together against us, don't worry."

"I used to feel bad after I got the money from Goldy," Billy said. "Sometimes I was nearly afraid to spend it."

"I felt good when I got the money," Ken went on. "The only times I feel bad is when I haven't any. Sometimes it seemed that when I swiped some stuff from the junk yards I was swiping it from McDonald. That first night when we got the dough from Goldy it was like getting my week's pay back."

"I wish I could feel like that," Billy said. "My old lady is sore as hell at me. She always used to say that she hated a thief worse than anything. I didn't like to see her come up here last Sunday. She just sat there and looked at me, half cryin', while the old man lectured me all the time."

"You'll be all right, Billy, after it's over. The only thing is don't get mixed up with Mclsaacs."

"I ain't going to. I'm finished with this kinda stuff."

"So am I," Ken said. "The only crooks that get away with it is the kind like McDonald."

The four of them were found guilty and remanded another week for sentence.

On the morning they appeared in court to be sentenced Ken was wearing his good secondhand suit, which Mabel had brought up to the jail. Billy Addington also wore his Sunday suit, but Bob Mclsaacs and Les Winters were still dressed as they had been on the night of their arrest, except that now Bob was wearing a shirt and tie instead of his hockey sweater.

They were brought up into the prisoners' dock from the basement bullpen, where Mclsaacs had met an old friend of his who was waiting to appear in County Court on a charge of assault with a deadly weapon. Bob Mclsaacs told the others, "There goes a real guy. He knocked off a guy in charge of a cash-and-carry icehouse, with a tire iron. His name's Ellis, from Seaton Street."

The court officials were busy with remand procedures from the previous case, and Ken glanced around the courtroom from his place on the wooden bench inside the dock. The crown attorney and their own lawyer, Mr. Rapaport, were talking and smiling together. The magistrate wore a flowered necktie beneath his black robe, and he looked up now and again across the top of his glasses from whatever he was reading. An old fat policeman wearing glasses but no revolver opened the door at the rear of the courtroom and admitted a Salvation Army woman.

Finally a clerk sitting below the magistrate's bench rapped gently on his desk with a gavel and read the charges against the boys, as a policeman whispered angrily to them to stand up. The magistrate stared at the prisoners for a moment before he spoke. Ken glanced over his shoulder, looking for his mother. Right behind the prisoners' dock sat a red-eyed Mrs. Addington and her daughter Belle, while a little to one side but in the seat behind them sat Mr. and Mrs. McIsaacs. Mabel Tilling was nowhere to be seen.

The magistrate shot his French cuffs and picked a piece of thread from one of them as he began to speak. "During the past two years we have been faced in this country with a time of increased unemployment and its attendant hardships. Our boys and young men—" He fixed the quartet with an over-the-glasses stare. "—including you who stand before me today—have left school and have found yourselves part of a society which can offer you little in the way of steady employment and its attendant remuneration. There is nothing more tragic to my knowledge—" He raised his eyes to the spectators' benches. "—than to be young, and eager to take one's place among men, in a decent civilized community, and find the way barred by the economic barrier of unemployment." Facing the boys again— "However we cannot allow our knowledge of these things, or our sympathy with the accused, to sway us from our task, which is the protection of society from the anarchy and lawlessness that parallels the upward swing in our crime rate."

He consulted his notes before going on. "Lester Winters, I am told that you come from a motherless home. You have been brought up by friends and neighbours, and for a time you were the ward of an orphan asylum in another town. Your boyhood has not been one which you can remember with a great deal of pleasure, and your associations have not been of the best. I have taken these factors into consideration because I recognize the need for this court to show full appreciation of the background that has contributed to your standing before me today." He cleared his throat, and reached for a glass of water. Ken stared from the clerk and the court stenographer, both busy over their notes, then over his shoulder to where a Catholic priest was leaning over speaking to Mrs. McIsaacs.

The magistrate began again, "Kenneth Tilling," and Ken swung around to face him, standing at rigid attention. "You have received the advantages of two and one-half years of secondary education, but you also come from a broken home. When you testified on your own behalf you laid the blame for your crime solely on the factor of unemployment. I had the feeling then—and I have not lost it yet—that you went into this with your eyes open to its financial rewards, if it succeeded, and its consequences if it did not. You seem to me to be possessed of an above-average intelligence, but one which for some reason you refuse to utilize for your own good. Your testimony was honest and forthright, but the honesty of a confession under law does not atone for the dishonesty of the act confessed. You possess no previous criminal record, and I do not believe that you can yet be classed as a criminal, socially at any rate."

Ken felt a sense of relief making him want to smile, and he turned his gaze from the magistrate's face and watched the court stenographer flip his notebook to the next page.

The magistrate went on. "William Addington, you, unlike the others, cannot claim unemployment as a reason for your act, nor can you claim a disadvantageous homelife. True your salary is picayune but many others are labouring under the same, er, disadvantage, without resorting to the breaking of the law to implement their small stipend. You have shown weakness of character and a willingness to be led, but your past good record is also in your favour. The fact of your refusing to divulge the name of the truck driver might be a praiseworthy gesture in the criminal world, but the protection of an accomplice is not looked upon in the same light in a court of law.

"Robert McIsaacs, you have received the benefits of a decent upbringing in a good Christian home. I have heard the testimony of character witnesses on your behalf. However after hearing them I was surprised to note that your record of crime is a lengthy one for a youth of your age. Up to now your offenses have been nothing but petty misdemeanors, but each succeeding one has been more serious than the one previous. If you continue on this path the consequences might well be the gallows. You, the oldest member of the group, were its leader, and as such the greater blame must be laid to you." The magistrate paused and searched his desk for something. Finding it he looked out across his glasses and said, "I will now read the sentence of this court."

The policeman whispered snottily to the boys to face the magistrate, even though they were already facing him.

"The crime of which you all have been proved guilty is punishable by incarceration in a federal penitentiary. I am not going to send youths there to mix with older hardened criminals. I think that you have all learned a lesson." He stared down at the boys. "Lester Winters, Kenneth Tilling and William Addington, I sentence you each to six months in the Ontario Reformatory—sentence to be suspended. Robert McIsaacs, I sentence you to six months determinate and three months indeterminate in the Ontario Reformatory."

The boys stood for a moment in the dock, uncertain what they were to do. A policeman opened the gate, took Bob McIsaac by the sleeve, and led him down the steps to the cells, as Bob gave a wave and a hard half-smile to his parents. Their lawyer walked over and led the other three boys from the dock. Ken noticed that the priest and Mr. McIsaacs were trying to comfort Bob's mother, who was sobbing wildly. A man whom Ken took to be Les Winters' father came bearing down on his son, while Billy Addington joined his mother and sister on the bench where they sat. Ken watched the others for a moment or two, then he walked along the aisle to the doorway, thinking that his mother had probably been too drunk-sick to come to court.

He shrugged off his aloneness, letting it be replaced with the independent mantle he had worn since early boyhood, and hurried into the snow-covered street. On the opposite sidewalk, under a metal awning outside a side door of Eaton's department store, an unemployed man wearing a pinned-up suit coat, a row of war medals on his chest, was selling five-cent apples from a cardboard box.

**9**

During the rest of the winter Ken
and Billy Addington, who had been fired from McDonald's
Wholesale after the trial, spent most of their weekday mornings in
the employment office and their afternoons at the skating rink in the
park. Once or twice a week Ken made his way east across the Don
River to the public library, carrying home as many books as he was
allowed to borrow on his library card. He became interested in
North American Indian tribes, and read all the books he could find
on the subject. He drew a freehand map of North America and wrote
the names of the tribes and their approximate territories on it. The
Plains Indians were his favourites—the horse-riding Sioux,
Arapahoe, Crow, Apache and Cheyenne.

Two evenings a week he and Billy attended two different young
people's groups, one of which met in the parish hall of a large
downtown church. This church was an old one which had been
surrounded by office buildings and factories, and its congregation
had died off or moved away many years before. The children of its
old parishioners were now among the most influential and fashionable in the city, but they made use of the church now only for social
occasions such as weddings and fashionable funerals. Most of the
time the church premises were used only by the neighbourhood
underprivileged.

Ken and Billy learned to dance on the floor of its parish hall, and
it became a warm and friendly place in which to escape cold and
snowy winter evenings.

During the spring Ken received an unexpected letter from a Mr. Clarence Gurney, a caseworker with the Friendly Uncles Club. It took a few minutes for Ken to recall who Mr. Gurney was, but then he remembered that a couple of years before the man had visited Timothy Place and had talked Mabel into allowing him to go to a summer camp sponsored by the Uncles. Mr. Gurney stated in his letter that he had been informed that Ken had "been in difficulties" during the winter and, though Ken was getting over the age limit for help from the Friendly Uncles, he would be pleased if Ken could visit him at his home where they could perhaps plan something to his benefit. Mr. Gurney suggested an evening soon, and gave his address.

On the night in question Ken put on his Sunday suit and a clean shirt, though he hated dressing up when his attempts were pitiful secondhand substitutes for the real thing. On his way uptown he imagined that every idle glance from a passerby was a critical appraisal of his appearance, and he had an urge to throw his necktie away and scuff dirt on his shoes. He wished he'd ignored Gurney's invitation and gone bike riding with the gang.

He passed out of the shabby working-class streets of Cabbagetown, crossed Parliament and into the Moss Park neighbourhood where the houses were bigger but just as shabby as the smaller ones of his own district. Moss Park, which had once been a well-to-do residential area when the city was young and Cabbagetown was a close-in suburb of the much smaller city, was now a transient neighbourhood, its big houses showing ROOMS TO LET signs, but many of them converted to cheap office premises and the homes of esoteric sects, societies and foundations.

As he ambled slowly along Dundas Street Ken eyed the houses he passed with their signs in the windows proclaiming their faith, fad or fatuity: Sunday Seances, Toronto Anabaptist Society, BRITISH ISRAEL, Ontario Heart & Lungs Foundation, SALON DE DANCE, 126th Battalion Club, Lupino's School of the Hawaiian Guitar, Milady's

Hair Bobbing, ASTROLOGY, Ont. Theosophical Society, and ROOMS FOR MEN—25c.

He crossed Sherbourne Street into the heart of the city's criminal, drug and prostitution district, a neighbourhood that not only led the country in most crimes, but also in its incidence of tuberculosis, venereal disease, illegitimacy, incest and percentage of social welfare recipients. It was a neighbourhood of common-law unions, hamburgers, the deserted and deserting spouse, the lonely drinker and the lonelier sleeper.

The scenes were familiar to him: the slack-breasted whores standing before the lunch-counters, the toothless drunken harridans, the crippled old men and their pinch-checked younger counterparts, most of them conditioned and institutionalized by charity and beggary, the flotsam that flowed from all parts of the city and from other parts of the whole country itself.

Ken glanced into the interiors of restaurants he passed, envious of those who could afford to eat in them. What he wanted most in the world was to be dressed in new clothes, some money in his pocket, and Myrla Patson on his arm. He and Myrla would enter a restaurant, sit down at a table, and he would order a meal. While waiting for the waitress to bring it he would light a cigarette and look across the white tablecloth at Myrla, who would smile back at him—

He turned north into a neighbourhood that was undergoing its transition from genteel shabby rich to genteel middle class; its residents the left-behind, the immovable, the disinherited, disconnected remnants of a society that was gone or scattered. Among these had infiltrated the poorer climbers, the socially misplaced, the maiden dilettantes, the pretenders to whom a street name and number were more important than the lodgings themselves. These newer denizens rented rooms, flats, or "studios" in houses that were now too big and too decrepit for their former inhabitants. The neighbourhood had the look of decay, the smell of senility and the transitory tackiness of residences jerry-divided into low rent "apartments."

To young Ken Tilling the district represented a way of life that he would never know, and which he didn't really care to ever achieve. He was satisfied to remain a member of his class and station in life, and it never entered his head to want such cultural appurtenances as oil paintings, symphony records, books of his own, social status or a membership in a club or social milieu. He was convinced that the people of Cabbagetown got more fun out of life, raised the prettiest girls and had fewer ulcers and breakdowns than the social and financial strivers up here. When the stock market panic had run its course he would be quite content with a steady job, a weekly pay envelope and a girl like Myrla. His step took on the buoyancy of spring and the carelessness of youth as he hurried now past Carlton Street and the girls' college that stood abutting the sidewalk on the west side of the tree-lined street.

Clarence Gurney called to his sister from behind the closed door of the bathroom, "Bernice, where is the darned toothpaste?"

"On the top shelf of the medicine cabinet," she answered, turning up the volume of the Gothic-cabinetted superheterodyne radio that stood on the living room mantel. She turned the dial, choosing a station that poured forth the muted music of a dance orchestra playing "I'm Dancing with Tears in My Eyes," and lay back on the afghan-covered sofa. The radio music blotted out the sound of running water from the bathroom that had been built into the closet space beneath the third-floor stairs of the sub-divided large old house.

When her brother came out of the bathroom she asked, "Are you staying in this evening, Clarence?"

"Yes," he answered.

"I have to go over to Dorothy's for bridge. Which reminds me, Lenore asked me last week why you don't belong to the bridge club. I'm sure you'd enjoy it; the Curries go, and Alfred Noon, and some of the—"

"You know darn well, Bernice, that I can't stand that man!" Clarence said, stamping his foot. "I'm really too busy to bother with that crowd."

"What are you going to do, listen to the A & P Gypsies?"

"Probably not. I have to interview a boy for the Uncles."

"I hope he's cleaner than the last one you brought here. I'm afraid that one of them may bring vermin into the apartment."

"Now, Bernice, you're exaggerating. The young chap who's coming tonight is the one that Merv Rapaport spoke to me about last week, who was up on the theft charge last winter. One of the four boys Merv was appointed to defend in court."

"A criminal! You know, Clarence, I wish you'd give up the Friendly Uncles; charity has its uses but—"

"Not that again, please!"

Bernice stood up and pulled on her coat. "Perhaps I could meet him myself. A young criminal. It might be interesting."

"Some other time, Bernice. You know how I hate an audience when I'm engaged in casework."

"Yes, I know." She opened the door, then adjusted her hat before the narrow mirror on the wall next to the apartment entrance that opened into the tiny living room. "I'll see you later," she said, closing the door behind her.

Clarence Gurney was a bachelor in his middle thirties whose athletic body was running to seed. He worked as a bookkeeper for a large insurance firm and spent most of his spare time as an athletic instructor at a West-End settlement house and doing part-time casework for the Friendly Uncles. He would have liked the easy opulence of a bachelor flat and an Oriental "man" but the market crash had wiped out the small estate his father had left him and his sister, so they were forced to share the small apartment. They wouldn't have been able even to live like this if Bernice wasn't employed as a grade school teacher. Clarence liked to think of himself as a civilized, if slightly corpulent, man of letters who had been paid once for an essay that had appeared in the American *Social Workers' Digest.* He loved to lounge around in a dressing gown listening to Brahms on his electric phonograph.

Before Ken arrived he hurried around the small room emptying the ashtrays and straightening chair cushions and the afghan cover on the sofa. He brushed up some cigarette butts that his sister had tossed carelessly into the fireplace, and opened the living room window from the top. Then he went to his room and changed his trousers, carefully knotting a necktie on his white shirt, and robing himself in a green silk dressing gown with a paisley pattern, tying a loose knot in its wide sash. When he was finished he settled himself on the sofa with a book.

When he heard the knock at the door he opened it and admitted Ken Tilling, who smiled up at him as he hesitated in the narrow hallway.

"Come in, come in!" Gurney invited.

"Thank you."

When the boy had stepped inside, Gurney closed the door and said, "Well, Kenneth, you've certainly grown up to be quite a young man, although you're not much taller, are you? Let's see, it must have been three years ago that I saw you last."

"It wasn't that long ago," Ken answered, taking in the apartment through the corner of an eye. To him its tawdriness was everything he had ever wanted in a place to live.

"I thought it was back in twenty-seven or -eight," said Gurney.

"No." Ken was surprised at Gurney's wearing a dressing gown over his clothes.

"Here, take a seat, Kenneth," Gurney invited, stepping aside with a little hop and pointing to the sofa.

"Thank you, sir."

As the boy faced away from him Gurney noticed his rundown heels and his long hair that fell below the back of his collar. "It has been quite mild today, hasn't it?" he asked, sitting down at the other end of the sofa.

"Yes, sir, it has."

"Did you walk up?"

"Yes, sir," the boy answered, thinking that he would have walked up even if he'd had a lot of money. This neighbourhood was only a couple of miles northwest of Cabbagetown, and he could have run up if need be.

"Is that all you can say, Kenneth? You don't have to be so polite and—distant with me you know. I wish you'd call me Clarence as the other boys do."

Ken brushed aside the first little whisper of suspicion and said, "I'd much sooner say sir."

"All right then," the man said, smiling with his lips. "It's quite a long walk up here but I don't suppose you mind it on a nice evening like this?"

"It's not bad. I like walking; I walk everywhere, all the time."

"Do you?" asked Gurney as if this commonplace revelation had suddenly buoyed him up. "It's frightfully good exercise." He patted his belly. "Are you a Scout?"

"No, sir."

"Scouting is frightfully good fun. I had a troop once." He went into a short history of his connection with the Boy Scout movement, and told Ken how much he had enjoyed the weekend hikes with "the good bunch of sports" in his troop, and the fun they had had at summer camp. He tossed back his head as if to further enjoy "the frightfully good times" they'd had.

"I was a Cub once," Ken said. He thought back on the few weekly Cub meetings he had attended one winter at St. Hubert's church. He had given it up when his mother could not afford to buy him a uniform, and he had felt out of place being the only boy at the meetings without even a little green-and-yellow cap to wear.

"The Cubs are very good training," Gurney said. "Scouting too. Of course you're getting a little too old now for the Scouts. Let's see, you must be seventeen now?"

"I'm eighteen," Ken said.

"Over the age of consent?" Gurney asked archly. The remark failed to bring any response so he became suddenly solicitous. "I'd like you to tell me about your unfortunate escapade last winter."

Ken didn't answer for a moment, then he said, "I'd rather not talk about it, Mr. Gurney. It was just one of those things. After you haven't had any money for quite a while you get desperate I guess."

"If you don't want to talk about it, Kenneth, you don't have to. Have you any immediate plans?"

Ken shook his head.

"I was enquiring about employment for you at the office today. I've been able to find jobs for a couple of boys who are friends of mine. I'd do a lot for a young man who proves to me that he wants to be a sincere friend. Of course with times as they are it's very difficult—"

Ken noticed that the man had been squirming around on the sofa and was sitting much closer to him now. He pressed himself against the arm of the sofa.

"What do you want to do, Kenneth?" Gurney asked, sitting still now and wearing a social worker's sympathetic look.

"I don't know exactly."

"Isn't there anything?"

"I want a job first. I guess I would have liked to have become a draftsman. I was very good at drafting at Tech."

"With times as they are there just aren't any jobs to be had. Would you like to join the YMCA?"

"I don't know. I guess I would, sir," Ken answered.

"We'll see what can be done about it then," said Gurney. This started him on a long spiel about the Y and its benefits in shaping young men both physically and mentally. He spoke about the facilities for exercise and about the "splendid types" it produced. Ken had some ingrained ideas about the YMCA, having belonged once, temporarily, on a boy's card given to him by a charitable institution.

"The Y produces many splendid God-fearing young men," Gurney went on.

Ken nodded, but Gurney's use of the term God-fearing brought back to him suddenly and vividly his utter dejection as a small boy when he had spent a whole month at a Salvation Army camp at Lake Simcoe. He had been sent out first for the regular two-week period but his mother had been arrested as a common drunk towards the end of the two weeks and this had meant an enforced stay there for another two weeks. Looking back on it he knew that it was the most miserable month he had ever spent in his life.

The Salvationist camp staff had used the boys' enforced imprisonment to proselytize them mercilessly, able for once to gather a large number of male slum children into their midst and by strict regimentation to make them listen to their scary propaganda. The neurotic members of the Army staff, ignorant, piously cruel and fanatical, had worked on them until, through a fear-inspired dread of heavenly vengeance, Ken, along with many of the other boys, had gone forward to the mercy bench and had prayed for release. Thus, "saved" as the Salvationists joyously proclaimed, "another group of souls had been delivered to Jesus."

For months afterwards, Ken, with a child's fear of heavenly vengeance if he slipped back into his former ways, desisted from swearing, prayed many times a day, and refused to go to the movies on Saturday afternoon with the other kids on Timothy Place. One evening the following summer, after a long hysterical fight with his mother who wanted once again to send him to the Salvation Army camp, he had accepted a Cubeb cigarette from a package that Bob Mclsaacs had bought or stolen, and broke once and for all the neurotic bonds that the Salvationists had forged.

After puffing the Cubeb down to a lip-burning butt he had shouted every swear word in his vocabulary, feeling that only by indulging in these "sins" could he erase the terrible things that these adults had done to his childhood. The following Saturday afternoon he went to the matinee at the Idle Hour Theatre, cheering lustily as Art Acord foiled the villains, and secretly rejoicing that his downfall was complete. He still said his nightly prayers but they were becoming nothing but a mumbled habit.

"Health is very important," Gurney was saying, breaking into Ken's memories. "We must watch our health."

Ken didn't think Gurney looked too healthy himself, but he answered, "Yes, sir."

"We must guard against the temptations. What we call the temptations of the flesh," Gurney went on, his face white and his eyes boring into Ken's. He rearranged his dressing gown over his lap.

The boy's suspicions were now confirmed. "Yes," he answered.

"You must watch that no woman gets a chance to spoil you, Kenneth. You know that you're quite good-looking, don't you, Ken?" The man laid a fat trembling hand on his knee.

"I don't think I'm good looking at all," Ken said, staring down pointedly at Gurney's hand, which was slowly withdrawn.

Gurney smiled a placating smile and asked, "Have you a girl friend, Kenneth?"

"No!" Ken shouted, causing Gurney to pull back quickly. He didn't want to talk about Myrla Patson, or any other girl, to Gurney. Somehow it would have cheapened or dirtied them.

"You're smart, Ken. Stay away from them."

The boy was becoming embarrassed, and he had to fight an urge to jump to his feet and denounce Gurney there and then. "I don't bother much with girls," he said.

The man was becoming obviously wrought up, squirming around on the sofa, his hands fluttering, first sitting bolt upright and then lying back against the cushions, twisting the afghan cover. Finally it was Gurney who jumped to his feet, and keeping his back to the boy asked, "Would you like a glass of lemonade, Kenneth?"

"All right."

"I find that it's getting quite warm in here, don't you?"

Ken nodded.

The man hurried out of the room.

Ken stared around him now at the room. It seemed shabbier now than it had when he first entered it, and even he could tell that the landscape hanging on the wall above his head was only a cheap print. Somehow the room was as spurious as Gurney was, with his pretence at social consciousness. Ken hadn't had much traffic with social workers outside his own house and in their offices, but he decided that the Friendly Uncles Club was just a front for Clarence Gurney, whose motives were far from giving a hand to what the Friendly Uncles liked to call "underprivileged boys."

His eye was caught by several group photographs ranged on either side of the radio above the fireplace. He got to his feet and looked more closely at them. Most were enlarged snapshots of boys and young men wearing bathing suits or sweatshirts and shorts. He picked out a thinner Clarence Gurney standing with his arm around another young man under a rustic archway bearing a sign reading Camp Oweewo.

Gurney entered the room carrying two glasses of weak lemonade, one of which he handed to Ken. Gurney then threw himself down on the couch, holding his glass precariously in his hand. Then he jerked himself into a sitting position and asked, "How do you like it, Ken? Cooling isn't it?"

Ken took a long gulp from his glass. "Yes, it's great," he said.

"There's some more in the kitchen if you want some."

Ken nodded, taking another drink. The lemonade was weak but quite cold. The room was much warmer than it had been.

Gurney sipped at his glass, staring at Ken. He said, "I'll bet the girls are crazy about you."

"Oh—I don't bother much with them."

"That's right. You have to watch yourself. Women and girls give horrible things to young men. We had a chap one year out at camp who went into town and got mixed up with a girl there. We had to ship him back to the city rotting with disease."

"Yeah?" Ken asked without emphasis. He wondered if Gurney was talking about the clap. Several young men he knew in Cabbagetown had had it, but none of them looked as if they were rotting.

"Of course we can't help our appetites," Gurney went on indomitably. "We have to have some outlet."

Ken finished his lemonade.

The man raised his glass to his lips and stared over the rim of it at Ken, who was still standing in the middle of the floor. "Are you sport enough not to ever mention it to anyone if I show you some pictures I have?"

"I was looking at those on the mantel," Ken said.

"Not those kind." Gurney gulped his lemonade. "Just a minute, Ken." He hurried from the room, his dressing gown swishing behind him.

When he reappeared he was carrying a brown envelope in his hand and had a blue necktie hanging over his arm. "Here's a tie you can have, Kenneth. I noticed the one you're wearing doesn't tie very well."

"Thanks very much, I need a tie."

Gurney sat down on the sofa and patted the top of it. "Come and see my pictures, Ken," he invited. He was very excited and Ken noticed that his upper lip was beaded with sweat. With nervous hands he opened his envelope and pulled out several photographs. "You won't mind looking at these for a bit of fun, will you, Kenneth?"

Ken shrugged and joined Gurney on the couch.

Gurney leaned close to him and handed him the photographs. The first one was of two nude young men standing on a diving board, the second was an older man, with an erection, holding a teenage boy by the hand. The others were of males engaged in coitus and various sexual aberrations. Ken noticed that they were all amateur snapshots, and seemed to have been taken in the northern woods.

As he handed them back to Gurney, Ken said, "What are these, fun and games at Camp Oweewo?"

"Oh no. My goodness nothing like this goes on up there. They were given to me by a friend, I find them very funny."

"Yeah?"

"Do they make you—you know?" Gurney asked through quivering lips.

"No, they don't bother me."

"You're a funny chap," Gurney said, slipping his arm around Ken's shoulders. "Other fellows get a kick out of them. Don't you get a kick?"

Ken shook his head. "No."

"You have beautiful brown eyes."

Unable to control himself, Ken burst into laughter.

Gurney withdrew his arm. "Why do you laugh?" he asked.

"I don't know." The whole thing was ludicrous and he laughed again.

Gurney began to smile a strained smile and placed his hand once again on the boy's shoulder. Ken pushed him aside and stood up.

Gurney busied himself cramming his snapshots back into the envelope. "You're not angry with me are you, Kenneth?"

The boy looked down at the back of the man's head but didn't answer. He crossed the floor to the door.

"Please stay for a little while longer," Gurney pleaded.

"No. I've got to go."

"I'm so lonely. I live here all alone with my bitch of a sister, and I'd like to talk to you for a while. I'm sorry for—for—Your eyes made me—"

"I'm going," Ken said, grasping the doorknob.

"Will you come again?"

"Sure," Ken answered, wanting only to get out into the spring night.

"And you're not angry at me, Kenneth?"

"No," Ken answered, opening the door.

"Tell me you're not angry with me," Gurney pleaded. His face had fallen and he stood in the room as if stricken.

"No. Goodbye, Mr. Gurney," Ken said, pulling the door closed behind him.

Outside the spring evening was noisy with the sounds of the downtown city. The wind blowing up from the lakefront was clean and fresh on Ken's face, and he faced into it, heading south. He suddenly felt sorry for Clarence Gurney, and for all the Gurneys of the world, and he felt glad he was what he was. Just above Gerrard Street a middle-aged whore weaved in his direction and asked, drunkenly, if he wanted a good time.

"Not tonight, Ma," he answered laughing. On an impulse he handed her Gurney's blue necktie.

"Whassis?" she asked. Then shouted after him, "Ya goddam cheap punk!"

He turned east on Dundas, wondering why he had given Gurney's necktie to the hag on Jarvis Street. He needed a necktie too.

Theodore East was seventeen years old in the summer of 1931. Despite the depression he still worked for the boxboard company and his salary had gone up steadily from twelve to fifteen dollars a week. He had ambitions that seemed grandiose to those who knew him in Cabbagetown, but no real talents with which to achieve them. Instead he had the gall and brashness of the social climber and a native cunning that told him that by practising little favours for others he could worm his way into their good graces. For some reason he had placed Ken Tilling among those he wanted to ingratiate himself with.

One weekday afternoon he went down to Timothy Place to ask Ken to go with him to the amusement park at Sunnyside. The door was answered by a sick and frowzy Mabel.

"Is Ken in, Mrs. Tilling?" he asked, startled by his first sight of his friend's mother.

"No. I guess he's up in the park," she said.

"Oh well thanks a lot. I'll find him up there."

"He's been gone about half an hour," Mabel added. She was pleased that her son had such a clean and well-mannered friend. Most of his friends were either curt or surly towards her.

"Right. Thanks again, Mrs. Tilling."

As he retreated down Timothy Place Theodore was surprised that a woman like Mabel should be Ken's mother. He understood now why Ken was reluctant to invite anyone to his house.

Riverdale Park was full of the unemployed. Small groups of men were clustered around the cages in the zoo, staring with time-killing indolence at the equally apathetic animals, putting off their return home to their wives and families. Below the zoo, on the flats west of the river, a few young men played softball, with an audience of old men who sat on the bleachers and watched them.

Theodore crossed the stinking little river on the footbridge, his eyes searching the almost empty playing fields of the flats for a sign of Ken and the other members of the gang. Looking up along the footpath that curved through a lightly-wooded rise to Broadview Avenue, he spied Ken and some other youths lying in the grass,

When he arrived Billy Addington asked, "What's the matter, Easty, you not working today?"

"No, I'm on my holidays."

"D'you get paid?" one of the other youths asked.

"Sure. We get two weeks in the summer, with pay, and a bonus at Christmas."

"Not bad."

"My old firm used to give us a week's holidays that we paid back by a month's unpaid overtime," somebody said.

"Not many firms give holidays any more," Billy put in.

"Not many firms even give jobs."

Theodore sprawled on the grass beside Ken, listening to the five or six unemployed members of the gang talking about different small jobs they had held in the past. Inevitably the subject changed to girls, and they talked openly about the girls they had picked up recently, and the sexual conquests they had made. Billy Addington and a fellow called Wanscott who lived in the Riverdale district east of the park had a date that evening with a pair of out-of-work sisters in their teens who were known to the gang as "pushovers." They spoke with lascivious eagerness of their coming walk with the sisters up the Don River Valley.

To Theodore, who was still a virgin, the mere accessibility of such things was a revelation. He would have to begin accompanying Ken Tilling up to the park in the evenings.

"Listen, Wanscott, tonight we're going far enough up the Don to get away from the spotters," Addington said. "Right up underneath the Bloor Street viaduct."

"There's plenty of bushes around the swimming hole at the red bridge," somebody else said. "The spotters are too thick down here in the park."

Although the large city park, which sits along the river in a wide valley, contained many secluded spots for couples to hide in, one of the bugaboos of alfresco lovemaking was caused by the large numbers of spotters, or elderly voyeurs, who combed the hills and gullies to spy on the trysting couples. Some of these spotters or scouts, as they were known to the park regulars, sneaked around in pairs, led a dog on a leash, or were bold or brave enough to sneak close enough to a couple lying prone in the grass to almost touch them. The gang, and all the other young people who used the park in the evenings, detested them.

Late one evening Ken Tilling and a girl called Joanie Brutt from Sydenham Street, who was a willing recruit to the scheme, lay down together in a secluded section of the park, while four or five members of the gang took up a position in the darkness, also lying on the grass about fifty feet away. Ken rolled himself a cigarette and lighted it, letting the match burn out by itself to draw the attention of a spotter. Joanie was wearing a white dress which could be plainly seen from some distance away against the dark grass.

While Ken and Joanie waited they whispered together, and after a while Ken used the opportunity for a little petting. Ken was becoming more interested in Joanie than in the plan itself when suddenly the girl gasped and pushed him away. Standing over them was a man, who looked enormous from the ground. Ken rolled away from his feet, afraid of being given the boots, and squatted on his haunches while Joanie adjusted her clothes.

"Who's the girl?" the man asked roughly.

"She's a friend of mine," Ken answered.

"How old is she?"

"Tell him, Joanie," Ken said.

"I'm sixteen."

"What's your name?"

"Charles Dawes," Ken told him, praying that the other members of the gang were still around. "Who are you?"

"Police. Get going, buddy, and be thankful I'm not running you in."

"How about my friend, she can't stay here. I've got to take her home."

"Never mind her. I'll see she gets home," the man said, grabbing the girl by the arm and pulling her to her feet. Ken straightened up and kicked the man in the groin, missing with his first kick but feeling his second one hit the mark. He jumped back and shouted, "Hey, guys, a spotter!"

The man let go of Joanie and tried to grab Ken, but when he saw the other youths coming at him from the darkness he turned and tried to escape. A big fellow named Billings from Allen Avenue grabbed the man by the shoulder and pulled him around, punching him in the mouth. Billy Addington kicked the man in the head as he fell, and some of the others gave him the boots in the ribs and belly. The man lay huddled on the grass, shielding his face with his hands, and pleading with them that it was all a mistake.

Billings pulled him to his feet and asked, "Are you a cop?"

"No. I was just having a bit of fun with the boy here," he said, looking for Ken in the crowd.

"You're a liar," Ken said. "You know what you were after."

"Honest, kid, I was only foolin'. I wouldn't a hurt the girl. I'm a married man with kids a my own."

The gang jeered, knowing that some of the scouts or spotters drove the boy away and then attacked the girl. Usually their victims were too ashamed or frightened to report it to the police.

"Let's put the boots to him good," one of the boys said.

"Just a minute," said Billings. He turned to the man and cautioned, "Listen, you dirty louse, if we ever see you around this park again we'll really kick the Jesus out of you. Maybe the police won't do nothing to help us, but we can handle guys like you ourselves. Understand what I mean?"

"Listen, fellows, I wasn't go—"

Billings punched him as hard as he could in the face. The man moaned, covered his face with his hands and stumbled away in the direction of the street lights marking the dirt road along the railroad tracks.

"That'll learn him a lesson," Billings said.

To Theodore the talk about spotters was something entirely new, and the fact that just as many girls as boys made the park their evening hangout was something he hadn't realized until then.

Two young girls came across the grass and sat down with the gang. A short dumpy girl with blonde hair, wearing a boy's sweatercoat and a blue skirt, was called Anne. The other one, who was taller with a good figure but with a slight cast in one eye, was called Terry. They laughed and joked with the boys, and Theodore noticed that the boys' language cleaned up considerably after their arrival.

He wondered if these girls were as free and easy with their favours as the others that the gang had been talking about. He became excited at the thought of being so near to girls who were no longer "innocent" as it was called. He moved close to the tallest one and tried to start a conversation. She answered his first questions, but finally asked the others, "Who's this guy anyways? Maybe he'll ast me what colour pants I got on soon."

"You probably don't wear any," Ken said.

"You'll never find out anyways, Tilling. Is he a friend of yours?"

"He lives near me. He's one of the few around my place that still has a job."

The dumpy blonde said, "If you don't want 'im, Terry, shove 'im over here."

When they were walking home Theodore said nothing about going to Sunnyside. He questioned Ken about Anne and Terry, and Ken told him they were just a couple of the Janes who sometimes hung around with the gang. Theodore asked Ken if he'd ever been out with them, but his friend answered that he couldn't be bothered; there was nothing doing there anyway. Before Ken left him Theodore made him promise to pick him up after supper and take him to the park.

After washing himself above the waist and running a razor over his almost hairless face Theodore dressed himself in the bedroom he shared with his older brother Paul. He could hardly sit still, thinking of the trip to Riverdale Park that evening with Ken Tilling, and he went to the window and stared into the backyards below.

Two young women were talking across a gray board fence that separated their back steps. One of them was thin almost to the point of emaciation but the other one was more than plump with wide hips and unfettered pendulant breasts. Theodore watched the thin one's mouth moving quickly with a choice bit of gossip, and imagined how it would look to somebody nearby, showing the bad teeth and the spittle-covered lips. The sight of the woman disgusted him, but he moved his eyes to the swinging breasts of the other one and stood watching as he became tumescent.

He hated the neighbourhood, and especially the backyard squalor that was typical of its streets. He also hated the noise of the hordes of children, and the dirt and stupidity of most of its inhabitants. More than anything else he hated his address, even though his own family's house was not as shabby as the ones around it. He particularly hated having to live in Cabbagetown.

His mother shouted from the downstairs hallway, "Ted!"

"Yes, mother."

"There's a boy waiting for you on the veranda; I can see him through the screen door. Are you coming down?"

"Yes, right away." He left the window, felt in his pockets to make sure he had his wallet, comb and handkerchief, and hurried downstairs.

"Where are you going?" asked his mother from the kitchen doorway.

"Oh nowhere, mother, just out."

"Stay out of mischief, and don't be late coming home."

"No, mother, I won't." He waved a greeting to Ken and smoothed his hair before the hall-stand mirror. "Goodbye, mother," he said, heading toward the front door.

"Theodore!"

"Yes, mother," he answered, a sick feeling coming over him.

"Have you forgotten something?" she chided.

"Be with you in a minute, Ken," he shouted through the screen door. He hurried back to the kitchen and kissed his mother.

She would have been horrified had she known what making him do this in front of one of the gang made him think of her. Having this to add to their taunts about his sissiness was intolerable.

When he and Ken began walking up Sumach Street Ken asked, "Listen, Easty, where you going—to a party?"

"We're going to pick up a couple of babes aren't we?"

"We're gonna try, but you didn't want to get dressed up for it. I'd like to see your clothes afterwards, if we score," Ken said laughing.

Theodore looked down at his neat suit, then at Ken who was wearing a pair of unpressed trousers, no necktie, and with his shirt-sleeves rolled above his elbows.

Before they reached the park Theodore asked Ken if he'd had any news from Bob McIsaacs in the reformatory. Ken told him he'd written one letter, but had received no answer to it. Had he seen Myrla Patson lately? Ken answered that he'd seen her walking through the park with a guy a couple of times, but hadn't been close enough to speak to her. Theodore said he'd heard from somebody that Myrla had been laid off from her job at Frosst's and was in domestic service somewhere. Ken pretended disinterest and changed the subject.

Theodore ran into a small grocery store near Gerrard and came out with two packs of cigarettes, handing one to Ken.

"What's this for?"

"I thought you might like a tailor-made for a change. Having to roll your own smokes isn't so good on a date."

"Well, thanks," Ken said, not knowing what to make of the other's generous action.

Theodore then offered Ken a stick of gum.

"Holy jeez, Easty, you're really prepared. Who do you think we're going to pick up, Mary Pickford?"

"No, but I like a chew of gum. It sweetens the breath too."

"Yeah I guess so." Ken bit off half a stick, placing the rest in his shirt pocket. He lighted a cigarette and blew a satisfied cloud of smoke. "You oughta come on more dates, Easty," he said.

When they got to the park they didn't search out the rest of the gang across the river, but sat in the bleachers at the ball diamond watching a pair of factory teams play softball. Ken looked over the terrain, especially along the path that led from the footbridge to the zoo, ready to spot likely pickups. There were two or three promising girls but each was a single. Theodore was searching too, and he plucked at Ken's sleeve once or twice and pointed out pairs of girls. Ken however, because he knew them too well or because they did not look the type, shook his head each time.

Theodore pointed to a pair of pretty girls sitting alone at the end of the bleachers. "There's two, Ken. Why don't we go over and sit beside them?"

Ken gave them a cursory glance. "They're no good, Easty. They're probably girls from one of the factories that's playing ball."

Theodore's face fell.

"Don't worry, I'll spot two before it gets dark. You get so you can tell right away what they are. You've got to stay clear of the ones who just want to flirt but have to be home early. All you get from them is a veranda goodnight and a peck on the cheek. They're all right if you want a steady or to get married or something. Then there's the type that only want you to take them to an ice-cream parlour, and after that they get on a streetcar or something and leave you standing at the stop."

Theodore stared at his friend.

"Another type that's no good is the ones that tell dirty jokes and sound like pushovers till you get them alone. They're the cock-teasers. Don't waste your time with them. The best ones are the quiet-looking kinda older ones like that one there." He pointed to a young woman who was strolling along the path with an exaggerated nonchalance. She halted and pretended to watch the ball game but before moving on again took a quick look behind her to see if she was being followed. Two young fellows approached her from the direction she was going, and one of them spoke to her. She ignored him completely but after they'd passed her face broke into a close-lipped smile. Ken said, "See what I mean. She's a pickup. If I was alone I'd try her myself."

Theodore could not keep his eyes from her as she strolled along by herself, slowly and temptingly, her figure enticing him through her thin summer dress.

After the ball game ended the two Lotharios stood against the wooden fence surrounding the duckpond and tossed wisecracks at the girls who passed. When Theodore wanted to follow some of them Ken detained him. Two girls who had smiled at their wisecracks stopped along the path obviously waiting for the boys to catch up to them. They kept looking back and whispering and giggling together.

Theodore pleaded, "Come on, Ken, there's a couple of easy ones there. What are we waiting for anyway?"

"Don't be nuts, can't you see they're sisters," Ken said. "Sisters together's no good. They're each afraid the other'll snitch on them."

"How about the two sisters Addington and the other guy are taking up the Don tonight?"

"They're different."

"It'll be dark soon, Tilling!" Theodore exclaimed in a panic. "Look there's hardly any girls left in the park!"

"This is just the right time. The girls that are left are all out for a bit of fun."

The young woman who had walked past so slowly during the ball game returned with a girl friend.

"Hello, beautiful," Ken said.

The other young woman looked around and said, "Why don't you go roll a hoop, sonny? Isn't it past a little boy's bedtime?"

Theodore laughed at the reception Ken's greeting had received.

"Aw to hell with them!" that young man said.

Just before dark two girls about sixteen years old came hurrying along the path. They both giggled at a remark Ken made as they passed, and the boys followed them, close enough to let the girls hear their smart sophisticated repartee. Now and again one of the giggling girls would steal a glance over her shoulder.

As they were crossing the footbridge the boys drew abreast of them, one on each side, and Ken took his partner's arm. The girls stopped then and with pretended annoyance asked the boys what was their big idea. The boys talked fast, especially Ken, asking them if they were going to a fire, and did they know that it was unsafe for goodlooking girls like them to be alone in the park that time of night. For a moment or two the badinage went on, as the girls sized them up and made up their minds whether or not to drop them right there. When they began walking again they had split up into couples, Ken with one who told him her name was Della, and Theodore with the other whose name was May.

As they strolled along across the grass of the playing field

Theodore asked May where she lived and where she worked. She told him she lived downtown and stayed home to keep house for her widowed father and two older sisters. He told her to call him Ted, and described his job at the boxboard plant. She took his arm, telling him she felt nervous in the darkness of the park, and Theodore felt protective and pulled her closer.

May said she hardly ever came to the park, especially at night, but her girl friend Della had coaxed her that evening, and she'd had nothing else to do. This was the first time in her whole life she'd ever allowed a boy to pick her up, and she hoped it didn't make him think she was cheap. Her father was very strict and made her come home early, but she was soon going to leave home and go into training for a nurse. Her father had wanted her to complete high school and go on to college, but she'd decided that nursing was the only thing she wanted.

Theodore believed everything she told him. He thought how fortunate it was that he'd picked up a girl like May on his first attempt. He began to feel she was too nice for him, and felt that his motives were rotten. He told her about his interest in music, and she said she liked Guy Lombardo, and thought that Art Jarret was a better crooner than Russ Columbo. He blurted out that this was the first time he'd ever picked up a girl himself, and she turned then and stared hard into his face.

Ken and his partner led the way across the flats to where the ground rose up towards the street in a series of steep grassy hills. The grass here was uncut and gave reasonable protection from the view of everyone but the most dedicated of spotters. When Theodore and May caught up with the others, halfway up the lowest slope, Ken said, "You two stay here. We'll go along the hill a bit farther."

After the others had gone May and Theodore sat down in the grass. He offered her a cigarette but she shook her head. He lighted one and lay beside her, using his smoking as an excuse for his shyness and lack of knowledge of what to do next. Now that he was face to face with the reality he had craved, he found himself scared and tongue-tied. May lay back on her elbows, saying nothing and staring into the darkness. Theodore crushed his cigarette in the grass and looked at her.

"Whadda you think you're looking at?" May asked.

"I was just looking at you. You know, you're beautiful lying here where it's nearly dark and everything."

"Well, I like that!"

Theodore sat up. "I didn't mean it that way, May. I'm sorry if you took me wrong."

May giggled and circled his neck with her arm, pressing him back into the grass and kissing him on the mouth. Theodore grabbed her awkwardly and began kissing her neck and face, his hands groping over her surprisingly big and firm breasts. May mumbled "Don't!" a few times but made no attempt to stop his hands, which were now exploring beneath her dress. He hardly noticed how free and easy she seemed for a nice girl, and he felt, along with his urge to make love to her, an overriding certainty that she would not have acted this way with anyone else. Once she drew away from him slightly and he halted his efforts.

She was wonderful, with soft warm skin and a smell that was clean and enticing. All the things he had ever heard about such occasions were false and insignificant beside the real thing. He lay beside her not wanting to go on. She was too clean and pure to entertain the dirty thoughts and motives that he had.

May seemed hurt and surprised by his sudden refusal to carry on, and she pushed herself against him in wanton abandonment and kissed him passionately. He tried to tell her that his thoughts were not only physical, but she stopped his words with her mouth. She helped him to remove her flanellette bloomers, arching her back as he rolled them down her legs with a trembling hand.

When it was over he lay beside her staring up at the stars, for the first time in his life felt that he now knew the secrets of the universe, and that all the questions were answered.

From a short distance away in the long grass came the sound of scuffling, and Ken's girl giggled in the darkness. May fixed her clothing and lay against Theodore, stroking his cheek. She didn't seem quite as wonderful as she had a few minutes before, but he kissed her, thinking it was expected of him. They didn't talk now, but lay beside each other staring at the sky. Theodore took out his cigarettes again and lighted one.

He and Ken left the girls at the zoo entrance to the park, after making an unlikely date with them for the future. Ken asked Theodore if he'd given his partner his right name.

"Sure, she gave me hers too. Why, didn't you?"

"No. God you're a dope, Easty. Supposing you've got her in trouble."

Theodore hadn't given a thought to this possibility until now. May not only knew his name but even the place where he worked! He worried about it all the way down Sumach Street.

**11**

Myrla Patson drew her last pay envelope from the company cashier's wicket and carried it along the hall to the women's locker room, where she placed it in her purse. She took off her grease-spotted smock and wrapped it in a piece of the morning paper that she found on a bench, then with the small parcel under her arm she left the factory building.

She felt no loss yet at being laid off, looking forward to the adventure of finding a new job. She did not know how her mother would take the news, what with her father now being out of work, but she was certain she would find another job within a few days. Her board money, small as it was, had spelt the difference between a few small food luxuries and the unvarying relief diet.

She walked straight into the kitchen where her mother was ironing one of young Donnie's shirts. Bertha Patson placed the iron on its stand and pulled the plug from the light socket. "You're home early, Myrla," she said, afraid to ask why.

"I've been laid off," her daughter said.

Bertha said nothing but placed the big kettle on the stove.

Myrla said, "I've been expecting it, but I didn't want to say anything until it actually happened."

Bertha asked, "Did you eat your lunch?"

Myrla nodded.

"I'll make you a pot of tea," Bertha said. "It never rains but it pours. Mrs. Travis down the street was taken to hospital this morning in the police ambulance. They say she looked like the wrath of

God. What they'll do with the kids I don't know. Mr. Travis is nearly out of his head, Mrs. Robinson was saying."

"What was the matter with her?"

"I don't know; she's been poorly a long time. She kept putting off going to the hospital because she had nobody to look after the bairns. Now, poor soul, she'll probably come out of it in a box."

"Oh, Ma, you say that every time anybody goes to the hospital. Golly, they cure some people you know."

Myrla took off her coat and hung it on a hook in the hallway. When she returned to the kitchen she took her pay envelope from her purse and emptied it on the table, counting out the six dollars and twenty-four cents it contained. "I see they paid me for the whole day today anyhow. Three days this week, but you'd have thought they could have let me stay on till Saturday at least." She picked up the change and a dollar bill and gave the five dollars to her mother. Bertha shoved the new crisp bill into her apron pocket.

When the tea was made Bertha filled a cup and placed it on the kitchen table in front of her daughter. "It's weak," she said, "but we'll never make it last until Friday if I make it strong enough. There's two pieces of baloney left outside from what I bought for your lunch. Do you want a sandwich?"

"A cup of tea's all I want," Myrla answered, stirring some milk and sugar into the cup.

Bertha began ironing again, but Myrla noticed that she had neglected to put the cord plug back into the light socket. She said nothing but sipped the scalding tea.

Lately she had seen her mother pause as she did her housework as if she was thinking deeply of something. Once or twice a week she had noticed Bertha going upstairs only to reappear a minute or so later with her eyes red from crying. At these times Myrla had hurried out of the house, sick with the inability to help her mother, who was becoming a thin worried bag of nerves.

"Where's Dad, is he out today?" she asked her mother.

"Yes. He's not taken his household cleanser with him today though. He thinks he'll be better selling some of his paintings, so he took them he had in the cellar."

"Oh, Ma! Didn't you try to stop him! My God, nobody'll buy those things!"

"He won't listen to me," Bertha answered. "I'm afraid all this trouble is sending him daft. I said to him, 'Geordie, you can't sell them old things that's covered with coal dust from laying in the cellar so long.' He said, 'By—by Christ, if they won't buy summat to keep them clean maybe they'll buy summat that's dirty!' Since Monday morning he sold only three tins of cleanser. Nobody'll answer their door to pedlars any more. I'll bet there's even ten or twelve of 'em come here every day. In this neighbourhood!"

When George Patson had answered the want ad for salesmen to sell household cleansers from door to door, the family had joked about getting their cleanser at cost price. George had been full of hope then, his eyes lighted with a sense of purpose after weeks of enforced idleness. The first week he had earned seven dollars in commissions, and he had thought after perfecting his sales pitch he would be able to earn as much as he had made towards the last at the silversmiths. He had said, "It's really only a stopgap, a stopgap. While I'm going around with the cleanser I can keep an eye peeled for a decent job. Anyhow it's better than just sitting around the house."

Despite his enthusiasm and the increased hours he put in, he only made three dollars the following week. His commissions had remained around that level ever since. Once he had come home waving four one-dollar bills in his hand that he had received for cleaning up the basement of a church. This job had been the only real one he had found in the past nine months.

The bright eager George of two years before had deteriorated into a slow, painfully shuffling old man whose old clothes hung on a thin emaciated frame. Bertha's observation that she thought her husband was going daft corroborated what Myrla had been thinking. Her father took hardly any interest in anything now, a strange departure from the days when he had hurried home from the silversmiths on Saturday to busy himself with the British football pools, then after supper to go down into the cellar to paint.

Nowadays George sometimes didn't shave for days on end, and he flew into fits of anger in which he cursed and ranted against the "big shots" whom he blamed for his plight. He would refuse to speak to any of the members of his family unless spoken to, and seemed to ignore them all completely. Then at other times he would sit down at the table and, as if possessed by something secret but happy, would talk about his day's adventures, later playing with the children. Lately he had begun to retreat into the parlour after supper with the paper, and Bertha had gone in to him after doing the dishes only to find him staring at the wall, the unopened paper on his knees.

"I think I'll go upstairs and lie down," Myrla said. "I can't do much about looking for work this afternoon anyway." Then she added as an afterthought, "I guess I'd better wash out my stockings. I'm supposed to go to a dance with a fellow tonight."

"Leave your stockings down here and I'll rinse them out for you," Bertha said. "I don't know what to get for supper. Is there anything you'd like?"

"I don't care—anything. Get some fish-and-chips."

"They're pretty dear," said her mother. "A whole order costs us fifty cents. When I think that we used to buy them back home in Dumfries for fourpence-a'penny before the war. The fish was better too, not this old cod or salmon they're palming off on you today. It used to be good halibut fillets, and fresh too."

"You know, Ma, you and Dad should go back to Scotland. You'd be much better off there than here, at least you'd get the dole. Take the young kids with you and stay there till times get better."

"I'll never go back until I can go with money in my purse and a return ticket to Canada. I'd never let my folk see me come crawling back," Bertha said defiantly. "I can hear them saying to one another, 'There's Bertha Sinclair come back finally from Canada. They say they've had to sell every stick they owned to get their fare home.' No, Lass, I'll not go back now, not if I have to starve to death here!"

Myrla went up to her room and lay beneath the patchwork quilt thinking how different the future had looked just a few short years ago. She and the other girls in school had all been going to leave home at eighteen and marry tall handsome young men who could afford a nice apartment and a maid. Not that they actually believed it would happen, but there had been a definite possibility for some, and Myrla had been assured by some of the girls that she might.

She thought of the other girls, of Olive Fergus and Bunny Raines whom she supposed were still running back and forth along the looms at the hosiery plant, coarsened now from listening to two years of the women's dirty stories and from dodging the saucy hands of the fixers and bobbin boys. Poor Olive and Bunny, still eating the dried-out sandwiches in the fifteen-cent box lunches and still dreaming of a man, tall and handsome or not, who would take them away from the clickety-clack-clack of the machines and away too from the decaying shanties on Bright Street and Arnold Avenue. And she wondered what had become of Fritsy Bruckstein. Was she still slaving with her needle in the rear of her father's small Queen Street CLEAN & PRESS—HATS BLOCKED store? What tall handsome young Jewish stranger would ever see her plying her quick little fingers while she was hidden from the world behind the wallboard partition at Queen and Sherbourne Streets?

They had memorized all the fine flower-filled poetry, but had never read the adage, "When poverty comes in the door, love flies out the window." Miss Cox, their middle-aged, middle-class spinster teacher, had tried to drill into them that cleanliness was next to godliness, but she had never been up against the situation where she had to carry a galvanized washtub upstairs, fill it with hot water heated on the kitchen stove, and then cool it with cold water that had to be lugged from the kitchen sink. Miss Cox had also told them that virtue was its own reward before most of them knew what virtue meant, and dear old naive Miss Cox had never had to choose in her life between virtue on the one hand and reward on the other.

Myrla was only out of work two weeks before she found the job at Mrs. Leroy's. For eighteen dollars a month all she was asked to do was the housecleaning, the washing and ironing, and to look after the baby three nights a week. Mrs. Leroy did the cooking, for as she told the other ladies of her bridge club, she really loved to cook. Of course the dirty pots, pans and kitchenwear were left for Myrla to wash after the meal was over.

Mr. Claude Leroy would have missed his wife's fancy meals if Alice Leroy had been forced to wash up the messes she left, but he didn't realize this, and sometimes called his wife "my perfect little housekeeper."

Alice Leroy had too much nervous energy and too much spare time to herself to be a good employer. She didn't really need a servant at all for she had enough energy herself to do all the work and more, but she had to keep up her prestige among her friends. All day long she would chastise the girl in the low polite tone which maddened Myrla, "Must I tell you again, dear, not to throw away those celery leaves," or, "Please, Myrla, use a chamois on my good glassware." Some days it was the floor wax that had stuck to a table leg, or some tea leaves that were stuck to the inside of the garbage can lid. Myrla looked forward to wash-day for Mrs. Leroy seldom came down to the cellar.

Strangely, as the summer lengthened Myrla began to get along better with Alice Leroy, for she no longer gave the woman the opportunity to chide her that she had done at first. On her evenings and Sunday afternoons off she went out with one or the other young men she knew—in the evenings to a movie or a dancehall, and on Sundays for a walk. The Leroys' baby was a girl named Sandra, and Myrla, who played with her most of the day in her kitchen or placed her in the yard in her playpen where she could watch her from the open kitchen door, grew to love the little girl.

On bridge-party afternoons, after she had served the tea and small sandwiches to the guests, Myrla would go into the basement and stand and listen to the talk that went on upstairs. Sometimes she heard a woman refer to her looks, and warn Mrs. Leroy to keep an eye on her husband. What the middle-class bridge players had to say they said better than the women of Cabbagetown, but it was the same women's talk she'd heard as a small girl listening to her mother and the neighbours.

Claude Leroy was a forty-year-old department store auditor with a growing paunch. Once or twice he had asked Myrla how she spent her dates with her boy friends, but his questions were usually impersonal and he had never tried to go any further, even on the couple of occasions when they were alone in the house. She knew he found her attractive though, and sometimes she lay in her bed and wondered how she would act if he should come to her during the night.

Twice a month she visited her family, usually for Sunday supper. Her father sometimes asked her with a sneer how she liked living like a queen among the toffs uptown while her family was existing on relief. She always bought young Margaret and Donnie a chocolate bar apiece, and once she took her mother some old dresses of Mrs. Leroy's, though she never saw Bertha wearing them. After supper she and her mother would talk for fifteen or twenty minutes, then they would wash up the supper things before she left. Each month she slipped Bertha a five dollar bill, which she knew her mother spent on extra food or clothes for her father and the children.

One evening in September the Leroys held a party for some of Mrs. Leroy's peers and superiors from the department store. After a light dinner Myrla bathed the baby and put her to sleep, then dressed herself in the maid's uniform she hardly ever wore and answered the door to admit the guests. By nine o'clock most had arrived and the house became warm and smoky. Myrla found it hard to walk through the downstairs rooms with the drinks and sandwiches, and she had to refuse the invitations of some of the men to dance with them.

As the party became livelier and noisier Myrla watched the fun from behind the kitchen door, ready to hurry out with a new tray of drinks when Mrs. Leroy called for them. When it was quite late Alice Leroy came into the kitchen and told Myrla to open another jar of olives, stick them with toothpicks, and take them out and place them on the dining-room buffet. Myrla noticed that she was quite drunk, and that she was staggering around the kitchen with a finger on her lips as if wondering what she had come for. She kept saying, "Don' mind them, Myrla, they're all good scouts. Everybody here's a damn good scout."

Myrla smiled and nodded.

"They're all damn good scouts even if they are my frien's, Myrla."

"Yes, Mrs. Leroy."

"Do you drink, Myrla?" the woman asked.

"No thanks. I've never drunk liquor in my life."

"You'd better have a drink, Myrla," Mrs. Leroy said. She stared into the girl's face with tipsy inquisitiveness. "I'll bet you think I'm an old bitch sometimes, don't you?" She laughed and waved a finger at the girl. "I'm not too bad to work for though, am I, Myrla? You're damn right I'm not. An' you're a good scout too, Myrla." Then she said, "Don't mind me, Myrla, I'm drunk."

Mrs. Leroy took a bottle of Scotch from the sideboard and poured half a tumbler full, filling the rest of the glass with ginger ale. "Here, Myrla, have a drink," she invited. "You're a good scout, an' I want you to know that I know it too. We're both good scouts, an' you gotta drink with me!"

Myrla stood looking down at the tumbler in her hand.

"Go on an' drink it," Mrs. Leroy commanded.

Myrla raised it to her lips, hating the smell of it, but not wanting to offend her drunken employer. She took a deep breath and before she could taste it almost drained the glass. It came back into her nose and throat and burned them, and she closed her eyes and held her breath until the burning eased and her stomach settled.

"Feel better now, Myrla?" Mrs. Leroy asked with a wink. She walked with exaggerated steadiness from the kitchen, while Myrla supported herself against the table and fought for a moment against the waves of nausea that rose from her stomach. When the nausea had passed she began sticking the olives with toothpicks.

Soon she felt herself floating on a feeling of excitement and good spirits and, was smiling happily as she carried the plate of olives to the dining room. A young man said in her ear, "Lo and behold if it isn't Helen! How many ships did you launch today, Helen?" She felt herself being encircled in his arms. Suddenly the room was a blur of embarrassing sound, but beyond the noise she heard a man's voice say, "Kiss her, Rod, kiss her!" The young man turned her around and did just that. She laughed a little too loud and broke away from him.

As she placed the olives on the buffet she thought, "I guess I should feel bad about being kissed like that in front of all these people, but I don't." She giggled to herself, and avoided the young man on her way back to the kitchen.

She began trying to wash some of the used glasses but found that she no longer wanted to, and laughed at this as if it was the funniest of jokes. She sang the words to a few bars of dance music she could hear coming from the radio, and told herself, "To hell with everybody! I'm going to have a good time too!"

She pulled a stool from beneath the table and poured herself another drink, but not as large a one as Mrs. Leroy had poured for her. She sat there eating olives out of the jar and spitting the stones on the kitchen floor.

From the direction of the front door she heard Mrs. Leroy bidding goodnight to some early-departing guests, and she wondered who had given them their coats. "Not coats—wraps," she said to herself, imitating Mrs. Leroy.

For the next hour or so she went through the motions of her job, carrying drinks and food to the remaining guests, seeing some of them out of the house, everything happening in a dizzy wavelike fog in which she moved, sometimes overly dignified and at other times wearing a bemused smile. Finally she retreated to the kitchen where she lay her head on her arms on the table and slept.

She awoke to find the house strangely quiet, and despite the rocking of the room she climbed unsteadily to her feet. Setting a course for the door she entered the empty dining room, and made her way to the living room. All the guests, and the Leroys too, had left. She made sure the front door was locked and headed back along the hallway to the stairs. As she passed a small room that Claude Leroy called his study, she looked in and saw Leroy sitting behind his desk with a drink in his hand. He was staring at her, a smile on his face.

"Where is Mrs. Leroy, sir?" she asked.

"I neither know nor care," Leroy answered with a laugh. "I think she went out with some of the others for coffee and hamburgers."

She found it funny that they should have gone out for hamburgers, with all the good food in the house. "If you're waiting up for her, Mr. Leroy, I guess I'll go up to bed," she said, leaving him.

She looked in on the baby, covering her and leaving the nursery door ajar, and went to her own room where she threw off her clothes dragged on her nightgown and dropped on to her bed.

She was awakened by Claude Leroy's voice in her ear, and she felt the mattress sag as he got into bed beside her. Everything seemed confused and unreal, but when he turned her face to his and kissed her she kissed him back. She felt his hand on her breasts, and this brought her part way back to reality, but not enough to care. She sensed his eager nervousness and held him off until he coaxed her not to stop him.

"Do you love me?" she asked him, giggling.

"Yes, Myrla," he answered, breathing hard against her neck.

"More than you do your wife?"

He did not answer, so she pushed him away.

"Yes, Myrla," he vowed. "More than I ever loved any other woman in my life."

She laughed drunkenly, so loud he had to shush her.

During the fall Myrla and Leroy carried on their affair, meeting downtown once a week and taking a room in a shabby hotel in the west end of the city. Claude Leroy, through fear of his involvement with the girl being revealed to his wife, was an easy mark for Myrla's scarcely-hidden blackmail, and he gave her money, clothing, and even once paid a forty-five dollar dental bill that Myrla had acquired in getting all her teeth fixed. For Christmas, Claude gave her a fur-collared cloth coat that he bought at a discount at the department store.

Myrla not only enjoyed receiving this money and the gifts from Leroy, but enjoyed even more the knowledge that she was sharing him with his wife Alice. The giving of herself to Leroy the night of the party had been an accident that both could blame on their drinking, but their continued affair was carried on by both of them with their eyes open. Though not particularly passionate by nature Myrla enjoyed her meetings in the hotel room with Claude, her satisfaction being both physical and psychological, with the latter being uppermost. She enjoyed frightening her lover with angry threats when they quarrelled, but enjoyed most of all her hold on him and her victory over Alice Leroy.

Since losing her job at Frosst's, and the obvious decline of her parents under the poverty and hopelessness of hard times, her former sense of moral and ethical values had been greatly eroded, and things that had once been unthinkable were now accepted by her as natural aids to survival. She took Mrs. Leroy's orders now with a supercilious acceptance that puzzled her employer and caused small suspicions to cross her mind.

Myrla and Claude quite often changed the hotel rooms they rented on the evenings of her day off, for Leroy tried to plan everything so that the risk to him was reduced to the absolute minimum. What he could not help was his fear of Myrla's giving him away to his wife. This fear made him drink much more than he had done before, and acquiesce in her constant "borrowing" of money.

One evening at the Royalcourt Hotel, a small second-rate place on the outskirts of the downtown hotel district, there was a knock at the door following Claude's departure. Myrla opened it to find a bellhop standing there. With a nervous glance up and down the corridor he asked the girl if he might have a word with her, and she let him in.

With much hesitation he told her that on the few occasions she and her boy friend had rented a room there he had noticed that "Mr. Lanark" had left before the evening was over.

"So what?" Myrla asked.

"Well, it's quite unusual," the bellhop said, sitting down uninvited on the edge of the bed. "It's—it might mean that your friend is a married man."

"Is that so?"

"Don't take offence, miss, but—well, what I mean is, he's not the only man who likes a girl's company. Know what I mean?"

Myrla laughed. She was both startled and flattered that the man took her to be a prostitute. Whores, to her, were fabulous young women who lived an easy life and made money doing it. She told him she was not what he took her for.

"I'm sorry, miss," he said, jumping up. "Don't take offence."

"I'm not offended," she answered him, and laughed again.

He laughed too, and she noticed now that, unlike her lover, he was young and darkly handsome. She offered him a drink from an almost-empty bottle Claude had left on the dresser, and he accepted.

They talked for a few more minutes, and finally the bellhop, who told her his name was Tony, said he had to go.

"You know where to find me," Myrla said, as she let him out of the room.

"I'm on till midnight," he said.

From then on when she and Claude shared a room at the Royalcourt, Tony dropped in to see her when he came off duty at midnight, once or twice staying until morning, but most times only for an hour or so. When Claude began finishing his bottle of liquor, or taking what was left home with him for the morning, Tony brought his own bottle from his locker downstairs.

During the winter Myrla discovered she was pregnant. For the next few days she went about her work in a daze, making plans one minute and discarding them the next. She had almost resolved, once or twice lately, to break off the affair with Claude, but she had put it off too long. Their evenings in the hotel rooms in surroundings that she looked upon as being almost luxurious, the deference of the hotel staffs, the dinners in the hotel dining rooms, had been things she had not wanted to bring to an end. She had enjoyed the feeling of putting something over on Alice Leroy, but now this feeling was gone, and lately she had experienced twinges of conscience in the woman's presence.

After they had had dinner and gone up to their room on their next date she told Claude of her condition.

His face lost some of its colour and he sat on the edge of the bed, one of his shoes drawing pictures on the carpet. "Are you sure, Myrla?" he asked.

"Yes. I haven't seen a doctor but I'm sure just the same."

"You could be wrong you know," he said. "Perhaps you're making a mistake."

She shook her head.

He got up and paced the floor. "Why didn't you take more precautions, Myrla? You must have known what this could mean. Didn't you see that something like this would complicate everything?"

She caught the whine behind his words and she almost screamed, "*Me* take precautions! How about you? You were so damned drunk all the time that you hardly knew what you were doing. It was all right when you were having your fun, now it's me that's to blame!" Tears of self-pity rolled down the sides of her nose, and she wiped them away with her sleeve.

"Myrla dear, I'm not blaming you," he said, hoping to keep her quiet. "I realize I'm as much to blame as you are. What's done is done and we can't change it now." He placed his arm around her shoulders. "You're not far gone yet; I can probably get a doctor to fix you up and—"

"No!" she shouted.

"Myrla, you're only eighteen years old. Don't you see how this would alter your whole life? You'd have the child of a man that you could never marry. Your relatives and friends would all give you the cold shoulder, and you'd have nowhere to go." Then triumphantly, "How would you support a baby?"

She read the look on his face and answered him scornfully. "I'd support my baby myself if I had to. I can work, and I could leave this rotten city and go somewhere nobody knows me."

"Myrla, you're distraught now but you'll feel different later. We'll find a safe, easy way to make things all right."

"I'm not going to do anything to stop it," Myrla said.

"You'll change your mind, Myrla," Claude said, taking off his jacket.

Myrla turned away and stared through the window. How she had ever allowed him to father her child was now a mystery. The sight of him, with his fattening belly and glasses and his easy insistence that only he knew what was best for her, filled her with a mild loathing.

"Did you get a bottle, dear?" he asked.

His easy use of the word "dear" jarred her nerves. He said it in the same habitual insincere way he said it to his wife. The thought of Alice Leroy maddened her, a woman much older than her, with a bad figure and quite ordinary looks, but now the winner because she wore his wedding ring.

"The bottle is in the top dresser drawer," she said.

Claude poured two stiff drinks, nearly filling the glasses with cold water in the bathroom. He handed one to Myrla and gulped his. Then he said, "There's nothing like a drink to scare away the blues. Drink up, Myrla."

For the next half-hour, possessed of a logic that came out of the bottle, Claude tried to reason with her, but Myrla just shook her head. She told him that she knew the consequences better than he did, but her mind was made up.

He began to see a Myrla he had not known before. Despite the cheapness of her speech and actions he now sensed that behind them, and behind her Cabbagetown background, was a strength of character he had not dreamt she possessed. It was something he had overlooked or failed to notice before: it was human dignity.

He took her in his arms and stroked her long dark hair, perhaps really loving her for the first time. The whisky that had stifled his fears now filled him with a masculine pride that this beautiful girl was going to be the mother of his child. Then a doubt assailed him, could he be certain that the baby was his?

He turned her face to his and asked, "Myrla, are you sure I'm to blame?"

"What do you mean?"

"Could it have been somebody else—one of the other chaps you've been out with?"

She thought of Tony but said, "It's yours! Don't worry, Mr. Leroy it's yours all right! The fellows I go to dances with sometimes don't make love to me like you do!" She dissolved into easy tears. "What do think I am anyways?"

He tried to console her. "I was only asking."

Her tears turned to sudden anger. "Don't worry, you won't get out of this! You're not going to leave me or make me get rid of it or anything else! If my life's going to be ruined so is yours!"

"Myrla—the people in the next room will hear. Don't cry, my God, I'm going to help you if you'll only give me a chance."

He poured himself a tall drink and drank it straight.

After a while he took her in his arms and they lay down on the bed together. When her sobs subsided he told her not to worry, that he would figure out something.

Among the East-End Toronto facto-
ries that drew many of their workers from Cabbagetown, and
Riverdale across the river, was "the soap works" on the east bank of
the Don, near the spot where it empties into the Bay. There were two
large soap manufacturing plants in the East End, both of them international in reputation and both manufacturing various kinds of
laundry, face and specialized soap, soapflakes and allied products.
Soap is a relatively inexpensive product to manufacture, and most of
the sales dollar was turned back into a large advertising budget that
cajoled, frightened, coaxed, and persuaded the pimpled, odorous,
star-struck, socially conscious wallflowers of both sexes into buying
one or the other of their products. Their laundry soaps and soap
flakes, in the days before detergents, had become household words
and needed less advertising than their face soaps—body cleanliness
being closer to both godliness and success than clean laundry was at
the time.

The soap works was a much better place to work than, say, the
steelwares or the wirebound-box company, where too many plant
workers bore foreshortened fingers and arms from their labour on
the presses. The copper and brass foundry was not as dangerous, but
finding a job there was almost as difficult as finding a job as a city
garbageman, whose unbelievable salary was twenty-eight dollars
and eighty cents a week.

Ken Tilling secured a job at the soap works through Theodore
East's older brother Paul, a five-year member of the maintenance
gang. Ken began work as a packer in the Flako department, which

was a separate corporate department from the Soapy packing room. The job paid thirty cents an hour for a ten-hour day and a five-and-a-half-day week, or sixteen dollars and fifty cents weekly, quite a sum during the late fall of 1931.

Ken gave ten dollars a week to his mother and with what was left he clothed himself and went to the movies and the Greek lunchroom on Parliament Street with either Theodore or Billy Addington. He felt an obligation to Theodore, who had really found him the job, but Theodore often bored him with his egotistic patter about musical concerts or the big shots' sons he had met as a member of the Orange Young Britons.

The job at the soap works was quite simple. Ken stood at the end of a long low wooden table, a large pile of folded cardboard cartons on the floor beside him, and two chutes emptying on to the table from several packing machines. As the boxes of Flako came spilling out from the chutes, Ken placed them in an unfolded carton, sealed its top with a wide gummed-paper strip that he wetted with a paint brush and piled them beside the table to be moved away by another youth who piled them on a wheeled dolly and ran them out to the shipping floor.

Enough Flako was spewed out from the seven boxing machines in the small room every day to wash every dish and pair of silk stockings in a city the size of Sodom or Gomorrah. The soap was manufactured, flaked and boxed by mechanical means; but Ken was the missing link in the technological manufacture and distribution of soap flakes, for as yet there was no machinery in the plant to mechanically take the boxes from the chutes and pack them into cartons. Why should there have been when Ken was young, agile and had perfect eyesight which could discard broken boxes, did not have to be oiled or repaired and could work a fifty-five hour week without breaking down.

The pair of wide chutes from the machines poured the Flako on to the table in a never-ending stream. If Ken had difficulty in assembling a carton in time, or had to stop to blow his soap-filled nose, the boxes would come together on the table and pile up like a log-jam, grinding together, breaking, and tossing some boxes high in the air. Ken would have to wade into the jam and pile the boxes around him on the floor to keep the chutes clear, clearing the leftovers up when he had once again caught up with the machines. The difficulty of once catching up again when the steady rhythm was broken was too big a penalty for blowing his nose, so he'd let it wait for his ten-minute break period, lunch hour or quitting time. It was hard on his sinuses but much easier on his nerves and muscles.

The foreman of the Flako packing room was an odious little cockney named Trenton who had worked for the same company, in the same room, and for almost the same pay, for the past twenty years. Trenton would yell through the babel of noise, "Hey, you there, Tilling! There's too many rejections 'ere! We cawnt 'ave so many as this. Some of these bloody boxes ain't even broke at all, only dinted. If yer cawnt 'old yer puce we'll bloody soon get somebody that can!"

Sometimes Ken would remove the gauze mask that he, along with everyone else in the room, wore in place of the non-existent ventilating system, and shout obscenities back at Trenton, hiding them behind a beatific smile. Trenton, who was slightly deaf, saw the smile but did not hear the words.

Working in the Flako packing room was a high price to pay for new clothes and occasional movies and snacks of coffee and pie. Ken had to battle against a natural inclination to stuff a box of Flako down Trenton's throat and run out into the sunshine and freedom. To relieve the overpowering monotony of the job he acquired the habit, that sustains all such workers, of allowing his thoughts to escape into the world outside the factory walls. He reviewed what he had read and seen, planned escapist trips into far-off places that had not yet heard of Flako and planned sadistic revenge against the foreman. Most of the time however his fantasies were sexual, and he made imaginary love to most of the girls he knew, their mothers, and figures as unattainable, to him, as the deaconess of St. Hubert's church and Mrs. Wells, his next door neighbour. Long hours were spent in an imaginary courting of Myrla Patson, which stopped, however, short of actual love-making with her. His thoughts of Myrla were as pure as the spilled Flako around his feet.

When he began working at the soap works Mabel Tilling stopped drinking, for the first time in years. The neighbours were surprised but not half as surprised as she was herself. Roy came around a couple of times but he soon tired of one-sided conversations with a Mabel who refused to join him in a drink, and he came no more.

The energies that Mabel had spent on drinking were now sublimated in work, and she bustled around the house cleaning and scouring and fixing things that she had ignored up to then. Ken came home to find a hot meal waiting for him, had a lunch of sandwiches put up for him every night and had his clothes washed, ironed and mended as they had never been before.

Mabel spent most of Ken's ten-dollar board money on food and little odds and ends they had needed so long around the house. She became a regular Monday evening patron of the Idle Hour theatre, and every week brought home a piece of chinaware to add to their almost non-existent stock of dishes. She bought herself a second-hand winter coat at a rummage sale at King Street Presbyterian Church, and a Mrs. Audrey Bainbridge, the wife of the minister there, gave her a job doing her washing and ironing one day a week for two dollars and her carfare. Each week she hid the two dollars away to save for Christmas.

Mabel's sobriety melted the puffiness from her face and neck, and she told everyone she hadn't felt so good in years. On Thursdays she and Mrs. Bainbridge, who was a few years younger than Mabel, talked about the small towns each of them had come from, chattering away like schoolgirls about their younger days in the country. It felt a little odd to be treated as an equal by a minister's wife, but it only pointed out to Mabel what a waste her life had lately become, before she gave up the booze.

One morning at home Mabel had placed the large galvanized washtub on two chairs in the middle of the kitchen, and she was carefully rubbing the collar of one of Ken's workshirts on the scrubbing board when there was a knock at the front door. She dried her hands on her apron and mumbling about it probably being "another poor devil peddling calendars or needles" opened the door.

A middle-aged woman stood on the steps, holding a heavy leather briefcase in one hand and blowing on her other hand to warm it. "Good morning," she said. "Are you Mrs. Mabel Tilling?"

"Yes."

"I'm from the City Welfare, Mrs. Tilling. May I come in?"

Mabel nodded and stepped back from the door. She followed the woman into the middle room. "The place is a mess," she said. "I'm washing this morning. Everything's upside-down."

"Oh don't worry about that, Mrs. Tilling. I wonder though if I could warm my hands over the kitchen stove? They get pretty cold carrying this." She indicated the briefcase.

Mabel led the way into the kitchen, and the woman circled the washtub and held her hands over the stove. "I don't usually come down this far," she said. "This is Mr. McAllister's territory but he's off this week with the flu." She sighed. "There's a lot of flu going around this time of year."

"Yes there is," Mabel said, giving the woman a chair to sit on.

"Thank you. I'll sit right here if you don't mind," the woman said, unclasping the briefcase and bringing out a sheaf of papers. She selected one and placed it the top of the pile. She asked the usual relief investigator's questions. Names, landlord's name and address, how many in the family, any income, were the employment cards stamped. Then she looked up and asked where Ken was.

Mabel hesitated a moment and then said, "I guess he's down at the employment bureau."

The woman toyed with her pencil a moment before she asked, "Are you sure he's not working, Mrs. Tilling?"

Mabel didn't know what to answer. "He-he's got a—he's got a small job," she said. "He's been working for three weeks now. I've been hoping to get on my feet so I didn't say anything about it to the other inspector. It's the first time in two years he's had a steady job." She appealed to the woman. "You know how hard it is to get back on your feet. He gives me a few dollars a week and we've been eating things we've missed for a long time. He's had to buy himself some clothes too—" Her voice trailed off as she realized the hopelessness of going on.

The woman didn't look at her, but tap-tapped with her pencil on the edge of the briefcase. "I'm sorry, Mrs. Tilling, but there's nothing else I can do. Somebody must have tipped off the department. All I know is that there was a report on my desk about Ken's job this morning."

"Will we be cut off right away? Mabel asked.

"Not wholly, but your relief will be cut down considerably."

"How do they expect people to get on their feet?" Mabel asked nobody in particular. "You start to get a few things, and save a few dollars for Christmas, and then they cut you off."

"I know how you must feel, Mrs. Tilling. I was at a house on St. David Street this morning where the mother has to go away to a sanitarium with tuberculosis. She has five small children, the youngest still a baby. The landlord got an eviction order, so we're trying to place the children somewhere quickly. The poor woman's furniture will have to be stored too." She stood up, buttoning up her coat. "As you say, they should allow a reasonable time for people to get on their feet. I get actually sick at some of the things I see on the job. I can't do anything though."

After the woman had left, Mabel finished the washing. Then she dressed to go out and took the six dollars she had saved, from her dresser drawer, and went downtown to Bergiotti the bootlegger's place.

When Ken came home from work he found the fire out, the house cold, and no supper. It wasn't Thursday so Mabel wasn't working at the minister's house. He stood looking through the kitchen window at the snow-covered back fences, and prayed she hadn't started drinking again. Then he roused himself and went down to the cellar to chop some wood to start a fire in the stove.

Mabel came home two days later.

**13**

One evening Ken and Billy Addington went skating on the big artificial pleasure rink in Riverdale Park. As they slid and tumbled down the snow-covered hill to the flats, their skates and boots swinging from their laces around their necks, they were brought up short by the sight of a thin gray-haired man making solitary runs down the sloping footpath on a pair of skis, pushing himself along with a pair of poles.

"Hey, look at that guy," Billy said.

"Yeah."

"That's the first time I ever seen that," said Billy. "He's got real skis."

"Maybe he's some kinda nut," Ken said. "We used to go down the hills over near the icies on the other side of the park on barrel staves, but I never saw anybody with a real pair of skis before."

"Skating's better," Billy said.

The boys paused for a minute or two and watched Les Winters and some other youths playing a pick-up hockey game in one of the fenced-in hockey cushions, then headed for the heated pavilion to put on their skates.

After they had thawed their cold feet and put on extra socks beneath their skates in the overcrowded smelly pavilion they headed out on to the rink. Pushing off into the slowly circling throng of skaters they followed each other around the ice. Both waved enthusiastically at people they knew, letting the cold air colour their cheeks while their exertions warmed the rest of their bodies.

Billy asked a neighbourhood girl to skate with him, and they linked arms and glided away together, matching their steps into a gliding unison. Ken circled the rink once more by himself before pulling into the middle of the rink where some of the gang were congregated.

"Hello, Tilling, how's a boy?"

"Hi, Mac, what's the matter, tired?" Ken asked as he braked to a stop.

"No. Fat an' me are waiting for Helen Billings an' her girl friend. You oughta see her girl friend, eh, Fat? Boy, is she a peach."

"Who is she?" asked Ken, skating small circles around the two boys.

"Dunno, I never seen her before," Fat answered.

"Where's Billy gone?" asked the youth called Mac.

"He's skating with some Jane," Ken answered.

Mac said, "I seen Myrla Patson a coupla minutes ago, passing here by herself. Jeez she's cute! She might be picked up by now."

Ken's heart slowly turned over at the mention of Myrla. He stared around him, trying to catch sight of her. He just had to find her and ask her for a skate. "I guess I'll shove off," he said, leaving the others.

He circled the rink slowly, hands in pockets, looking for Myrla. Billy and his partner passed him, and he returned their waves. He made almost four circles of the rink, growing panicky now, before he spied her, wearing a heavy white sweater and a blue skirt, a blue-and-white toque covering her black hair, coming down the steps from the pavilion.

He circled the ice behind her, afraid that some other youth would ask her to skate with him; but her beauty and the months of thinking about her making him frightened to approach her and be rebuffed. His fear of losing her again beat out the fear he had of speaking to her, so gathering his courage he skated alongside her.

"If it isn't the Patson girl," he blurted.

She looked at him without recognition.

"Remember me. Ken Tilling. I was at your party a couple of years ago."

"Sure I remember," she said, breaking into a smile.

"May I have this skate with you?"

She took his arm and they began circling the rink. She wasn't a very good skater and had a hard time at first adjusting her stride to his.

"What have you been doing the last couple of years?" she asked.

"Not much, there's a depression on you know. I'm working down at the soap works right now." He could feel her soft breast beneath his upper arm, and he stared at her profile as he answered. She was easily the most beautiful girl in the world. "What have you been doing lately?" he asked.

"I was laid off at the Frosst plant last spring. Since then I've been working for a family in North Toronto." She added hurriedly, "You couldn't get me back in factory work."

Ken sensed that she was trying to hide the fact of her comedown to domestic work. "How long do you intend to work there?" he asked.

"Oh I don't know. I'll probably leave there in the spring."

"What'll you do then?"

"I've had an offer to travel with a family."

"Gee that must be great. Just travelling around with no worries or anything like that."

Myrla looked at him and said, "Yeah, it won't be bad."

"How come a good-looking girl like you doesn't get married?"

She laughed. "I'm waiting for the right fellow," she said.

"How about me?" Ken asked, only half joking, and afraid of what her answer could be.

The girl was sober as she said, "Let's wait till we get to know each other."

They skated until after ten o'clock, stopping only twice to rest on the park benches that were frozen into the ice around the light standards. They talked about their jobs, their families, the young people each of them knew in Cabbagetown. When the lights were turned off they skated to the steps leading up to the pavilion, and Ken told Myrla he'd wait for her at the door until she took off her skates.

In the men's dressing room he noticed that Billy Addington's shoes were gone from under the radiator where they both had placed their shoes. Only then did he remember that he hadn't thought of Billy, or of anyone else, since meeting Myrla again. When he had his shoes on he sat near the open door and waited for Myrla to emerge from the ladies' dressing room.

When they came out from the pavilion the rink lights were still off and city workmen were flooding the lower end of the rink. They walked across the ice, and Ken took her skates and carried them with his own under his arm. When they reached the refreshment booth that was really a large old frame house containing a kitchen, counters and a large lunchroom, they went inside and Myrla sat at a table while Ken bought hot dogs and coffee.

When they finished their hot dogs Ken asked her if she would like another.

"No thanks, Ken," she said. "You don't want to spend all your money on me."

"You sure?" he asked. If hot dogs had cost a million dollars apiece he wouldn't have minded buying her another one right then. He was glad that she thought of saving his money though.

When they left the refreshment booth Myrla said, "Let's walk over to the other side of the park; maybe there's still some bobsleighs and toboggans going down the icies."

"Okay. I think they've turned off the lights over there though."

As they crossed the footbridge Myrla pulled him to the railing, and they stared down at the dirty ice of the river before walking on.

"How old are you, Ken?" she asked.

"I'm nineteen," he answered. Then to hide his confusion at having to admit such a ridiculous age he added, "and never been kissed."

She pulled him off balance and laughed. "I remember one time you were kissed—playing Postman at my party."

"Yeah. I've never forgotten that."

She stared into his face before she said, "I wish you were older. I'll be nineteen myself in the spring."

"I'm old enough," Ken said, knowing that he wasn't. A girl of nineteen wanted an older man, twenty-one or even twenty-four maybe.

"I didn't mean it like that," she said, pressing his arm with hers. "I mean when you're young you can't do everything you want, like getting married, things like that."

Ken didn't know what to think. Surely a beautiful girl like Myrla didn't need a husband, especially not one like him. He wondered what she'd meant.

As they climbed the path to Broadview Avenue Myrla said, "I like this time of year, don't you? The snow makes things nice. In the winter it covers all the dirt."

"I think I like the summer best," Ken said. "The park here's nice in the summer. Sometimes on Sunday mornings I come up here, maybe walk through the zoo, then up through the Rosedale Ravine where the rich people ride their horses along the paths. Down here in the park there are old men walking their dogs while their wives get Sunday dinner ready. There's some young fathers and their kids too. People seem to feel good on sunny Sunday mornings, and some of them smile and say good morning."

"Ken, you ought to be a poet or something," Myrla said.

"It's not poetry. I hate poetry—"

"Don't get mad."

"It's just life I guess," Ken went on. "People feel good on Sundays because they're their own bosses then, and can do what they want. They seem to walk slower and see things they don't see other times, and—I guess you must think I'm nuts or something."

"No I don't. I think you're swell," Myrla said, clinging closer to him. "You'll be very successful some day, and then you'll forget you ever knew me."

Without facing her he said, "No I won't, Myrla. I'll never forget you. I—I've been crazy about you ever since the night of the party. I've thought of you lots since then."

Neither of them spoke, each walking along thinking their thoughts.

Myrla stopped and faced him. "May I kiss you, Ken?" she asked him.

"May you!" he exclaimed, dropping the skates to the snow and pulling her into his arms.

They stood together on the pathway locked in each other's arms. When Myrla heard some mocking laughter from down the hill they broke apart, and looked back. Two laughing young couples, their skates dangling in their hands, were approaching them along the path. Ken picked up their skates and they hurried up the hill.

When they reached Myrla's house they stood beside the front door and kissed again many times. Before they said goodnight they made a date to meet on Myrla's next evening off, at the Leroy house.

Ken wondered if every young man faced the same trepidation and indecision he did when he looked forward to a date with a girl. He wondered if he was dressed well enough to call for her where she worked, whether she had changed her mind, whether she had just been joking about seeing him again. The things he had said as they walked home from the rink sounded silly now as he repeated them to himself. They must have given her a laugh.

On the way to the Leroy house on the streetcar Ken fought an urge to get off and walk back to Cabbagetown. Why should a beautiful girl like her go out with a poor skinny little runt of nineteen who had nothing better to offer than a thirty-five cent movie. Several suitors must have called her up since he'd seen her last, asking her for dates.

He walked along the street the Leroy's lived on, out of place among the middle class houses that lined it, feeling more miserable with each step. He rang the bell at the side door of the Leroy house, hoping perversely that she'd gone out with somebody else. A light was switched on above his head and a man's footsteps came down a short flight of stairs.

The door opened and a plump middle-aged man asked, "Yes, what can I do for you?"

"Is Miss Patson in please?"

"Yes. Was she expecting you?" The man looked him over with what Ken felt was wry amusement.

"I have a da—she told me to call for her here," Ken answered.

"Won't you come in then?" the man invited. Ken followed him upstairs into the kitchen. "Myrla won't be long I'm sure. Just make yourself at home here. I'll let her know you're waiting."

After the man left, Ken gazed around him at the most wonderful kitchen he'd ever seen outside the movies. Everything was painted green and white, with built-in cupboards and counters, and a green clock set in a china plate ticked away pontifically. There were a white electric stove and fridge, and even radiators under the windows. Until then Ken had never really thought of a kitchen being heated by anything but its stove.

There were no ashtrays to be seen so he didn't light a cigarette. His snowy shoes left two small puddles on the linoleum, so he went back to the stairs and wiped them again on the doormat.

He was still staring around him in the kitchen when Myrla came to the doorway and gave him a friendly smile. He smiled in return but instead of going to her stood rooted to the floor. She half smiled then looked up at the clock. "I won't be long," she said. "You're a little early you know. I'll go and get my things."

When she returned they left by the side door. Ken wondered if he should have offered to kiss her when she entered the kitchen. She must think he was crazy.

As they walked along the quiet street Myrla mentioned that another fellow she knew had phoned and asked her to go with him to a dance at the Forester's Hall.

"Why didn't you?" Ken asked. He wondered why she had mentioned it at all.

"Well, I had this date with you, didn't I?"

"Then why did you bring it up?" He was suddenly unreasonably angry with her. "Maybe you should have gone out with him."

"Maybe I should!" she said. "If you didn't want to see me why did you come all the way up here? I wanted to go out with *you*, that's why I didn't go out with him."

"I really didn't expect you to keep the date with me," Ken said, exulting in acting like a fool.

"Why not?" Myrla asked, letting go of his arm. "Did I give you any reason to think that?"

"Let's not talk about it," he said, beginning to walk faster.

Myrla had to hurry to keep up with him. She gave a tentative laugh and said, "You're certainly in a hurry."

He walked on, not answering her.

She took his arm again and slowed him down. "Ken! What's the matter? What are you mad at?"

"I'm not mad," he said.

"Then don't pout. You don't look nice when you pout. If I hurt your feelings telling you about the other fellow, forget it. I wouldn't have gone out with him anyway."

"I wasn't worrying about him." He didn't know what had made him angry. He was so much in love with her that unless he could have her all to himself he wanted to hurt and humiliate her.

She smiled up at him. "Okay then, Ken, what is worrying you then?"

"I don't know. I'm just nuts I guess."

"You did want to come out with me tonight, didn't you, Ken?"

He smiled then. "Sure I did, Myrla. I was afraid you'd have changed your mind though." He wondered how his moods could change so quickly. No other girl could make him act as he was doing now.

Before they reached the corner of north Yonge Street Myrla asked Ken where they were going.

"I thought maybe you'd like to take in a show," he said.

"Say that'll be great! I don't want to go downtown to see that new horror picture, *Frankenstein*, though."

"Hey, why not? I hear it's great. Billy Addington saw it last week."

"No, Ken. Let's find a nice quiet little picture at a nice quiet little picture show," Myrla said.

They took a streetcar downtown, and found a small neighbour-hood movie that advertised a rather old talking-picture called *The Leather Pushers* that starred William Haines, one of Ken's favourite movie stars. They held hands, and whenever there was a funny line in the dialogue Ken would glance at Myrla to see if she was enjoying it. Once her knee actually brushed his and he pulled his leg away for fear she would think he was trying to be fresh.

After the show they sat in a small restaurant and had date turnovers and coffee, later talking as they each smoked a cigarette.

"How much Flako did you pack today?" Myrla asked.

"I don't know, but it was too much."

"Do you like working at the soap works?"

"No. It's probably the most boring job in the world. I've been fed up with it since I got the job. The only time I like working there is during the evenings when I have money in my pocket for a change, but during the day I hate it."

"Do you want to quit it?"

"Not tonight I don't. I see fellows down there who've been doing the same thing for years, and will be doing the same thing, over and over, till they quit or die. I'd run away if I thought that was all I had to look forward to."

Myrla said, "Most factory jobs are rotten. I hated every minute at Frosst's. Maybe most of the men down at the soap company are married, and they have to stay there. They're probably thinking just the same things you are, but they can't afford to give in to their feelings."

"I don't want to get married then, if it makes you like that."

"Some people don't belong in a factory. Take my father for instance. He worked for years doing the same monotonous job every day, and hating it, just because he needed the money he brought home to bring up his family. When he worked at the silversmiths he used to come home at night and try to paint pictures in the cellar. On Saturday afternoon and Sunday he'd go up the Don Valley, when the weather was warm and even in the winter sometimes, and paint scenes up there. I don't think he's a very good painter, but it kept him happy. It let him forget about dipping racks of cutlery at the silversmiths. Now that he's not working any more he can't afford to buy paints. He doesn't know what to do with himself."

"I never knew your father was a painter," Ken said.

"You couldn't call him a real painter I guess. One time, after he was laid off, he tried to sell some of his paintings from door to door. I guess the people only laughed at him or pitied him. He burned them all in the furnace after that."

"Gee whiz! I'm sorry, Myrla."

She toyed with her spoon in her saucer. "You're the first person I ever told that to," she said. "I was always ashamed to let people know that my father had ever sold things like cleansers and stuff from house to house. I guess I was ashamed to let anybody know that he thought he was a painter too."

Ken nodded. He knew all about being ashamed of things. Myrla seemed closer to him than ever now she had told him about her father.

"Why do we keep lying all the time? When I worked at Frosst's I once told a girl named Ruby that worked on the next machine that my father was a jeweller. Now I don't know why. I had nothing to be ashamed of telling people he worked at the silversmiths. One time a girl in my class at school told us all that her father worked at the city hall. We were coming out of the art gallery one afternoon, all of us in the class, and her father passed us driving a garbage wagon. He waved at his daughter, but she pretended not to see him. I saw the look on his face, and I was ashamed of her from then on. Maybe girls do more of that kind of thing than boys do."

Ken wondered whether or not to mention his mother's drinking, but decided not to.

"I guess when you get older you get more sensible about things like that," Myrla said.

"I guess so."

Myrla watched Ken staring down at the table and stirring a small pile of ashes and cigarette butts in the ashtray. He looked so young. She asked herself if she was in love with him, or ever could be. She didn't know, or whether it would be any use her loving him, even if she did. Lately she had felt a need to be loved by somebody.

Ken was certain to find out about her pregnancy before long, and it might be best to tell him now before they became more involved one with the other. She remembered his telling her he loved her, the other night walking up from the skating rink, and she knew now that he did. She didn't want to hurt him, but it seemed inevitable.

During the rest of the winter she and Ken went out together once a week, sometimes to the movies, or skating, or just for walks along the downtown shopping strects. On a couple of occasions when the Leroys had gone out, Ken and Myrla spent the evening at the Leroy house, listening to the radio or rolling up the living-room rug and dancing. They sometimes engaged in what was beginning to be called "light petting" but so far Ken had not tried to consummate their affair.

To Ken Myrla was above this sort of thing, or so he rationalized his fear of going further with her. He had placed her in a category above that of the pickups he had made love to in the past. He was unsure of what was motivating him to act like this, but merely being in Myrla's company, holding her tight and kissing her, was enough.

Myrla was quite aware of his fears of going too far, and though they puzzled and sometimes aggravated her she was grateful to know that it was because of his love for her as a woman and his wish not to use her merely as a sex object. Claude Leroy had asked her several times about her feelings toward the boy, and she knew he hoped she would get Ken to marry her and pass her baby off as his. Though Ken was in love with her she knew he was not fool enough to be taken in by such a shabby trick. Besides, she liked Ken too much, even if she was not sure that she loved him, to entertain such an idea.

One spring afternoon she was sitting at the kitchen table polishing some of the larger pieces of silverware, wearing old cotton gloves and a turban made from a duster. Mrs. Leroy came in and filled a glass with orange juice from a pitcher in the fridge.

"You don't need to be too fussy with that, Myrla," she said. She pulled a chair up to the table and sat down facing the girl. After sipping the juice she asked, "How do you feel these days, Myrla? You're not ill are you?"

Myrla looked up quickly and asked, "Why?"

"You don't look too well, that's all," Alice said.

"I feel all right."

"Are you sure, dear?"

"Yes, Mrs. Leroy. There's nothing the matter with me." She looked at the woman, wondering how much she knew.

"I heard you retching in the bathroom this morning, and not for the first time either."

"Something didn't agree with me last night. I probably ate too much before going to bed."

"Are you sure it was something you ate, Myrla?" asked Alice. She felt sorry for the girl, and found it difficult to talk like this to her. "Have you been to a doctor, dear?"

"No. If I was sick I'd go to a doctor, don't worry," Myrla answered trying to smile.

"Myrla!"

"Yes?"

"You know very well what's wrong with you. It's no use trying to fool me. Why, it's written all over your face. How long have you been this way?"

Myrla slowly peeled off the cotton gloves, as Alice came around the table and placed her hand on her shoulder. "You poor kid," she said. "Who was it, that boy Kenneth who comes here?"

Myrla shook her head.

"Well whoever it is we'll see things are made right. When did you first know, in February?"

"No, in January," Myrla answered.

"Does your mother know about it?"

The question startled Myrla and she looked up quickly. "No. I just can't tell *her*."

"You can get the young man to marry you. Why, any of the young men you've gone out with would jump at the chance of marrying a pretty girl like you," Alice said. She wondered why working girls were so silly about such things. Did they never think of the consequences? She asked, "Who was the young man, Myrla?"

Myrla didn't answer.

"What are you going to do?" she asked, trying to keep the exasperation out of her voice. "Let's see," she said, counting on her fingers. "The baby will be coming along in October. Myrla, you should really do something soon."

"I'm going to," Myrla whispered.

"You can't wait very much longer. No matter who the boy is you'd better make some sort of arrangement with him." The girl's attitude began to anger her. "Will he marry you, Myrla?"

Myrla stifled an hysterical urge to laugh and answered, "He can't."

Alice almost shouted, "It's his duty. Does he know you're this way?"

Myrla nodded.

"What's the matter then?"

"He's married already."

"Oh, you poor dear." Then as a suspicion struck her that she was afraid to contemplate and wanted dismissed immediately she asked softly, "Who is it?"

"Don't keep questioning me, Mrs. Leroy, please. I don't want to answer any more of your questions right now. I'll leave here right now if you want me to, but I'm not answering any more of your questions."

"Yes you are," Alice Leroy said, backing away from the girl and falling into her chair. "Who is it?"

Myrla stared across the table at the stricken woman, whose face had now become white and ugly. She pulled the duster from her head and stood up.

"Myrla!" the woman cried, her face suddenly old and strained.

"Leave me alone!" Myrla sobbed, turning to leave.

Mrs. Leroy jumped from her chair and clutched the girl's shoulder. "Tell me! Tell me who's responsible!" She made a sound that was not a sob or a wail. "Do you hear me!" she cried desperately. "Tell me, you dirty little trollop!"

"Don't you call me names!" Myrla shouted, knocking the woman's hand from her shoulder.

Mrs. Leroy was now half crazed with the knowledge that it was her husband who was to blame. Her eyes were fixed on Myrla, and they flashed such hate and venom that the girl stumbled away from her. "You dirty little bitch!" she cried. "Are you trying to tell me it was my husband?"

"I'm not trying to tell you anything," Myrla answered, frightened by the woman's crazy unreasoning anger. Any sorrow she had felt for Alice Leroy disappeared now.

"Tell me! Tell me! I've got to know!" Alice cried. "Don't think you can protect him. I've known all along there was something between you. You couldn't fool me!"

Myrla was sickened by the woman's clumsy effort to save her pride.

The woman cried, "How could he! How could he with the likes of you!" Then she said, "You must have got him when he was drunk! That was it, wasn't it?" She tried to smile triumphantly.

Myrla took a step forward, holding the advantage now. "What do you mean, the likes of me?" she asked angrily, her eyes running up and down the woman who faced her. "I didn't have to get him drunk," she said scornfully. "It was you who got *me* drunk the night of the party and then ran off with that young squirt you'd been flirting with all night. You might have made Claude believe you'd gone out for a hamburger but—"

"Claude," Alice repeated, his name sounding strange coming from the lips of the girl. She collapsed into the chair that Myrla had been sitting on.

"Get me my money," Myrla said, "I'm leaving here."

When the girl had gone upstairs Alice Leroy tottered into another part of the house, took some money from her purse, and went slowly upstairs. She opened the door of Myrla's room, and without looking in threw two ten-dollar bills on the floor.

When Myrla had packed her suitcase and placed a few things in a shopping bag, she carried them downstairs and phoned for a taxi.

Ken continued seeing Myrla now that she was back in Cabbagetown, and he became the Patson's most frequent visitor. Now that she was getting to know him better Bertha Patson's ideas about him began to change, and her first impression of him, made at Myrla's party, slowly gave way to a more trusting and friendly one.

Bertha's main concern was that Myrla should soon get married, but she thought that Ken was still too young and unset in his ways to marry her daughter, even with his steady job at the soap works.

Being Myrla's steady had made Ken's happiness complete. His fellow workers in the Flako packing room often heard him singing over the rattle of the obsolescent machinery. The new eagerness and zest he put into his job even partly mollified old Trenton the foreman. The noisy, boring loneliness of the job was forgotten now as

Ken's prurient fantasies gave way to thoughts of the evenings and weekends he would share with Myrla.

Myrla had succeeded so far in keeping the secret of her pregnancy from both Ken and her family, but she knew it was only a matter of time before Bertha would know. Even now, sometimes, she felt that her mother had found her out and was keeping silent for reasons of her own. There were many nights that she lay awake sick with apprehension of the time she must confess her condition to her mother. Since her discovery by Alice Leroy she had heard nothing more from her, or from her husband. She lived in hopes from day to day that something, almost anything, would happen to end her dilemma.

Even more than her worries of what was to happen to her and her baby was what she was doing to Ken Tilling. She had not loved him at first, but more and more as time went on she found herself falling in love with him. No matter what either of them thought about the other, or how deep Ken's love for her had become, she knew there would have to be a showdown soon—and how could she justify her condition to him? But more important how could she excuse her actions in leading him on?

On a beautiful June afternoon Ken called for her and they took the streetcar to the Museum, joining the large crowd that pushed through the clicking turnstiles, and wandering hand-in-hand through the exhibit rooms, more interested in being together and part of the crowd than they were in the exhibits themselves. The cases of precious stones, and a room filled with archeological artifacts did not interest them, but Ken slowed her down as they strolled through an exhibit of armour and ancient weapons of war.

They were mildly interested in the Egyptian bas-reliefs and the crumbling mummies in their sarcophagi, but the exhibitions of Chinese art and sculpture, for which the big provincial museum was world-renowned, hardly slowed them down at all. On one floor Myrla pulled Ken into a large room lined with forms in glass cases upon which were draped English and French court dresses of the sixteenth, seventeenth and eighteenth centuries. They both found the natural history exhibits interesting, especially the lifelike sets that showed the animals and birds in their natural habitats.

After wandering through most of the floors Ken drew Myrla to a halt beside a showcase full of insects impaled on pins. Both were amazed at the size of some of the tropical insects.

Ken said, "Look at the size of that dragon-fly, Myrla !"

"It's the size of a bird."

"I remember when we were kids, catching them in a milk bottle down near the waterfront. We called them 'darning needles,' and we believed that if they lit on your face they'd sew your lips together."

Myrla said, "I used to be awfully scared of them. Donnie brought one home one time and it flew all over the kitchen before my mother knocked it down with the broom."

"We used to catch grasshoppers and make them spit tobacco in our hand. We'd hold them by their back legs and say, 'Spit tobacco, spit tobacco, or I'll kill you!' I guess we were pretty cruel, 'cause we used to nearly always kill them anyway, whether they spit tobacco or not."

"Look at the big spiders, Ken! I hate spiders!"

"So do I. I'd be scared of those real big ones."

"Do you believe that if you kill a spider it's sure to rain?"

"I dunno. It's sure to rain sometime anyway. Maybe they only come out before a rainstorm or something."

Ken wandered from case to case as if looking for something.

"What are you looking for, Ken?"

"A very common insect," he said. "The one I hate most."

"What, flies?" asked Myrla, pointing to a whole case of them.

"No, they're common enough, but what I'm looking for is a bed-bug."

"Ooh!" Myrla exclaimed. "They wouldn't have one of *them* in here. Or a cockroach either, I bet."

"Yeah, I forgot about cockroaches. My mother can smell when a house has bedbugs. One time we had them, and she used to soak the bedsprings in coal-oil and set fire to them. She'd roast—"

"Ken!" she said, pulling him away from the insect case.

They had coffee in the basement cafeteria and then left the Museum and walked down through Queen's Park behind the provincial legislature. To the west of the park, through the new-leafed trees, they could see some of the gray Gothic façades of the University buildings.

"It must be nice to go to university, "Myrla said. "Just to go to school, with no worries about getting a job or anything. Would you have liked to finish school and gone on to university, Ken?"

"I guess so."

"What would you have liked to be?"

"I don't know." He thought the question over. "I once thought I'd like to be an architect, but now I don't know."

"Would you like to be a doctor or a lawyer?"

"No. No, I don't think so. I'd like to be a student though. I'd like to learn everything there is. Maybe it doesn't really matter what you study as long as you've been to university. It's like belonging to a trade union or the Masons. If you've been to university you can get a better job, if not—"

"There's even lots of university men out of work today," Myrla said.

"Yeah I guess there is."

"My father used to say it was the system that was wrong. He blamed the big-shots in the government for the unemployment. When he was a young man back in Scotland he was a socialist. Do you believe in socialism, Ken?"

"I don't know anything about it. I think the socialists and Communists are a bunch of soreheads. Don't worry, if they had the money they wouldn't want to give it away to anybody else."

Myrla asked, "Why did you want to be an architect?"

"It's hard to say. I've always liked the idea of planning buildings. Sometimes, even now, I get the odd book from the library on architecture."

"You need a good education to be something like that," Myrla said. "What started you off on that idea anyway?"

"I don't know. I guess it was while I was going to Tech. We took drafting periods, and I found out I was one of the best draftsmen in the school. I won second prize for my drafting portfolio one year."

"You should have followed it up."

"Yeah I should have. I was crazy I guess. Anyway it's gone now, so let's not talk about it on a nice afternoon like this."

They paused and read the tags on some new wreaths placed around a regimental war memorial. When they began walking again Ken ran over and bought two bags of popcorn from a peanut vendor.

"My hands are getting all greasy, Ken," Myrla said. "You're terrible taking me out on Sunday and buying me something like this."

"Lick your fingers," he said.

They strolled down University Avenue, past the big General Hospital. Ken pointed to some dilapidated old houses on the east side of the street, and in the voice of a tourist guide said, "On your left is the birthplace of Mary Pickford."

"Where?" Myrla asked.

"It's one of those houses over there. I'm not sure which one."

"She knew what she was doing when she moved out of that," Myrla said.

They crossed Dundas into the Sunday silence of the city's downtown.

Ken asked, "What would you like to eat, Myrla, a Chinese dinner or spaghetti?"

"I don't care; I haven't eaten Chinese food for a long time."

"Neither have I. We'll go over here to Chinatown and try one of the restaurants."

"I used to be afraid of Chinamen," Myrla said. "When I used to go to the little laundry on Sackville Street for my father's stiff collars when I was a little girl I always left the door open behind me."

"It's crazy how people scare kids about things," Ken said. "The Chinese are just about the same as anybody else. They sure give you plenty to eat too."

Myrla clung tighter to his arm as they turned down Elizabeth Street into Chinatown. They passed the big restaurants and entered a small upstairs one down near the bottom of the street. Both of them enjoyed their meal, and when they were finished they lighted cigarettes and drank their tea. Myrla spied a Chinese woman and her baby in the kitchen doorway and said, "Look, Ken, isn't that little baby cute!"

Ken turned and looked behind him over the top of the booth.

In a complete non sequitur, as she often did, she said, "Those women's costumes in the museum were wonderful. I don't know how they ever walked around in some of them though. One of them must have weighed fifty pounds I'll bet."

"Did you like going there, Myrla?"

"Yeah. Sure. You know, that was the first time I ever went there. It's funny how you can live all your life in a city and never see half of it."

"We'll go to the Art Gallery some Sunday afternoon."

"Okay, but I've been *there* before. When I see the pictures I think of my father and it makes me sad. I guess he'd be the happiest man on earth if one of his paintings was hanging in a gallery. I think that losing his job was nothing compared to having to give up his painting. Nobody like my father, an ordinary unskilled working man, should ever try to be anything else I guess. All anybody down in Cabbagetown should want to do is work for wages, smoke, drink, or do simple things like that." She saw that Ken was unconvinced. "You know it's true, Ken. Nobody down there ever gets anywhere. They work hard all their lives and at the end they own an old living-room set and maybe a piano, and if they're lucky they might have bought a house and put a bathtub in it. I don't want to live like that."

"I wouldn't mind it if I could find a nice little place of my own," Ken said. He looked across the table at her. "I'd be satisfied if I only had you."

Myrla stared hard at the floor. Then she picked up a paper napkin and tried to rub a spot from the table top.

"I guess I shouldn't have said that," Ken said.

She didn't answer.

"I'm crazy. I don't say the right things. Maybe I should have shot you a line of baloney about wanting to get ahead, and having plans for us both, and things like that. I guess I should try to put myself over with you like—well, like Theodore East would do with a girl. I can't do that. This job at the soap company doesn't mean a thing to me, and never will. I hate it!" He gave a short bitter laugh. "I'd probably give it up the day after I got married."

She toyed with the rolled-up napkin, not looking up.

"I don't want to lie to you, Myrla." Again his short sobbing laugh. "I've never before heard of a guy proposing to a girl by telling her he's no good. All I know is I'm in love with you; I guess I'll never feel this way about another girl in my life. Maybe you're saying to yourself that I'm just a crazy kid, and pitying me. I don't care, Myrla. If that's the way you feel, just tell me."

She looked up and faced him then. "I don't think you're crazy, Ken. You'll never believe this after I'm finished but I've wanted you to say these things to me." She saw his face soften as he began to smile, and she hurried on, trying to finish what she had to say before he could interrupt. "Ken, just a minute. I could never marry you. Last winter when I met you at the rink you were just a nice-looking kid and I was there alone—"

He nodded, and began, "Myrla, listen—"

"On our way home through the park—remember?—you said something about going for walks on Sunday morning." She gave him a hurried smile but his face remained drawn and blank. "I guess it's my turn to be crazy now. Anyway when I heard you talking about things like that I felt you were different than most fellows I've met. After I kissed you I began thinking serious about us both." He made as if to speak but she shushed him and went on. "I'll be honest too. Sometimes I wondered if I was in love with you or not, and I've said to myself, 'You're not in love with him, Ken's just the one who happens to be around right now when you need somebody bad.' Lately though I think I feel the same way about you as you do about me."

"Myrla, then what—?"

"Ken—listen, Ken—haven't you noticed any change in me since last winter?"

"I think you're prettier, and—"

"Can't you see I'm different? God almighty, Ken, you've got to notice and try to understand!" She pushed herself back in the seat, her hand still playing with the napkin.

He turned his sad face to hers and said, "Myrla, what's—what are you trying to tell me?"

She turned her eyes from his and speaking quietly said, "I've got to tell you something, and when I'm finished you can get up and leave me. Someday you'll meet a nice girl and get married, and you'll look back on today and think what a lucky guy you were."

He shook his head. "If you want to get rid of me, Myrla, just say so right out."

"No, no, listen!" She paused for a moment. "I haven't any excuses. Everything happened before the night I met you again at the rink. If it had happened after that, you'd have been the one. I've got to make you believe that, Ken."

He stared at her, uncomprehending.

"I'm going to have a baby," she said.

He understood the words but it was another girl sitting in a booth of a cheap Chinese restaurant who was telling a guy sitting across the table from her that she was going to have another man's baby. She was telling him that for four months he had gone out with her and had been afraid to make love to her—too much in love with her to spoil it by a wrong word or gesture—too much in love with her to even notice she was pregnant—still holding her to be too pure and sacred—being a blind stupid fool—being a poor goddamned stupid unseeing fool—

"Ken, please don't look at me like that! I'm not worth even thinking about. Ken, what can I say or do to make you understand?"

The world had fallen away, leaving him sitting there with nothing left that could hold him in his seat. If it wasn't that—if it was just something that wasn't so final—if she'd only said she didn't love him, and he could hope—

"Ken!" she cried.

"No, Myrla, don't say anything else," he mumbled. He picked the check up from the table, dragged himself to his feet and stumbled across the restaurant to the cashier's counter. Throwing some money down with the check he pushed open the door and ran down the steps to the street.

*City of Toronto Archives, Fonds 1244, Item 108*

## BOOK TWO

# TRANSITION

JUNE 1932—OCTOBER 1933

1

Theodore East had been considering leaving his job at Thomas and Listowel's now for some time, to spend the rest of his life in music. The Juilliard School in New York was out of the question but a musical friend of his had mentioned a school in Chicago where the entrance requirements were much less stringent and from which a musical degree could be obtained. He spoke of this to his piano teacher, "Professor" Luigi Falzoni who had a studio in an empty store on College Street West.

The little piano teacher, who with his stiff wing collar and shabby suit was the epitome of accepted failure, asked him, "Why do you wish to go to Chicago, Mr. East? Do you think that the study of piano is something which improves from a change of geographical location? Do you think the instruments there have a better tone?" Then sharply, "Do you believe that going to Chicago makes a mediocrity into a genius?"

"Listen, Professor—"

The kindly patient smiling old man fixed him with a quizzical eye. "Do you believe it will be easier for you there? No, no, Mr. East, I do not think that. If it *was* one of those reasons I would say to you, 'Go, if you wish.' But I don't think these are the reasons at all. Do you know what I believe?" He swung around on the piano stool and faced the crestfallen Theodore. "I believe, Mr. East, that you want to go to Chicago for reasons that have nothing whatever to do with music. You want everything that youth wants: change, a strange exciting city, the companionship of the girls you may meet there, a room of your own and a sense of personal freedom."

The little old man smiled a nostalgic smile, then looked up as if he had just reminded himself that Theodore sat before him. "Go to Chicago, Mr. East. Go anywhere you wish, but leave your music at home. Restless youth and music don't mix; it is only when the musician has mastered his instrument that he can afford other things. Stay here and study piano. Work hard at it. If it is other things you need, go into the streets on Saturday night and find them. But do not try to mix the two."

"I didn't want to go there for those reasons, Professor. It's just that I want to devote all my time to—to my art."

"Art!" The little man swung himself around in a circle on the stool. "Mr. East, please don't speak of art until you are at first a craftsman. When you are an artist you will no longer be my pupil. Right now you are—" He stared into Theodore's face and shrugged. "You are a pianist of sorts, that is all." He jumped down from the stool and walked over to Theodore and patted his shoulder. "Next Thursday, Mr. East, unless you have gone to Chicago."

At Professor Falzoni's school he had met a young Italian called Bagnato whose father owned a Sicilian fruit store on a West-End shopping street. Young Bagnato was convinced that nothing could save civilization but his hero's, Benito Mussolini's, brand of political socio-economics. One evening a couple of weeks after his talk with the professor, Theodore met Bagnato again, and the young man invited him to attend the next meeting of the National Canadian Youth.

"What sort of a club is it, Italian, Catholic, or what?"

"No, nothing like that. We're a bunch of fellows, and girls, too, of course," he said, winking, "who are damned sick and tired of the way the government is treating us. We're going to put a government up in Ottawa that will rid this country of the Commies and of the Yid financiers too. Come along and look us over."

Theodore had wanted to quit the music school after that little fool Falzoni had told him he was only a piano player of sorts, but not to go to Chicago. He had found out the cost of the trip, the fees of the Chicago school, and when he added to this the fact that he would have to give up his job and find another, if he could, in the American city, the odds had been too great. The following Monday evening he went downtown to the large clubroom over a block of stores that was rented by the National Canadian Youth.

The clubroom, apparently used as a dance hall on some evenings of the week, was decorated with fading paper streamers and bunting left over from some previous entertainment. The orchestra platform had a pile of folded music stands and chairs piled against its rear wall, and a wooden lectern had been placed on it facing the room. Sitting around the walls on wooden chairs were the members of the group, about sixty or seventy of them, for the most part young men from eighteen to thirty years of age. About a dozen girls and young women were scattered among them.

When the meeting was called to order, the crowd merely carried their chairs into the middle of the hall and sat on them in crooked, haphazard rows. Theodore looked them over and carried his chair to a spot behind three well-dressed young men and a rather flighty girl, who had spent the time since she had arrived in the hall waving gaily to others in the room and posturing from group to group. To him they were the livewires, and he watched them carefully from his vantage point, noting their actions, ways of speaking, and even their carefree ways of smiling. He categorized most of the National Canadian Youth members as either young white-collar men like himself or university students.

Theodore understood very little of the procedure at first. A young man stood behind the lectern and opened the meeting, then called on an older man, who sounded foreign, but who spoke heatedly about "the great steps forward being made in Germany, Hungary, the Baltic States and other countries where forms of national socialism were thriving." When the chairman and the foreign-sounding speaker were finished, young men would pop up in the audience and make a motion on something or other, while another person would second it. Theodore found himself raising his hand with the overwhelming majority when the motions came to a vote, completely unaware what the voting was for.

There was talk about getting a public swimming pool "restricted," and a vote was carried to send a letter of commendation to the federal government for the "show of national discipline" against a group of hunger marchers "and their Bolshie agitators." The general meeting soon ended, and the chairs were carried back to the walls.

In one corner of the room a group seated themselves around a felt-covered table and began playing poker with chips they bought from the man with the foreign accent. Georgie Bagnato, who had come in late and had sat at the rear of the room, joined Theodore and, in answer to his question, said that the man with the foreign accent was a Latvian-Canadian who acted as treasurer, while the chairman of the meeting had been a young man called Jack Sharpe, the son of a wealthy Toronto family. Theodore and George Bagnato strolled over and watched a game of ping-pong between mixed doubles on the shallow platform. Some of the young people left, but others sat around in small groups engaged in conversation.

Theodore asked what happened next, and his friend said that because this was the first Monday in the month it was merely a general membership and business meeting. On other Monday evenings the group held dances, listened to a guest speaker, or on occasion held a smoker. Bagnato dismissed the dances as being rather mild affairs, but he entranced Theodore with his descriptions of the last smoker the youth association had run, mentioning beer, the amount of food and especially some French and South American films that a member had run off on his movie projector.

Bagnato took Theodore to meet Jack Sharpe after a while. Sharpe jumped to his feet and pumped Theodore's hand warmly. "Glad you're with us, East," he said, smiling warmly. "You'll find us strange around here at first, but you'll get used to us. What part of the city do you live in?"

"The East End," Theodore answered, making it as vague as he could.

"Good! Tell your friends out there that we're keeping an eye on the situation in Kew Gardens. We know what it's like having *them* try to infiltrate your neighbourhood. I particularly know what it's like, living up in Forest Hill."

Theodore didn't understand the allusion to "them," but he smiled and nodded. George Bagnato had told him that Sharpe was a member of one of the real socially prominent groups in the city, but his easy approach to Theodore and his obviously enthusiastic camaraderie warmed Theodore.

"George here tells me you play piano? Good! We can often use a good man on the old grindbox up here, especially for our dances. By the way, have we got your address and phone number yet?"

Theodore said hurriedly, "To tell you the truth I'm in the process of moving right now. I'd suggest the club use my business address."

"Of course," Sharpe said, with a conspiratorial wink. Then he called a girl over, whom he introduced to Theodore as Mildred. "Milly is our recording secretary. She'll take it down." Theodore gave the girl his name, and himself a promotion to junior accountant, his mailing address as Thomas and Listowel.

Sharpe said to the two young men, "Remember it's dance night next Monday. If you have any friends who might be interested in our program bring them along. I don't have to tell you of course that we want only Gentiles here." He was joined in his laughter by the others. "I don't suppose you're a Commie, are you, East?" As Theodore shook his head in vehement denial, everyone laughed again.

After they had strolled away from the president and his retinue Theodore said to George, "He's a nice guy."

"Yeah. He never puts on the dog, even though his father's worth scads. He'll be prime minister of this country some day. A man who spoke here a couple of weeks ago hinted that the Conservatives might find him a seat in the provincial house at the next election."

On his way home Theodore basked in his thoughts about the new friends he was making, and how their membership in the middle class didn't stop them from accepting him as one of them. He was slightly puzzled about the president's mention of the trouble in Kew Gardens, but had been ashamed of his ignorance and hadn't asked Bagnato. It had something to do with the Jews, he supposed, and now as he remembered the numbers of them who took the street car out there on Sundays, littering the lawns and beaches with lunch boxes, banana peels and other refuse, he began to understand.

He hardly knew any Jews, for the only ones around Cabbagetown, to his certain knowledge, were a few Queen Street storekeepers. They were dirty, loud and money-grubbing, but the only one he had ever really known at all was Sarah Rabinowitz whose father owned an electric-light fixture store on Parliament Street. Thinking back on Sarah among the other girls in his class at Park Public School he could not remember any traits, good or bad, that separated her in his mind from the others.

A girl called Doris Cranford whom he met at one of the Monday dances held by the National Canadian Youth invited him to her house one Sunday. He accepted the invitation before realizing what it meant, having to hide his living in Cabbagetown, not having a car to get out there in, his total lack of all the social graces. He was going to phone her and make his excuses, but Jack Sharpe happened to telephone him at the office to get him to play piano at a recruiting drive the group was holding, and offered to drive him up to Doris's place. Theodore told Sharpe, whose girl friend was going along, to pick him up at Bloor and Yonge Streets.

Despite his nervousness and fear of social discovery Theodore thoroughly enjoyed himself at the Cranfords'. Most of the afternoon was taken up with tennis, played by Doris, Jack Sharpe, and his girl friend whose name was Greta. Theodore regretted his inability to play. Mr. Cranford was a mining promoter, and he spoke to Theodore at some length about the rosy future of the mining industry, while Mrs. Cranford, who was very gracious and made him feel at home, took him out to her garden and showed him some of her blooms. He successfully parried all her questions about his family.

After dinner a man who was introduced to Theodore as Mr. Thomas Mundy, and who seemed to hold a good position in the provincial government, asked him, "Where are you employed, Mr. East?"

"I'm with Thomas and Listowel, the boxboard people."

"Oh yes. They're down on Commissioner Street, are they not? A smelly place down there, tanneries, chemicals and things. I drove down there less than a month ago. Being interested in urban blight and social questions in my job at Queen's Park I saw some real eyesores down in that section of the city, places that really need cleaning up. Take that slum neighbourhood north of there, Cabbageville is it—?"

"I think so," Theodore said.

"An eyesore. People living in filth and squalor. A regular breeding place for disease and discontent. It should be burned to the ground. Do you know the place I mean?"

"Oh, yes, sir. I've been through it."

"I feel very bad about it; it gives our city a bad image. It's costly too, why nearly half the families are getting welfare assistance. Think of it! If it weren't for the economic panic I'd recommend that it be razed and a low-cost housing development built in its place. Of course just now our hands are tied, there simply isn't any more of the taxpayers' money to be squandered on philanthropic projects. The people down there wouldn't appreciate it anyhow. I heard of a recent housing development in England where they found the people using their new bathtubs for coal bins. Can you imagine that!"

Theodore clucked his tongue and shook his head slowly. The

slight feeling of treason toward his neighbourhood, and even to his own family, was pushed aside by his desperation to keep his background hidden. What had his crummy neighbourhood ever done for him anyway!

"We're interested in forward-looking young men in my department, Mr. East," Mundy said. "Young people like you and Jack Sharpe who are trying to do something in a political sense. All we can offer as a start is something in the clerical end of things, but—"

"I'm anxious to get away from Thomas and Listowel, and into something with, well with a bigger future than paper boxes."

Mundy laughed. "Good man!" He gave Theodore his card. "Think it over and drop in and see me at Queen's Park."

He and Mundy played a game of croquet against the Cranfords. Between turns Mundy spoke loudly and at boring length about conditions and trends to which he was privy, "through my position," in both national and international fields. He had some highly unorthodox views on the causes of the market panic, as he called it. He was very much convinced, he told his listeners, by an American scientist's theory that sun-spots were responsible for economic trends.

Later in the living room as they sat listening to Eddie Cantor on the radio, all except Jack Sharpe who apparently boycotted all Jewish entertainers, Mundy turned to Theodore and pontificated, "If people would only realize that prosperity is just around the corner, and get behind their government, we'd be back to plenty in no time. The unemployed, and those who claim to be but wouldn't work if work was given them, are being enticed by foreign agitators into hunger marches and foolish demonstrations. A lot of them—not all, but a lot of them—should be thrown into prison."

Appropriately, Eddie Cantor broke into, *Just around the corner there's a rainbow in the sky. Let's have another cup of coffee, let's have another piece of pie.* Completely impervious to its sarcasm, Mrs. Cranford began humming along with Cantor.

*"Let's Have Another Cup of Coffee," 1932, from *Face The Music*, words and music by Irving Berlin.

Doris Cranford drove Theodore back downtown in her Model-A Ford, and he had her let him out north of Bloor Street. Before leaving her however he kissed her, and her sophisticated kissing technique surpassed anything he had come in contact with yet with his few conquests in Riverdale Park. Even comparing Doris with the girls in the park was sacrilegious, for she had looks, breeding and a glib familiarity with current events that he construed as advanced intelligence.

"You know, Doris, I could fall for you very easily," he said.

She laughed.

"You're laughing at me."

"Not at all, Ted. I think you're very sweet," she said.

He walked down to the Bloor Street streetcar stop, past the quiet working-class and rooming-house streets such as Yorkville and Cumberland. As he walked he kissed Doris over and over again in his thoughts. "Boy, she was really hot!"

Ken Tilling lay in the shallow shelter of the CNR boxcar's wooden walkway that ran from the middle of the roof to the top of the forward ladder. For three days the train had lurched, yawed and shuddered its way through and around the coniferous forests and blackwater lakes of Northern Ontario, heading west. The names of the small isolated division points were etched on his mind: Capreol—Hornepayne—Nakina—Sioux Lookout; but all he had learned so far was that the north country was a hungry country and that Canada would never run out of water or firewood.

Though it was early summer, nights on the top of the swaying boxcar were cold and the days were hot. He wore a shirt and trousers and a wool windbreaker, and his luggage and toilet articles were shoved into his pockets—a safety razor, thinned-out bar of soap and a small towel, which he wore around his neck at night. His peaked cap was pulled down over his ears against the grit and smoke, and his face was sunburned under its black bituminous coating. Scattered along the tops of the train of boxcars were a couple of dozen other hoboes, each one huddled down on the warm steel of the car roof, facing the rear of the train, impervious by now to the monotonous sight of lake and forest. They held themselves on with a hand gripping the catwalk.

After Myrla Patson had told him she was pregnant he had stuck with his job at the soap works for another week; then one afternoon, the day before payday, he had suddenly made up his mind to quit the job and to get as far as he could from Toronto for a while. The next time the foreman shouted at him he had smiled back at the man, free from his servitude at last and free forever from the ignorant importunings from the Cockney foreman to speed things up. The packing machines were speeded up to their top speed, and the boxes of Flako came tumbling down the chute onto Ken's table in a continuous avalanche that had him placing them in their cartons, sealing them up and folding another carton with a precision that gave him no time even to think. Late in the afternoon the boxes, which had been catching up to him slowly but inexorably since lunch time, began to pass him and, despite his efforts, the table began to fill up. The sweat ran down his forehead and under his gauze face-mask, and he tried a couple of times to get the foreman's attention so that the youth who wheeled the dollies of cartons away could give him a hand. The foreman was aware of what was happening but he was still angry at the breach of discipline that had caused Ken to answer him with a careless cheeky wave of the hand.

By the time he did pay attention he found that Ken had run out of cartons and that the boxes of Flako were rushing into a pile that overflowed the table, piled one on top of another on the table and the floor, and came together in a high volcanic peak before they spilled like lava, crushed and broken, into a mountainous snowdrift of broken boxes and spilled soap flakes.

For the first time the nasty little Cockney was speechless, but when he did find his voice it did no good, for the machine operators thought he was shouting for speed and more speed rather than the opposite. The foreman's shouts rose to piercing screams that could be heard but not understood over the clacking din of the machinery. Ken stood well back from the tumbling, tearing mess on the packing table and watched in awe as the machine-fed boxes of Flako ground together in a spreading jam that would have to be freed later with iron bars and shipping hooks.

When the machinery was finally halted half the packing room was hidden under grotesque piles of broken boxes and spilled soap flakes, and Ken was standing against the wall, his face-mask in his hand, gazing on it with a look of incredulous satisfaction.

When the foreman came wading through the piles of Flako, his skinny arms waving above his head, Ken just smiled at him.

"You're fired, Tilling! You 'ear me, yer fired, now, right now!"

"I know," Ken said.

He broke a path to the doorway through the Flako, winking at the machine operators as he passed them and feeling sorry for them, for the way the poor stupid bastards were feeling sorry for him. The next day he drew his last pay from the soap company, left most of it, with a short note, under the sugar bowl on the kitchen table, and went up to the CNR water tower in the Don Valley and hopped a westbound freight train when it stopped there for water.

During the afternoon the train broke out of the Ontario forests and the surface of the earth flattened out, while the trees became smaller and more sparse. Soon the wooded countryside was broken by small clearings that gave way to small farmsteads which in turn grew to larger farms with spreading fields, and the woods gradually disappeared to be replaced by prairie land. Ken sat up on the boxcar's top and breathed in the smell of the beginning West, its wider sky reminding him that Cabbagetown and the soap works were far behind.

When he jumped off the train at the edge of the railroad yards in Transcona he teamed up with a red-haired young man from Nova Scotia for the long walk along the highway to Winnipeg. It was already dark when they reached St. Boniface, and they made their way through the town to the hobo jungles along the bank of the Red River beneath the CPR bridge.

Some hoboes sat around a small fire, most of them foreign-born labourers by the looks of them and by the heavy pack-sacks they had spread around them on the ground. A younger man stood near the fire, feeding small sticks into the flames over which hung a small can of water. Ken and Red sat down inside the light from the fire and watched him.

The young man picked up a heavy stick and with much manoeuvring lifted the wire handle of the can so that he could grasp it in his hand. With his other hand he emptied a small fistful of tea into the can. After the tea had boiled for a moment or two he lifted the can from the fire and placed it on the ground.

"That's how to do it, boys!" he exclaimed to nobody in particular. "Boil it but not too long. That's what spoils jungle tea. Some guys boil it until the oil floats to the top."

Some of the foreigners spoke together in their own language and picking up their packs moved away through the trees.

The young fellow looked over at Red and Ken. "You guys want a cup of tea?"

Ken answered, "Sure, but we have no cups."

The host walked away from the fire but returned in a minute with two round tin cans which he handed them. "These are jungle chinaware," he said. "A couple of guys already used them at supper, but they washed them out after."

The hot tea tasted good to Ken.

"You guys goin' west?"

Red said, "Yeh, harvestin'."

"There's nothing much out there, boys. Nothing but hundreds of stiffs riding every drag. You're too early for the harvest yet anyways. Not that it'll be any good this year, what with the price a wheat, the drought an' the grasshoppers. They say the goin' wage'll only be a buck a day for stookin' and a buck an' a half for threshin'."

"Maybe I'll beat my way out to the Cariboo," Red said.

"That's tough country too now. Everything's on the bum. I was up in the Cariboo last winter. Do you aim to do a little pannin'?"

"I never thought of it," Red answered.

The young man was tall and thin, and wore a heavy plaid shirt and overalls. His face was narrow, with high cheek bones like an Indian's.

"I seen about a hundred guys pannin' for gold down along the Fraser," the young fellow said. "There's lots of Chinamen pannin' near Boston Bar."

"I don't aim to do no pannin'," Red said.

"You two guys just come off a drag?"

"Yeah," Red answered: "We walked in from Transcona. None a them fuckin' hunkies would give us a lift on the road."

The young fellow straightened up and stared at Red. He said, "Don't crack too wise about the fucking hunkies! I'm a fucking hunky myself—a Polack."

"I didn't mean nothing personal."

"That's the trouble in this goddam country, nobody sticks together. The Englishman hates the Frenchman, an' the two of them hate the Jew, and the Jew hates everybody, and everybody hates the hunkies. The only guy that benefits is the capitalist. He loves to see us all hating each other 'cause it stops us hating him."

"Yeah, you're right," Red said. "I'm sorry I made you sore. I didn't mean I hate all foreigners."

"Forget it. Did you guys eat yet?"

"No, not yet," answered Ken. "That long ride through the bush is sure a hungry one. All the towns are bummed out dry."

The young fellow pulled some paper-wrapped sandwiches from his pack and handed them to Ken, who shared them with Red.

"They'd only dry out on me," the young man said.

Later on the young man took their tin cans and climbed the bank of the river behind the jungles. When he came back he placed the cans along with the one he had used in a low fork of a tree near the fire. "There's all the dishes washed," he said. "The next guys to come here'll have something to mug-up in. If everybody'd do that when they stop in a jungle it'd be a better country to bum in. Live and let live is my motto."

He slung his pack on one shoulder and said, "I'm going down to the stockyards to get me a drover's pass to Montreal. Take care of yourselves."

After he had gone Ken said, "He was a pretty good guy."

"Yeah. He wasn't bad for a Hunky."

Ken found a job as a haying hand outside Winnipeg, and worked there two weeks. He had to learn the knack of keeping the hay on the tines of his fork as he twisted it up from the ground, then make its weight work for him as he lifted it back over his head and onto the wagon. At night he threw himself down on his cot in the farmer's empty granary, tired to death, his arms and shoulders aching with weariness and his hands raw and blistered from his grip on the fork.

During the times he had a chance to think he tried to rid his thoughts of Myrla Patson. Sometimes, even when he was exhausted, the memory of her kept him from falling asleep. At these times he would toss and turn on the narrow cot, remembering their last conversation in the Chinese restaurant, trying to recapture his feelings for her before she told him she was having a baby. He tried to rationalize it by saying to himself, "It's happened before to thousands of young men. It's really only an incident in a lifetime that you'll forget later on. There's other girls." But the memories of her and of his feelings for her were too recent, and the ragged edges of the wound he had suffered too raw.

On the third morning at the farm he awoke to find his hands stiffened into claws, under the broken blisters the raw red flesh having dried and pulled together so that it was torture to have to straighten them to lace his shoes. He knew he couldn't stand another day in the hay fields and made up his mind to collect his back pay of a dollar a day and hitchhike back to town.

After breakfast he showed his hands to Mike, a big Russian hired hand. Mike said, "Gee, kid, them hands is hurt sure. I tell you what to do. You piss on 'em make 'em tough like leather."

Ken was skeptical of Mike's nostrum, afraid that the man was making a goat of him. He had already learned that while a farmer is treated as a rube in the city, a city fellow was also treated as a dumb slicker on the farm. Some of the local members of the haying crew had kidded him only half good-naturedly at mealtimes already, calling him a "ribbon salesman" and such.

Mike insisted, "Go on, kid, you do like I say. I not fooling you, kid. You see!"

Ken found an old grain measure and urinated in it. After a moment's hesitation he plunged his hands in it to the wrists, feeling each blister sting as though it was immersed in iodine. He followed Mike's instructions however and kept them submerged until the liquid was cold. When he took them out he was surprised to find the blisters were eased and his hands flexible again.

The following day they were not quite so stiff, and in a few days they had improved so that the unbroken blisters had formed into hard callous and new thick skin now grew where only proud flesh had been before.

On the second Sunday afternoon at the farm most of the other hands had gone home for the day, and the farmer, Mr. Eckhardt, and Mike had gone somewhere to get a part for the mower. It began to drizzle and Ken lay on his cot in the granary reading some old farm papers he had found, and listening to the rain spattering on the granary's metal walls. When the rain abated he went outside and took a walk around the yard. From inside the house he could hear Mrs. Eckhardt singing something in German which sounded like a hymn. When she spied him through the window she came to the kitchen door and invited him into the house.

She busied herself around the stove making him a cup of tea. She was middle-aged with graying hair and heavy legs and hips.

"Why are you always so quiet, Ken?" she asked him.

"I dunno. Do I seem to be?"

"You worried about your girl maybe?"

He laughed. "No. Nothing like that."

"I think so," she said, turning to him and smiling. "Yes I think it is a girl." She carried the teapot to the table and stared down at him. "How many years have you, Ken?"

"Nineteen," he replied.

"You are still baby. Don't you worry about any girl. Lots of girl all over. You good-looking boy, Ken, have no trouble with womens. Lot of womens are—" She groped for a word. "—are lonely, eh?"

She took two mugs from a cupboard and placed them on the table. "Was this girl who make you sad, pretty girl?"

He nodded.

"They are all pretty. I too was pretty womans when I was young. You don't believe it?" she asked, though he had not doubted her. "You drink some tea, eat some biscuit, I show you how I was pretty before. My husband he thought I was pretty before, now he forget."

Ken took a sip of his tea.

She left the room and came back carrying a large envelope full of photographs from which she extracted some snapshots one at a time. He looked at the photographs of a young slim woman with her thick dark hair and clothing cut in the styles of twenty years before.

"This one was in Chermany before I was married," she told him. "In this one I was at the seashore on my marriage trip—what you call it, honeymoon, eh?"

Ken nodded and made appropriate remarks.

"Do you think I was pretty womans then?"

"Yes, very pretty, Mrs. Eckhardt," he answered.

"I was here in Canada twenty-five years now. All this time I go to Winnipeg only three time. My husband not want me no more now I am old." She began sobbing, her sobs shaking her heavy frame, the tears running down the sides of her nose. It embarrassed the boy, who didn't know what to do or say. Then she picked up her photographs and left the room.

Mrs. Eckhardt's tears had not awakened any sorrow in Ken, but only a slight disgust that any woman should show him the depth of her feelings in this way.

Later on when he had finished his tea and biscuits he heard the woman rising from a bed or couch in another part of the house. When she returned to the kitchen she had stopped crying but her face was red and swollen. She stood beside the table and said, "I am too old. For everybody now I am too old."

Ken toyed with his spoon, not knowing what to do. She took a few quick steps across the floor and fell beside his chair, her face on his knees and her arms clasped around his legs. He stood up, pulling her to her feet. She kept her face averted and tore the front of her dress, showing her large soft breasts. She pulled his face down on to them and mumbled endearments in German, her hand stroking the back of his head. Then she arched her belly against his, and after a moment or two she twitched and shuddered, murmuring over and over, "Baby, baby, baby, baby—"

When she let go of him she turned away, standing in the middle of the floor, her hands dropped to her sides, the tears running unchecked down her face. "Please go, Ken," she said. "Please leave me. It is not good that an old woman should act like this to a young boy. I am so shamed."

Later he sat on the edge of his cot in the granary and lived over again the huge softness of Mrs. Eckhardt's breasts against his face, and her hand stroking the back of his head. Now that the moment was passed he knew that she had wanted him to make love to her, and he too felt ashamed, and angry with himself that he had not. He consoled himself with the fact that he would get another chance, though he did not.

When the haying was finished Mrs. Eckhardt made him a large

lunch of cheese and jam sandwiches wrapped in newspaper, and Mr. Eckhardt drove him into Winnipeg, paying him fifteen dollars for the two weeks he had worked on the farm. When they parted Mr. Eckhardt told him to come out and see him at harvest time if he was in the neighbourhood, and Ken waved him goodbye from the sidewalk in front of the employment office as the farmer's old Ford sputtered away along the street.

Ken stayed in Winnipeg for a week, sleeping at night on a stained old palliase on the floor of the Immigration Building. During the days he took long walks along Portage Avenue, dropping into the department stores, sitting on park benches around the provincial legislature, and once taking a streetcar ride as far as he could go along Portage to the western outskirts. His early evenings were spent on or near the skid road, Main Street, where one evening he was picked up by an aging chippy in a restaurant, who took him to an empty lot near the river, where she lay down and pulled her dirty housedress above her skinny breasts for fifty cents. He went through the motions with her, but she only served him as a surrogate for Mrs. Eckhardt. She smelled of sweat and cheap perfume, and when they were finished he left her lying in the weeds. He worried for the next two weeks about catching a disease.

On the evening he decided to head west he walked out along Logan Avenue to the CPR freight yards, along with seven or eight others from the Immigration Building. They lay on the platform of a freight shed until the train was made up and ready to go. When the engine attached itself to the head of the train and highballed its signal that it was leaving, Ken and his companions moved out into the yards to jump it. As the long train of empty cars eased through the myriad switches toward the far-off diamond and the main line, Ken with a couple of other hoboes moved farther back into the yards where there would be less competition for the ladders. Ken watched the cars slipping past, faster and faster as the train picked up speed.

He fixed his eye on an oncoming car and prepared to begin his parallel run along the ground when something sharp struck him across the backs of his legs.

For a scary second or two he thought he had been hit by a train on the track behind him, but when he swung around he found himself face to face with a young Royal Canadian Mounted Policeman who was swinging a riding crop. Losing no time he charged past the young fuzz-faced cop and began jumping the intervening tracks that lay between him and the nearest city street.

As he ran he saw that the yards seemed full of Mounties, some in red tunics and others in brown uniforms. They were running back and forth along the side of the departing train rounding up the hoboes. He avoided most of them, running as fast as the uneven railroad tracks would allow him, but was finally confronted by two Mounties who came from behind a string of boxcars and tried to bar his way. He dodged to the side of one of them, and felt the cut of a riding crop through his shirt and windbreaker, but ran on. He had almost reached the street when he heard running footsteps catching up behind him. A voice commanded, "Stop—you—little— bastard!" but he ran on, harder than ever. Once, twice, he felt the slash of a riding crop across the backs of his legs, and he let out a high cry of pain. He hurried on, pivoting and changing course, but just before he reached the gate in the railroad fence two Mounties stepped out and blocked his escape. He came to a stop and with his breath shuddering up from his lungs, waited for the other cop to come up to him from behind.

The young Mountie's face was red and he was sweating from the chase. He grabbed Ken's windbreaker and twisted one sleeve of it into a snaffling grip. Then, both of them winded and hardly able to walk, they went down the yards to where other policemen had rounded up a large mob of hoboes who stood like a herd of reluctant cattle surrounded by police.

"You had quite a chase, Constable," said an older man in an officer's uniform, to the young cop who held Ken. "Hold on to him. He was resisting arrest."

Ken was so out of breath from running, and his legs smarted so badly from the cuts from the Mountie's whip, that he no longer cared what happened to him.

Other policemen brought small groups of hoboes over from deep within the yards, and they were all made to stand within the circle of policemen.

The officer, strutting and preening himself like a gorgeous bird, shouted, "Where the hell do you people think you're going anyway? Why didn't you stay home where you belong? Were you afraid you'd have to work or something?"

The hoboes watched him apathetically.

"I want all of you to know that I'm sick of complaints from the railways about you bums riding these trains!" He slapped his riding boot with his leather crop and puffed out his cheeks like a Colonel Blimp. "You're all guilty of breaking the law! Every damn one of you! Do you know that you're guilty of stealing from the railways every time you sneak a ride on a train? Well you are! I'm going to make an example of some of you. We'll see what a month's honest toil will do to straighten out your silly heads and toughen your crummy hides! If I had my way I'd send you all to Stony Mountain for a stretch!"

"We're looking for work, that's why we're here," said a voice from the crowd.

"Who said that! Constable, bring that man out here!"

A policeman pushed into the crowd and brought out a wizened-looking little man carrying a big khaki pack.

"Who the hell asked *you* to say anything?" asked the officer, stepping towards the little man.

The man stood solidly under the weight of his pack, his legs braced as if he expected a blow. He looked the officer over insolently from his highly polished boots to his Boy Scout hat. "Nobody asked me to speak," he answered, his voice loud and distinctive. "If I waited to be asked I'd have to wait forever. You called us bums. Listen, brother, I fought for four years for this goddamned country, and for this bloody railroad too. We're all looking for work or none of us'd be riding these freights and living like pigs. And I don't like being called a bum!"

The officer found his voice and said, "Get over there, you!" and pointed to a place near Ken. The officer then picked out about a dozen others, mostly foreigners, and lined them up along with Ken and the little man. Then he gave instructions to the policemen and they herded the other hoboes into the street.

When the main group of hoboes had gone, Ken and the little man were marched over, along with the dozen others who had been picked from the group, and were shoved into a line of police cars. Ken found himself in the back seat of a car with the little man and another man. The little man's pack made it a tight fit.

After a short drive they were unloaded before the main police station on Rupert Street, and taken inside where their names were copied at a desk, then they were taken upstairs in an elevator. They were herded down a corridor and pushed into a large barred bullpen, and the door clanged shut behind them.

The little man threw his pack to the floor and sat on it. "This is going to be a little more comfortable than riding the tops tonight," he said.

"How much will we get?" Ken asked him.

"I dunno, son. Hard to say. It depends on the labour situation out at the farm. If they need labour for the potato crop we'll probably stay to harvest their spuds. If not they'll probably let us go in the morning."

"I liked the way you stood up to them," Ken said.

"Oh hell, there ain't nothing to it. I could see that officer was just a windbag. He's like all the other scissorbills I ever met in my life, being a cop has warped his hayseed mentality. Most a them Mounties are stubble-jumpers from Saskatchewan or somewheres.

Give his kind a gun and they'll shoot their own grandma if Ottawa tells 'em to." He chuckled. "Joining the Force was safer than joining the Army in 'fourteen at that."

Ken rolled his windbreaker into a pillow and stretched out on the warm floor. Then he pulled up his pant-legs and looked at the wide red welts on the backs of his legs. The little old man said, "I guess they're your first wound stripes, kid. Always remember what they look like."

"Sure, Pop," Ken said, laughing and puffing down his pant-legs again.

"Good night, fellow worker," said the old man.

Ken tossed and turned on the hard floor, unable to go to sleep. He thought back over the events of the evening, and of the little man who had stood up to the police. The bright lights in the ceiling shone down into his eyes, and two of the other hoboes soon began snoring raucously. From another part of the building came the angry yowls of a drunk and the banging of a steel door. The welt across his shoulders began to burn so he turned on his side. Then he found that his shoulder ached from its pressure on the floor. He heard the little old man sit up and begin to roll himself a cigarette so he turned and faced him.

"Tell me, mister, are you a Communist?" he asked the man.

"Hell no, son. I've got no use for any of the legal parties in this scissorbill country; I'm a worker that's all."

"Oh," Ken said, wondering what could be more radical than Communism.

"Here, look at this!" the little man said, pulling a red card from an inside pocket. "That's what I believe in, son." Ken took the card and read the face of it. It was a membership card in an organization he hadn't heard of before, The Industrial Workers of the World.

He handed the card back to the man without reading his name on the back of it.

"There's not many of us left, son," the old man said. "I'm a Wobbly. Been one since nineteen-ought-nine."

The next morning the prisoners were given a cup of raw, bitter tea and a large slice of stale bread which they dipped in a tin plate of blackstrap molasses. About ten o'clock the turnkey came to the door and let them out. They went down to the main floor again in the elevator, lined up before the desk sergeant who ticked off their names on his list, and walked out into the sunshine. Ken and the little man bid each other goodbye at the corner of Main Street, and Ken watched the other walking north, almost hidden under his heavy pack.

That afternoon Ken caught a manifest freight in the CPR yards and headed west.

# 3

During the two months since she had last seen Ken Tilling, Myrla Patson had lived on the verge of a nervous breakdown. At first she had thought of him constantly, but later her more immediate worries had driven him out of her mind. She was not sure she had fallen in love with him or not, but knew that he had been in love with her. Though she had not wanted to hurt him, she had known that a sudden and final break would be less cruel than a gradual one.

Her mother had not yet spoken to her about her now obvious condition, but Myrla had known for a long time that Bertha knew she was pregnant. She was sure that her mother was keeping quiet about it in the hope that her daughter would leave home on her own, so that the younger members of the family would not discover her condition.

Most of the day she avoided Bertha as much as was possible in the confines of the tiny house, though doing her share of the housework. Lately she had retreated even further from contact with her mother, staying in the sink corner as much as possible when they were both in the kitchen, washing the dishes or her underthings, waiting on pins and needles for Bertha to begin berating her for getting in a family way.

George Patson had dropped out of the family's affairs, and spent most of his days peering through the front-room curtains at the few things that went on in the street. He sat sunken into one of the heavy chairs, alone with what black thoughts Bertha could not imagine. He had given up smoking weeks before, and now his wife and daughter noticed that he refused to read the newspaper. He sat quietly like an old, old man, coughing or clearing his throat at times but refusing to make any other sign that he was alive.

At meal times George crept into the kitchen and sat down quietly, eating, without apparent appetite, whatever was placed before him. The children ate in silence while their father was there, and Myrla scarcely looked up from her plate. Bertha kept up a pretence that nothing had changed, and would ask her husband if he wanted more macaroni or beans or whether his tea was warm enough. When the meal was over George would rise silently from the table, and either go back to his chair in the front room or, on most evenings, pull himself up the stairs to bed.

After George had left the table Bertha would clear off his plate and sit down in his empty chair. The table would brighten up now as the children talked about school, or their mother urged them to reveal items of neighbourhood gossip. Even Myrla broke out of her self-imposed retreat at these times and joined in the conversations.

One morning after Donnie and Margaret had gone to the Regent Street playground and George was ensconced in his front-room chair, Bertha sighed and asked her daughter quietly what she intended to do. This was the moment that Myrla had been dreading for months, and she wiped her soapy hands on her apron, turned from the sink, and sat down opposite her mother at the table.

"I don't know what to do," Myrla said, not looking at her mother.

"You'd better do something quick," began Bertha quietly, then her voice rose as she went on, "Whatever in the world possessed you to allow anything like that! What kind of a daughter did I bring up anyhow? I've seen it coming, young lady, don't worry. I've been watching you since you left school. I always knew that some day, if I didn't get you married first, that this would happen. There's nothing like this ever happened to any of my family before! Maybe because my father would have heat our arses with a whip if it had!" She jumped to her feet, picked up a rag, and began to wipe the top of the gas stove like a woman possessed.

Myrla sat staring down at the worn linoleum.

"What will the neighbours think? What do they think already! Did you ever give that a thought? My God, I'm ashamed now to even step out in the street!" She began sobbing, and Myrla suddenly realized that it was the first time she had ever seen her mother crying openly like that.

To Bertha Patson the Supreme Diety had always been her neighbours. She could think of no worse atonement for the sins of her family than to have them paraded before the judgement of the families that lived around her.

"What did I ever do to deserve all this?" Bertha asked from behind her apron which she had raised to hide her crying. "First your father loses his job and then you. Now your father's out of his head and you're—like you are! There's a limit to what a body can take! I don't know what to do—where to turn. Maybe I should take the bairns and go away somewhere by myself, where I can look people in the eye!" She began crying horribly, loud wails divided by breathless gasps.

Myrla stared at her mother's head bowed into her apron. Through her thick brown hair were streaks and patches of gray. The backs of her hands clutching her apron were thin and rough with standing blue veins. Myrla realized now more than ever what a long fight her mother had been making to keep them respectable, denying herself, pretending that adversity could not defeat her, holding her family together with a strength and power her daughter did not possess.

Bertha's crying stopped, and she wiped her reddened eyes on her apron. "Does Ken know?" she asked.

"Yes he knows. That's why he went away," Myrla answered. "He wasn't to blame though. It happened before I started going with him."

"Who was it?" her mother asked, showing her amazement. She fell into a chair.

Myrla didn't answer.

"Who was it!" Bertha screamed.

"Oh Jeez, Ma, what does it matter?"

"What does it matter!" Bertha repeated. "My God, girl, tell me! Or has there been so many you don't know!" She stood up and with anger and loathing flashing from her tear-reddened eyes she advanced on the girl.

"You can't say these things to me!" Myrla shouted. "I know who it was, but that's *my* business!"

"It's your business is it! It's my business too that my daughter does things like that. It's my business that I've got to face everybody and listen to their talk and stand their stares! It's my business that I brought you up and gave you a good home. It's not my fault that you went bad! I've done everything I could but there was a bad streak in you all the time! Now, if it's your business, get out!" She sat down again, limply, the anger drained from her by her flow of words. She was no longer crying but shuddering, all the colour gone from her thin cheeks.

When Bertha spoke again her voice was quieter and full of pity. "If your bairn is a girl I hope you'll never have to go through what I've been through. I don't wish you any hard luck, Myrla. I hope that both you and the young un'll do well. Let me see her some day. And—and God help you." She got up and crept from the room. Myrla heard her climbing the stairs, and then her bedroom door slamming behind her.

As the shadows from the tall elms and maples lengthened across the clipped grass of the park, and the traffic curving around the provincial parliament building thickened with the five o'clock rush, Myrla got up from the bench and crossed the grass to the corner traffic lights.

She walked slowly down wide University Avenue with its traffic artery divided from a narrower roadway by a wide tree-grown island that stretched in street-broken sequence down to the facing pawnshops and second-hand stores on Queen Street. She pushed unheeding through the groups of young women and girls who hurried north from their offices, their snatches of conversation and laughter only deepening the wedge of difference that divided them. She was alone, not a part of the crowd but only surrounded by it.

The office buildings and hospitals gave way to a neighbourhood of small factories, warehouses and clothing manufacturers, and Myrla strolled on, turning along this street and down another, trying to appear as if her stroll had destination and purpose. She felt weak from not having eaten all day, and occasionally she was almost overcome by short spells of vertigo which made her pause before going on.

She found herself at the foot of a street that ended with wide railroad yards spreading fan-wise from the Union Station to the east, and she walked west along a footpath on the south side of a parallel street overlooking the yards. A few yard engines steamed here and there in the yards, and to the south could be seen the railroad shops and roundhouses with their sunbursts of trackage on which stood lines of smoke-breathing engines. From the station snaked a long dusty green passenger train weaving through the yards.

Myrla crossed a long steel bridge and emerged from it at a highway along which ran the westward outpourings of the city's motor traffic. The corner was flanked with grocery warehouses, and to the east she could see the huge hulk of a grain elevator. Across the street some early spectators were arriving at the baseball park.

She walked east, past steel warehouses, the grain elevator, a large trucking company's parking lot, a cold storage building. She crossed innumerable railroad sidings, and passed uncounted factories, always heading towards the greasy waters of the bay. Now there were tethered lake steamers in the slips she passed, loading or unloading cargo or merely waiting there with fires out for cargoes they hadn't carried since the beginning of the Depression.

When she came to the Island ferry docks she watched the commuting residents and summer visitors rushing from the streetcars to the boats that would carry them across the bay to Centre, Hanlon's Point or Ward's Islands, which could be seen as a mile-off green belt to the south. The passenger wharves with their tied-up excursion boats came in view, and one of them, either the *Northumberland* or *Dalhousie City*, was pulling away for its final return trip of the day across Lake Ontario, to pick up its load of returning Sunday school picnickers at Niagara-on-the-Lake or Port Dalhousie.

It had been such a short time ago that young Myrla Patson of Mrs. Sangster's Sunday school class had embarked on the annual picnic of King Street Presbyterian Church, a shopping bag loaded down with sandwiches, and two fifty-cent pieces knotted in a corner of her handkerchief, to be spent by herself and her little brother Donnie who clung to her hand as they crossed the wide railroad level crossing to reach the docks. The level crossing had now been replaced by a raised railroad right of way that cut off the downtown city from the docks like a mediaeval wall.

A tall narrow-hulled, white-painted, three-decked excursion steamer was getting ready to carry a Moonlight Excursion into the lake that evening, and some deckhands were swabbing down the upper decks. Not so long ago a teen-age Myrla Patson had been one of the excursionists, hurrying with her escort up the gangplank, taking possession of seats on an upper deck abaft the deckhouse, eating hot-dogs washed down with orangeade as they waited for the trip to begin and the music for dancing to commence.

These things now belonged to an irretrievable past, and she quickly put them out of her mind.

Her reasons for heading for the waterfront had not been allowed to fully develop in her thoughts, but beneath them, almost hidden even from her subconscious, was the subliminal nagging that something desperate had to be done to end her indecision. If she had entertained the thought of suicide, even subconsciously, she now discovered that she would not be able to carry it out by throwing herself into the bay, not during daylight at any rate, and probably not after dark. In the first place she was too good a swimmer, and there were too many places to grab hold of and await rescue.

She headed through the subway under the railroad overpass, and into the downtown business streets. She walked painfully and as if in a trance, the new-lighted streetlights mixing with the multi-coloured flashes of the neon signs in a kaleidoscopic blur. Once she stopped and ran her eyes along a drugstore window display, allowing her thoughts to toy once again with suicide, this time with drugs. She turned from the window with a small hysterical laugh, realizing that she had no money, and that even suicide, in this way, was beyond her means.

After a few more blocks she paused to rest for a moment, leaning against the window of a shoe store.

"Hello, sweetheart," a male voice greeted her over her shoulder.

She kept very still, staring at the shoes in the window.

"How's about you and me goin' for a little walk, sister? Waddya say? Wyn't you break down an' admit you're lonely. I got a nice room, baby."

She turned and faced a cheaply dressed young man with carefully-waved hair. He looked into her face then his gaze fell on her swollen belly, and his eager smile changed to embarrassed apology,

"Gee, miss, I didn't know," he stammered. "I'm sorry—ma'am."

"It's okay." She had to smile at his discomfiture.

"I wouldn't have said nothing if I'd noticed. I'll be going. Sorry."

She moved on up the street. He hadn't been such a bad-looking fellow. Cheap, and thought he was irresistible. Probably lonely and needed a woman very much.

Through the loosely-curtained window of a mission that she passed Myrla saw a series of old, gray, bald, dirty male heads, while at a lectern at the front of a hall a young pimply-faced preacher ranted and threw his arms about. She could not hear the man's voice but she watched his hands, now upraised, now fallen to his sides, now pointing, thin and bloodless, up to heaven.

After walking aimlessly around the downtown streets for another hour or more she knew she had to sit down somewhere and rest or she would faint. She wondered where to go, but as she looked along the street she saw a winking electric sign that read Bus Depot. She pushed herself along until she reached it, pulled open the heavy glass door, and crossed the marble tile floor before falling gratefully into a space on one of the heavy wooden seats. She closed her eyes and luxuriated in the relief she felt, putting aside thoughts of ever having to get up and walk again.

A constant stream of bus passengers came and went through the waiting room, some of them brushing past her knees with their varied bags and bundles. A small wedding party entered from the street and stood near the doors leading to the platforms, surrounding a happy but nervous bride and groom. One of the group, obviously the family jester, made remarks at which they all laughed. Myrla envied their enjoyment, yet was too sick and scared to want to take part.

A young woman chased across the floor after a toddling baby, cutting off its advance and retrieving it in a hug when its little legs carried it too far from where she was sitting. Some middle-aged men passed her, probably autoless salesmen, trying to show the world that they were still seasoned travellers, with their expensive bags and the practised way they bought cigars and magazines for their trip.

By the time the hands of the big clock over the door reached eleven Myrla could stay awake no longer and she fell asleep, her head lolling on to her shoulder.

"Missus, hey, missus!" a woman's voice said in her ear.

She straightened up quickly and looked around, wearing a slightly startled smile. She turned to an old woman who was sitting beside her.

"I was afraid you might miss your bus," the woman said. She was a heavy woman with a big bosom, wearing a white summer dress and white shoes. She held a folded raincoat on her lap, while at her feet rested a large basket of peaches and a shopping bag full of small parcels.

Myrla glanced at the clock, which told her it was twelve-fifteen. "I'm not taking a bus," she told the woman. "I came here to meet my husband. He was supposed to arrive at twelve o'clock."

"What bus was he coming on?" the woman asked.

"On—the one from Barrie."

"Did you ask the girl at the desk. Maybe it's late."

"No. He may take a later one. Sometimes he does."

"I don't think there's any more arriving in tonight. I'm going to Oshawa. I believe there's only a couple more buses even leaving." Even as the woman was speaking Myrla had noticed her looking for a sign of her wedding ring. She clenched her left hand on her knee.

"I'll go and enquire at the desk for you if you like," the old woman went on. "You're probably tired, dear, what with that," nodding to the girl's protruding front, "and everything."

"Oh no, don't bother please!" Myrla exclaimed frantically.

"Well—all right."

Myrla said, "When I came out tonight I didn't bring a darn cent with me. I really should phone home and have my father come down in the car and pick me up. I'd appreciate it very much if you could give me a nickel so I could use the phone."

The woman dug into her purse and after searching its bottom handed Myrla a dime.

"Thank you very much. I'll change it at the cigar counter."

Myrla pulled herself to her feet and walked across to the cigar stand. Then she went into a phone booth and closed the door behind her. She pretended to insert one of the nickels and dial an imaginary number. Putting the receiver to her ear she glanced through the glass of the door to see if the old woman was watching her. Instead she was bent over gathering together her basket of peaches and her shopping bag. A loud voice intoned over the public address system,

"Bus for Pickering, Whitby and Oshawa, now ready on platform seven! A-a-Il aboard!"

Myrla said a fervent prayer of thanks as she watched the old woman in white make her exit through the doorway to the platforms. She stayed a moment longer in the phone booth then went into the lunchroom.

She bought herself a cheese sandwich and coffee with the two nickels she'd received for the old woman's dime, and with the worst pangs of her hunger now alleviated she sat down once again on a bench in the waiting room. She felt drowsy, and she lay her back against the bench and fell asleep again. She was awakened once momentarily by a janitor who mopped the floor under her raised feet, but fell asleep as soon as he had passed.

When she woke up the clock said seven-twenty and the waiting room was filling up with people. Early morning sunlight streamed in through the Bay Street windows. Her neck felt stiff, and she shook her head slowly to limber it. Her mouth was dry and bitter-tasting, and she pulled herself to her feet and went into the ladies' washroom, where she was glad to find herself alone. Before coming out again she washed her hands and face and combed her hair.

She walked the downtown streets again until nine o'clock. She told herself that something had to happen today, for she couldn't go on walking the streets, sleeping on waiting-room benches, and warding off starvation with dimes begged from kind old ladies. She paused in front of a police station, debating with herself whether to go in and give herself up as a vagrant, but decided to put it off until later in the day.

As she stared unseeing into the window of a department store there was a slight tap on her shoulder and she turned quickly to find herself facing Mrs. Plummer from Timothy Place.

"Hello, Myrla," the woman said, smiling through her badly-fitted teeth.

"Hello."

"What are you doing, window shopping?"

"No. Just killing time."

Mrs. Plummer looked her up and down. "My God, Myrla, have you got yourself married?"

Myrla coloured to the roots of her hair.

"I'm sorry, pet," murmured the agitated woman. "I'd have sooner bitten off my tongue than said that. You know how I am, always gabbin' and shootin' off my big mouth."

"That's all right, Mrs. Plummer," Myrla said. "I've left home. I slept all last night in the bus station."

"My Lord! Oh you poor child! What's the matter, did your father kick you out?"

"No."

"Well it certainly wasn't your mother, I know. Bertha's too fine a woman for that. How is your mother, Myrla?"

"She's fine. They're all fine."

"That's good. But my goodness I almost forgot. What are you going to do now?"

"I don't know. I thought about it all day yesterday and all last night."

"You poor little devil! Why don't you go to the Salvation Army, they've got a place for girls like—that get—into trouble, like you have. Have you been to them yet?"

"No. I don't want to go there if I can help it."

"I don't blame you a bit," said Mrs. Plummer. She went into a diatribe about all charitable institutions, the money they made, what they claimed they did, but didn't do, for the poor, and how she refused to ever give them a cent, a red cent.

Myrla listened, her own worries making her impatient with the old woman's ideas.

When she finished her long winded lecture Mrs. Plummer said, "I'll tell you what, Myrla, you come to my house. Elizabeth is working in Detroit now you know. I've got lots of room, and though it's not any Buckingham Palace it's a place to eat and sleep. I'd never forgive myself if I just left you to wander around the streets." She sighed and said to herself, "God knows we've all of us got our troubles these days." She grabbed Myrla by the arm and led her to a streetcar stop.

In the streetcar Mrs. Plummer rambled on about everything and everybody in Cabbagetown. She told Myrla that she'd heard Ken Tilling was out West working on the harvest, and that his mother was drinking now more than ever. She knew the whys and wherefores of every bit of scandal.

Myrla pretended to listen, but instead was thinking how lucky she'd been to meet Mrs. Plummer as she had. The Mrs. Plummers of the world were poor and ignorant, loud voiced and gossipy, ill-mannered and ill-dressed, but there was probably a special corner of heaven for women like them. The Mrs. Plummers were almost everything they said a woman shouldn't be, but they were really the salt of the earth.

Theodore East had been working now at the provincial legislature for four months. His job was not very much different from his previous one at the boxboard plant, but the pay was higher and, as he sometimes said, he was making valuable contacts. His boss, Thomas Mundy, seemed to be well satisfied with his work, and had let this be known to those higher up, including the Minister.

During the summer he had visited the Cranfords occasionally, but his relationship with Doris had cooled, and he had not heard from her in weeks. However through the parties at her house he had met some young people whose friendship he now enjoyed. He worked hard at keeping from them the fact that he lived down in Cabbagetown.

Through a growing friendship with Jack Sharpe, the president of National Canadian Youth, he became a fixture around the club and attended most of the meetings, dancers and smokers held in the club rooms. Jack had told him that only his age was a barrier to his becoming an officer.

He was now convinced that the foreigners and Jews were to blame for the Depression, and as a member of the club he had boycotted a large West-End swimming pool all summer because the owners let it be used by the dirty, greasy kikes.

He had tried to win over the other members of his family, but his father, for one, dismissed his arguments as immature.

"You know it's true, Dad! Who owns all the theatres and big companies? Look at all the lawyers and actors who are Jews. They're the ones who run the country. Nearly everyone works for them."

His father looked up from his supper and said, "I don't work for them. It isn't the Jews who own the telephone company."

"I'll bet it is at the top. Most of the money in the company'll be Jew money."

"No it isn't" said Mr. East. He said, "Hey, Mother, where's my tobacco tin?"

When his wife brought him his tobacco he slowly filled his pipe and smiled across the table at his son.

"There aren't many companies, Dad, that aren't owned by Jews."

"Don't talk so foolish. There's plenty of companies right in this town that won't even hire a Jew."

"I'm glad somebody is getting wised up. If all the companies were like that maybe a white man might be able to get a job."

His father stared at Theodore and shook his head. "I'd like to know what started you hating Jews all of a sudden. What has happened to you lately, did a Jew do you in for something or what? It wouldn't be that club you joined would it?"

"It's not just the club," Theodore answered. "Everybody knows what the Jews are like."

"Who runs this club of yours anyway? If I were you I'd find out who's behind it. People who try to stir up hate usually have a reason."

"There's nobody behind it. Not like you mean."

"I'd think it would be hard to keep an outfit like that together if all you ever do is hate something."

"We don't hate things," Theodore answered. "We believe in things like—like patriotism and good fellowship. We have speakers from all over. Last month we had a young fellow who has just come back from Europe. He sure opened our eyes about the Bolsheviks and things."

"The Bolsheviks! Well, well, I'm glad you're learning about other things than jazz and stuff. While we're on the subject let me tell you something, Ted. I don't think all this hatred is right, understand? I don't believe in hating other people, but that won't make me try to stop you going to your club or belonging to any organization you want to. Just use your head, and don't believe everything you hear." He relighted his pipe. "And so you think the Jews and hunkies are the ones who're making times hard?"

"Sure they are. Everybody knows *that*."

"I don't know it. I'd like to take you to one of our union study groups and let you hear some real economic theories. I don't know who the people in your club are, but it's a cinch they don't know what they're talking about."

Trade unions were things that Theodore thought were a waste of time. He hoped Jack Sharpe never discovered that his father belonged to a union, and listened to Bolshies and agitators. "What do union leaders do but spout off a lot of Communist propaganda!" he exclaimed.

His father laughed. "My union happens to be a company union," he said. "There's no more Communism spouted at our meetings than there is at the Board of Trade." He stood up and said, "Hurry up, Mother, and let's get up to the Crown in time for the first show. I want to give the Jew capitalists another half a dollar." As he walked around the table he patted his son on the head. "We'll argue it out in another five years, Ted," he said. "I'd like to bet your ideas will have changed by then."

"No they won't!" Theodore shouted. "My ideas will never change."

"You be a good boy while we're gone," Mrs. East said. "If you go out make sure you lock both doors."

Twice a week all summer Theodore had practiced tennis on the courts behind the YMCA. With more enthusiasm than skill he had now reached the point where he could play a set or two with his new friends. At the beginning he had worn his white duck trousers, white cable-stitched sweater and white tennis shoes to the Y across the river, but the stares and laughter of the kids on Myrtle street had since made him carry these things in a club bag.

Though he despised the people in Cabbagetown he detested standing apart from them. During the past few months he had learned that to be looked upon as a gentleman meant being indistinguishable from gentlemen in habits and dress. Having to conform with the dress, habits and mores of people who lived in Rosedale or Forest Hill was one thing, but how could he be expected to change chameleonlike whenever he left Cabbagetown for an uptown neighbourhood, or even to the downtown clubrooms. Tennis clothes stood out like a bandaged nose in Cabbagetown.

He had considered moving from Myrtle Street to a downtown room, and only the opposition from his mother had kept him at home until now. His address was a source of constant embarrassment to him, and he had to go to fantastic lengths to keep his new friends in the dark as to where he lived.

At a club meeting one evening Jack Sharpe presented a young man named Bob Leveritt, who told the meeting that he was a deputation of one from the East-End Beaches district who had come to try to gain the club members' participation in a scheme that was to come off the following Sunday.

He told the meeting that he was a representative of many Beaches young people's groups, churches and businessmen's associations. These Christian groups were eager to rid the beaches, and particularly the park known as Kew Gardens, of the weekly influx of Jews.

Leveritt said, "We are tired of being driven from our own park and beaches every Sunday during the summer by large mobs of Jews who come there from the Ward and other downtown Jewish neighbourhoods, take up all the picnic tables and benches, and scatter their old paper and herring bones around the grass and sand.

"We are tired too of our Christian wives and girl friends being leered at by every Abie and Izzy who ogles them on the boardwalk as they walk by. The sight of big fat Jewesses calling to Rachel and Sammy around our neighbourhood has got to stop! We don't want to persecute the Jews—"

"Why not?" somebody in the audience asked, to the accompaniment of loud laughter.

Leveritt smiled and went on. "All we want is that the Jews stay in their own section of town. We Christians can't go to the Islands or Sunnyside any more on weekends because of the hordes of Jews, but we won't stand for being driven out of our own neighbourhood facilities by them too!"

There were loud cheers from the members.

Leveritt held up his hand for silence, then said, "Now, fellows, I've taken up your time, but before I conclude I'd like to tell you of our scheme. On Sunday we'll all gather together at the gates of Kew Gardens on Queen Street at three o'clock in the afternoon. We have some signs painted, reading, JEW, STAY AT HOME!, A CHRISTIAN NEIGHBOURHOOD FOR CHRISTIANS!, and so on. We don't want any tough stuff, unless they start it, but only to march through the picnic grounds displaying our signs to let them know they're not wanted down there. Of course, if any of the smart ones try to get funny I guess you fellows know how to handle yourselves.

"Other neighbourhoods are only awaiting our leadership. It's up to us to show them what can be done without using undue force and without giving the police an excuse to break us up. I want to thank you, Mr. President and members of the National Canadian Youth, for your attention. I ask as many of you who can, to come down to the Beach next Sunday afternoon. Don't forget we meet at the Queen Street gates at three o'clock. Thank you."

Leveritt was given a wild ovation, and the rest of the meeting was buzzing with conversations about the Jews, and boasts of what would happen to them the following Sunday afternoon.

Theodore arrived by streetcar at the park gates at a quarter to three, and joined a group formed by Jack Sharpe and other members of the club. Most of the young men who cluttered the sidewalk were strangers to him, and he took them to be members of the neighbourhood groups.

At two-fifty-five Bob Leveritt and two or three other young men came out of the park carrying signs that were nailed on sticks and wrapped in paper. The paper was torn off and the signs distributed to those eager to carry them. Theodore reached in and took one which read, JEW AND GENTILE CAN LIVE—BUT NOT TOGETHER!

The young men formed into a long narrow column and advanced down a crushed stone pathway of the park, being stared at and cheered by crowds of Sunday strollers who had gathered there to see the fun. These were mainly Anglo-Saxon citizens of the Beaches district, members of the skilled working class or white collar members of the lower middle class. The crowd followed the sign-carriers as they marched down the path towards the picnic grounds.

Theodore felt proud of himself when they started out, but after advancing a hundred yards or so he began to feel a little silly, as people pointed at his sign and laughed. He began to feel as he felt members of the Salvation Army felt, accepted by most and sympathized with by some, but always remaining a small minority unable to interest more than only a few. He began to sense that the crowd felt they were just a silly group of boys. The attitude of the crowd, and its implied condescension, angered him so that he held his sign higher and strode forward more erect and purposeful than he had at first. These fools had no idea what they were laughing and sneering at. Soon everyone would recognize him and his friends for the patriots they were.

An old man wearing an Oxford gray suit and clerical collar stood on the grass near the path and looked them over as they passed. His face betrayed no emotion as he stared at each marcher individually, trying, it seemed, to search each one's face for a psychological clue to his behaviour.

"Come on with us, sir!" cried a marcher.

The old minister stared into the speaker's face, then pointedly turned his back in a gesture of contempt and walked away across the grass.

"The old guy looked peeved," said a young man who was marching beside Theodore. "You'd think we were going after the Christians."

"He's too old," Theodore said. "He should be pensioned off."

"You said it! Do you live around here?"

"No. I came down here with some of the fellows from our club. We're sympathetic to you people down here."

"We're certainly glad to have your support. A lot of our bunch must have got cold feet at the last minute. It's getting bad around here; the place is beginning to stink of the Jews."

As the procession neared the picnic area Theodore noticed some young Jews catching a softball. When they saw the crowd with its signs approaching them they stopped catching the ball and began walking to where the other Jews had taken all the picnic tables. Theodore and the others carrying their signs marched through the middle of the picnic area.

A heavy silence had fallen on the Jews, who sat on the benches or stood near the tables staring with a hypnotic sadness at the parading young men. A large crowd of Gentiles stood back from the area, the young girls in it laughing loudly.

Theodore watched the Jews, who were staring silently at the signs. Some Jewesses grabbed up their children and pulled them closer to the tables. From the beach and the boardwalk other younger Jews and Jewesses came hurrying across the grass towards the picnic area. The marchers walked between the tables once, turned around and retraced their steps, then came to a halt.

Leveritt climbed to the top of a table and held his hands up for silence. "We have come here today to make it known that this is a Christian neighbourhood," he shouted. "We don't aim to start any trouble with anybody, but we're giving a final warning to those who come down here from downtown every Sunday—and you know who you are—that you will not be tolerated in the future."

There was a cheer from the marchers, which was taken up mockingly by members of the large crowd that was now gathering some distance away.

Theodore stood looking up at Leveritt, his sign held high in the air. From the crowd of spectators came a loud cry, and it broke up as it disintegrated into running figures heading towards the beach. Theodore looked behind him and saw a fight in progress near the boardwalk, then the running crowd hid it from view.

The Jews began shouting then, reaching for their children, their possessions, their picnic things, the women wailing and crying their children's names. Many of them began to run away across the grass to the side street at the east of the park, while others began to run in the direction of the beach. The marchers also broke up, and led by Sharpe and Leveritt broke into a run in the direction of the fight.

The young Gentiles met some young Jews in bathing suits who were running away from the beach, and several individual fights broke out. A small group of young Jews tore a sign out of one of the marcher's hands and broke it, then retreated across the park being chased by some of the spectators.

Theodore threw away his sign and took after a small middle-aged Jew who had become separated from his fellows and was heading towards the beach. Theodore looked over his shoulder and saw that several other marchers were also hurrying to catch the Jew. They chased him across the boardwalk and through the heavy sand of the beach until he saw he was outflanked, turned to face them, not sure which way to run.

The Jew was wearing a vest and his shirtsleeves were rolled up from his hairy forearms. The sweat was running over his face from his white bald head. Some of his pursuers were waving the sticks from their signs, and the Jew stared at these in terror, his pale fat features working with his fear. As they closed in on him he retreated into the waters of Lake Ontario, wading out about twenty-five yards until the water covered him to his waist. He stood there crying, stumbling now and then as the small waves made him lose his footing on the slippery gravel bottom.

Somebody threw a stone, which splashed close beside the Jew, and the others followed his example, picking up stones from the sand and pelting the Jew with them. The ugly little man in the water raised an arm to cover his face, and cried out each time a stone found its mark. Theodore couldn't hit him at first, but finally managed to skim a flat rock off the Jew's shoulder. A group of girls gathered on the board-walk and screamed at them to stop.

Theodore bent over in the sand to pick up a stone and a sharp kick from behind sent him sprawling on his face. He looked up startled, and found a lifeguard wearing a red bathing suit and blue trousers turning away from him to chase the others from the sand. Theodore scrambled to his feet and followed them, brushing sand from his clothes.

When he and the others had crossed the boardwalk and reached the grass of the park again one of the fellows said, "I never had so much fun in my life. That was the funniest-looking Jew I ever saw."

Theodore agreed. He felt possessed of a strange elation.

In the picnic area the tables had been overturned, and paper and sandwiches, jars of pickles and other Jewish food were scattered around the grass. The crowds of participants and spectators had broken up into small groups, and two or three fights were still going on among the debris. Seven or eight young men had a Jew backed against a tree and were pummelling him with their fists. A small group of Jewish women and children were huddled together, the women crying and screaming and the small terror-stricken children trying to hide in their skirts.

As Theodore and the others who had been pelting the Jew with stones reached the picnic area they saw several policemen in uniform and plain clothes driving a group of young men before them towards the park gate. When they tried to join the others three policemen cut them off and told them to leave the park by the side entrance.

Theodore and the others walked up the side street and around to the main gate on Queen Street just in time to meet the larger group who had been driven through the park. He saw Jack Sharpe, and pushed through the crowd to him.

"Hello, East, how did you make out?" Jack asked.

"We drove a kike into the lake," Theodore answered. "You should have seen him standing out in the water and crying. It was the funniest damned thing I ever saw."

"Good stuff! I managed to get one of the dirty sheenies. Look at my hand where I hit him!" Theodore glanced at the skinned knuckles of Sharpe's hand.

"I didn't get a chance to get that close," Theodore said. "I sure bounced some rocks off the one in the water though."

Jack offered him a ride home, but Theodore made the excuse that he was going to visit with a friend on Bloor Street. Jack said he could drop him off up there, so Theodore climbed into Sharpe's sports roadster and they pulled away.

During the drive they talked about the events of the afternoon.

"I'll bet we've taught them a lesson," Jack said. "I was interested in the psychology of the crowd. At first they were against us, or seemed to be. That Beaches district is peopled by good solid Anglo-Saxon Protestant Orangemen, pretty insular and stupid actually. They are the kind who need a leader to show them the way, but then they're ready to follow. That first fight was probably started by one of the kikes, but before it was over a lot of the Beaches people were into it, chasing the Jews and breaking up their picnics. The Jews know now what to expect when they start throwing their weight around with the Gentiles."

# 5

As the summer passed into fall, Myrla Patson's time drew near. She had put on weight since moving into Mrs. Plummer's house, and she told everyone who asked her that she had never felt better in her life. The Victorian Order nurse called to see her regularly and had placed Myrla's name on the city welfare rolls.

A church organization had sent her a small layette, and she had added to it herself, making dozens of diapers, more to keep herself busy than because she thought she would need so many. Put away neatly in a drawer were belly bands, knitted pink booties, nightgowns, baby's shirts, pink woollen sweaters, and pillow cases and a pair of pink blankets on which she'd inscribed "Baby" in needlework. The reason she expected a girl, she thought, was that her mother's last words to her had been, "Let me see her some day." She preferred a girl to a boy, who she was afraid might grow up to look like Claude Leroy.

She had not seen her mother since leaving home, but she knew that Bertha sent young Margaret to visit her every week or so, using the child as an emissary to take back reports to her while saving her own pride. Margaret told Myrla that her father took no interest at all in her, and that she was just not mentioned in his presence.

Mrs. Plummer was away all day at her job in the mail-order division of a large department store. Myrla did the cooking and the housework. On Saturdays Mrs. Plummer scrubbed the floors, spread newspapers around the rooms, and kept up a steady chatter about her job, the neighbours, and people she had noticed on the streetcar. She was a compulsive talker.

Mrs. Plummer was short, neither thin nor stout, with a frightful taste in clothes. For some reason she still favoured blue serge skirts and white silk blouses in the mode of the World War, and her unbobbed hair was worn in a severe bun on the nape of her neck. She never once mentioned to Myrla her son Charlie who was in the penitentiary, but each week she sat down at the kitchen table and laboriously wrote him a long letter. Once in a while the postman dropped a letter from him through the letterbox, and Myrla studied the envelope carefully before propping it against a bowl on top of the chiffonier in the dining room. She wondered how a young man could stand being in jail for years.

As she came in one evening from work, Mrs. Plummer said, "I saw Mrs. Tilling tonight down on Queen Street. She was as drunk as an owl, and was staggering along with her boy friend, that little fellow called Roy. You never saw such a sight in your life. I was in the street-car, thank God, and everybody in it was gapin' at them. I think she's gettin' worse since Ken's been gone."

"I wonder where Ken is?" asked Myrla. "The last time I heard he was working on a farm in Saskatchewan."

"Wherever he is he's better off than living with that old sot. I seen him come home from work last winter and have to make a fire and cook his own supper. Mabel'd be out, God knows where, drinkin' God knows what."

"It's too bad Ken having a mother like that," Myrla said.

"I told Mrs. Wells that lives next door to them, time and again, that it was his mother was holding him back. Ken was a smart boy. He was always very polite too, to me anyways. When he got mixed up with the McIsaacs' boy, stealin' and stuff, you'd have thought it would have woke her up. When he started working at the soap company she stopped drinkin', but it didn't last long. She'll be found dead on the street one of these days, mark my words."

Myrla's labour began one morning in October, and she lay quietly in her bed, not wanting to awaken Mrs. Plummer. During the long intervals between the spasms she went over the list of everything she'd prepared. Everything was clean and ready at hand, according to the instructions she'd been given by the Victorian Order nurse.

She lay in the dark, nervously remembering all the stories of pain and danger she had heard the older women of the neighbourhood telling each other. The first pains were bad enough, and she hated to think they could become much worse. There was no clock in the room, and she had no idea of the time. After a couple of more spasms she got up and tiptoed down to the kitchen and put a kettle of water on the gas stove. When it warmed she washed herself in the sink, and brushed her teeth. The kitchen clock said only three-thirty, so she went upstairs again and crawled into bed.

She heard Mrs. Plummer get up at seven o'clock, and go downstairs, and Myrla could hear her puttering around the kitchen and lighting the coal stove. In a half hour or so she came upstairs again and went into her room.

Myrla called to her.

The woman came into the room. "What's the matter, Myrla?" she asked. At that moment another spasm of pain crossed the girl's back and centred deep in her belly. She winced, and shut her teeth tight.

"Oh, so that's how it is, is it?" Mrs. Plummer asked cheerily. "My God I'll never forget how it was when I had Elizabeth. When did they start?"

"Around two o'clock I guess."

"Mmm. Well, it won't be long now. I'll bring you up a cup of tea," she said, hurrying from the room.

When she returned with the tea she said, "Sit up, Myrla. Look, I'll put this pillow at the back of the bed. There, isn't that better? There's nothing like a cup of tea. It beats me how women got along without it before them Hindoos or whatever they are started growing it." After a minute Mrs. Plummer went on, "I'll stay off work today of course. I'll only run down to the corner store and phone in. They get mad if you don't phone in."

"It's no use staying off work. Nothing might happen until tonight," said Myrla. "You might lose your job."

"Don't worry about me losin' my job. A store that big can get along without me for a few days. I lived before I heard a them an' I'll live again even if they do fire me."

Mrs. Plummer phoned the nurse, who arrived during the afternoon. She told the old woman what to do and when to call the doctor, and said she'd drop in the next morning.

Myrla became very frightened as the time lengthened and yet there was no sign that the baby would be born soon. She prayed to God for forgiveness, and promised Him that if she could have a fine healthy baby she would never sin again. She wished her mother was with her, but was ashamed to have Bertha see her like this.

At supper time Mrs. Wells brought a saucepan full of thick soup across the street. Myrla ate a few spoonfuls of it, and lay there listening to Mrs. Plummer tell once more of her own childbirths. Mrs. Wells, who was childless, had to be content with telling the long gruesome story of her sister Aggie's last confinement.

About nine o'clock in the evening, leaving Mrs. Wells with Myrla, Mrs. Plummer ran down to the corner grocery store and called the doctor, who arrived a half-hour later.

The doctor, an old dishevelled man, examined Myrla and soothed her with his joviality. He told her she was the fifth confinement that week. He said, "I'm thankful they were all considerate enough to have their babies at a decent hour. I'm getting too old to leave my bed in the middle of the night."

Soon Myrla could think of nothing but the searing pain, and in the shortening intervals between spasms she fell back on her wet pillow exhausted, the sweat on her forehead running cold. Later she dug her nails into her palms and cried and moaned to God and her mother to help her. When the pains seemed to be tearing her in half she screamed shrilly.

The baby, a small well-formed boy with the Patson looks and a hearty pair of lungs, was born at eleven-thirty. After the baby was examined by the doctor Mrs. Plummer wrapped it and placed it in the quilted clothes basket Myrla had prepared.

Myrla lay as if in a coma, her face ashen against the pillow. The doctor sat beside the bed staring at the girl. Finally he stood up and said to Mrs. Plummer, "Go and phone an ambulance. That girl is very sick. I'll stay here with her." He gave her the number of a hospital and what to tell them.

Mrs. Plummer ran down to the corner but found the grocery store closed, and had to make her phone call from a Queen Street drugstore. When she returned she found Myrla awake but looking deathly sick.

The old doctor said, "I was just telling this pretty young lady that we'll be taking her to the hospital in a few minutes where we can fix her up right. She's scared, but there's really not much to be scared about. She might need a blood transfusion that's all."

"Am I very sick?" asked Myrla, her voice trembling.

"Not too sick," the doctor said.

"I'm afraid. I'm not married."

"Do you think I don't know that?" asked the doctor, laughing. "Do you think that makes any difference to the baby?"

"Maybe I'm being punished," the girl said, turning her face to the wall.

"Punished!" asked the doctor. "Who would punish you for having a baby? I think you've had enough punishment for one day. We're going to take you to the hospital now and fix you up."

Myrla was cheered by the doctor's reassurance. "For months I thought about this moment," she said. "I thought the first thing I'd want was to hold my baby. For a few minutes there I almost hated it."

"Why not? He gave you a lot of trouble," the doctor said.

"Is it a boy?" she asked.

"He's a lovely big boy that looks just like you, Myrla," Mrs. Plummer said.

"I was so sure he'd be a girl," Myrla said. "Can I see him?"

"You just lie still for a while," the doctor said. "Do you know anybody we could ask to donate some blood down at the hospital, any friend, school chum, a brother maybe?"

"Nobody has a phone," Myrla said in a weak, faltering voice.

"We'll steal a pint from you then," the doctor said to Mrs. Plummer.

"Oh laws! I've always been afraid of them big needles."

"Have you ever given blood before?" the doctor asked.

"No, doctor."

"Well, after tonight you'll be able to brag that you have."

When the ambulance arrived Myrla was placed on a stretcher and taken down the stairs and on to Timothy Place and placed inside the Public Health ambulance. Mrs. Plummer, carrying the baby, was placed inside also, and sat on a small folding seat. The ambulance had to back out of the narrow street.

It was all very confusing to Myrla at first. She remembered being sick, and now she noticed a small vomit stain on the front of her nightgown. She had half awakened a couple of times, once to see flashes of white coats near her bed and masculine voices, and another time to hear the sound of babies crying in the room. Gradually she began to realize where she was—in a hospital ward. She called weakly for a nurse, and the woman in the next bed said, "I'll ring for her, honey."

When her baby was placed in bed with her she gazed for a long time into his face. He was sleeping, and she let her eyes run over the contours of his cheeks and his funny little nose. She drank in the sight of him hungrily, hardly able to contain the happiness that now flooded her. She opened up his blanket and gazed at his limbs, feeling his feet and arms and sending up a silent prayer that he was whole and unmarked.

Later a nurse came over and peeked under the covers. "Has Mr.

Patson eaten supper yet?" she asked Myrla. Myrla was self-conscious as she tried to give him the breast, but the nurse pinched his cheeks and pulled at his chin until he awoke and gave a lusty cry of protest. Then he began feeding, and Myrla kissed the top of his head.

The next morning she met her eight ward mates, who were occupying beds on either side of the ward. Some of them talked incessantly, especially a fat happy woman in the next bed to Myrla, whose name was Carruthers. She told Myrla, her huge bulk wriggling as she laughed, that she had nine children, one every year so she could get a week's rest. "My annual vacation," she called it.

During the day the women, or most of them, talked back and forth to each other. One young woman in a corner however kept quiet and hardly ever spoke. Mrs. Carruthers told Myrla that the woman's husband had not been to see her, and she thought he was going around with another girl while his wife was there in the hospital. Myrla thought that perhaps the other girl was unmarried, as she was, and she was glad she'd bought herself a cheap wedding ring in a pawnshop before the baby was born. When she was asked, she told the others that her husband was working in Vancouver, and that she was going out there to join him as soon as the baby was old enough to travel. Mrs. Plummer sent her some flowers, and Myrla told her ward mates they had been sent by her husband.

Mrs. Plummer and Mrs. Wells visited her nearly every evening. They brought her some second-hand magazines and the latest Timothy Place gossip. Mrs. Plummer told her that her sister Margaret had asked about her. "I didn't tell her about you havin' that haemorrhage though. I said both you and the baby was doin' fine, an' that he was a big healthy boy. I didn't want to worry your mother."

"I looked at the baby on my way in," Mrs. Wells told her the first time she came. "He looks the spittin' image of you, Myrla."

"He'd better, after all the trouble we had to bring him into the world," said Mrs. Plummer.

"Listen to her, Myrla!" exclaimed Mrs. Wells. "You'd think *she* had the baby instead of you."

"I'd have sooner had a baby than them needles," Mrs. Plummer said. "Believe me, if it hadn't been for the blood I give, this young lady might not a been here today."

Mrs. Wells looked as if she had heard the story many times before. "My, Mrs. Plummer, you're a bloody heroine, ain't ya?" she asked.

"This is a nice hospital," said Myrla quickly.

"Yes. My daughter was in here once. St. Michael's. They say Catholic hospitals is best, at least the Catholics say that," said Mrs. Plummer.

Mrs. Wells snorted. "They're all the same. All except the General. I wouldn't send a dog to the General. When I was in for my goitre—"

The two women enjoyed their visits, and Myrla knew that besides coming to see her and the baby they came to gather verbal ammunition for their conversations. Hospitals, like funerals, were a great attraction to them, and they let few opportunities slip by to attend both.

After Myrla came home from the hospital the weather grew cool and Cabbagetown acquired its Between-seasons drabness. The grass on the small lawns was wet and matted into small gray patches, and the streets were dirty and spotted with the decaying residue of the previous summer, old leaves and twigs and wind-blown manure.

She was wheeling the baby along Dundas Street one day in the paint-worn wicker carriage somebody had given her when she met Theodore East.

"How is the baby, Myrla?" he asked her.

"He's fine, here take a look," she invited, pulling back the covers.

"She looks like you," he said.

"She's a he."

"What are you calling him?"

"Derek," she answered, tucking the baby in again.

"That's a classy name for this neighbourhood," he said.

She had always thought of him as something of a sham, and she watched him now with ill-concealed distaste as he took a cigarette from a cigarette case and lighted it.

He asked her if she'd had any news of Ken Tilling, and she said she'd heard he was in Vancouver.

"What is he doing out there?" Theodore asked.

"He's been in a relief camp since he worked on the harvest in Saskatchewan."

"I don't understand why he left his job at the soap company. He'll never get anywhere bumming around the country like a tramp."

"He's no worse off than if he'd stayed around here," Myrla said, defending him.

"At least he had a job here. He could have stuck it, after I had to beg my brother to get it for him. Maybe he doesn't want to work. A lot of the unemployed don't, you know. If they'd only take lower wages for a while, it would give business a chance to get on its feet. They should cut out the charity. That would bring them to their senses."

Myrla bit her lower lip and didn't answer.

He told her that he was working at the provincial legislature now. "Up at Queen's Park we're closer to the realities of the situation," he said, as if quoting some demagogue he'd heard on the radio. "What the people in this country need is more discipline. Until we get a good stable regime like they have in Italy and Germany, to keep the people contented with their place, we'll never get out of this slump."

Myrla thought of how her father had tramped all over the city seeking work—any kind of work. She wished she hadn't stopped to speak to this silly ass.

"Where are you coming from now?" Theodore asked.

"I was up Parliament Street to Woolworths. I'd like to buy my mother a pair of slippers for Christmas. Her feet bother her, walking around the house all day in a pair of broken-down shoes."

"We're buying mother an electric washer," Theodore said.

"That'll be nice," Myrla said, thinking that it would have to be something beyond the means of almost everyone else in the neighbourhood.

"Maybe I could come down some afternoon and keep you company," Theodore said.

"I don't think so. Mrs. Plummer wouldn't like it."

"What do you care what they say?" he asked.

She read the implication in his words, and began to move away from him.

"I'd have thought you might be happy to be asked for a date?"

"Yeah, but from a man, not a goddamn sissy little boy," Myrla said, turning away and hurrying along the street.

Theodore watched her go. He thought, maybe I should have offered to pay her. No wonder Tilling ran away after knocking her up. It's what the little bitch deserved.

**6**

On the morning before Christmas an inch of new snow lay on the streets. By noon the snow had melted, and by afternoon what should have been a fresh fall of Christmas snow came down as rain, washing along the gutters in dismal streams.

Bertha Patson entered her house, took off her wet coat and placed the meager contents of her shopping bag on the kitchen table. She put the groceries in a cupboard with the exception of some hamburger, which she dumped into a frying pan, adding a small dab of dripping from a jar.

Bertha had bought a baby's rattle and nightgown out of the family's relief-voucher money, and these were now wrapped in a brown-paper parcel along with a Christmas card addressed to Myrla. The card was part of an unsold stock that young Margaret had been trying to sell during the Christmas season.

As yet Bertha had not seen Myrla's baby, but Margaret had kept her up to date on his health and habits. She was dying to see him, but her pride would not allow her to ask her daughter to visit her, and whenever she passed Timothy Place she hurried by, looking straight ahead.

Unknown to anyone else in the family she had turned in an insurance policy on young Donald, and with the nine dollars she received had bought him a Toronto Maple Leaf hockey sweater and a hockey stick, and a needlework set and a cheap copy of *Little Women* for Margaret.

She had not known what to get for George, who now sat in his chair in the front room, neither smoking nor reading, a shadow of his former self, seemingly unaware of what went on around him. He wore none of his clothing out, and needed nothing, so she bought him a package of gum and some five-cent chocolate bars.

When Margaret came in Bertha asked her if she knew where Donnie was.

"Nope, I didn't see him around. I was over at Cissy's house. Boy, Ma, have they got a nice tree! It's all covered in stuff like snow, you know, the sparklin' stuff."

Bertha nodded, and continued stirring the contents of the frying pan.

"Are we gonna have a tree, Mama?"

"Not this year."

"Oh gee, Mama, Cissy's got a tree. Why can't we have one?"

"We can't afford it," said Bertha.

"I'll bet we're the only house in the whole world that hasn't got a tree," Margaret went on, petulantly.

"Well we can't have one this year, so that's that," Bertha answered, simulating anger to hide the sadness behind her words. "Maybe next year we'll be able to afford one. Your daddy'll be working next year and we'll get a tree."

"Everything around this old house is next year," the girl said. "Daddy'll not have a job next year."

"What makes you think that?" asked her mother.

"He's crazy, that's why."

Bertha swung around from the stove and pulled Margaret on to her knee as she sat down in a chair. "Who told you that?" she asked.

"Nobody."

"Who said your father was crazy? Tell me now. I won't be mad."

"All the kids in the street say it."

Bertha was silent for a long time. When she spoke again her voice was milder. "Don't you listen to the kids, Margaret, they don't know what they're talking about. Your father's sick but he's going to get better soon, and then we'll have a bigger tree than any of them."

She stood the girl on the floor and went back to the stove.

"What are we having for supper, Mama, liver?"

"No, hamburger and onions."

"Mama, are we gonna have a chicken tomorrow?"

"No, a chicken costs too much. You're going to like tomorrow's dinner though. Pork chops and apple sauce."

"Do you think Santa Claus will bring me my doll and carriage, Mama?"

"I don't know. He's got a lot of children to go to, you know. Maybe he won't have enough dolls and carriages left."

"When I shook hands with him down in Eaton's he promised me it, Mama," Margaret insisted.

"Well then, wait and see."

"Why does he always take the best toys to the richer kids, Mama?"

Bertha couldn't answer that question. "Come on, don't bother me with your silly chatter. Make yourself useful and get out the dishes and set the table," she said.

Donald came home, his clothes soaking wet. When Bertha asked him where he'd been he told her he'd carried some parcels home from Queen Street for a woman on Myrtle Street.

"Did she give you anything?" Margaret asked.

"None of your business."

Bertha noticed that he had something bulky in his coat pocket, but she said nothing. When the table was set she brought George in from the front room, and the family sat down in silence to eat.

During the evening, after the children had left the house, Bertha placed tags on the presents she had hidden in an upstairs cupboard. She wished now she had saved a quarter to buy a tree, for it seemed a shame to have a box of tree decorations and not use them. The bulbs and ornaments were getting dull and the silver foil was tarnished, but a decorated tree would have made it more Christmasy just the same.

She took some red paper strips and folding paper bells from the box of decorations and hung them up in the dining room. There was one big red paper ball that she usually hung in the front window, but she was afraid it would cut off some of George's view, so she hung it in the doorway between the hall and the dining room.

The few decorations made the house seem more cheerful, and a bit of the old spirit of Christmas returned to her. A month ago she had been despondent about the coming holiday, wondering how on earth she'd be able to buy anything for the children. Then she had heard a woman in a grocery store talking about cashing in an insurance policy, and it had given her the idea.

All her life she had believed in the adage that God would provide, and indeed He always had. Faith in this had been the staff on which her grandmother Sinclair had leaned during the many crises that beset her family, when Bertha was a girl. When she had grown up and had a family of her own she had clung to her, and her grandmother's, belief, and it had helped her many times.

As soon as the children came home she packed them off to bed. For a long time after they should have been sleeping she could hear them whispering and giggling between themselves. When they began a loud argument about something she climbed the stairs and entered their room.

"Now listen here, you two," she said. "If you don't go to sleep soon Santa won't come here at all. I'll give you both a good whipping if you wake your father!"

"It's not me, Mama," Margaret said. "Donnie says that Santa Claus is only your own mother and father."

"Gee you're a snitch-cat, Margaret!" Donald exclaimed from beneath his bedclothes.

"Sssh, both of you, before you wake your father. Donnie doesn't know what he's talking about. If I was Santa Claus you know you wouldn't be able to get anything. Now if you're both good and go to sleep, Santa'll have been by the time you wake up. Now, not another word out of either of you till morning, d'you hear!"

From downstairs she could still hear them whispering together.

When she was sure they were both asleep Bertha began filling their stockings. She placed two or three bright new pennies in the toes, and filled the feet with an orange apiece, an apple, and some candies. She stuffed the bottom of each stocking with red tissue paper, though she felt like a cheat doing it. Into Donnie's stocking she stuffed the blue-and-white wool hockey sweater, and into Margaret's she jammed the small needlework set. Then she printed their names on small pieces of paper which she pinned to each stocking and laid them out at the edge of the dining room table, laying the hockey stick and *Little Women* on the table top. When she had finished she backed up to the doorway and surveyed the scene as it would look to the children in the morning. Then she promised herself that next Christmas would be better, even if she had to steal to make it so. She sighed, turned out the lights, and went up to bed.

She could not sleep, but lay in bed beside George thinking back on other Christmases when there had been a fifty-cent tree in the parlour and beneath it the separate small piles of presents for Myrla and the other children. There would be a turkey or goose in the oven, bowls of nuts, candies and crackers here and there throughout the two front rooms. George would remain seated at the table after their Christmas dinner, smoking a cigar and wearing a paper hat that had been the prize in a cracker he had pulled. Remembering Margaret's question about rich children, she realized why poor kids could not understand Santa's obvious unfairness. She wiped a tear from her cheek before falling off to sleep.

When she awoke the bedroom was still in darkness. From downstairs came the noise of Donnie and Margaret scampering about and shouting and laughing. She slid quietly from the bed and dressed herself in the darkness, the children's excitement laying hold of her.

As she tried to sneak downstairs the stairs creaked and gave away her approach. Margaret ran into the small hallway and shouted, "Look Mama, Santa Claus brought me a sewing set and a book!"

Bertha smiled, and placed her finger on her lips. She entered the dining room and picked up the book, gazing on it admiringly. "My goodness; Santa Claus has been good to you. A sewing set too!"

"He didn't bring me my doll and carriage though," Margaret said. "I guess you've got to be rich for him to bring you things like that."

"What kind of way is that to talk, young lady? You ought to thank your lucky stars that he came here at all, with so many kids getting nothing."

Donnie was wearing his hockey sweater over his underwear, and he weaved around the room checking with his hockey stick and shooting imaginary goals into the doorway.

Bertha sat down and the children brought her their few things to see, touch and admire. "My goodness you kids are lucky. Santa didn't miss us this year after all."

"Can I go out with my sweater on?" Donnie asked.

"Not yet, it's still dark outside. My goodness, what time is it anyway?"

Donnie ran into the kitchen. When he came back he said, "It's five o'clock."

"Good gracious! How long have you two been up?"

"Quite a while I guess," Margaret said. "Mama, did you hear Santa Claus come?"

"No, I didn't hear a thing. Did you?"

"I heard his reindeer."

"That was only an old milk wagon," Donnie said.

"It was not!"

"Hey, hey, you two, no fighting this morning," Bertha said.

Donnie handed her a small, crudely wrapped parcel. Then from a hiding place in the hallway he brought Margaret a bag of shelled peanuts.

"What's this, a present for me !" asked Bertha, with pretended breathlessness.

Donnie turned away shyly and began playing with his hockey stick.

Bertha took layer after layer of paper from her present, and revealed it to be a small gold-colored thimble. "Well, my goodness, that's the nicest present I ever saw! Look at it, Margaret, it glitters like ten-carat gold! Now, Margaret, we've both got to thank Donnie for his presents."

Margaret mumbled her thanks.

Bertha said, "Thanks, Donnie, very much. I wasn't expecting a thing."

She went into the kitchen and shook the stove before putting on some coke. The kettle was still warm, and when it came to a boil she made herself a cup of tea. Then she stirred up a pot of porridge and made herself a slice of toast over the open fire. The children were almost too excited to eat their breakfast, and Bertha had to tell them they couldn't leave the house until they did.

After the children had eaten she brought George down, and fed him. When she placed him in his chair in the front room she gave him the package of gum and the candy bars. She returned to the front room in a moment or two and found he had put the whole five sticks of gum in his mouth at once and was chewing like mad.

Later in the morning Margaret came in from the street, and Bertha gave her the small parcel containing the presents for Myrla and the baby. "Now you go straight down to Timothy Place with this. And don't drop it."

When Margaret returned, she brought Donnie in with her.

"Gee, Mama, I'm starved," he said.

"You're never anything else," his mother said. She spied a fairly big parcel that Margaret was carrying, and asked the young girl what it was. Margaret handed it to her.

Bertha opened the parcel carefully, and found a book of cut-out dolls for Margaret, a pair of heavy gray wool socks for George, a small hammer and saw attached to a cardboard sheet for Donnie, and at the bottom, wrapped in white tissue paper, a red and blue patterned apron addressed to her.

"Bless her heart," she said.

The children were trying to show her their presents but she pushed them away gently and left the kitchen. They heard her hurrying upstairs to her room.

7

After a bleak New Year's holiday things in Cabbagetown settled down again into the dreary monotony of January. The weather was successively cold, wet, mild or dry, and only enough snow fell to form ugly hummocks along the curbs and in the front yards—not enough to cover the enervating sight of the earth and pavement beneath it. Despite the promises of fat politicians and well-fed idiots in all phases of society, things did not get better but worse. Those who still held salary-reduced jobs held on to them, and unemployment gradually became a chronic way of life.

After Christmas Myrla Patson had taken young Derek to see her mother, and Bertha, though inclined to be reserved and shy at first, had soon warmed to her grandson. George Patson had taken the baby on his knee and dandled it, though seemingly not aware of his relationship to it. After their first coolness Myrla and her mother had talked for a long time over cups of tea in the kitchen, and had wiped out what vestiges remained of their falling-out that had kept them apart for the last few months.

Billy Addington found a steady job at seven dollars a week at a small candy company that specialized in penny candies. Since the previous summer he had been subject to dizzy spells, and the doctors at St. Michael's hospital clinic had diagnosed it as malnutrition, and told his mother to feed him two raw eggs and a quart of milk a day. Mrs. Addington applied to the relief office for a medical increase in her voucher, and they allowed her an extra pint of milk a day, which Billy drank faithfully for nearly a week before giving it up.

Theodore East won a second prize in the Young Mens' Singles Badminton Championship at the Broadview YMCA. He received an illuminated scroll, which he hung on the wall of his bedroom beside the fading photograph of his brother Paul's fourth grade school class.

Bob McIsaacs was sent down to Kingston Penitentiary for five years on a charge of breaking into a Danforth Avenue drugstore and stealing a quantity of cigarettes and cosmetics.

Mabel Tilling received a letter from Ken in Vancouver. He said he was sleeping in a mission on Pender Street and eating his meals on transient relief. He said he was thinking of letting them ship him out to a transient relief camp near Kamloops until spring. There he would be issued old army fatigue clothes, and given twenty cents a day, which would keep him in tobacco. He said he was getting sick of the sight of the mountains anyway, and intended to work his way east again on the freights in the spring. He was lonely for the East, where at least it snowed white snow not black wet slush.

Winter dragged into a slow on-again off-again spring. By April the small patches of hard-packed snow and ice that remained behind the shading trees and billboards melted into dirty pools. The muddy rivulets that ran from the lawns across the sidewalks dried up, and the gray sodden grass showed a sign of green here and there. The returning sun shone into the dirty windows and warmed the airless shabbiness of the little houses.

The signs of spring gave a new optimism to such people as newspaper editorial writers, who had dozens of panaceas to end the Depression. Politicians tried to echo the new uplift that had gripped the United States since the election of Franklin D. Roosevelt as president, but all they came up with were the silly second-hand slogans. 1933 promised to be the worst year yet.

The unemployed got up in the morning and as though following a senseless migratory urge followed each other along Queen Street to the new government employment offices that had had to be enlarged to accommodate them. They knew without leaving their houses and flats what the answer would be but they went through the useless ritual of going, to show their haggard wives their willingness to work.

Mr. Howard Wells of No. 7 Timothy Place left the government employment office at noon. Since eight-thirty he had been sitting on a plain wooden bench in the basement "chin-wagging" with some of his cronies and waiting for a nonexistent call for a job from the man behind the counter. He was glad to get out into the air and sunlight of the street after three and a half hours of the smell of cheap tobacco, spit, unwashed men, and the peculiar offensive odour of the cleansing agent that made every government and municipally-owned building in Toronto stink like a new-scrubbed morgue.

He walked with a slight limp, a legacy of the war. He was forty-five, an Englishman, and a patternmaker by trade. He and his friends had been talking all morning about the war veterans' canteen funds, and he had learned that if he wished he could go down to an office and draw ten dollars merely by signing a form disclaiming any further claim on the funds.

He hadn't yet made up his mind to draw the ten dollars, and as he headed east along the depressing store fronts of Queen Street he was angering himself into a lather thinking of the fat political ex-brass-hats who were living like millionaires on the money he and the other men in the trenches had spent on beer, tea, buns and Brasso in Belgium and France. He made up his mind to write an angry letter to the *Telegram*, exposing the racket.

Some of the old men from the Catholic home on Power Street stood on the corner in front of St. Paul's Church, leaning their slight weight on their canes, their old rheumy eyes following every passing car. There was nothing else for them to do. They had been left behind and pushed against their will into the role of spectators, and they accepted it as they accepted their aging aches and pains, philosophically and uncomplainingly. The new warming sun burned through their misfitting second-hand coats and raised the hackles on their dried-up backs. They mumbled nonsense through their toothless gums to one another, pointing with their canes at the passing traffic and the store windows, pretending they were still part of the rush of life around them, afraid to admit to themselves they were only waiting to die.

"I'm not going to end up like them," Howard Wells said to himself. "Next summer, if I get the chance, and I'm working again on the CNR extra gang, I'm going to drop an eighty pound rail on my foot. I'll make this one good, not like the piece of shrapnel at Hill 70 in 1917 that only gives me ten dollars a month for a stiff knee. This time they'll have to cut my leg off, and I'll get a good compensation pension that'll keep me an' Rose—" He put the painful thought aside.

A woman came out of a grocery store and bumped into him. "Hello, Mr. Wells," she said.

"Good morning, Mrs. Tilling."

"Are you on your way home?" she asked, falling into step with him.

"Yes. I've been down to the employment."

"No luck I guess? I saw your missus going to work this morning." She sighed. "Things is getting worse if you ask me. Jimmy—that's Mr. Cluff the man what rents my back room now—hasn't worked for a month. He expects to be taken back on at the foundry next week though."

"There's no work anywhere except at these twenty-cent-a-day relief camps," Mr. Wells said angrily. "Slavery, that's what it is. Bloody slavery."

"That's what I say too. Ken was in one out near Vancouver the last time I had a letter from him."

"How's young Ken getting along?"

"He's coming home as soon as the weather warms up."

"He's been gone nearly a year now; you'll hardly know him."

"I'll be glad to see him back though. I'm nervous all the time he's riding them freight trains. Dorothy—that's Mrs. Cluff—was telling me she read in the paper that the police is stopping the unemployed from coming east. I guess old Bennett's afraid they'll go up to Ottawa and shoot him. Not that he don't deserve it. Say, Mr. Wells, does my roomers make too much noise?"

"Oh they do sometimes; the walls are pretty thin you know. Me and the wife hears 'em spattin' now and again."

"They fight all the time. Since he's been laid off she's been a holy terror. I'd give 'em notice only it's nice having somebody in the house," said Mabel.

When they turned up Sumach Street they passed a truck parked in front of a house and piled with furniture. Most of the load looked like barrels and boxes tied up with clothesline. A man came down the steps from the house carrying a bag of coke on his back.

"Them poor devils haven't much to move," said Mabel. "They must have been given their notice. If I ever have to move I might as well set fire to my junk. All I've got that's any good is an old trunk."

"There's a lot of them moving," said Mr. Wells. "Where to I don't know. That one'll move out of there and find another landlord to take him in, then somebody'll scrape up a month's rent and take that old shack. Next month the landlord'll ask for the rent, an' they'll tell him they're on relief. He'll either have to be satisfied with the rent vouchers from the relief department, or give *them* their notice. Everything's gone to pot."

"Did you hear that Mrs. Plummer is selling out and moving to Detroit?" Mabel asked.

"Yes, the wife was telling me yesterday. Lizzie got married down there eh?"

"She'll be better off," said Mabel, referring to Mrs. Plummer. "She's had to work hard, poor soul, since her husband died. It's going to be tough for Myrla though."

"What is she going to do?"

"What can she do? She'll have to move, that's certain. She could go back home if her mother'll have her, or she could put the baby in a home. It'd be a shame though to put such a nice fat baby up for adoption. Sometimes I wonder what keeps the kids so healthy around here, not that there isn't plenty of sick ones mind."

"When Ken comes home he should settle down," said Mr. Wells. "Running around the country'll do him no good."

"He's just like his father was," Mabel answered. "I don't think anybody coulda kept *him* at home." Then with a typical non sequitur, "I bought a tin of salmon for my dinner. Now that I'm alone I have a hard time knowing what to buy for myself. If I buy too much of anything it spoils, and the little bit of meat and vegetables I eat isn't worth buying."

They turned into Timothy Place. Mr. Wells bid Mabel good morning and entered his house.

After Mabel had taken off her hat she put the catch on the door that separated the front hall from the downstairs rooms. From the cupboard in the middle room she took a bottle of rubbing alcohol and carried it into the kitchen. She rinsed out a tumbler and poured a good stiff shot of the rubby-dub into it, then filled the glass with water. The liquid became milky white in color, and she stirred a teaspoon of sugar into it, closed her eyes and downed it in one long gulp. She took the glass from her lips, made a wry face, and shook her head.

The salmon can was hard to open, and she nicked her thumb with the can opener. She swore at it before she managed to pry back a hinge of lid, and when she tried to empty its contents on to a plate the fish refused to leave the can. Throwing it down on the table she poured herself another drink.

After she'd stomached the second drink she felt better, and her movements became brisk and businesslike. The stove was out so she decided to do without tea, and the breadbox held only a week-old crust, which she threw into a corner.

Her head now felt clear, and she could see no shake to her hands as she held them out before her. Laughing at this she filled the kitchen with peal after peal of happy laughter. Her laugh stopped as quickly as it had begun, and now she sat staring at her hands. "That's good medicine," she said to herself. "Good for what ails you." Again her drunken laugh filled the little room.

She pulled the bottle along the table top and read the label. JOHN T. WILSON, SONS, *Prescription Pharmacists. Rubbing Alcohol*—NOT TO BE TAKEN INTERNALLY.

"Oh no! That's what *you* think, Mr. Bloody John T. Wilson! And your bloody sons too!" She drained the bottle, this time not waiting to add either sugar or water. The bitter stuff scorched her throat and made her gasp for air. When she recovered she held the bottle up to the light, and making sure it was empty threw it against the stove where it smashed to pieces.

"Mrs. Tilling! Mrs. Tilling!" shouted Dorothy Cluff through the covered stovepipe hole in the ceiling.

"Aw shut up!" cried Mabel. "I on'y dropped my med'cine bo'll!"

There was silence again from upstairs.

She pulled the can of salmon across the table and tried to empty its contents on the table, but only succeeded in spilling some gray water and a few bones and scraps. She got up and stumbled to the sink, returning to the table with a wet greasy fork. With this she pulled out some fish and stuffed it into her mouth.

After she had eaten enough she threw the can into a corner and lay back in the hard chair and began to cry, her sobs rising in angry drunken bawls. Her eye fell on the plate and she swept it crashing to the floor. Then she cradled her head in her arms and cursed and blubbered into the small puddle of bones, fish and water on the table.

**8**

Before Mrs. Plummer left for Detroit, Myrla Patson went to see her mother again and asked her if she could leave the baby with her. Bertha tried to hide the joy she felt at having her grandson, and told Myrla that she'd take him if it was the only alternative to having him placed with strangers. Myrla told her she'd pay five dollars a week for his board as soon as she found a job. Neither of them talked about Myrla's going back to live in her parents' house, both of them understanding that Myrla would find lodgings of her own.

Mrs. Plummer sold a few things here and there, for a pittance, and gave away most of her furniture to the Salvation Army, which sent a small truck to pick it up. "You know, Myrla, if anybody'd told me a few months ago that I'd give nearly everything away like this I'da thought they was balmy or something. Now I don't give a damn what happens to it. If you ask me we scratch and scrape all our lives to pick up a few bits of furniture, and what we call treasures an' keepsakes, and it's all crazy. It's like Mrs. Wells with her bloody chinaware acrost the street. She takes care of it as if it was going to be left to the Royal Ontario Museum when she kicks off. Do you know what it is? No? It's a bunch of cheap gewgaws from Brighton an' Blackpool an' places like that that she brought with her all the way from England. It'll all end up either in the garbage or in a second-hand junk store window when she dies. Believe me, Myrla, I've found out that nothin's worth saving except yourself, an' sometimes we can't even save that."

Before putting Mrs. Plummer on the Greyhound bus for Detroit Myrla found a job as a waitress in a restaurant on Queen Street West.

Her boss was a short chunky man of fifty with a nearly bald head. He was a Macedonian who claimed to be a Greek, or the other way around. He wore heavy tortoise-rimmed glasses when he checked the invoices or read his New York newspaper with the queer-looking print. His name was Mike.

During the mornings after the breakfast rush was over, Myrla and the other regular waitress, a tall washed-out blonde called Annie, filled the sugar bowls, the paper napkin containers, swept the floor and served the coffee customers who sat at the counter. They took the ketchup bottles to the kitchen and wiped them down before filling them with cheap watered ketchup from a two-gallon can. The ketchup in the can was not the expensive kind the labels on the bottles said it was.

Very soon she learned the other little dishonesties that Mike practised: the using of scraps, the mixing of condensed milk with the coffee cream, and with the butter to make it spread farther on the toast, the inclusion of veal scraps with the chicken in the sandwiches and salads, and the tuna fish sandwiches made from cold cod fillet—

One morning during the summer, when Mike had gone out to the bank, Annie asked Myrla if she'd ever been out with Mike.

"Mike! My God, no."

"He's got his eye on you," Annie said. "I've seen him watching you lots of times."

"Oh you're crazy, Annie. Why, he's never even hinted to me that he wanted to date me up."

"He will, you wait and see. His wife is an invalid, you know, and he's quite a gay old bird for his age. Yesterday, when you were talking to that salesman that was sitting in the front booth, Mike looked as if he'd like to choke the guy."

"For crying out loud! I was only kidding Harold about his pie. My God, if I can't talk for two seconds to one of the regular customers I'll quit."

"Don't get excited, Myrla. But I noticed. He never gets mad when *I* talk to anybody, because I'm not his type. But he's got his eye on you, and don't forget it."

From then on Myrla imagined that Mike's eyes were boring into her back every time she turned away from him, but after a while without noticing any awakening of interest in her she began to think that Annie had been talking nonsense.

The other waitress's words, though, could not be brushed aside. The idea of being Mike's girl was not without its appeal to her. The young men she met were too demanding, and none of them had any money. A man like Mike could make things much easier for her. She had made up her mind after the baby was born never to repeat the mistake she had made with Leroy. Any future affair would involve a bigger return for her favours than a few affectionate words or a fur-collared coat.

One evening as she stood in the restaurant doorway, sheltered from the rain and watching for a streetcar to come to a stop across the street, Mike opened the door behind her and said, "Wait there a minute, Myrla, and I'll drive you home."

In a couple of minutes he came out and they climbed into his car that was parked at the curb. On the way to her rooming house Mike spoke about a letter he had received from his sister in the old country. He asked her how her baby was getting along, and mentioned his only son, who was going to college in the States. He drove her to her door and bid her goodnight, telling her he'd see her in the morning.

Myrla knew now that Annie had been wrong. He hadn't tried to proposition her, as she'd expected, nor had he even tried to kiss her. Though she had been prepared to turn him down, her ego was hurt by his actions.

While she was spending a Sunday afternoon at her mother's place young Donnie said to her, "I saw your old boy friend yesterday."

She looked up from bathing Derek on the kitchen table. "Who do you mean?" she asked.

"Ken Tilling. Who'd you think?"

Something of her old warm feeling for him came back for a minute. "Where'd you see him?"

"Down on Myrtle Street talking to that guy Theodore East."

"Oh. Did you speak to him?"

"Sure. He asked me how you were."

"What'd you tell him?" Myrla asked, looking up.

"I told him you were fine."

"Did you say anything else?"

"Nope."

"Are you sure, Donnie?"

"Gee whiz, sure I'm sure. What do you think I'd tell him? Gee whiz, Myrla, you think you're the whole cheese!"

Later in the afternoon Bertha took Margaret and Donnie down to Cherry Beach, leaving Myrla at home with the baby. She washed out some of the baby's things, and placed them, damp, in the clothes basket to be hung out in the yard the next day. Her mother would not allow anything to be hung on the line on Sunday.

While she was busy washing the clothes in the sink the baby crawled out of the kitchen, and she could hear him playing on the floor of one of the other rooms. She tiptoed into the dining room and saw Derek sitting on the floor before her father's chair, staring up at his grandfather with a puzzled expression.

She was suddenly afraid, for no reason at all, that George might hurt the baby. For a moment she stood frozen with fear and apprehension, staring into the front room.

Her father's hand slid slowly from the chair arm towards Derek's head, and she bit her knuckles to keep herself from screaming. The hand moved slowly, so slowly, towards the child. Derek seemed to be watching it too, as fascinated as his mother was. George's hand seemed to take hours to move the few inches between the arm of the chair and the baby's head. When it settled on the top of the baby's head, it patted it. Derek's face broke into a grin and he smiled up at his grandfather, his two front teeth showing white in his open mouth. The hand lingered a moment on the soft hair of the baby's head, then was drawn back out of sight.

Myrla crept back into the kitchen and fell into a chair. She trembled now as the reaction began. As soon as she had recovered she went to the doorway and called to the baby, who came crawling across the floor to her. She asked herself what did her father's gesture mean? Was her father just pretending a disinterest in things around him? No, nobody could pretend that for so long. Perhaps he wasn't as—as bad as they all thought. She kept the baby with her in the kitchen for the rest of the afternoon.

At supper time when her mother and the children returned from the beach, Myrla took her mother aside and asked her if she'd ever noticed George paying attention to the baby.

"Yes I have," Bertha replied. "I didn't want to say anything about it to you in case you got frightened. Derek often goes into the front room, and your father plays with him. I've never seen him try to pick him up, and I'd never go out and leave the baby alone with him. I've never even let your father know that I know. It's funny, he never says a word to any of us any more—for all we know he's deaf dumb and blind, but he seems to like the baby. I guess the poor man likes to watch the baby play."

Mike drove Myrla home from the restaurant several times without making a pass at her, or trying to make a date. Then one evening he asked her if she'd care to go with him on a drive down to Niagara Falls the following Sunday. She told him she'd like to very much, except that Sunday afternoon was the only time she spent at her mother's with the baby.

"Let's make it Saturday night then," he said. "Saturday I close up early, and we can go for a drive along the Lakeshore highway to

Hamilton and back. You don't get enough fresh air, Myrla. A drive in the country will do you good."

When they closed up the restaurant on Saturday evening they drove through the city and out along the Lakeshore Road through the western industrial suburbs of the city. After they crossed the bridge over the Humber River, Mike pointed to some tourist cabins between the highway and the lake. "Cabins and motor courts are the coming thing," Mike said. "When the depression is over there'll be a lot of people traveling on this road, or on one like it. I see in the papers the other day where they're already talking about building a new highway north of here, to Hamilton."

As they went through Port Credit and Oakville Mike pointed out things to Myrla, especially spots where he thought a roadside restaurant would make money.

They stopped for a Coca-Cola at a roadside stand, and the youth who served them stared at Myrla as if he was mentally noting the difference between her age and Mike's. She placed her half-empty bottle down on the counter and turned away.

"What's the matter, Myrla, you not thirsty?" Mike asked.

"I guess not," she answered, with an attempt at a smile. She told herself she'd have to get used to being stared at by fresh punks when she was with Mike.

Near Hamilton Mike drove into a large park and took Myrla for a walk through the rock gardens. The flowers were beautiful, and the landscaping was something she had never seen before. She knew from what Mike told her that the rock gardens were famous, but strangely she had never heard of them before. As they moved slowly with the crowds, mostly American tourists, she caught the eye of several people, and tossed her head with pretended disdain. She supposed that the ones who didn't stare took her and Mike for father and daughter.

On the drive back to Toronto Mike said, "I guess you thought it was funny for an old man like me to ask you out, eh, Myrla?"

"I don't think you're that old, Mike," she answered. "I'd sooner go out with a man who doesn't—who doesn't try to get fresh all the time than with some young guy that can't keep his hands to himself. I enjoyed the drive tonight very much."

"So did I. It does me good to take a pretty girl like you out. Lately I've been very lonely."

Myrla nodded.

Mike then told her about his wife falling and injuring her back nearly ten years before, and about the small fortune he'd spent on specialists without any of them being able to help her. Gradually over the years following her accident his wife had become more and more helpless until now she was totally bedridden.

"It must be awful for her, being in bed all the time," Myrla said.

"It is bad for her, and for me too," said Mike. "But don't let me make you listen to my troubles. You're out for fun, eh?"

He then told her about Greece when he was a young man there, and about driving a mule team during the Balkan War. He had arrived in Halifax with twelve dollars in his jacket and had got off the train in Toronto without knowing a soul in the city. He had seen a Macedonian name above a restaurant, had gone in and had been given a job washing dishes for his meals, tobacco and a place to sleep in the cellar. Myrla found his story fascinating.

She was pleasurably surprised when he let her off in front of her rooming house without having once made a move to seduce her. During the following week he drove her home twice, and the following Saturday he took her to a neighbourhood movie.

Later in the summer they went for a short drive on a Saturday evening and came back to the city early. As she stared through the car window at the crowds on the Sunnyside boardwalk Myrla smiled to herself, for she knew what was coming.

Though Mike had acted very properly toward her up to now, she had always known that his propriety was caused less by his fear of offending her, or by the fact that he had placed her on a pedestal as

Ken Tilling had done, than by a well-conceived plan of an older and not very attractive man to win her. Since going for the first drive with him she had known that Mike was wooing her by his careful actions so that she would be placed in a position where refusing to go the final step would seem to her ungrateful if not dishonest.

"Would you like to go somewhere and have a drink, Myrla?" he asked her quickly, as if the thought had just occurred to him.

"Where? I don't care much for beer, Mike," she said.

"I know where I can get some good liquor. Do you want to?" His voice was eager, but the rest of him was tensed for a refusal, his hands clenched on the wheel.

"All right," she said.

They drove to a small downtown hotel, where Mike registered. They were taken up in the elevator by a bellhop, and Myrla was glad she could let him see the wedding ring she always wore. In the room Mike spoke to the bellhop, who returned in a few minutes with a bottle of whisky hidden inside a towel. Mike paid him, and poured drinks for himself and Myrla.

The setup reminded Myrla of the nights she had spent in similar hotels with Claude Leroy, and she luxuriated in the slightly shabby surroundings and the strange feeling of power and well-being it gave her to be there.

Mike turned on the small radio on the bed table and said, "Do you want to dance, Myrla?"

She stood up, and he circled her shoulders with his arm. They took a few amateurish steps around the room, then Mike gently backed her against the door of a closet. He held her tight and kissed her hard on the mouth. She felt his solid strength beneath his clothes, and she tightened her arm around his neck. Mike was shuddering as he covered her face and neck with kisses.

Myrla struggled with him then, and finally pushed him away. Then she sat down in a low chair. "Pour me another drink, Mike," she ordered.

He brought the new drink to her, and bent over her, trying to kiss her again.

"Oh, Mike, don't!" she said petulantly. "Let me drink this first. Gee whiz, let a girl catch her breath at least."

"Excuse me, Myrla, I forgot. You're so beautiful, Myrla, I forgot I'm not a young man these days. Maybe you don't like Mike so much, eh?"

She sipped her glass slowly before she answered. "I'm not used to this stuff, Mike, while you're an experienced man. I'll admit I made a mistake once, but I was younger then and didn't know what I was doing." She dropped her face in her hands. "Why is it that every man thinks that all a girl thinks of is that kind of stuff. I thought you were different. I thought you liked me for—for other things. You've been a gentleman to me up to now, Mike, please don't spoil it."

"I wasn't thinking just because you got in trouble that time that I could do anything I wanted," Mike said. "Don't you think that, Myrla. And because you work for me don't mean nothing either. I wouldn't try to make you do anything just 'cause I give you a job. You believe me, Myrla?"

She was silent, her face still hidden in her hands.

"Myrla, please!"

She got up and walked to the dresser. Taking a comb from her purse she began pulling it through her shoulder-length hair. Her eyes were still dry, but the face that looked out at him from the mirror was sad.

Mike asked, "Do you forgive me, Myrla?"

She nodded sadly.

Mike took off his jacket and hung it over a chair. "You don't mind do you, Myrla? It's warm in here after the drinks."

He walked over to her and took her in his arms, turning her to him. He took the comb from her hand and threw it on to the dresser. They stumbled around on the rug, Mike's mouth pressed down on hers. He picked her up and carried her across the room, dropping her on the bed.

"Mike!—no—no—oh, Mike, no—no—please!"

He made no answer.

"Mike oh, you're mean! don't do that! no, please please!"

"It's been so long, Myrla," he mumbled against her hair, his hands fumbling with her clothes. "Every day—I watched you—I couldn't wait any longer."

He was too strong for her. Almost imperceptibly she tightened her arms around his neck and began kissing him, hungrily. Later she lay naked on the top of the bed waiting for him to undress.

When he took her in his arms again, she said, "Mike dear, I'm afraid. Be careful, dear. Have you got any safes with you? Mike—"

"I got some. Don't you worry, Little Myrla." He turned out the light.

A week later Mike found Myrla a small two-room apartment on a West-End street not far north of the restaurant.

The waitress, Annie, said, "I see that you made it, Myrla. Didn't I tell you he had his eye on you. Try to find out for me whether any of his friends need a sweetheart."

9

During the first month after arriving home from the West Coast Ken Tilling reported to the employment office every morning. Each day he went through the silly routine of having his card stamped, then lounged around the office waiting for a job to be announced by one of the men behind the counter. He finally gave up this routine as a waste of time and, instead, tramped the city by himself seeking a job on his own.

A friend he met on the street one day told him that a downtown brewery was building an addition to its plant and needed labourers. At seven o'clock the next morning he queued up with twenty or thirty other men outside the construction company's shack. He felt very young and inexperienced as he looked around him at the older men, most of whom were dressed in overalls and were carrying lunch pails or even thermos bottles in their jacket pockets.

"How many men are they taking on?" he asked a man standing behind him.

"Hard to say. For all I know they might have enough now. Some a these guys bin here since five o'clock this morning. Imagine havin' to stand here for three hours for a lousy job at forty cents an hour. The timekeeper'll probably hire hunkies or wops anyways, and they'll slip him a couple bucks apiece on pay day."

"Yeah. That's what they do I guess," Ken agreed.

"Sure they do. You ever worked at pick-'n-shovel, kid?"

"Only in relief camps. I was out in B.C. all winter. I worked swingin' a banjo an' wheelin' a barrow all winter near Kamloops."

"Then you know what it's like then." The man rolled a cigarette. "You want a makin's?" he asked Ken.

"Thanks a lot. I'm fresh out."

"How are these relief camps, kid, tough?"

"No, not too bad," Ken told him. "They're not too bad out West. The guys out on the Coast wouldn't stand it a minute."

"My brother-in-law worked in a camp down near Trenton," said the man. "They're building that big RCAF airport there. The biggest in the British Empire they say. Most of it is bein' built on twenty-cent-a-day labour. Imagine men havin' to work for five bucks a month! The sooner we get together an' throw those fakers outa Parliament the better! My brother-in-law's a cabinetmaker by trade, and now he has to work for twenty lousy cents a day."

"Bennett'll never get in again," Ken said. "The farmers out west hate his guts. They've knocked the bodies off their old cars and put a wooden box and shafts on 'em, and now they drive them like a wagon, behind a horse. Bennett-buggies they call 'em."

"I heard that. I guess it's tough all over. My wife is sick, but do you think I can get any bloody satisfaction outa the pogey? They tell you, if you want medicine go here, then they send you somewheres else. The doctor says there's nothing wrong with the wife. I told him, 'No, there's nothing wrong with her except she needs some grub, and for me to find a job.'"

"There's even doctors on the pogey, they say," said Ken. "Sure, an' lawyers, stockbrokers, even locomotive engineers," the man said.

Before eight o'clock those who were already working began to arrive. They glanced shamefacedly at the line-up in front of the timekeeper's shack before sitting down, away from them, against the fence. They talked and laughed together, self-consciously smug that for a few moments at least they were better off than somebody else.

At eight-fifteen two big men pushed themselves through the queue and let themselves into the shack. Ken could see them, through the window, laughing and talking together. One of them showed the other something in the newspaper, and they laughed their hearty well-fed laughs. They talked together over the blueprint table, pointing down at some plans and bending close to read the prints, ignoring the line-up of men outside.

Ten minutes passed. A few of the latecomers broke away from the queue and walked away down the street. The men began to grumble.

"I remember that big fat guy," said an elderly man farther along the line than Ken. "His name's Delaney. He's the engineer. He's the dirtiest son of a bitch in the country to work for. He was down on the Beauharnois job till they fired him for drinking. A big French-Canadian caisson worker cut him down with a chair one night in a Valleyfield tavern."

"Who's the other guy?" someone asked.

"He's the timekeeper. I don't know him."

Another half-hour passed before the engineer came to the door of the shack and looked over the line of waiting men. "There's no use standing around here," he shouted. "We've got all the men we need."

Ken felt all his own anger and frustration well up in his throat at the sight and sound of the man's brutal, coarse callousness. "Why the hell didn't you tell us that when you first arrived, instead of letting us stand out here like a bunch of dogs!" he shouted.

"Who asked for any of your lip," the man shouted back. "Anyways we don't want a goddamned skinny little runt like you."

Some of the men in the line laughed their fawning obsequious laughs.

"You're a big fat bastard !" Ken shouted.

The engineer began to push through the line-up to get at Ken.

"Stay there, Delaney, if you know what's good for you," said the elderly man who knew him.

Delaney stopped as he heard himself addressed by his name. He looked over the crowd, then as if thinking better of going among them, he turned and re-entered the shack and shut the door.

The queue broke apart slowly, as some of the earliest arrivals seemed reluctant to leave their place. Most of them walked away singly and in pairs.

"That's the stuff to give 'em kid," said a man, patting Ken on the back.

"You shouldn't have made him mad," said another. "He won't hire nobody now that he thinks we're against him."

"Oh hell, what's he going to do, import bloody Chinamen to do his goddamned labour?" Ken asked. "What do you want to do, go on kissing everybody's arse just to be allowed to live in this country!"

Ken walked off by himself in the direction of home. Before he reached the next corner he looked back at the construction site. Five or six men were still queued up outside the timekeeper's shack.

Theodore East sat with Ken in a booth near the rear of a small Chinese restaurant one evening in August. He told Ken why he had stopped taking music lessons from Professor Falzoni. Ken's face, peering at him from across the table, was thin and wan beneath its tan.

"You should have kept up your studies, Ted," Ken said.

"I don't know. There wasn't much use of it when I didn't intend to make music my career. I still play a bit, over at the Y, places like that. Maybe someday I'll change my mind again."

"I don't know the first thing about music," Ken said. "I've never been too interested in it."

Theodore shook some salt on his side dish of chips. "Music is beautiful, Ken. You should go with me some night to the concerts at the stadium. You'd love it once you got to know a little about it."

"Maybe I would, but I couldn't go there dressed like this." He pulled the lapel of his old gray suit. "They'd make me go in by the tradesmen's entrance."

"Let's forget music for now. Tell me something about your trip to the wild and woolly West."

Ken took a sip of his coffee. "There's not much to. tell. I worked last summer haying near Winnipeg, then on the wheat harvest near

Weyburn, Saskatchewan. I made the big sum of a dollar a day for stooking, and a dollar and a half for threshing."

"What's stooking?" Theodore asked.

Ken told him.

"That doesn't seem to be hard work."

Ken laughed. "That's what you think, Easty! You start out early in the morning with a sweater on over your shirt. By eight o'clock you take off the sweater, and by ten you have to take off the shirt. You wear a pair of leather gloves—if you have a pair—and the sweat runs down your arms and into your gloves. Then the small bits of chaff fly into them and stick to your hands with the sweat. If it's barley you're stooking it's not chaff but barbs. You begin to itch all over. The chaff gets under the waistband of your pants, and every time you move it itches and scratches. Then the sun bakes you, and the sweat under your arms dries into salt patches that rub you raw. Clouds of grasshoppers fly into your face as you bend over to pick up the sheaves. The sheaves get heavier every hour during the morning, and every ten minutes during the afternoon. While all this is happening you're trying to keep up with the farmer on his binder, or maybe two or three of them. He keeps going around and around the field, and every time he passes you he stares over to see how much you've done. You can't possibly keep up with him, or a gang of stookers can't possibly keep up with several binders. The windrows get longer each time the binder comes around. It's a terrible job."

"Yeah, it's tougher-sounding than I thought," Theodore said. "What else happened on your trip?"

Ken told him about being slashed with the Mounties' riding crops in the CPR yards in Winnipeg, and about some of the young fellows he'd met on the road, in Vancouver and in the relief camp. He tried to tell him the way he'd felt one chilly night when he'd heard a young hobo singing "The Sweetheart of Sigma Chi" near a hobo jungle campfire outside Revelstoke, B.C. It had been a few moments that he knew would remain with him as long as he lived, but the story lost something in its telling. He knew that it was impossible to transport the scene and the way he had felt from then and there to here and now. He was silent as he smiled to himself, thinking back on the quiet dirty-faced men lying on the ground and the young man's beautiful voice rising in the mountain air.

"Go on," Theodore said, breaking the spell.

Ken glanced across the table, suddenly realizing that Theodore was a million miles away from him, and probably always would be.

He told Theodore about the middle-aged farmer's wife near Winnipeg, and Theodore sat up and asked him to give him every detail of her behaviour.

"She sure must have been hot stuff," Theodore said.

"At first I was surprised, then I guess I was disgusted. Afterwards, though, when I thought about it I felt very sorry for her."

"Sorry for her? Why?"

Ken said, "You wouldn't understand, Easty."

"I guess not."

Ken then told the other about a boy getting his foot crushed in the couplings between two flatcars on a CPR freight train approaching Broadview, Saskatchewan on his way out west.

"Was it cut off?" Theodore asked.

"No, but it was terribly crushed. We had to wait until the car was topping a grade, and the couplings let out their slack, before we could pull it out. They took him off the train at Broadview—one of the 'bos had gone back to the caboose and reported it—and there was an ambulance waiting. I guess they had to cut the kid's foot off later."

"It must have been awful. Did he faint?"

"No. He had to hang on, same as the rest of us. It was raining cats and dogs, and his foot was in the couplings for more'n a half hour. All he did was pray and curse, and sometimes you couldn't tell where the praying stopped and the cursing began."

"Did you have any narrow escapes yourself, Ken?"

"Sure. Everybody that goes on the bum has narrow escapes."

"Did you ever meet any girls riding the rods?"

"Two or three," Ken told him.

"Did you ever travel with one?"

"No, I left them severely alone."

He tried to satisfy Theodore's prurient questioning by giving him a highly coloured version of his bout with the Winnipeg chippy and a girl he had met one winter day on the bathing station deck at Vancouver's English Bay.

"It must be quite an adventure traveling around like that," Theodore said. "I'm going to travel someday, but not by freight train. I'd like to go to Rome."

"Rome, Italy? What the hell for?"

"Oh, I'd like to see the ruins, and St. Peter's. I'd love to visit the Sistine Chapel, and go to Florence. A chap up at the Parliament Buildings took a trip to Italy last year. It didn't cost him much, tourist class."

"You sure get some high-falutin' ideas, Easty," Ken said, laughing. "What do you really want to do anyway?"

"First of all I want to get out of Cabbagetown. Just move somewhere I won't be ashamed to tell people I live. Then I want to make enough money to travel a lot and enjoy myself. Like some of the people I know down at our club. After seeing them it makes me sick to have to come back to this lousy neighbourhood."

"Do you think you'll make enough money working up at Queen's Park?"

"There's ways and means to get ahead for those who want to. And I want to and intend to, one way or another. People can say what they want, it's the end result that counts."

"You sound ashamed of your philosophy," Ken said.

"I'm not ashamed of anything. Anything that is but living around here. People seem to believe everybody ought to be a Boy Scout and going around doing good deeds. I think a person's first duty is to himself. If we live in a dog-eat-dog society, like the Reds and agitators say we do, then I want to be one of the dogs that eats not one of those that gets eaten."

"Watch out who you try to eat," Ken said. "Out West I got pretty tired of guys trying to push me around. I've come to the conclusion that the most pushing bastard of all is the little guy who thinks he can hold his crummy job longer or get more smiles from the boss by being a heel to his fellow man."

"You're a Red," Theodore said.

"No I'm not. I believe a lot in what they believe in, but unlike most Reds I've talked to I don't put the working stiff up at the top of the noble pile. I'm a working stiff myself, and like you I was brought up among them, and I believe that some of the worst sons of bitches in the world are other working stiffs. And they're that way because they're both scared and because they know they're inferior."

"Well *I* think that!" Theodore exclaimed.

"Yeah, but you'll never get yourself in a position where rosy-cheeked boyish bastards, who are Saskatchewan stubblejumpers before they join the Royal Canadian Mounted Police, can whip you across the legs on behalf of other bastards like Bennett."

"You should stay at home where you belong, then those things can't happen. Don't worry, Tilling, if you had a job now at twenty-five or thirty dollars a week you'd forget about all that stuff."

"All the jobs in the world won't make me forget the things I've seen. If I ever get a job that makes me fat between the ears and satisfied with the way things are, I hope it kills me."

"Stop before I get you a soap-box!"

Ken laughed. "I get mad sometimes," he said.

"You know, Ken, I can't understand why some people are content to live down in this neighbourhood. God, I'm not a snob or any-thing, but I wonder why they don't have more ambition."

"There's not much use if they haven't got a job."

"But it's their outlook."

"Their outlook isn't much different than mine," Ken said. "Don't forget that both of us are the same as they are. We live around here too."

"But we're not the same as they are, Ken. Don't you see, you and I might be different from one another, but we're both different from most of the people around here."

"We might think we are. Maybe sometimes we try and forget we aren't. Maybe we feel a little smug because we've read a few books or know the meanings of a few more words than the majority of them do, but we're no different."

"I have nothing but contempt for the poor," said Theodore. "If they were smart they wouldn't stay poor all their lives."

Ken gave his friend a sardonic look. "I don't see any thousand dollar bills sticking out of your pockets, Easty. I've met old bums on the road who could quote you and your downtown friends more erudite sayings in a day than you could get into your heads in fifty years. Hell, Theodore, if you hate the poor so much why don't you just move up with your high-toned friends, and quit eating the grub that your poor contemptible father earns and your poor Cabbagetown mother cooks?"

"There's no use talking to you," Theodore said. "Have you seen Myrla Patson since you've been home?"

"No."

"Do you feel like seeing her?"

"It's hard to say."

"You were lucky you didn't marry that bag, Ken. She was never any good."

Ken's eyes narrowed, but he shrugged it off.

"She works in a restaurant out on Queen West near Daylor Avenue. I thought maybe if you didn't want to see her you might want to see the baby."

"The baby! Why?"

"Listen, Ken, it's none of my business, but after all."

Ken laughed. "You think it's *my* baby! You crazy bastard, if Myrla had been going to have *my* baby, what makes you think I wouldn't have worked down in the Flako room forever?"

Theodore didn't look convinced.

"How can I prove I'm telling you the truth? Ask Myrla. Do you think I'd lie about something like that?"

Theodore stared at the other. "I thought all the time it was yours. So did everyone else I guess. Though Myrla didn't seem to be sore at you or anything." He said, "Who was the baby's father then?"

"I don't know. Somebody she met when she was working as the maid up in North Toronto I guess." He suddenly wondered if Mrs. Patson or his mother also thought the baby was his.

He parted from Theodore at the corner of Myrtle Street. When he arrived home he made up his bed on the couch in the front room, but tossed and turned unable to sleep. He didn't know whether his mother was still out, or in bed in the room upstairs. From the front upstairs room he could hear Dorothy Cluff moving around. He savoured all the possibilities he now had with her when they were alone in the house. He heard the faint click as she put out the light, and he turned to the wall and lay there thinking of her and trying to picture her naked.

# 10

When the clock on the wall of the mixing room said 11:55 Billy Addington removed his long chocolate-spattered apron, and washed the dry brown crust from his hands at the washstand in the corner.

Billy was happy that today was Friday, for two reasons. Friday at the Besty-Tasty Candy company was payday but, to one receiving only seven dollars a week, the particular day on which it was grudgingly given was no cause for special elation. It was not that. Billy was happy because Friday was a date night with Susan, and the day before Saturday, on which he only worked half a day.

The mixing room was heavy with the smell of chocolate. The walls, the floor, the machinery, even Billy, reeked of it. It permeated his clothing, hair, and even his comb, nail file and wallet, so that he was a permanent olfactory advertisement for Besty-Tasty products. His appetite for chocolate had been satisfied forever during his first week in the mixing room. He had imbibed his fill, not only by mouth and gullet but by absorption through his pores. Now he could no longer even smell chocolate, for it was his own body odour.

Billy took his thin lunch package from a shelf and, before leaving the room, read the dials on the three open vats that were bubbling, made minor adjustments to the steam valves and went to lunch.

The Besty-Tasty Candy company was a small wildcat operation that lived on the crumbs of the candy trade ignored by the national companies. Its specialty was penny candies, and cheap chocolate bars for the sports and carnival trade. Because of their high mark-up and lack of competition, the hawkers at the stadiums and county fairs pushed the Besty-Tasty line to the limit, with little regard for either the taste or the digestive health of their customers.

Billy carried his lunch through the packing room, waving to Mrs. Butler, the candy packer, who tried to smile at him around a mouthful of apple. Her assistant, Lila, was bent over the wrapping table reading the funnies in either *The Globe* or *The Mail And Empire*. Lila's smock was twisted above one knee, and Billy had the satisfaction of glimpsing an expanse of lard-like thigh above the roll of her stocking. He continued on to the shipping room and sat down on a box across from Larry Bell.

"Hi, Billy," greeted Larry. "How's the mix coming, boy?"

"So-so," Billy answered, opening his lunch wrapping and looking to see what kind of sandwich he had.

"D'ja see what the paper says about Johnny Recco? He should be able to take that nigger in the first round. That's one fight I'd like to see. Jeez, that Johnny is a smooth fighter. Talk about footwork! Boy, he travels faster'n you can see."

"Hu-hu," Billy answered, preparing to bite into his chopped-egg and onion sandwich.

"You ever go down to the fights, Billy?"

"No, I see enough around where I live. For free too."

"Aw, there's a lotta difference between a street fight an' a real bout in a ring." Larry went into a long discourse on boxing. When Billy finished his sandwich he peeled an orange and listened.

When Larry finished both his lunch and his lesson on pugilism he handed the sports section of the morning paper to Billy and looked at his watch. "I'm going downstairs to Louis' Gifts & Smokes to play the slot machine. Yesterday I got three plums, forty cents. On my first handle too. See you later, Bill boy." Larry left the shipping room doing a poor imitation of Bing Crosby singing "Time On My Hands."

Billy screwed his lunch paper into a ball and threw it down the freight elevator shaft. He glanced disinterestedly at the sports head-lines in the paper before placing it beside him on the floor.

It had been three days since his last fainting spell, or whatever it was. The attacks came on without warning, everything beginning to turn—then faster and faster until things were revolving so quickly that they became a black blur. He generally had time to sit down on the floor before he fell and hurt himself, and it was really not an unpleasant sensation. He was never unconscious more than a frac-tion of a minute. When he came to, and found that others had seen him taking the spell, he was ashamed; but if he had not been seen he felt better when his senses returned, as if awakening from a satisfying sleep.

Tonight he and Susan would go for a walk, as they usually did on Friday. On Sunday evenings they sat in the Brooks' small parlour with Susan's parents and listened to Eddie Cantor on the radio. Tuesday evening was their movie night, and every Tuesday they went across the Queen Street bridge to either the Teck or the La Plaza movie house. Billy preferred the La Plaza, where there was always a stage show put on by a small theatrical group known as the DeWitt Musical Players.

Billy had read somewhere that protruding front teeth in a woman gave her sex appeal, and he believed this, for Susan's front teeth had a slight protrusion, and she had sex appeal as well. When she took off her glasses she was quite attractive, and she was more refined than most Cabbagetown girls. The only thing that marred his evenings with her was his fear of taking one of his spells.

Since Ken Tilling had arrived home from the West Coast Billy had been out with him once or twice. He envied Ken his devil-may-care attitude and his ability to leave a job or leave town and go anywhere he pleased. Lately though, Ken had been spending most of his time at the public library, and every time Billy saw him he seemed to be carrying a book. He often used big jaw-breaker words in his conversation, and Billy hated him when he tried to put on the dog like that. Ken had also picked up some queer ideas from bumming around the country, such as that Billy was a fool for working for seven dollars a week. Once he'd said to Billy, "Why the hell don't you steal half the chocolate bars and sell them yourself, if the owner of Besty-Tasty won't pay you enough." He'd told Billy too that the fellows out West and on the bum wouldn't stand for the stuff they pulled in Toronto.

One time, when Billy had described Susan to him, and told him that they were thinking of getting married, Ken had laughed in his face. "How are you going to eat?" he had asked.

Billy had told him that Susan also worked.

"Another few years of depression and we'll have an Amazonian economy," Ken had said.

"You sure have picked up a lot of funny notions, Tilling," Billy had told him.

"I've picked up the first grade of my education that's all."

Billy didn't trust Theodore East's friendship with Ken. East was a stuck-up who tried to act better than the other people in the neighbourhood. He was always talking about symphonies and tennis and crap like that. The members of the gang had never really liked East. They'd always half believed he was a pansy, or the next thing to it.

Now that his sister Belle's husband was out of work, the two of them had moved into the Addington house, ruining Billy's plan to marry Susan and move her into his parents' house himself. He prayed every night that his brother-in-law would soon find another job, and get out.

He had grown so thin the last few months that he was ashamed now to wear his bathing suit. The smell of chocolate or something had spoiled his appetite, and he could no longer eat as he used to. It was not very appetizing to have everything from sardines to cabbage tasting of chocolate. He believed his job, and the constant smell of chocolate, brought on his fainting spells, though the clinic doctors down at St. Mike's didn't think so.

He got up from the box on which he'd been sitting and sauntered into the wrapping and packing room. Mrs. Butler was busy with her knitting, so he stopped beside Lila and said, "Hello, beautiful."

"Hello, Billy, how's tricks?" She made room for him beside her on the bench.

"What's on tonight, Columbus Hall?" asked Billy, sitting down.

"Yep. Every Friday is my night to howl. I met the cutest boy there last week. Tall, blond, wavy hair. Wow!"

"He probably gets it marcelled," said Billy, brushing his straight black hair back from his forehead.

"Maybe he does, lots of them do," said Lila, pursing her lips to think about it. "You'd be cute, Billy, if you had your hair waved."

"Not me."

"I think you'd look swell with wavy hair," said Mrs. Butler, dropping her knitting to her lap and smiling mischievously.

He laughed. "I'll get it marcelled tomorrow."

"Where's Larry gone?" asked Mrs. Butler.

"Down to play the machine at Louis'."

"The darn fool! I'll bet he's spent a dollar and a half in that thing this week. He puts a whole quarter in and if he gets three nickels back he thinks he's lucky."

The door opened and a very excited Larry Bell careened across the floor. "I done it!" he cried. "I done it!"

"Not the jackpot!" Mrs. Butler exclaimed.

"Yes siree!" He pulled a handful of nickels from his pocket. "Two-sixty-five! Lila, how'd you like to go to the Royal York tonight?"

"Boy, are you lucky," said Mrs. Butler, with a touch of envy.

"I'm going to play every slot machine in the city," Larry said. "This beats working by a mile."

His winner's enthusiasm was contagious. The other three were warmed temporarily by the proven knowledge that wealth was just around the corner, in the words of the song, as close as Louis' Gifts & Smokes shop. If such good fortune could happen to Larry Bell, what was to stop it happening to any of them?

When the hands of the packing and wrapping room clock said 12:30 they went back to their jobs in a mood of gaiety. Being poor was only a temporary misfortune after all.

Ken Tilling worked a dart-game concession for the two weeks of the 1933 Canadian National Exhibition. It was one of a similar row of games of chance owned by an old carnival hand named Bowie. The old man, who shuffled around in a pair of frowzy Indian moccasins, a black sweatshirt and shapeless panama hat, was reputed to be a millionaire. If he was he was one of the richest legitimate thieves at the CNE, which is no small feat.

Bowie took Ken aside the day before the fair opened and impressed on him the importance of not giving away, except under duress, any article in the "flash"—the carny name he gave to the display rows of alarm clocks, parasols, blankets, binoculars, toasters, "pearl" necklaces and large stuffed animals.

"Dat stuff is on'y to draw the crowd, see. If dey win a prize, give 'em some a the slush, small stuff like canes or ticklers, see."

"What'll I do if somebody wins a big prize?" Ken asked.

"Don't let 'em win. If it looks like he might, see, walk in front of 'im, see, an' spoil his aim. Or pull his darts out quick, if he gets t'ree in a square, see. Use yer head. An' when ya spiel, let's hear it clear down ta de end of the midway, see."

Ken was afraid that his lack of business on opening morning would make Bowie fire him. Though he shouted lustily to the sparse straggling crowds of early arrivals, he found few players. Everyone seemed in a hurry to pass by the games and make their way to the sideshows and rides. He kept up an incessant patter, making himself hoarse.

"Don't waste your voice yet, friend," said a young fellow who came to spell him off for lunch. "Never mind trying to pull in any of these people. This afternoon you'll get a fair tip, but tonight'll be real big. Save your pipes for then."

During the afternoon Ken's nervousness left him, and he duked in quite a number of players. When Bowie came around to collect the large bills from the cash drawer, Ken handed him two tens and five fives.

"How's it goin', boy?" asked Bowie, leaning across the counter in his opening day finery which was a rumpled seersucker suit.

"Not bad," Ken answered. "I'm getting used to it."

"Keep up the patter, see. Murdock'll be around later to let you get a bite to eat, see."

For supper Ken ate two hot-dogs washed down with a paper cup of coffee. He strolled down the midway, pausing to see the ballyhoo acts outside the sideshows. He joined the gathering tip outside the Showboat show, and gazed critically at the bare bug-bitten legs of the dispirited Negro chorus who shuffled indolently to the music of a small Negro band.

The blare of the music, the press of the crowd, the smells of cotton candy, hamburgers and taffy-apples gave him back a sense of elation and excitement he had always felt at a circus or carnival. He loved everything about it, from its entertaining phoniness to the litter of Krackly-Nut boxes underfoot. The spiels of the carny talkers, the screams of the girls on the roller-coaster, the noise of the calliope at the merry-go-round all blended into a happy discordant symphony that welcomed him as a part of it.

In the evening the midway became a solid mass of pushing humanity, and he took in fistfuls of dimes while shouting hoarsely to the eager mob, "Oh, oh, oh, looky here a lucky lady! Forty-five is the big winnah! Nearly made it that time, sir! Oh, oh, oh, who's next to win, who's next to try! Win kewpies, win candy—you play, we pay!"

Individuals in the crowd disappeared into a thick gray mass that pushed forward hands clutching money, or drew back to throw a dart. He kidded them, scolded them, begged them and lied to them, and had as much fun as they did. The money piled up in the cash box under the counter. There were young fellows trying to win their girls a blanket or a plaster-of-Paris doll. Some of the players were old men, serious gamblers eager to win a prize. The young girls threw their darts with wild abandon in the general direction of the dartboards. He handed out canes and whistles and snake ticklers as if they were the biggest prizes on the midway, and the crowd carried them away with expressions of nose-wrinkling yet happy disappointment.

As the evening lengthened the crowds became even thicker, some sports carrying armfuls of cheap prizes that had only cost them ten times what they were worth. Ken took the dimes from the young fellows who, cigar in mouth, took their stance and shot their darts into the cork-backed boards, handing them the junk they won, his voice gravelly but still strong with the excitement that was endemic to them all.

Much later on when the fireworks signalled the end of the day, and the crowds thinned as they left the midway for the streetcar loops at either end of the grounds, Ken stopped shouting and stood draped across the counter, tired but happy, gazing out across a white trodden carpet of old boxes and paper. From down the midway came the music of the calliope playing "Don't Blame Me" and "Annie Doesn't live Here Any More" and the high broken notes of a trumpet in the Negro band at the Showboat show.

During the next couple of days Ken's voice took on the gravelly timbre of a tugboat captain's, and his spiel now came out of its own accord, a meaningless amalgam of doubletalk and carnival patter.

One evening Theodore East was passing with a party of his friends when he spied Ken. He brought them over, and some of them tried their luck at the dart game, though Theodore didn't acknowledge his friendship with Ken. One of the young men, whom Theodore called Jack, repeatedly addressed Ken as "boy," so Ken in turn addressed him as "Sport." He tried disdainfully to refuse the small prize Ken offered him, but Ken forced it on him, a broken snake tickler that somebody had returned earlier. When they left Theodore linked his arm with a tall, tanned girl and favoured Ken with a wink across her shoulder. Ken ignored him.

He had a few narrow escapes with the customers, until now having avoided giving any big prizes from the still-virgin array of flash. One afternoon, however, when the crowds were light and the sun shone in on the dartboards two young fellows began to play. The first threw his trio of darts carelessly, but the other took his time. He aimed each one, and all of them entered the inch-square spot on the board marked with the number 15. This meant that the thrower had his choice of any prize on the shelves.

Ken, who was keeping a close watch on the board, walked over almost as soon as he heard the third dart struck and quickly pulled all of them out. "You nearly had it that time, fella," he said, mustering all his nerve and gall. "Another eighth of an inch and anything on the stand was yours. Try again, sir."

"Try again, hell !" exploded the young man. "The last dart was in the same square as the other two."

"Sorry, sir. It may have looked that way from there, but it was just outside."

They argued hotly for a few minutes, and Ken was almost ready to call in the fellows from the next concession, when they walked away.

When Bowie next came around, Ken told him what had happened.

"You did right. Try to pull 'em out quick, see, before they can be sure, see. If ya get into trouble, see, give a shout to the boys in the other games. On'y if there's a big crowd, see, an' de whole lot gets mad, then you c'n give 'em somep'n else, see."

"I haven't given away any of the flash yet."

"You ain't esposed to. Don't worry about these clems, see. They don't care nuttin about winnin, see."

Ken saw all right. The game was difficult enough, and when the one skilled player in five thousand won a decent prize he was supposed to cheat him out of it. He realized that the carnival business was one in which honesty was not a policy at all. He began to slip change and bills into a pocket during heavy play. On the streetcar going home the first night he counted the money and found it added up to almost ten dollars. From then on the three dollars a day he got from Bowie was supplemented by ten to twenty more.

Late one evening he turned from pulling some darts from a dartboard to find himself face to face with Myrla. He was too surprised to speak.

"Hello, Ken," she said.

He managed to mumble something.

"I'm surprised to find you working here."

"It's good dishonest work. I'm surprised to see you too." He moved along the counter and took care of some other players. When he came back he gave Myrla three darts. She threw them but won nothing. "Too bad," he said. "How's things?"

"Everything's fine. How are things with you?"

"Oh great!"

When he returned from another trip along the counter he asked, "What are you doing down here?"

"I'm with a friend," Myrla answered. She pointed behind her at a middle-aged Greek or Italian who was standing behind the crowd.

"Your boy friend?" Ken asked.

"I work for him." She saw the disgust on Ken's face. "I've got to go now. Come and see me. The Union Jack Grill on Queen West, near Daylor."

"Be seeing you," Ken said. He watched the man grab her by the arm and steer her away through the crowd. The name of the joint would have to be something corny and patriotic like Union Jack, he thought. As he watched them disappear into the crowds he saw the man looking angry and saying something fast into Myrla's ear. She'd opened up the old wound, and now his head and his heart were full of love for her.

After he closed down the joint he walked to the lakefront and sat on a bench smoking one cigarette after another, not even noticing the fireworks bursting in the sky above him.

Why had she let him see her with that old greaseball, whom he could now picture kissing her, undressing her, making his old dirty love to her? Maybe she was just as he sometimes thought her, a cheap little tart he should try to forget.

A woman sat down beside him on the bench. She opened her purse and took out a pack of cigarettes. "You got a light, honey?" she asked, in a wheedling voice.

He noticed that she was drunk. "Here," he said, tossing her a book of matches.

"D'ja need to throw them, honey? If you was a gennelman you'd give a lady a light."

"Go to hell!" he said angrily, getting up and walking away.

Before the Exhibition ended he went with Murdock and a couple of Negro girls from the ballyhoo chorus of the Showboat show to Murdock's room in a sleazy hotel near the exhibition grounds. Ken and his girl slept on the floor, covered with the counterpane from Murdock's bed.

"Christ, you're rough!" Ken's girl exclaimed once. "You'd think you hated women or somep'n."

"What makes you think that?"

Ken hid the nearly one hundred and fifty dollars he'd stolen from Bowie in the cellar at home. Later on he gave some of the money to Mabel and bought himself a new suit, topcoat and shoes. One afternoon he went to a downtown movie showing James Cagney in one of his cocky, lady-killer roles. Ken came out of the movie house into the sunshine feeling just as Cagney had acted in the picture. He lighted a cigarette and took two or three long drags of it. Then, carelessly, with his coat unbuttoned and a hand shoved into a trouser pocket, he sauntered down to the corner.

The picture had lifted him out of himself. He remembered now how years before he and the others in the gang had run from the side exit doors of the Idle Hour, shouting and shooting their imaginary six-guns in imitation of the cowboy stars of the day. This feeling of emotional oneness with the characters portrayed on the screen had always stayed with him. On leaving a movie he liked he almost unconsciously copied the mannerisms and attitudes of a character, and for a few minutes he ceased to be the very common, unsuccessful Ken Tilling, and was instead transported by the fantastic make-believe of the screen into something else.

While still the brash Cagney-portrayed hero he decided to go and see Myrla. On the streetcar going out to the Union Jack Grill he practised his approach to her, his remarks witty and contrived, yet carrying an undercurrent of maliciousness worthy of James Cagney himself.

After getting off the streetcar he stopped before the front of an old store now inhabited by a Gypsy fortune-teller. His hands were sweating and his mouth tasted of dry felt. He glanced into the window at a crude lithograph of a human hand and a phrenological chart of a human head. A young Gypsy girl, her loose bodice showing a sweat-stained cleft between her dirty breasts, motioned to him from inside the door. He shook his head and walked along to the Union Jack.

He hung up his coat and sat down in a booth at the rear of the narrow grill, having seen nobody yet but an old man drinking tea near the front of the counter. He pulled a menu from behind the sugar and napkin containers but dropped it when its flutter gave away the shaking of his hands. Somebody came through the kitchen doorway and stood at the end of his table. He looked up at a tall washed-out blonde.

"Yes, sir?" she asked, in the tired tone that long-time waitresses acquire.

"Oh, get me a Coke I guess."

When she brought it she asked, "Will that be all, sir?"

"Yes thanks. By the way, where's Myrla Patson today?"

"Do you want to see her?" the blonde asked. She went into the kitchen. He sipped at the drink to dampen the felt lining in his mouth.

Myrla stood in front of the kitchen door and glanced first at the booths near the front of the restaurant before spying Ken seated almost at her elbow.

"Well, for crying out loud! Hello, Ken," she said, turning to him.

"Hello, Myrla."

"I'm sure glad you came to see me." She smiled a questioning yet triumphant smile.

"I was out this way so I thought I'd drop in and see you," he said.

She pushed into the booth and smiled at him across the table. She looked at his hanging topcoat then at him. "Gee, Ken, prosperity must have come from around that corner."

"You don't look bad yourself. Where's your boy friend today?"

"Who Mike—you mean the man I was at the Exhibition with?" she asked. "He's gone to Buffalo."

"I see you pick 'em young."

Myrla stared at him, on the defensive now. "He's my boss. Anyway I guess I can go out with anybody I like."

Ken didn't answer, but sipped his Coke.

"How's things at home? Is Mrs. Wells still working?"

"Yep."

"I was down to my mother's place on Sunday. Dad's still the same as he was when we—when you used to come."

He nodded. All the smart stabbing things to say stuck in his throat.

"You never saw my baby did you, Ken? Gee he's cute. He's walking now."

"I heard he was a cute kid," Ken said. "I guess he's nearly a year old now?"

"Next month."

"Theodore East thought he was mine."

"I figured some of them would think that. I told my mother and Mrs. Plummer that he wasn't yours."

"Have a Coke on me, Myrla," he said, to change the subject.

"I think I will. Just a minute." She walked behind the counter and took a bottle from the cooler.

As he watched her cross the few feet of floor he was remembering the night at the party four years before, and the taste of their first kiss came back to his lips. The night they had met at the rink in Riverdale Park. All the evenings until he had left her in Chinatown the afternoon following their visit to the museum. They had been the happiest days of his life.

She slid into the opposite seat again. "How's your mother?" she asked.

"She's getting worse all the time. I don't think there's much hope for her any more."

"I'm sorry for her, and for you."

"Where are you living now, Myrla?"

"Not far from here." Then as if to change the subject, "Do you still go around with Billy Addington?"

"I see him occasionally. He's going steady with a girl on Sackville Street."

"Do you still read a lot, Ken, like you used to?"

"Not as much now as I did when I first came home from the West. The library is running out of my kind of books, I guess." He shrugged. "Or my tastes are changing."

"Why don't you try to get the kind of job that would interest you? I think you can do something very well, if you'd only make up your mind what it is."

"I used to want to be an architect," he said. "Now I don't know."

"What *are* you going to do, Ken?"

"It's hard to say. Theodore East was harping on that the last time I saw him."

"Oh him!"

He laughed. "Maybe it's a good thing I don't know what's going to happen to me. Most people look ahead to some kind of security, meaning money. I don't know any other way to make more money than I've made in the past, not permanently anyway. Bob McIsaacs and Charlie Plummer both tried it the hard way, with a gun, and look where they are. Theodore East—" He saw her curl her lip and laughed again. "—East is trying to find his place in society by toadying to a bunch of rich men's sons, or maybe just richer-than-us men's sons, or their daughters. Poor Billy Addington's case is hopeless."

"Do you think your own case is hopeless, Ken?"

"No, not at all. I haven't figured what I want to do yet, but something will turn up. And what about you?"

"Believe me, I'll get ahead no matter what I have to do. This is the God's truth, Ken, the only person I care for now in the whole world is my baby. I'm going to make sure he doesn't have the childhood we—I had."

"I'd like to know how you're going to do it without marrying a rich man," Ken said, shaking his head. "There isn't one of us who stands a chance of breaking out unless something happens soon to change things. Those we know who are working, especially the fellows, are doing two men's jobs for half a man's pay. The girls are either marrying guys who make twelve bucks a week and decaying in a single crummy room, or letting themselves be laid by anybody with a dollar and a pack of tailor-mades—"

"Meaning me?" she asked, her eyes narrowing.

"No. Myrla, believe me there's nothing personal in anything I'm saying. Billy Addington got mad at me for telling him he was a damn fool working like he does for a few bucks a week." Banging his fist on the table top—"We've got to wake up, Myrla. We're all chumps. We're all living, we young people who should be alive if we're ever going to be, as if we're numbed by what is happening to us. Except for the degree, we're all doing the same thing as your father."

"What big solution do you have to offer?"

"None. Plenty. Everybody has to find their own."

"Maybe I'm finding my own solution in my own way," she said.

"I hope so, Myrla. I'll let you know five years from now."

"Where do you think you'll be by then?"

"In 1938? Probably in Cabbagetown. Probably spending my days dreaming escapist dreams, and my evenings chasing little chippies through Riverdale Park. I'll be as honest as my fear of prison makes me, but I'll steal when I can get away with it, for I have no moral scruples about stealing any more—"

"You don't mean that. If you thought for a minute that you'd be living like that five years from now you'd cut your throat."

He laughed.

"Tell me honestly, Ken, what you're going to do?"

"I don't know, Myrla. My plans are pragmatic, immediate. Maybe I'll go down to the States for a while, just for a change of scene. When I was out West, sleeping in boxcars and flop-houses, I had a feeling of freedom and, yes, even cleanliness. I didn't mind the dirt and squalor I was living in because it was temporary. The next day I'd be a couple of hundred miles away. It's like the difference between being broke and being poor. The same thing."

"Now that you're getting older you've got to think of settling down."

"Do you mean like Theodore and Billy Addington? Listen, Myrla, the way I figure it I can give everyone we know a hundred years' head start and catch up with them in a week. Do you think that Easty or Billy are any further ahead of me than one week's pay cheque?"

"They will be."

"Let's wait and see," he said, laughing. He stood up.

"Are you going, Ken?"

"I guess I'd better. I've said enough for one afternoon. Every time I meet somebody I know, like you especially, the conversation sooner or later gets around to what we've been talking about. I'm becoming a bore on the subject."

"I quit work at seven. Do you want to see me then? We can go up to my place and talk."

"No, Myrla. When I came here this afternoon I did, but now I know we'll never go out together again."

"Why? What did I do?" she asked, grabbing him by the hand.

"You didn't do anything. This may sound nuts, but now I realize there's no way we can be the way I once hoped we would be. I don't want you any other way but that. I guess if I was some guy in a book or movie I'd say I wanted to remember you as you were, or something like that." He pulled on his coat. "So long, Myrla."

She stood up. "If it's because of me going with Mike, we don't need to let *that* stand between us."

"Please, Myrla."

"I'll come down and call for you at your house."

"I'll be leaving in a few days."

"Won't you see me again before you go?" She pushed her hand up his sleeve.

"I don't think so. Goodbye, Myrla."

"You always were scared, weren't—"

He walked out of earshot. He paid the blonde waitress for the soft drinks, and ignored the look she gave him. When he reached the sidewalk it struck him that this was the second time he and Myrla had parted in just about the same way. But this time it was an anticlimax, as everything had been an anticlimax since the Sunday afternoon when she had told him she was having another man's baby.

He felt free once more. Myrla still had the power to hurt him, but she no longer had the power to draw him back.

As he passed the Gypsy fortune-teller's he smiled at the young girl peering through the dirty curtains over the door. She stuck her tongue out at him.

A week after visiting Myrla Patson at the Union Jack Cafe, Ken Tilling arrived home one evening from the public library across the Don and found his mother lying in a drunken stupor on the front-room couch. He fixed himself something to eat, and sat down to read the evening paper.

The Depression that had started almost four years before with the collapse of prices on the New York Stock Exchange (Black Thursday as the financial world called it) had now spread over most of the globe. The Chinese rickshaw coolie, the Bantu miner outside Johannesburg, the Paris pawnbroker, the Wyoming rancher, everyone in the world, in one way or another, was affected by a world economic collapse that nobody understood, and nobody knew how to cure. The poor took the brunt of it, as they always did in any cataclysmic upheaval, natural or man-made.

There were food riots in Bombay, veterans' marches in Washington, unemployed treks to Ottawa. In Germany the people had made Adolph Hitler, a nationalist fanatic with a mystical hold on them, their Chancellor. Strangely, though nobody seemed to know it at the time, the rise of Hitler and Germany's subsequent attacks on Poland, the Low Countries, France and Russia, which formed World War II, would prove to be the only cure for the Depression.

The Depression was no longer euphemistically called the slump, the panic, the recession or such things. Hoover's "chicken in every pot" had been flushed down the same drain as "just around the corner there's a rainbow in the sky." The poor of Cheapside, Harlem,

Berlin's Wedding, St. Henri, the east side of Vancouver, the north side
of Winnipeg, and Cabbagetown, took their unemployment stoically,
as they had always taken disaster. Some chose apathy, some revolt,
some fatalism, and some "took care of number one."

In Cabbagetown, as in most parts of the civilized world, the poor
took care of the poor, and of themselves. They ran block parties and
rent parties and they formed vigilante committees to prevent the
bailiffs from evicting their neighbours. Marxism, which had, outside
of the Soviet Union and some European countries, been up to now
an intellectual concept, came down into the streets. There were those
who became Communists, those who became socialists of various
sorts, from "Christian" to utopian, and others, like Theodore East,
who without knowing what it was, became cryptofascists.

Ken Tilling called himself a cynic, though his political concepts
leaned toward the anarcho-syndicalism of the Wobblies. He had
taken part in a few eviction fights, but as a noncommitted individual.
As a natural loner he sympathized with the friendless and helpless,
but refused to join any group. He had transferred his cynical distrust
and hatred of the bureaucrat, the YMCA secretary, the Bible-
thumper, and all their middleclass minions, into a distrust of politicians of all political hues and aims.

When Mabel woke up she walked into the kitchen, a little unsteady
yet on her feet. After looking to see if there was any tea left in the pot
she poured what remained into a cup, shook the fog from her eyes
and drank it. She was pale and weak, and only her hands and face
had been washed in days. Her eyes looked heavy and bloodshot
within the dropsical flesh of her face, and her cup of tea threatened
to spill from her trembling hands.

"What did you have for supper?" she asked Ken.

"I made myself some toast and cheese," he answered, not looking
up from the paper.

"Is there any more left?"

"There's some cheese there beside you on the table."

She made herself a sandwich. "It's getting cold out," she said.

"Yeah."

"I hate to think of another winter coming."

"Yeah," said Ken. He was more interested in his reading than in what she was saying.

"Did you look for a job today?"

"No."

"What are you going to do?"

"Huh?"

"What are you going to do I said, or am I talking to myself?"

"I'm going away in the morning. To the States."

"To the States? What for, things are as bad down there as they are up here. My God, Ken, running around the country won't help you. You should try to find a job here."

"I don't want a job here," Ken said, lowering his newspaper.

Mabel took a bite of her sandwich. "I guess you're glad to be leaving me. You never did consider me."

"I'm going away tomorrow that's all."

"What am *I* going to do? You're just like your father was. I wish I was a man and could run away too."

"Don't start that stuff again. I'm going away tomorrow that's all."

"You'd think you'd have some consideration for me," she whined.

He kept his head buried in the paper.

"Are you listening to me!" she asked sharply. "I'm talking to you!"

"I heard you," he said.

"Why the hell don't you answer me then? You think you're so goddamned high and mighty. Don't forget that it's me that brought you up. That slaved for you and kept you, when I could have been out having a good time like other women. You don't think of that, do you?"

"I wish you *had* left me," he said.

"Oh you do, do you? You're ashamed of the mother that bore you and brought you up, ain't you? That's it, ain't it?" She leaned across the table towards him, crying with self-pity.

He got up and went into the front room, staring through the window at the empty stretch of pavement and the ugly brick houses across the alley. Somebody, perhaps the kids on the street, had broken the big front window of Mrs. Plummer's old house, and the landlord had patched it up with tape. The long crooked scars across its face made the house look grim and forbidding in the light of Timothy Place's one lone street light.

When he returned to the kitchen he found his mother sitting where he'd left her, staring at the stove, her hands trembling in her lap. He took two dollars from his pocket and handed them to her. She kept her tear-stained face averted from him as she got up, and splashed some water on her face at the sink, and wiped it on the torn bit of towel hanging on a nail in the wall.

She left the kitchen then returned wearing her hat and coat. "I'll see you in the morning before you go," she said.

"Yep. All right."

He heard her feeling her way along the hallway in the darkness, then the closing of the front door. He took a can of brown shoe polish and two old rags from a small box behind the stove and began polishing his shoes.

After tidying up the table he washed the dishes, and put them away. Then he washed, shaved and brushed his teeth. He placed a bar of soap, safety razor, toothbrush and paste, and a clean handkerchief into a small towel and wrapped them up, placing them where he would not forget them in the morning. Except for the clothes he was wearing, and a suit coat, he wrapped his other clothes in newspapers and placed them in the dresser drawers in the front room. Then he stood listening to the steady thump, thump of an orchestra over the Wellses' radio from next door.

Into the dresser he also placed various papers that bore Canadian addresses, and everything else that might incriminate him or give him away when he reached the States. He tore the labels from his suit and topcoat and threw them in the stove. When he counted the money in his wallet he found he still had a little over seven dollars.

His preparations made he sat down on the couch and leafed through a copy of a national magazine.

A short story began: *Roland Boyce peered across the hedge that stood like a long green sentinel between his own rolling lawn and that of Clarissa Maybee. Her rambling Cape Cod bungalow shone white behind its green mantle of Virginia creeper, and on its flagged terrace the slim, tanned form of the beauteous Clarissa herself lay languid on a pink beach chair—*

"Crap!" he said to himself, and threw the magazine into a corner. He pulled on his coat and turned off the lights and left the house.

Two young Italian kids were shooting a noisy game of Boston pool near the rear of the Queen Street pool hall, while an old man sat on a long bench against a wall reading the *Racing Form.* Joe, the pouch-eyed proprietor, leaned on his almost empty cigar counter and talked to another man.

"Hullo, Tilling!" cried Les Winters as Ken entered from the street.

"Hi, Les."

"Ain't seen you around lately," Les said. "Where you been keeping yourself?"

"Oh I've been around."

"You workin'?" Les asked, noticing Ken's new clothes.

"Not since the Exhibition. I'm leaving town tomorrow; guess I'll go down to New York."

"There's nothing to stick around this dump for. Gonna shoot a stick?"

"I might shoot a couple games of snooker. You gonna take a cue?"

Les took off his coat, and chose a cue carefully from the rack on the wall. Joe came over and pulled on the lights above the snooker table. Then he racked up the balls.

"You guys got dough I hope?" he asked in his hopeless way.

"Whaddya think? We look like a coupla deadbeats?" Ken asked.

"Never can tell these days," Joe said. "I got too many games put on my eye awready. They never come in an' square up."

"I know, Joe, the country's in a hell of a mess," Les said.

They played two-handed snooker until eleven o'clock. When he arrived home he made a saucepan full of coffee, and filled the stove with coke so that it would stay on until morning. While he sat in the kitchen drinking coffee he heard Dorothy Cluff moving around in her kitchen up above.

Since coming back from the West he had been secretly lusting for Dorothy, and had already made love to her a thousand times in his fantasies. The knowledge that on most nights the two of them were alone in the house had been a challenge to him. Her calculated carelessness in her dress and exposure when she occasionally came downstairs, or when she seemed to arrange to come down the stairs just when he was entering the house, were sexual come-ons. Now that he was leaving in the morning it had to be tonight or probably never.

He climbed the stairs and looked into his mother's room to make sure she was still out, then walked along the darkened hallway and knocked at Dorothy's front bedroom door.

"Is that you, Ken? she asked.

"Yes. Are you in bed?"

"Yes. I just come to bed."

"I've made some coffee downstairs. Would you like a cup?"

"I hate to get up now," she said. There was a short silence. "Bring me one up, will you?"

He went downstairs and poured a cup of coffee. On his way upstairs again he felt his belly knotting with excitement, and before he reached her room he saw that she had pulled on the light. He knocked, and she told him to come in.

She was sitting up in bed wearing a torn silk nightgown. Her clothing was scattered around on the floor.

"This is service," she said, reaching for the coffee. "Sit down and make yourself at home. It's about time you came up to keep me company once in a while."

"I thought you might like a cup of coffee," he said. "This will be the last time I'm seeing you for a while. I'm going away in the morning."

"I heard you telling your mother. What do you want to go away for?"

Each time she raised her arm he could see the unshaved black hair in her armpit, and the heavy press of her breast against her night-gown. The hair on her head was blonde except for an eighth of an inch against her scalp.

"I just want to get away from here," he said. "This isn't my idea of life at all."

"Do you want to take along a partner?"

He smiled. "It might make it hard to pick up lifts."

"I'm a good hitch-hiker," she said. "Before I was married my girl friend and I hitch-hiked to Rice Lake. We had no trouble getting rides."

"That was because you didn't have a guy along."

"I wish *I* could get away from here," she said, staring into her cup. "Believe me, Ken, I wouldn't stay here a minute." She told him about her girl friend who had married a butcher in Hamilton. "What did *I* marry?" she asked. "Do you think I like to be stuck in these two rooms all day, afraid to make a noise in case I wake Jim? And then be stuck here all night by myself while he's down at the foundry? Believe me, if I could find a sugar-daddy with some money I'd get out of this life in a minute."

Ken's eyes had been drawn to a worn spot in her nightgown which now and then revealed part of one of her brown nipples. She caught him staring at it and smiled, and he took his eyes off her and looked around the room.

"The place is a mess," Dorothy said. "There isn't room to put any-thing, especially in the back bedroom we use as a kitchen. I keep my milk and butter and things like that in a box on the window sill. Yesterday the butter was covered in coal dust that must have blown up here from the gasworks, or maybe from the trains down in the Don Valley. This whole neighbourhood is covered with soot and smoke all day."

"It's too bad Jim can't get back on day work," Ken said.

"He's lucky to be on nights. At least it's steady. They laid off three more men on the day shift yesterday."

"It's the same everywhere."

"What we need is somebody like Roosevelt. Those birds in Ottawa don't care about you and I, so long as they're getting theirs. I get so goddamn mad sometimes. Don't worry, they'll have a revolution before long. Look what they did to the hunger marchers. Jim says half the men at the foundry are joining the Party.

"What party?"

"The Communist Party. They're the only ones that do anything for the working class. Look at them down here, how they organize the people for the eviction fights. You should join them, Ken."

"I don't believe in parties," he said. "I think the old bindle stiffs had the right idea. I believe in direct action. I'd like to see the hunger marchers and the unemployed burn the Parliament Buildings down, with every two-bit politician in it."

"That wouldn't do any good. What we need is a workers' government, and, by God, within five years we're going to have one."

Ken laughed. "I'm surprised to hear you talk like this, Dorothy."

"I'm waking up, at last. We need a strong party that'll give the workingman something to rally to. And the discipline he needs too."

"Discipline? Like Mussolini in Italy gives the Italians? A friend of mine, who lives right here in Cabbagetown, said the same thing about giving the workers discipline. He's against the Communists, as a matter of fact I think he's against the working class."

"You talk to Jim about it some time. He goes to weekly cell meetings out in the East End, above a show near Greenwood Avenue."

Ken stood up, took the coffee cup from Dorothy's hand, and placed the cup on the bedside table. She was wearing a heavy cheap scent that excited him as if he'd touched her flesh.

"Have you seen Myrla Patson lately?" she asked.

"Do you know her?"

"Just when she lived over at Mrs. Plummer's."

"I saw her a few days ago."

"She's the prettiest thing. You used to go with her, didn't you?"

"I used to."

"I'll bet when a person gets to know you you're different than you seem." She smiled at him, a warm inviting smile. "Usually the shy ones turn out to be the devils. Why don't you come over here to the bed and sit down. I won't bite you."

He sat down on the edge of the bed as she pulled over to the wall to give him room. "Now you're getting friendly," she said.

They were both shy, waiting for the other to move first.

"Has your mother gone out?" Dorothy asked.

"Yes."

"Where?"

"I don't know. Wherever she goes when she drinks."

"She's going to go crazy if she doesn't stop drinking that cheap wine. She'll end up out in nine-ninety-nine Queen West."

"I know. She *has* stopped at times, but she goes right back to it. I don't think she'll ever really stop."

"Have you got a cigarette, Ken?"

"Yes. I've got a pack downstairs." He picked up the coffee cup and left the room.

When he returned the light was out, and the blind was up on the window, making the room dim but not dark.

"Here's a cigarette," he said, entering the room.

"Give me a kiss first," Dorothy said. He saw her walking towards him naked. She pressed her body against him, and he felt her big brown nipples harden against his shirt. Her mouth searched his face until it found his lips, and her tongue then opened them. Her hands ran over his flanks and then began to unbutton his fly.

City of Toronto Archives, Series 372, Sub-series 33B, Item 84

## BOOK THREE

# EXODUS

## OCTOBER 1933—FEBRUARY 1937

# 1

For the six months she had been living as Mike's mistress Myrla Patson had found reason to question the adage that it was better to be an old man's mistress than a young man's slave. Mike paid the rent on her tiny apartment but other than this he gave her little. She still worked full time at the Union Jack Cafe, and in return for her favours she was receiving only $25 a month in rent from her lover.

Her biggest happiness came from her weekly visits to Derek and her family. She bought Derek a new steel stroller, the latest thing, and made or bought him the items that made up a winter outfit. When there was no snow she took the baby for long walks downtown, along Queen Street East, or up to Riverdale Zoo. She watched his baby interest in the traffic, and she would stop and let him look at the horses they passed, not as many as there were on weekdays, but the occasional one pulling a milk wagon. She delighted in his happy arm-waving enthusiasm over every dog or cat they met.

Her mother seemed to accept the family's reliance on the relief vouchers now and, since Derek had been living in her house, appeared more lively and younger than she had before. Her father still sat in the front room chair, his fringe of hair much grayer now, immersed in his silent world.

The winter passed uneventfully. One evening in the spring she sat in her flat and read a letter from Annie, the other waitress, who had been married before Christmas and now lived out of town. She heard Mike's key being turned in the door, and she lowered the letter to her lap. Mike entered, followed by another middle-aged Greek. Myrla was surprised, for this was the first time he had brought a visitor.

"Here's my little girl, Myrla," Mike said.

She noticed that they were both half drunk.

"We just came from a party, Myrla. This is a good friend of mine from Sudbury. Nick meet Myrla."

The other man took off his hat, and gravely shook her hand. Mike showed his friend over the small apartment, talking to him in their own language. Myrla couldn't understand what was being said, but she knew Mike was letting Nick see that everything, including herself, was his. She watched them, becoming angrier by the minute. They sat down on the sofa, ignoring her, and began laughing and carrying on like a pair of schoolboys. She got up and went into the bedroom out of sight.

After a minute or two Mike called, "Hey, Myrla."

She entered the sitting room and he said to her, "There's a bottle of gin in my coat pocket over there. Make us a couple of drinks. Go easy on the ginger ale though, it's hard on our stomachs." He laughed and slapped his friend's knee.

She mixed them each a gin and ginger ale, and they sat and talked between themselves for more than an hour. When they got up to leave she helped Mike with his overcoat.

"You've got a good girl there, Mike," Nick said.

"Sure I have, you bet. Look at her, she's the prettiest girl in Toronto, and I'll bet in Sudbury too, eh?" He grabbed her by the shoulder and pulled her around to face him. "You got a li'l kiss for Mike eh?" he asked. She smiled as if it was a joke, but tried to break away from him. He held her though and kissed her wetly on the mouth. "How's that, Myrla, eh? You go to bed early, Myrla, and keep yourself fresh for Mike, eh."

Nick laughed. "Come on, you old fool," he said. The two of them left, slamming the door behind them.

Myrla stood in the middle of the room, looking at the door. Then she wiped the back of her hand across her lips, and spat the taste of Mike's kiss from her mouth. She fell into a chair and began to cry. How could he bring another man there and show her off, like something bought and paid for? An ugly old Greek bastard like him! Pawing at her and bragging to his friend that she was his, all his!

Later on, when her anger had had a chance to cool, she thought things out carefully. She had to keep her job, no matter how Mike humiliated her, but she no longer felt she owed him anything. The smart thing to do would be to keep the job, and the apartment he paid for, and in the meantime go her own way, unknown to him. What was the difference between being Mike's mistress and the mistress of other men whom she could choose herself? Besides, Mike gave her no money she could call her own, except her small wage at the lunchroom. She knew how to earn some money, and when she had saved a few dollars it would make her independent. Then she could pay Mike back, and show him she wasn't completely reliant on him.

She picked up the phone book and found the number of the Hotel Royalcourt.

When she dialed the number a man's voice answered, Hello."

"Is that the Royalcourt Hotel?"

"Yes."

"Have you a bellhop by the name of Tony working there?"

"Yes, madam. Do you wish to speak to him?"

"Please."

It took some time for Tony to come to the phone. When he did he said, "Hello?" in a questioning tone.

"Hello, Tony."

"Hello. Who is this?"

"An old friend of yours. Don't you recognize my voice?"

"I'm sorry. I don't believe I do."

"It's Myrla Patson."

"Who?"

"Myrla Patson." She snapped, "Don't tell me you've forgotten me?"

"Oh, Myrla! Say I'm glad to hear from you. What are you doing these days?"

"Nothing much. How's things with you?"

"Oh so-so, you know. Still on the same old grind. I thought you were married or something when I didn't see you for so long. Where've you been?"

"I've been in town all the time." She began to regret calling him up. "I guess you're wondering why I'm calling you up like this?"

"Well, it is kinda funny. It's years since I seen you last."

"Not quite, but never mind that. Listen, Tony, I know you can't stay on the phone too long. What time do you quit?"

"Twelve midnight."

"Come up to my place and see me." She gave him her address. "I want to talk to you about something."

"Do you live there alone?"

"Sure I do."

"I'll come up after I quit work," he said.

**2**

Theodore East walked with his friend Jack Sharpe along the downtown streets from the National Canadian Youth Club, their feet sliding on the small patches of ice that remained here and there on the sidewalks.

"This Miss Summers I'm going to meet, is she a sympathizer?" Theodore asked.

"Don't use the word 'sympathizer,' East, it sounds too Commie. Miss Summers supports our club that's all. And try to stop making us sound like an 'ism or something."

"All right. Does Miss Summers come down to any of our dances?"

"No. She's getting too old to come to our dances, especially among a heterosexual crowd. I think she's an old dyke, but she foots some of our bills."

"We seem to have a lot of homo supporters. Like the party you took me to, full of fairies."

"Yeah, I'm sorry about that one. It's really impossible to do much with people like Clarence Gurney and his crowd. They have no political opinions at all; all they think about is sex. Gurney bragging about his conquests. I think they're all underprivileged kids he catches through that Friendly Uncles Club of his. I'd like to kick out every fag we attract. They spoil the meetings with their simpering and giggling. The first thing we know the *Daily Worker*'ll be tagging us The National Canadian Faggot Society."

"I can't stand fairies at all," Theodore said. "I try to keep out of their way."

"So do I. I don't expect there'll be any up at Barbara Summers' place. She usually has an artsy-craftsy crowd, you know, writers, painters, a few screwballs, maybe even a campus Commie or two from the university. Don't let any of their opinions get you down."

"Where does this Barbara Summers live anyhow?"

"Not too far now," Jack answered.

When they arrived at an apartment house in the north-central section of town Jack Sharpe pressed a buzzer, and the front door clicked open. As they climbed the stairs a woman leaned over an upstairs banister and shouted down a greeting. They continued up the stairs until they reached her floor.

"Hello, Jack, glad you could come," she said.

Sharpe presented Theodore.

"Glad you could come too. I'm always glad to welcome any member of your club."

As she led them along the hallway to her apartment she said to Sharpe, "I sometimes have some very tiresome old fuddy-duddies here you know. A little youth is so welcome. Mr. Bracket is here tonight, and Paulson, and that campus Communist, Rogers. There's Goldie Beatty, Eileen and a friend of hers called Lillian, Tommy Wright and, let's see. Oh yes, Jake Creighoff. I'm sure you'll both enjoy yourselves."

When they entered the small apartment Theodore was presented to those he didn't know, which was practically everyone standing or sitting around the living room and in the narrow hallway leading to the other apartment rooms. This was his first exposure to the arty crowd, and he was determined to make the most of it. Jack Sharpe spoke to a short pretty blonde called Goldie.

Their entrance had interrupted a discussion, which resumed. A tall bony young man wearing a cheap suit and a workshirt was holding forth. Jack Sharpe whispered to Theodore that he was John Paulson, a young and coming novelist. Theodore listened to him with increased interest.

"—all art, despite the medium used, is the delineation of things. An artist is one who can transcribe his senses on to canvas or paper, clay or a sheet of music, with the greatest degree of accuracy."

"True, but only to a point," began a round-faced man sitting in a corner.

A young gray-haired man sitting next to Theodore said, "I don't hold with it at all."

A plain-looking young woman sitting next to him patted his arm and said, "Now, Tommy, don't begin that again please."

Barbara Summers said, "Let's hear what Mr. Bracket has to say."

The round-faced man in the corner said, "What John has just said is true to the extent that it is true of very few artists. Realism, or naturalism if you will, can change art to illustration and writing to journalism."

"I disagree strongly with that premise," said the tall young novelist. "Take Dos Passos. Is what he calls 'photographic realism' not art?"

Theodore now noticed that the speaker was wearing heavy wool work socks inside a pair of bedroom slippers.

"Art, art, art !" exclaimed Goldie. "Perhaps if we had fewer Artists—with an upper case A—in this town, and a few writers instead, we could begin to like our so-called Canadian literature."

"Goldie, you have the artistic sensitivity of an editor of *The Home Journal*," Paulson said.

Goldie stuck out her tongue at him and laughed. "We're all of us Philistines," an older, Jewish-looking man said.

"Not all of us, Jake. Some of us are definitely Hebrews."

The round-faced man in the corner spoke again. "Perhaps if all the writers and painters I know would stop talking, and thinking, of such things as Art and Philistinism and ivory towers and such claptrap we'd be better off. As a nonartist I'm attracted to books and paintings by their contents and not because their creators are conscious of their work as art. How many worthwhile literary craftsmen have written informative and entertaining books without ever becoming known as artists?"

"None," said the young man known as Tommy.

"Oh nonsense!" Goldie exclaimed.

"The only ones who are not artists are those without talent or those who have not yet found their medium," Tommy said.

"There you are, Steve," said Goldie to a young man slouched on the floor. "The masses are all potential artists."

"Thank you. We have always claimed that the masses contain not only potential artists but scientists, statesmen and everything else."

Theodore realized he must be one of the Communists. The young man known as Steve was dressed in very poor clothes, if for effect. Theodore had seen too many poor people to be fooled as to how they looked.

As the conversation went on Theodore found himself only half listening at times. He envied these people their apparent worldliness and knowledge, though.

After a while Goldie sat down beside him. "Are you bored stiff listening to our small talk, Mr. East?" she asked. "We're all show-offs here trying to pose as intellectuals. Rogers there used to be an intellectual before he pretended to become one of the workers." She looked at Rogers as she spoke, trying to catch his attention, but the young man was talking to the Jew named Jake.

Theodore liked Goldie. When he looked around at the others he decided he also liked Mr. Bracket. Aside from these the rest were what Ken Tilling would call "phoney baloneys."

Theodore wondered where Ken was tonight. Probably riding a freight train somewhere, or mixing with fellow hoboes and derelicts in a flophouse somewhere. He began to pity Ken. This was the sort of company his friend should be cultivating, not the useless people he had escaped to. Escaping from Cabbagetown to a life of riding freights and bumming meals and cigarettes was no escape at all. He wondered why Ken couldn't see it that way. He smiled thinking to himself of how the sparks would fly if Ken Tilling ever confronted Rogers at a party such as this.

Later in the evening as the small crowd sat or stood around eating sandwiches and pouring themselves cheap domestic wine from two gallon jars standing on a sideboard, Goldie asked him, "What do you do for a living, Mr. East?"

"Call me Ted," he said. "I work down at the Parliament Buildings."

"What do you do?"

"I'm only a clerk," he said.

"Why do you say 'only,' Ted?"

He shrugged.

"It's probably a very good job, as jobs go today. Do you belong to Jack Sharpe's club?"

"Yes."

"I went down to a dance there last fall. Do you belong to it for its social or political side?"

"A bit of both I guess."

Goldie's questions were innocent, but he had the feeling that she was writing down his answers.

"Does Rogers belong to the Communist Party?" Theodore asked her.

"It's hard to say. I suppose he does, though I think they'd be better off without people like him. When he speaks about the workers I could scream. My family is working class. He'd never get to first base trying to fool my father or my brothers."

Theodore felt himself being drawn even closer to this pretty girl. He had an insane urge to tell her he'd thought the same thing about Rogers, and that he lived in Cabbagetown, but he resisted it.

When Goldie excused herself and left him he was joined by the gray-haired young man he had noticed earlier. "East isn't it?" the man asked.

"Yes. Ted East."

"Did you come with Sharpe?"

Theodore nodded.

"Are you a Blackshirt, or whatever colour is popular in Canada?"

Theodore curled his lip.

"What is it you call your club, the National Canadian Youth? Tell me, why does a smart young sensible fellow like you want to belong to an outfit like that for? Are you still politically naive or what?"

"I believe in certain principles."

"Or the lack of them. Is it because you dislike Jews and radicals, or is it because some well-to-do people belong to it and are willing to cultivate you? A young fellow like you should be a radical. I was a socialist at your age. All young men are socialists or utopians of some sort or another at twenty-one. But perhaps you believe your own Oswald Mosley—*Sir* Oswald, pardon me—when he says that radicalism and socialism are doomed if we have to wait for every Hottentot to learn to sing "*Internationale*." But even Mosley was a socialist when he was your age. Have you ever made a study of the rightwing people today who once were socialists? It's quite interesting."

Jack Sharpe had approached them and had been listening. He said to Theodore, "Don't mind Tommy. He's a complete cynic."

"I see that."

"Were you eavesdropping, Sharpe?" Tommy asked, laughing. "I'd like to take you apart and see what makes you tick. But right now I'm trying to place you in my catalogue of fascist types."

"There's no such thing as types," Sharpe said. "Am I a type? Is Ted here? Is Barbara?"

"What goes on here?" asked Mr. Bracket, who now joined the group.

"Tommy is going to name the types who have nationalist leanings," Sharpe said.

"If you like," Tommy said. "Let's see. There are several well-defined types who are drawn to all nationalist-cumfascist movements. There's the rabid anti-Semite who might even be an apostate

Jew, or whose mammy was seduced by one, or who has been cheated in business by one. Then there are the native-born or immigrant nationals of countries that are fascist, and White Russians, Ukrainian Nationalists and other minorities of Uncle Joe Stalin who are anti-communist. Then there are some nationalistic French Canadians and followers of Roman Catholic corporate statism. And last—but the potential majority of fascists in this country—the professional war veterans, old hags who believe anything is patriotic that flies the Union Jack, psychologically crippled or impotent cranks, humanity-hating homosexuals and radical snobs to whom the working class parties are anathema because they represent the poor. Take your choice as to which group either of you fit."

The others laughed, but Sharpe was serious as he said, "Don't forget the patriotic young Canadians who are nationalists because they hate to see their country being slowly turned over to the Jew Bolshevists."

"That is a hard-core Nazi type which is fortunately in the minority," Tommy said, laughing and walking away.

Theodore walked through the small rooms pausing and listening to snatches of conversation from the small groups gathered here and there.

Paulson was talking to Creighoff the Jew. "How can I possibly work without tranquility? How can any artists? The writing of novels needs tranquility and freedom from economic pressures."

"Not in your case. You're not under a financial urge to write. You have a private income I understand."

"I have, but the sum involved is not as great as you think. But finances is only one of the disturbing factors that keeps me from working."

Theodore left them and peeked into a bedroom. Barbara Summers and Goldie were looking through the pages of a magazine. He wondered if Jack Sharpe had been right about Barbara, and she was a Lesbian? He had never met one of them down in

Cabbagetown, but perhaps there were some there, maybe Miss Pettipew the deaconess at the church was one. He supposed that all good little Lesbians, like the self-discovered fairies or "fruits" as they were known down there, soon moved out of Cabbagetown and up to neighbourhoods such as this.

The Communist Steve Rogers was holding forth to a group in the kitchen. "Art, true art, cannot function under this capitalist system. In the Soviet Union the writers embrace proletarian realism, which is the only real art there is—"

"Name one of your proletarian realists," Jack Sharpe challenged.

"Mikhail Sholokov," Rogers answered, from his place on the floor.

"Anybody else?" asked Tommy Wright.

"There are many. Isaac Babel, who wrote *Red Cavalry*."

Theodore wandered around, being ignored by most of the groups. When Goldie came out of the bedroom he tried to get her into a conversation with him again but she broke away from him.

On their way out of the apartment house Jack Sharpe said to him, "That Steve Rogers is a damn fool. I wish all the Bolshies were as stupid as he is."

"I guess most of them are," Theodore said. "They have to be."

"Some of them are like Rogers in some respects, especially the middle class Commies. Some of the leadership is smart though, or maybe astute is a better word. People who are financed from Moscow, like Tim Buck, Sam Carr, McLeod, Roy Davis, Kashton, and all that gang. The rank and file are plenty dumb though."

"I didn't like Paulson, or that Jew Creighoff either," Theodore said.

"What did you think of Goldie Beatty?"

"She's great! I was talking to her for quite a while."

"I saw you. She's a funny one. Sometimes I think she's a Commie who's trying to find out what she can about our group. I'm going to make some careful enquiries about her."

"I haven't met many writers and artists before," Theodore said. "It was just like you read about in Greenwich Village."

"It was meant to be. They're all fakes and imitations."

"The thing I noticed was that they all seem so—I don't know, so darned—ineffective. They talk about a lot of things, but none of them seem much concerned about what is happening to the country."

Sharpe nodded. "They're not. They're interested mainly in creating an impression among themselves. They like to think their conversations are Bohemian and stimulating, but all they stimulate in me is boredom. I told you they're mostly screwballs. You should see some of them who weren't there tonight, *they're* even worse. Unpublishable novelists, unhung painters—in more ways than one (Sharpe laughed)—and uneducated academics."

They parted at the corner. On his way to take a streetcar home Theodore thought of all the interesting people, screw-balls or not, he'd met since joining the club. People he wouldn't have known even existed if he'd stayed around Cabbagetown.

He bought the first edition of the next morning's paper and sat back in the streetcar to read it. On one of the inside pages his eye was caught by a one-column photograph of a familiar face, with the name "William Addington" beneath it in boldface type. He folded the paper and began to read the short paragraph or two beneath Billy's picture.

Shortly before five o'clock yesterday afternoon the body of William Addington of 16 Gore Street was discovered immersed in a vat of boiling solution at the Besty-Tasty Candy Co. on Richmond Street in this city. It is believed by plant officials that he was the victim of a seizure while working around the vats, and that while unconscious he toppled forward and met his death.

He was described by members of the firm as being well trained and a thoroughly reliable worker. Mr. Addington is survived by his parents and a sister who resides at home. Authorities decided no autopsy or inquest was necessary, and the body was removed for burial.

Theodore folded the paper in his lap. Death was an impersonal thing that affected only older people, until something like this brought it close. He held no great affection for Billy and, though they had both gone to Park Public School together, he had not known Billy well. All the way home he thought about Addington, for Billy was the first of his acquaintances to die. Already, even at the age of twenty, Theodore realized that a final reckoning was coming to them all, sooner or later. The shortness of life on earth, and the workings of blind unreasoning chance, were revealed to him now by Billy's death.

# 3

Myrla Patson formed a fee-splitting partnership with Tony, the bellhop at the Royalcourt Hotel. Almost any night she wished she could call Tony and, after Mike had left her place, could go down to the Royalcourt and sleep with a "trick," whom she preferred to call a client.

She recognized that she had become a whore but, though prostitutes like her were not yet known as call girls, they looked on themselves as being higher socially and morally than the girls and women who worked the streets or were inmates of a whorehouse. Generally speaking their clientele was of a higher order, socially and physically, than the tricks picked up in the streets. These men, who did not think of themselves as whoremasters, were usually salesmen, conventioneers or visiting members of the white-collar trades. When overcome by drink, loneliness or sexual hunger they would drop a hint to a bellhop that they wouldn't mind a bit of female companionship. If the bellhop was Tony he would call one of his girls, and if she was free she would come to the customer's room. Tony had five girls on his phone list, and of these Myrla, because of her youth and attractiveness, was by far the most popular.

Myrla accepted her new change in status philosophically, and the only thing she hated about the arrangement was the necessity, at first, of being down at the Union Jack Cafe in time for work in the morning. Over the course of weeks she met the other four girls whom Tony pimped for, all of them like herself casual prostitutes, or at least not what they would have called hardcore whores. One of the girls, a deserted wife with a small baby, worked as a saleslady in a department store during the day, two of them were factory girls, and the fourth was a childless divorcee who had formerly been the nymphomaniac wife of a socially prominent lawyer. The divorcee, whose name was Hazel, lived in a high class residential neighbourhood, often took double jobs with Myrla and taught the girl everything she needed to know about plying her trade.

Myrla began banking her money and looking forward to the day when she could quit her job at Mike's restaurant as well as tell him off for the way he was treating her. She enlarged on his actions the night he had brought his Greek friend to her flat, and used this humiliation as her excuse for her new life. Because she did not sell herself full time her change from waitress to whore was gradual, and minimized any qualms she might have felt about it.

One evening when she was sitting around her rooms, almost bored to tears, she called up Tony. She told him that Mike was spending the evening at home with his wife. About an hour later Tony called back and told her to go to Room 36 at the Royalcourt.

When she arrived at the small hotel she hurried up to the third floor and knocked at the door of No. 36. A young man opened the door and stared at her for a moment before inviting her inside.

When he had shut the door behind them he asked, "Did Tony send you?"

She told him yes.

"I didn't expect anyone quite so young and pretty as you," he said.

"I didn't expect anyone as young as you either." He looked to be just out of his teens.

The boy walked over to the dresser and picked up a pint of whisky. "Would you like a drink, miss?"

Myrla smiled and nodded.

"I don't drink hardly at all," he said. "I just thought you might like one." He poured a small shot into a glass, added ginger ale and handed it to Myrla, who sat down on the bed, the glass in her hand.

The young man was embarrassed and undetermined as to what to do next. After standing awkwardly in the middle of the floor he sat down beside Myrla on the bed.

"Are you from out of town, Mr—?"

Without telling her his name he said, "Yes I am. I'm going back home tomorrow."

"Do you come to Toronto often?" she asked, trying to loosen him up.

"Not very often. This is the first time in six months."

Myrla nodded. She drank the whisky and ginger ale, got up and placed the glass on the dresser. Then she took off her coat and hung it in the closet. When she sat down again on the edge of the bed she let her dress pull up above her knees, showing the tops of her rolled stockings.

The youth tore his eyes from her legs and said, looking down into his glass, "You must think I'm acting rather foolish for a person who asked Tony to send you here," he said.

Myrla smiled at him.

"As a matter of fact this is the first time in my life I ever did anything like this." He gulped his drink and made a wry face. "Briefly, I'm engaged to be married in June, and I've never—I've never been with a woman. Contrary to what they say, you know, experts like Dr. Marie Stopes and other marital advisors, I feel I'll be placed in a bad position on my wedding night if I don't have at least a cursory knowledge of—of what to do. It's pretty embarrassing for me to have to tell you these things, but I hope you'll understand."

Despite his country bumpkin air and his formal way of talking Myrla liked him. She smiled at him and nodded. Then she kicked off her shoes and rolled down her stockings, placing them with her shoes on the floor. She stood up and walked to the door of the clothes closet and faced him. She reached behind her and unhooked her dress and pulled it over her head and hung it up. Then she took off her slip and watched him as he stared at her in her pants and brassiere. She unhooked the bra, and pulled it from her breasts, throwing it on a chair. She paused for a moment, enjoying the way he was staring at her, then rolled her panties down her legs, throwing them after the brassiere. She smiled at him wantonly now, his obvious hunger for her feeding her own passion, hardening her nipples and twitching the muscles in her belly.

She had never made love to a virgin before, and she gave herself over to a fantasy in which she was this boy's bride, and they were together for the first time in a hotel room on their honeymoon. This had been something she had missed in reality, but she could live it now in her thoughts.

She walked over to the dresser and poured herself a bigger shot of liquor, topped it with ginger ale, and stood watching him. He still stared at her, his mouth slightly agape.

"Take your things off, honey," she said.

He unbuttoned his shirt while she took a drink, watching him over the rim of her glass. He took off his shoes and socks, and stepped out of his trousers. He hesitated over taking off his jockey shorts, but she smiled invitingly, noticing his tumescence.

"Have another drink, dear," she said.

"No really, I wouldn't care to," he said. "It would probably make me sick. I'm not antiliquor or anything. It's just that I've never done much drinking—either."

He looked so clean and youthful, in comparison with the men she usually slept with, that she allowed herself to believe the honeymoon fantasy she had created. We could be a newly married couple, she told herself, wishing just momentarily that they were. She hurriedly drew herself back to the reality of the present. His bride, whoever she was, might not thank her for what she was going to do, if she knew, but she ought to give her a vote of thanks, or say a prayer for her.

"Take your shorts off, honey, and let's see what you're hiding from me," she said.

When he did she put down her glass and walked to him. They kissed, and she parted his teeth with her tongue, while her free hand ran over his clean youthful quivering flesh.

"Take things easy, honey," she whispered. "Just follow me, as if we were dancing and I took the lead."

She laid him back on the bed, then pulled him into a position above her. When he entered her she cried, "Oh sweet jeezus, darling!"

Before she left him she taught him much more than he would ever have to know on his honeymoon, her feelings both masculine and evil yet her desires and satisfactions completely feminine as well.

When she left her bridegroom-lover before midnight, Myrla said to him, "Don't try this too often before your wedding day, or you might get to like it too much and forget about the marriage. Try to be gentle with your bride at first. She's got to learn, and you've got to teach her."

"I can't imagine Josie ever being as good as you."

"She'll be fine. But no matter how mad you get never tell her who *your* teacher was."

In the lunch counter across the street from the Royalcourt, Myrla gave Tony his cut of her teaching fee. She didn't mention the bonus she'd received from the young man in Room 36. An extra ten-dollar bill was rolled into the top of her stocking.

Contrary to what she had been led to expect, Tony never tried to bully or humiliate her, and never forced her into dates she didn't want to take. He seldom questioned her about money, and accepted what she gave him of her fees without quibbling. Except for the occasional Sunday evening, when she was not entertaining Mike, and Tony could get away to be with her, their relationship was a business partnership that both were content to keep that way.

Though the majority of her customers were much older than the young bridegroom-to-be most of them were jolly and easy to get along with, determined to enjoy their brief fling with another woman while away from wife and family. Myrla recognized that for most of them their hiring of her was not so much to assuage a sexual hunger as it was to boost their masculine ego. They enjoyed the feeling of male power that their acquisition of a young and pretty girl gave them.

The worst client she had met, up to then, was one evening when Tony called her and she went to the room of a man in one of the bigger downtown hotels.

When she arrived the man was drunk but not half as drunk as he pretended to be. As if impelled by some deep-seated psychological reason or, as Myrla thought, probably by a recent fight with his wife, he used all the foul language he could think of as soon as she entered the room. Then he began to abuse her verbally, making every perverted proposition that entered his distorted mind. He appalled her but she tried to ignore it at first, blaming it on the drink. Later though, as she realized that she was in the company of a pervert and psychopath, pure and simple but not much of either, she tried to get out of the room. The man was big and he blocked every attempt she made to escape. He knew she was at his mercy, and he openly gloated over his mastery of her. Once, after slapping her hard across the face for refusing one of his more perverted suggestions, he handed her the telephone and told her to call the police.

He made her mix him strong drinks of Scotch and water, and once when she went into the bathroom to mix water with his drink she looked into the usually empty medicine cabinet and saw a small bottle marked spot remover. Beneath the label was a skull-and-crossbones danger tag, and without knowing what the stuff could do to the inside of a human being, and caring less what it might do to the big gross man lying on the bed, she emptied a good dollop of it into his drink.

She remembered Ken Tilling once saying, "Myrla, if you live in the gutter, do everything down there—your loving, your learning, and your fighting. When you leave the gutter leave everything behind, but while you're down there live by its rules." She was in the gutter all right tonight, and that big fat pig would find she could fight by gutter rules.

It wasn't long after he downed his spiked drink, slobbering it over his chin and chest, that he passed out as if into a coma. Myrla dressed herself, taking her time with the application of her makeup, and when she was ready to leave the room she casually took the man's wallet from his pocket.

It contained about seventy dollars in cash, which she rolled into her stocking. Then she placed the wallet in her purse, took the elevator to the downstairs lobby and went home.

In the man's wallet was an identification card, containing the man's address, some club membership cards, automobile and driver's permits, snapshots, a few receipts and a checkbook. She scribbled a note, addressed to his wife and signed "Marjorie," and shoved it into the wallet, which she then placed in an envelope and ran out and mailed to the woman.

The note read, "George left this in the—Hotel tonight, so I am returning it to you, not knowing his city address. I took the small amount of cash it contained to settle my fee."

After mailing the wallet she realized that the man's name was familiar, and after thinking about it for some time remembered him as a member of the provincial cabinet. This frightened her, for she would be easy to trace through Tony. For the next few days she worried that perhaps she had killed him.

A couple of weeks later she was searching through the newspapers for mention of the man, as she had been doing since the evening in the hotel, and read where he was taking a leave of absence from his government seat and was going to Florida to convalesce from his recent illness. There was no mention of his being accompanied by his wife, which was what Myrla had expected. From then on she had a vague fear at times of being called to a hotel room and being confronted by him, and was always very careful when the man she was to meet was a stranger. A few months later she was surprised to read in the papers that the man had died of a long-standing kidney infection. She was glad, but she never did connect his kidney trouble with his mixed drink of spot remover and Scotch.

One morning at the restaurant Mike handed her a postcard that had just arrived in the mail. It was from Ken Tilling and gave as a return address, General Delivery, Los Angeles, California; but the card had been mailed from Ciudad Juarez, Mexico. Ken said the weather was very warm during the day, but not so warm to sleep out in at night. He said he'd "beaten his way" across the country, was having a good time, but was not getting fat on what he was eating.

The picture on the postcard was of a Mexican market square, with a two-wheeled wagon being pulled by oxen. In the background was a church. The figures in the lithograph looked like Mexicans, with the men all wearing sombreros, as she'd seen them worn in the movies.

That evening she wrote Ken a long letter, addressing it to General Delivery, Los Angeles. She told him she was still working at the restaurant, but was thinking of quitting soon to take a better job that had been promised her. She said merely that the other members of her family were just the same, but filled a whole page with news of young Derek. She talked of the cold and snow in Toronto, and said he was lucky to be where it was always warm. She warned him not to fall in love with any movie stars in Hollywood, but if he met any to be sure and write and let her know what they were like off the screen. She said he'd probably heard of Billy Addington's death, but wasn't it a terrible thing. It had nearly made her sick when she read about it in the paper.

She hesitated for some time wondering how to close the letter, whether to end it, "Yours always" or "Your Friend," or merely sign it "Myrla." She finally ended it with, "Lots of luck. Myrla," and drew a cross for a kiss beside her name. Because Ken had mentioned eating, she enclosed a five dollar bill. The next day she took it to the post office, registered it and sent it away.

**4**

During the winter a young immigrant couple had moved into No. 4 Timothy Place, and shortly afterwards the young wife had a baby. The women on the street felt cheated, for none of them had noticed the young woman's condition before the event took place.

The first inkling that the neighbour women had of what was going on was the appearance on the street one morning of a young foreign-looking man, carrying a doctor's satchel, who entered No. 4. He was spotted by Mrs. Gaffey who was sweeping the snow from her front steps. She ran indoors and turned off the gas under her wash boiler before hurrying to spread the news to Mrs. Porter in No. 2. This lady was baking a cake for Sunday dinner when Mrs. Gaffey gave her the news, but she left her baking and both women stood in the Porter front room, staring through the window and awaiting developments.

"Though I live right next door I never heard a thing," Mrs. Porter said. "I can't imagine what's wrong in there. They keep to theirselves and we keep to ourselves. What ain't our business we don't bother with."

Mrs. Gaffey agreed. "That's right too. It's no good poking your snout in what don't concern you, is what I always say."

"The poor souls. They never make a noise, Mrs. Gaffey. Never a sound do I hear from that house next door. I'd have a hard time hearing them anyways, what with my gang making a noise all day that'd raise the dead. My Hilda was awake an' bawlin' all last night with a toothache. It's them school dentists what does it. He filled her tooth about a month ago, and it looks like tin he's put in, if you ask me."

"You're better off if you can send them to a real dentist," said Mrs. Gaffey sympathetically. In Cabbagetown any doctor or dentist who was employed by the city or the Board of Education was known as a school dentist or city doctor to separate them from members of their professions who were in private practice, and who were known as "real" ones.

"When I was a girl I don't believe there was a night in my life when I didn't have a toothache," stated Mrs. Porter, exaggerating.

"That's what you have to put up with when you're poor. It's nothing but aches and pains and doctors' bills all the time. Now, when I had the specialist to look at Harold a few years ago—"

They became so interested in recapitulating their ills and those of their respective families that they completely forgot they were waiting for the reappearance of the doctor from next door. Just by luck Mrs. Porter spotted a public health nurse crossing the street on her way to No. 4. She hurried to the front door, and when the nurse arrived asked, "Hey, nurse, what's going on in there?"

"Confinement," the nurse answered laconically.

After shutting her front door again Mrs. Porter said, "She didn't have to be so snippety about it. That's the way they talk to you when you live around here. If we lived somewhere else they'd be afraid of being reported. Mark my words, they didn't act like that when we lived up on Broadhurst Avenue."

Mrs. Gaffey nodded in complete approval. "So the poor thing's having a baby," she said. "That's the same nurse what came for Myrla Patson."

"She didn't seem very big," said Mrs. Porter, referring to the woman next door. "She certainly carried it well. I'll bet it'll be a boy. Boys are always carried far back."

Instead of sickness their conversation switched to childbirth. Mrs.

Porter sniffed the air, and crying, "My lord, there goes my cake!" she rushed off to her kitchen.

During the afternoon Mrs. Gaffey and Mrs. Porter paid their first visit to No. 4. The door was opened by the young foreigner, who told them he was the young woman's husband. He led them upstairs to the front bedroom.

The pale young woman lying in the bed there hardly spoke any English, but she smiled a lot and looked pleased that the women had visited her. Through her husband she apologized for the house being upset, though neither of her visitors could see anything to apologize for. The husband lifted the baby from its bassinet, and the two women admired it. It was a boy, substantiating Mrs. Porter's prenatal prophecy.

Both women ooh'd and aah'd over the pretty baby things the man took from the dresser drawers to show them. Before they left, the husband brought them each a tumbler full of wine that he called "Tookey" or "Tokey" or some such foreign name, and they drank to the health of mother and baby.

The woman, through her husband, thanked them both for coming to see her, and they promised her to come back the next day. The husband thanked them at the front door, and gave them each a neighbourly pat on the shoulder as they left.

"They was certainly clean for foreigners," said Mrs. Porter when they were out of earshot.

"I don't think there's a cleaner house on the street."

That "foreigners" were dirty was an axiom among Cabbage-towners, when the direct opposite was true. Most European immigrants lived in the West End of the city, and few citizens of Cabbagetown knew any non-English-speaking families at all. The only "foreigners" around their neighbourhood were the Jewish storekeepers on Queen and Parliament Streets, and the Central Europeans who lived in a colony to the south near King Street.

These people, mostly immigrant males without families in Canada, also congregated in their own restaurants near the corner of Parliament and Queen, where they ate outlandish-smelling meals and spent their days arguing over Balkan politics or playing cards.

The "foreigners" were just beginning to spread into the city's East End, but it would be years yet before they ousted the Anglo-Saxon majority from the district immediately west of the Don River. When this happened some of the Cabbagetown women, who still could not be convinced that foreigners and Jews were not dirty, used to watch the European immigrant women washing down their front porches and steps every day, and put it down to showing off or being clean publicly to hide their houses' inside dirt. The sight of an immigrant woman placing her mattresses outside her windows to air them was looked upon as being a filthy and unhealthy habit. Most Cabbagetown housewives lived their whole lives and went to their deaths believing these things.

The truth was, of course, that the dirtiest families in the city of Toronto, and probably everywhere else, were the poverty stricken welfare recipients of English, Scots and Irish birth or descent.

"Of course they're by theirselves," Mrs. Porter went on, speaking of the new neighbours. "Wait till they got a gang like I got, I'll bet things'll be different then."

Neither woman had ever been in a foreigner's house before. The novelty of this had attracted them as much as the urge to see the new baby.

"I guess *some* foreigners is clean," Mrs. Gaffey said.

"There's good 'n bad in every nationality, that's what I always say," her friend corroborated.

"What's their name anyways?"

Neither woman had thought to find out.

When the wine the young man had given them began to take

effect they stood clinging together on the sidewalk, ignoring the cold, giggling and gossiping like schoolgirls.

In No. 5 Timothy Place Mabel Tilling's drinking went from bad to worse. At times she brought some of the bums who hung around on Queen Street near the wine store at the corner of Sackville Street home with her. They would have loud and profane parties there, getting crawling drunk on bottles of cheap Catawba wine or rubbing alcohol that they had bought with money cadged from passers-by on Queen Street or stolen from home or from their relief vouchers.

There are many gradations of the poor, and these members of the wino substratum of society were just about as low as a human being could get and still stay within the human race.

Over Christmas Mabel was sick in bed for a week from the effects of a paregoric binge. She was still fleshy but now her fat hung from her frame in ugly creases. Her face was puffed but sallow and her eyes stared redly from behind dark wrinkled pouches. Those neighbours who had spoken to her before now tried to avoid meeting her on the street, and when she was sober she could not look them in the eye, but passed them, muttering to herself under her breath. Jimmy Cluff, who through attending many Communist Party meetings had absorbed a great deal of Marxist phraseology, told his wife Dorothy that Mabel Tilling was a prime example of what happened to members of the working class under capitalism, a member now of the *Lumpenproletariat.*

Mabel had received three letters from Ken during the fall, but had answered none of them. The first had been mailed in New York City, the second from Memphis, Tennessee, and the third from Gladewater, Texas. In the third and last letter Ken had told her he was working as a dishwasher in a restaurant in Gladewater, which was a wooden sidewalk shanty town in the middle of the new East Texas oilfields.

Each time she had received a letter from him she had cried to herself, vowing that she would write an answering letter the next day.

However when the next day came she was either too drunk or sick for want of a drink to write him, and his letters had been lost. At times she cried because her only son had neglected her, and at others because she felt she'd neglected him. When she thought of him while she was drunk she cursed him for an ingrate who had taken advantage of her fine bringing-up, but when she was sober she cried for him because he was her only child and she had not treated him as a mother should.

She was arrested in March on her third common drunk charge, and went to jail for sixty days.

Ken Tilling arrived home at Timothy Place in June. He was thinner than he had been when he went away, but healthy and wiry, and his face and hands were browned from the California sun and the hot winds that had blown along the tops of Southern Pacific and Rock Island freight trains through Arizona, New Mexico and Kansas. He had long ago lost or given away or worn out the new clothes he had been wearing when he left home the previous October, and now wore a pair of khaki work pants he had been given by the Volunteers of America at their Los Angeles hostel, and a chamois windbreaker he had stolen from a parked car in East St. Louis, Illinois.

Dorothy Cluff pretended a disinterest in him she didn't feel when she answered the front door and let him into the house. He took her in his arms in the hallway, but she placed her finger to her lips and pointed at the ceiling, telling him that her husband Jimmy was upstairs.

She said, "I see the wanderer is home again. What brought you back here?"

"I missed the beautiful stink of the gasworks," Ken answered. "Last Hallowe'en I slept on an old car seat in the town pump house in Yazoo City, Mississippi. From outside I could smell the magnolias and jasmine and it reminded me of home, because it was so different."

"I don't believe you."

"I don't blame you. I'm lying. Although the sheriff did put me up in the pump house in Yazoo City. You wouldn't smell the magnolias that time of year, whether there's any in the town or not."

"What did you do with your new suit and topcoat?"

"I don't know."

"You don't *know*?"

"If you want the truth I sold the topcoat last winter in Fresno, California to an Armenian fig-packer for a half dollar, and my suit was stolen last fall in Phoenix, Arizona when I handed it in to be fumigated at the Sally Ann."

"Did you have a tough trip?"

"No. I enjoyed it very much. I saw all the places I wanted to see. I missed a lot of meals—"

"I can see that. You're thin as a rake."

"—I was chased by a lot of railroad bulls, including Texas Slim in Longview and Step-'n-a-Half in Marshall, Texas. They're two of the toughest railroad cops in the United States, on the Texas & Pacific. I've been half-frozen and half-baked, and I was lousy a couple of times. I had great fun. I left here a youth and returned a man."

Dorothy gave him a crooked smile. "It seems like a funny way to have a good time," she said.

That evening, after Jimmy Cluff had gone to work, Dorothy invited Ken upstairs, speaking down through the stovepipe hole in the ceiling. He stayed up there until early morning, and had to promise Dorothy to take her with him the next time he went away on the bum.

His mother was out of jail now, but she came home infrequently. Once she was brought home dead drunk by two small boys on their small play wagon. Ken had to steel himself to answer the door, burning with shame when the caller was somebody to report that his mother was lying drunk up an alley, or it was a good Samaritan who had brought her home in his car. What he hated most at these times, even more than the shame he felt for his mother, was the looks of pity on the faces of those who brought Mabel home.

About two weeks after arriving home he called at the Union Jack Cafe, where a new waitress told him that Myrla was no longer working there. He asked the Greek owner of the place if he had Myrla's address, but the man snarled, "Go and look for her down around Jarvis Street. If she's not there, it's where she should be."

During the summer he found odd jobs now and again. One job he liked was delivering handbills, and he was taken on more or less as a permanent part-time worker by a distributing company. He liked the work in the open air if the weather was good, and the walking kept him in trim. He didn't gain much of his lost weight back, but he was healthy, and he even had a few casual sexual encounters with lonely housewives, a bonus he had not expected. The dollar-and-a-half a day he received kept him in tobacco, and occasionally he bought his mother a thirty-five-cent bottle of wine when she was too sick to get up and go out.

Jimmy Cluff, like most of the new tyro Communists, was full of a missionary zest, and spent a lot of his time trying to proselytize the unworldly and unconvinced whom he met. He pointed out items in the newspapers to Ken, showing him the wrongs and injustices that were being perpetrated every day against the members of the working class. Ken would agree with him, but refused all Jimmy's invitations to go to party meetings.

"I don't want to join any party," Ken told him. "I'm really not very interested in politics."

"Come along and learn our program and objectives," Jimmy would plead. "There's plenty of literature you can read, and we hold weekly study groups too."

"No. I'm not interested. And another thing is that I don't like the Communists I've met. Last fall I was living down on the Bowery in New York, and in the evenings another guy and I used to go up to

Union Square at Fourteenth Street and listen to the Communist orators, and to the arguments that would break up afterwards. It was a
lot of fun and I learned a lot, but most of the Communists were
more interested in Russia and Germany than they seemed to be
about the working stiff in the United States."

"The problems of all the workers in the world are indivisible,"
Jimmy would quote pontifically and by rote.

Ken would laugh. "What's that, your fifth commandment?"

"You won't always laugh at the problems of the workers."

"Who the hell's laughing at that? Do you think that because you
carry a membership card in the Communist Party of Canada that
you're the only person who knows anything about the workers'
problems? I feel just as involved in them as you do. I've seen the
working stiff being kicked around all over the North American continent. In California I've seen the fruit-crabs—the Mexican fruit
harvesters—living in old packing cases and lean-tos made of flattened gasoline cans along the railroad right of way and outside the
company commissaries. Every back-breaking nickel they earn is
used to buy a bit of bread and baloney to ward off starvation for
their kids.

"All over the States there's Hoovervilles built on city dumps where
the people live like animals, pollocking stuff from the garbage. In
Mississippi the poor niggers are poorer than the skinny mules they
drive, and their flimsy cabins are worse than chicken coops.

"Last fall I met a guy riding a Baltimore and Ohio freight train
through West Virginia who'd had his leg broken by a company cop
during a strike in Cincinnati. You don't even have to go anywhere
outside this town to see that the system is rotten and has broken
down. Right here in good old Tory British Toronto you have the same
problems they have anywhere else. Just because I don't use Commie
words like 'labour power,' *petit-bourgeois*, or 'surplus value' doesn't
mean that I can't see what's wrong. I'm just not interested in your
new civilization or your new religion or your new politics, or what-

ever the hell it is. I'm just interested in pork chops for the poor, jobs for those who want to work, bugless beds and free hospitalization.

"I'll tell you this much, Jimmy. The one thing I *have* learned so far during my short but happy life is that all the help the poor will ever get is from each other or because they fought for it against the rich—"

"That's what I've been telling you!"

"—Despite all their goddam ranting and preaching the churches and uplift societies have never done anything for me, except for the Sally Ann and the U.S. Episcopalian Church giving me a flophouse bed and a meal ticket once in a while—paid for by the American government under transient relief—and getting a holy boot out of doing it. When I've been half-starved all they wanted to do was save my soul, and when I was almost dropping with exhaustion they wanted me to pray before I dropped into bed. A few years ago I had a son of a bitch called Gurney come here from the Friendly Uncles Club. He was supposed to be an investigator for the outfit, and they're supposed to be interested in rehabilitating poverty-stricken kids. He invited me up to his apartment, and when he got me there he showed me some French postcards, and tried to make me. He was a fag, a fairy. To hell with all that bunch."

All Jimmy's persuasiveness fell on deaf ears.

Ken promised Jimmy however that he would read all he could on politics, sociology and economics, and in the evenings that summer he read nearly every book on the Politics and Economics shelves of the Riverdale Branch public library. He began by reading George Bernard Shaw's *An Intelligent Woman's Guide To Capitalism and Socialism*, and followed this by reading everything the library had by John Strachey, Lenin, Kropotkin, Leon Trotsky, Beatrice and Sidney Webb, Engels, Stuart Chase, Leopold Blum, Fournier, and a dozen other writers who each had a different plan for ameliorating poverty. Some called it socialism, some communism, some Christian radicalism, some Social Credit, and others Technocracy. Ken Tilling remained an interested skeptic.

**5**

In September Cabbagetown was surprised and titillated by the news that one of their boys, Bob McIsaacs, along with another prisoner named Sam Spilluk had escaped from Kingston Penitentiary.

The news reports went on to say that the two escapees had been members of a work party engaged in cutting hay outside the penitentiary walls, and in a manner not yet discovered had made their getaway. They were believed heading in the direction of Toronto and all police forces had been notified to be on the alert. A cordon of roadblocks had been drawn up around the Kingston area. Their apprehension was expected in a matter of hours.

There was no further news on the escape until the following night when word was received that two young men, believed to be the escaped convicts, had stolen fifty dollars and his automobile from a Montreal commercial traveller who had been forced to halt his car for a passing train at a level crossing on Highway 2 near Port Hope, Ontario. The man had also reported the theft of the clothing he was wearing and a suitcase full of extra clothes, plus a sample case of ladies wear.

"Did you know McIsaacs?" Jimmy Cluff asked Ken, as they sat on the front steps watching the Enright boys and some of the Porter kids playing a noisy game of soccer with a rolled-up bundle of rags.

Ken told Jimmy of the time he, McIsaacs, and the others, had been arrested and tried for stealing the bathtub and wash basin.

"What's McIsaacs like? Is he as dangerous as the papers make out he is?"

"It depends, I guess," Ken told him. "He wouldn't go around killing or hurting women and kids. People around here wouldn't have to bar their windows at night. It might be dangerous though if somebody tried to arrest him. He's no different from the rest of the guys around here."

"He looks tough in his newspaper pictures."

"Those mug shots make everybody look tough. You'd look tough too if the cops had been grilling you for a couple of hours, not gently either. Then they took you out, slammed you down in a chair, and told you to look into the lens of a camera. Maybe Bob was groggy from being slapped around and didn't move fast enough, so a cop gave him another slap on the head and pulled his chin around. You wouldn't expect him to look like Ronald Coleman under those conditions."

"I thought the third degree was outlawed in Canada?"

"Sure it is. Just as social and economic inequality doesn't take place under our wonderful democracy."

"The cops *do* slap criminals around then?"

"The cops slap everybody around that they can get away with it with. They always have. Boy, for a Communist you're pretty naive. They do everything cops do everywhere else. What's the word of one poor guy against five or six policemen who are solid church-going citizens and family men, and members of the Masons, Orangemen or Knights of Columbus?"

"Everything is rotten under this system," said Jimmy.

"Everything is rotten for the little guy under any system, even Communism. When you Commies take over will you stop the police from slapping prisoners?"

"Not if they happen to be infantile leftists like you," Jimmy said, laughing.

"Infantile leftists. Another Commie phrase no doubt."

They argued for a while about law under a police state versus law under a democratic government. Ken jumped up from the steps and joined in the kids' soccer game. Mr. Wells sat in front of his house, laughing whenever one of the small boys took the "ball" away from Ken.

The story about the escaped prisoners faded from the front to the back pages of the newspapers, and then was dropped altogether. Ken tried to guess whether McIsaacs and Spilluk had made good their escape or whether the police were playing the story down for their own purpose. He noticed that there was an increase in the number of policemen in the Cabbagetown neighbourhood, and now the radio cars made more frequent trips through the streets.

One morning the *Mail & Empire* ran a story about the watchman of a cork company being robbed of his revolver, and a second revolver and box of ammunition being stolen from the company office. The watchman had identified McIsaacs and Spilluk as the men who had bound and gagged him.

The next afternoon the *Star* and *Telegram* reported that a milk bar and ice-cream shop on Danforth Avenue had been held up shortly after noon by two masked men who answered the escapees' descriptions. They had driven off in a car after cleaning the till of nineteen dollars, but had missed the receipts deposited in the office by milk-wagon drivers, which had been dropped in a milk can.

The milk company owner had his picture taken in a fatuously grinning pose, and he had stated to reporters that because of his adroitness he had foiled the bandits in their attempt to steal much more money than they had. He told the papers that he had told the hold-up men that the bit of money in the till was the day's receipts. They had missed more than two hundred dollars in the milk can.

"Look at old fat-gut standing there with a self-satisfied smile on his blubber mouth," Ken said to Jim and Dorothy that evening. "I'd like to go and hold him up tonight myself, just to wipe that smirk off his face. Why don't those storekeeping scissorbills ever wisen up? They're not satisfied just to save their hard-stolen money, but they have to brag about it, as if they'd done something brave. The hoboes call all storekeepers 'cockroaches,' and it's a name that fits. Because all of them are naturally grasping, and have the instincts of a pack rat with their money, they always seem to hide it away in their pocket or behind the canned peas or something, and then get their picture taken and brag how smart they are."

Jim said, "I often wonder what guys think of after they've robbed a place, and then read about all the money they missed, in the papers?"

"They think the same things anybody else would think. They make up their minds that the next time they stick up a place they'll be sure not to leave anything behind, in pockets, secret drawers or milk cans. So the next job they pull, if there isn't much money in the till, they go through the guy's pockets, and if they still can't find where he's hidden it they slap him around with their pistols till he's damned happy to tell them where he's hidden it. Guys like dough-head there are the ones who add violence to robbery."

"Do you think it was McIsaacs who pulled this job?" Jim asked.

"Search me. Perhaps he and the other guy are a thousand miles from here by now. They'll be blamed for every local hold-up anyhow."

Because the international news was undergoing one of its periodic moments of quiet, and people were getting tired of reading about Herr Adolph Hitler, the German Chancellor who was accused of persecuting the Jews, the papers gave a lot more space to McIsaacs and Spilluk than they normally would have done.

The Toronto papers ran highly-coloured and hyper-imaginative biographies of both of them.

Sam Spilluk was described as a young man who had lived most of his life in Western Canada. Both his parents were dead. He had been serving seven years in the penitentiary for the armed robbery of a bank in Northern Ontario. A married sister in Estevan, Saskatchewan described her younger brother as a quiet, thoughtful boy, who had sung alto in a Ukrainian male choir and had been interested in nature study and bird-banding. When he reached his teens he had been thrown from the seat of a binder by a runaway team of horses, and the accident had seemed to change him. From then on he had found himself in constant difficulties with the law.

Bob McIsaacs was pictured as coming from a fine clean Christian home, and had once served as an altar boy in St. Paul's Roman Catholic church. His parents were interviewed, and his mother claimed he had been a good boy until he met up with bad companions in Riverdale Park, who had led him astray. His father had refused permission to the newspaper photographers to take his picture. When he was questioned about his son, he stated that he knew no more than anybody else about Bob's whereabouts, but hoped he'd had enough sense to get out of the country.

One morning while Ken was scrubbing the kitchen floor there was a heavy knock at the front door, and he answered it. A policeman filled the doorway, and asked, "Are you Tilling?"

Ken nodded.

"They want to speak to you down at the station," the cop said.

Ken went back into the house, accompanied by the policeman, and took off the old piece of sacking he was wearing around his waist. He drew on a coat and gave his hair a quick going over with a comb.

When they went into the street, Ken was shoved into the back seat of the police car that was parked at the curb, and the policeman got into the front seat with the driver. As the car turned around in the narrow street, having to run up on both sidewalks to do so, Ken saw Mrs. Porter standing in her doorway, her hand held over her mouth. He smiled at the certainty that within a few minutes everyone on the street would be informed that he was under arrest.

"Can I smoke?" Ken asked.

The driver told him to go ahead. He rolled a cigarette and lighted it.

"What's this all about?" he asked.

"Dunno. They told us to come down and get you, that's all," the driver said.

The officer who had come to the door began telling the driver about laying a concrete floor in his cellar on Coxwell Avenue.

When they reached the police station on Dundas Street Ken was led into a big room off the main office. There was a row of lockers at one end of the room, and a policeman sat at a long deal table eating his lunch. Ken stared out of the window, past the Dundas Street fire hall, watching the traffic run along the street. In a short time a uniformed inspector with war medals on his tunic, and followed by two younger plainclothesmen, entered the room. The inspector told Ken to sit down.

One of the detectives asked him how long it had been since he last saw Bob McIsaacs, and he told him. The other detective asked him if he'd seen McIsaacs since he came out of the reformatory after their theft of the plumbing fixtures. Ken told them he'd seen McIsaacs once or twice on the street. They asked him the dates of these meetings, and he guessed dates within a month or so of the actual times.

"How come Leslie Winters saw him nearly a year after you did?" the inspector asked.

"I don't know, except that they went around together. I used to chum with Billy Addington. I only knew McIsaacs slightly before we swiped the bathtub. After we appeared in court neither Billy nor I saw him much."

They questioned him for almost an hour, asking him what other friends of McIsaacs he knew, and whether he had any idea where Bob was hiding out. He told them he had no idea.

When they finished their questioning the inspector told him to go. When he walked through the main room of the station he saw Mr. McIsaacs sitting on a bench.

"Hello, Mr. McIsaacs," Ken said.

"Hello, son," the old man answered. "Let's see, your name's Tilling, isn't it?"

"That's right."

"Have they been questioning you about Bob?"

Ken nodded.

"They've been pestering me for the last two weeks. I can't get it into their heads that I don't know where Bob is. The first thing I know I'll be losing my job. This is the second day this week I've had to take a day off work."

The desk sergeant shouted to Ken to get out if his business was finished. Ken glanced over the high desk at the red, beery, stupid face of the fat sergeant before turning again to Mr. McIsaacs.

"I'll be seeing you," he said. "I sure hope you won't lose your job. I'm sorry about—well, about everything."

"Thank you, son. I hope you stay out of trouble like this."

"Didn't I tell you to get out, you!" shouted the sergeant.

"Goodbye, Mr. McIsaacs," said Ken. Without a glance at the sergeant he walked out of the station as slowly as he could.

Over the next few days no crime in the city was too small or too different from armed hold-up not to be blamed on McIsaacs and Spilluk. The newspapers even tried to build news stories around the phone calls from nervous housewives who claimed to have seen strange men peering through their kitchen windows. Even editorial writers got into the act with their erudite conjectures.

At first Ken thought that the tapping on the kitchen door meant that it had blown open and was flapping in the breeze. He got up from the couch in the front room and walked through the middle room and the kitchen but found the door still secured on the small hook that held it shut. Then he heard it again, a slight tap-tapping on the wood as if made by fingernails. He crossed the kitchen and stood against the door listening.

"Who is it?" he asked.

"Open up, Tilling, it's me," somebody whispered.

"Who?"

"It's Mac. Open up, quick!"

He unhooked and opened the door. Bob McIsaacs pushed his way into the kitchen. He was clean-shaven and well dressed, but his face was pale and haggard under the bare light of the naked electric bulb hanging from the ceiling.

"Anybody else at home, Ken?" he asked in a whisper.

"No, they're all out but me. Even the couple upstairs."

McIsaacs let out his breath in relief.

Ken pulled a chair from beneath the table and said, "Sit down." He sat down across the table himself, opposite McIsaacs. "You don't look much different, Bob," he said.

"I guess you wonder what I came down here for."

"Well—"

"I'm hot as hell. I'm hotter'n a firecracker."

"I know," Ken said. "The cops questioned me last week. You took an awful chance coming here."

"I had to. You seen my old man?"

"He was up at the station the same morning as me. They've been questioning him a lot."

"Why the hell don't they leave him alone? He don't know where I am. How'd he look?"

"He's worried about losing his job. They keep bothering him."

"I knew they would," Bob said, banging a skinny fist into his palm.

"You took an awful chance coming down here," Ken said again.

McIsaacs laughed silently, pulling a pack of cigarettes from his pocket. He gave one to Ken and took one himself, then he lighted them both with an expensive lighter. He stopped laughing and said, "I try to make my chances fifty-fifty, and don't try to fill no flushes. Now that I got all this heat on me I'm careful. Tonight I hadda come down here or I wouldn'a touched this neighbourhood with a ten foot pole."

Ken now recognized the change in the way McIsaacs spoke. He wondered if it was prison talk, as hobo language was different from colloquial English. McIsaacs' hands were trembling as he puffed greedily on his cigarette.

"You know my mother, Ken?" Bob asked.

Ken had never met her, but he now remembered that Bob never called her "my old lady" like most of the gang; it was always "my mother."

"No, Bob, I don't know her."

"I got a message for her," the other said, staring at him. "You take a message to her?"

"Sure I will."

"Your door locked?"

Ken went through to the front of the house and locked the door, leaving the key in the lock. When he returned to the kitchen he saw that McIsaacs had placed the back of a kitchen chair under the knob of the back door. He sat down again.

"Here's an envelope with two hundred dollars in it," Bob said. "I want you to stash it somewheres for a while, and after the heat's off I want you to take it to my mother, understand?"

Ken nodded, and took the envelope Bob handed him.

"Don't deliver it until you hear from me, or until I'm pinched."

"Okay."

"I brought it to you 'cause I know you can dummy-up. I thought of Les Winters, but I don't trust him."

"I'll handle it."

"Good." He relaxed a little now. "How's things around, Tilling?"

"Rotten, everybody's on the bum."

"I see that. I been missing a lot a the Depression. There's always lots a work where I been."

"I guess so," said Ken, smiling.

"Not sensible work, but stupid stir jobs. Guys ast to be sent to the pen to learn a trade, but all they learn 'em is how to swing a mop."

Ken laughed.

"It's true." Then he said, "You don't mind me hangin' around here eh, Tilling? I'll blow if you want me to. I don't wanna get you into no trouble."

"Stick around a while. Everybody's out, and the couple upstairs won't be back for hours yet."

"I like talkin' to somebody I know—you know, like you. I been talkin' to a bunch a stir-crazy sons a bitches for so long I need a change. What's Addington doin' these days?"

"He's dead. I thought you'd have known."

"No, I never heard. What'd he die of?"

Ken told him.

"You mean to say he boiled hisself in a tub a candy?" McIsaacs shook his head. "He was a nice kid." Then after a thoughtful pause. "Sometimes I keep tellin' myself I'm a chump, but then I hear about guys like Addington that was workin' for seven lousy bucks a week, an' I don't think all the chumps is where I been."

"I guess we're all chumps. Around here you're born a chump."

"Yeah."

"Did you ever see Charlie Plummer down in Kingston, Bob?"

"I seen him a few times, but he's on a different tier, an' works on the mail bags. He's nearly ready to be sprung I think." Bob glanced around the room. "How's your mother?"

"The same as ever."

"That's tough. You workin' at all?"

Ken told him he delivered handbills once in a while. He saw that Bob was disgusted with the shabbily-furnished kitchen. "It's a hell of a looking place to live, isn't it?" he asked.

"You don't need to apologize," Bob said.

"I've always been ashamed of the places I lived. All my life I've been ashamed of my drunken mother and of the dirty stinking holes I've had to live in."

McIsaacs was silent.

"Sometimes I've felt like sticking up a joint just to get enough money to get out of this."

"Don't be a chump, Tilling. What you wanna do is get it legit. You was always kinda smart—you know, reading all the time and stuff.

Get it the way the big guys get it, be smart. You know what I mean? Beat it outa their hides with a whip 'stead of a gun, understand?"

"That's easy to say, but you can't get anywhere these days. I get so goddam tired a waiting. I get desperate."

"Give yourself time," said McIsaacs. "I've found out that it don't do no good to be impatient. Where I been you learn to wait. Take it easy, and look around."

They talked about the fellows and girls they both knew in Cabbagetown. Ken brought the other up to date on where everyone was and what they were doing. Bob listened, laughing sometimes, asking questions, banging a fist into the palm of his other hand at times.

They talked about their schooldays.

"Remember how you guys from Park used to beat up us micks from St. Paul's?" Bob asked. "Sometimes I used to wish I was a Protestant 'cause there was always more of you than there was of us. I seen in the papers where I was supposed to have been an altar boy, Hell, every mick that gets in trouble they say he used to be an altar boy." He laughed. "Old Father Tim Walker'd never have trusted me at no altar."

"They're giving you quite a play in the papers," said Ken.

"Yeah, you ever read such crap? The other night me an' Sam was readin' about some dame sayin' she saw us looking through her window. We laughed like hell at that. We wasn't closer'n twenty miles from her." His face hardened. "Some a the square Johns think we go around shootin' people for fun—and women an' kids too! You ever hear such crap?"

"What about the guy up on the Danforth?" Ken asked.

"I don't know nobody on Danforth. What guy?" McIsaacs asked, staring at Ken.

"Skip it," Ken said.

"I read about some guy that owns a milk bar an' a dairy company," Bob said. "He's a pretty smart guy. But I don't think the fat fucker had any dough in a milk can at all. Next time a couple a guys heist his place they might not like to see a man down on his fat knees cryin' an' blubberin'. He might not look so good in the papers the next time with both his cheeks busted."

Ken asked him if he ever thought of getting away, maybe to the States, and beginning life over again with a job.

"There ain't no jobs, nowheres, you just told me."

"I know, but if there was."

"For a long time I been thinkin' about things, Ken. I got lots a time to think. Sometimes I think one way, an' other times another way, but every time I end up thinkin' that if I was to start all over again I'd do the same thing, on'y without makin' the same mistakes. I can't ever start over again now. The next time I'm pinched they'll throw me the book."

"I couldn't stand being in jail for long," Ken said. "Would they really give you life?"

"I couldn't miss."

"I'd be worried stiff."

"You think *I'm* not? I worry all a time. Sometimes I get so jumpy I don't know what to do. If I had enough guts I'd go on the junk, but then if I got scooped I'd go crazy without a fix. You ever seen a junky when they wouldn't give him a fix?"

Ken shook his head.

"It's pitiful. I'm ascared of junk."

"What are you going to do now, Bob? Have you got any plans?"

"Plans! My head's full of plans. Every time I move from one side of a room to the other I gotta make a plan. I've got a thousand cops an' a million John Citizens lookin' for me. I can't trust nobody all a time but Sam, an' sometimes I can't even trust him. I'll tell you this much, I'm goin' a long way away from here soon."

"That's a good idea. Get away from this town and let them forget you. Settle down somewhere else."

McIsaacs smiled wryly. "All my life I'm gonna be on the lam, Tilling, or else in stir. Right now my mug is up on every post office wall in Canada. I've gotta keep movin' all the time. There's nowheres to go and I can't settle down. Anyways, maybe I don't want to settle down the way you mean. My old man settled down, an' what did he ever get for bein' an honest John? He raised us kids as well as they'd let him on the peanuts they paid him. When he kicks off he'll get a wreath from the company an' a coupla masses, an' that'll be the end a him." He sat punching his fist into his other hand. "When I was a kid I remember layin' awake at night listenin' to my old man and my mother talkin' downstairs. One night I heard my old man say that they were cuttin' down the staff at the plant. My mother ast him what he was gonna do if he got laid off. Do you know what he said?"

Ken shook his head.

"He said, 'If they lay me off after all these years I'm gonna burn down the whole goddam mill.' Lucky he wasn't laid off an' he didn't have to, but he would've. He's a quiet old guy, but I know my old man. He'd a done it in a minute."

"Listen, McIsaacs, you're a guy just like everybody else. Don't you ever want to have a wife and family some day—I mean, don't you even *think* of anything like that?"

"Sure I do, but it don't bother me 'cause it's no use. When people used to ast me if I wanted to be a priest, I used to say no, 'cause I knew a priest can't have no wife or kids or nothin' like that—you know. Well you can't have no wife or family if you spend most of your life in jail neither. A priest knows he can't have a woman so he forgets it, or tries to. That's the way I am, see? I don't even hardly think about it no more."

"Some guys that's been in jail settle down," said Ken, unwilling to give up.

"The on'y guy that can settle down is him that never should a pulled anything in a first place. A punk goes out an' heists a gas-station. Okay he gets caught. He does his time. He's finished then, see? It seems to me it was different with me. I started off thinkin' I could beat them. I did too! I'm beatin' them now, this minute, see what I mean, Ken?" His face lit up. "See, what you don't know is that I get a bang just outa beatin' them. I never worked for no seven bucks a week, an' I never tried to get ahead by lookin' down on my own people like this guy East, you was tellin' me about, does. I played it all the way by myself."

"You can't keep beating them though," Ken said.

"I know. Listen, Tilling, do you think *you're* beatin' them? They're beatin' you just like they're beatin' everybody else. They'll beat us both in the end, but they'll kill me quick and wear you down till you're dead."

"Not me," said Ken. "That guy McDonald I used to work for, he beat me once but he couldn't do it now."

McIsaacs laughed. "You think he's not beatin' you right now? Does he live like you do? Like hell he does. He's laughin' at you an' guys like Addington and my old man. He's laughin' at me too, but he don't laugh when I stand in front of him with a gun. That's another thing I like, see? When I poke a gun in their guts they ain't bigshots no more—it's me, see?" He jumped up and looked at his watch. "It's after eleven o'clock."

Ken said, "The woman upstairs'll be coming home soon."

"Yeah. I gotta go," McIsaacs said. He pulled some money from his pocket and handed Ken a ten-dollar bill.

Ken didn't take it. "You'll need it more'n me, Bob," he said.

"You take it. Don't forget to give that envelope to my mother."

"She'll get it." He put the bill in his pocket.

"Not till you hear from me, or I'm pinched."

"Okay."

"I come in over the fence from the ink company, so nobody'd see me on your street. I'll go back the same way, along the lane, and over the fence. I got a car parked over on River." He pulled the chair away from the door, and unhooked the catch. "You case the yard for me will you, Tilling?"

"Sure." Ken got up and went to the door. "Is everything okay? There's nothing else you want?"

"No."

"I guess I won't see you for a while?" Ken asked, offering his hand.

"Maybe you won't see me again, Tilling," Bob said, shaking hands with Ken.

Beneath his put-on air of bravado Ken could sense the other's fear and loneliness, and his hunger for ordinary untroubled companionship. Right then he felt much older than McIsaacs, who seemed like a little frightened boy trying to bluff his way past his fear.

Bob said, "Don't forget to see my mother."

"I won't. Don't worry."

Ken turned out the kitchen light and pulled the door open. He went outside and stood on the back steps for a moment until his eyes became used to the darkness, looking around the yard and along the tops of the fences. Then he re-entered the darkened kitchen.

"Everything looks all right," he said.

"So-long, Tilling."

Bob ran down the steps and across the small backyard to the gate leading to the lane. After opening it and looking around he turned to Ken and waved. Then closing the gate quietly behind him he disappeared into the darkness. Ken heard his footsteps for a moment or two, then went into the house, closing the door behind him.

**6**

On the Saturday evening following the visit by Bob McIsaacs, Ken Tilling lay on the day-couch in the front room where he slept, listening to the Toronto CBS outlet which featured every Saturday three or four hours of radio dance music coming from such New York hotels as the Taft, Pennsylvania, Roosevelt, the Central Park Casino, and Chicago's Trianon and Aragon Ballrooms.

Mabel Tilling had left the house after supper the evening before, taking with her the week's supply of bread and milk tickets from the Welfare Department. She knew somewhere where she could exchange them for a bottle or two of bootleg wine.

Dorothy and Jimmy Cluff had gone out to a Myrtle Street rent dance with Dorothy's sister and her brother-in-law. Ken could picture them, having paid a dime apiece to enter the house from which the bits of shabby furniture had been removed from the downstairs rooms, shuffling around in the crowd to the same dance music he was listening to on the old Gothic Rogers Batteryless radio he was listening to at home.

Why these ten-cent house parties were called "rent parties" puzzled Ken, for though he'd been to many he had never been to one where the handle or take was enough to even pay a day's rent on a dog kennel. Dorothy Cluff was a rent-party addict, destined in ten or fifteen years to become one of the perennial stalwarts at the bingo games held in the basement of St. Paul's Roman Catholic church.

Ken surmised that these crowded tawdry get-togethers filled some social need of Dorothy and Jimmy's, and as most of them were held on Saturday evening, the only evening Jimmy didn't have to go to work at the foundry, they were worth the twenty cents they cost, plus the odd nickel or dime that the dancers paid for cups of "pogey" tea or sandwiches from the kitchen.

Ken stopped thinking of the Cluffs, and lay back, hands clenched beneath his head, and listened to Wayne King, "The Waltz King," and his saccharine orchestra playing a beautiful new number called "Be Still, My Heart."

1934 had been a good year for popular music but the vintage year as far as Ken was concerned would always be 1933, for that was the year he had been in love with Myrla Patson. On walks together they had joined in duets, singing "Everything I Have Is Yours" and "It's Only A Paper Moon;" while some evenings, after George and Bertha Patson had gone to bed, they had sat in Myrla's front room and sang *sotto voce*, with the radio turned down, the song that they had agreed was truly their song: "Don't Blame Me."

Ken pushed himself into a sitting position on the edge of the couch, and angrily began rolling himself a cigarette. That wasn't just a year ago, it was a century ago, and it wasn't a stupid kid called Kenneth Tilling, but some nitwit he no longer wanted to remember.

The radio announcer in a good Chicago imitation of Ben Grauer, but with too many "beautifuls" and "spacious ballrooms" in his spiel, introduced Wayne King's version of "Flirtation Waltz." The violins began, undulating on, *I always knew, some day I'd accompany you . . .* and the reeds took over on the words of the title, when the music was shut off. A Toronto announcer broke in with a news flash.

"A police dragnet, stretching in an arc from Hamilton to Barrie to Bowmanville, has been ordered tonight to apprehend two cowardly desperadoes who shot down and killed Constable Charles Marsh of the Toronto Police Force, who surprised them as they were robbing a West-End grocery store in this city a short time ago.

"CFRB has been informed that Constable Marsh was engaged in trying doors on Bloor Street West, when the front door of the store owned by C. H. Hallund, near Landsdowne Avenue, opened to his touch, and he entered.

"These men are desperate! Motorists leaving the city in any direction are warned that all cars will be stopped. All provincial and local police units have also been warned to look out for the murder vehicle, believed to be a 1932 Hudson sedan."

The music returned to the radio, but Ken was no longer listening. He *knew* that the "two cowardly desperadoes" were Bob McIsaacs and his friend Sam Spilluk. He also knew that McIsaacs' running days were over, almost before they'd had a chance to begin.

Sammy's right hand was cut from punching in the front window of the grocery store. He usually wrapped his fist in an old sweater when there was a window to be smashed, but tonight there had not been enough time. There hadn't even been enough time for them to fill a bag with cigarettes, and all they'd got was the few dollars from the tin biscuit box under the counter where Sam had known the old man kept some of his Saturday receipts. The money was not enough for a getaway stake, but it would pay Scolley for the use of his garage for a little while longer.

"They'll be watching the Lakeshore, Sammy. We'd better turn on to the railroad tracks and go along them until we get to a street closer to the river."

"*Along* the railroad tracks? It'll ruin the tires."

"I know, but we've got to do it. They'll be waiting out at the Six Points, but as soon as we cross the river we'll cut down one of them country roads through the Chink market gardens an' back to the Lakeshore. If the city cops have a roadblock anywhere it'll be at the Humber bridge."

"Let me know when we get to the place where we're gonna take the railroad tracks."

"Yeah. How's your hand?"

"Pretty bad. It's hard changing gears."

"Maybe I can do it," said Bob McIsaacs.

"No."

The stolen car ran smoothly enough but the Saturday evening traffic kept them slowed down. Once a policeman waved at them from a corner but they cut around the line of traffic and kept out of his way.

"Do you think they know who we are?" Spilluk asked.

"Sure."

"Nobody seen us at the store, except the cop."

"They know though."

"It was a dumb move."

"There's always a dumb move," Bob said.

"The Provincials'll be looking for us too."

"Sure. I said it was dumb. Cops and screws are bad. You should never kill a cop."

"He shoulda been smart. How old was he, Bob?"

"Fifty, fifty-five."

"That's too old," said Sammy.

"He wasn't very smart. I wisht it had been somebody else like Billings back in the joint."

Sam swore as they were forced over by a car that was making a left turn. The Hudson swayed but kept on, but it hurt Sammy's hand to swing the wheel.

"Maybe I should take it, Sammy."

"No."

"You're bleedin' a lot."

"I know. You know how it is, Bob, I can't stand nobody else driving. I feel better if I know it's me."

"You want a smoke?"

"Light me one."

In the light from his lighter Bob could see where Sammy's knuckles had been laid bare, and the flesh turned back over the hand. Blood was running over his wrist and dripping on to his knee.

"You'll need stiches," he told him.

"I know. I don't like getting so much blood on me. It feels funny having your own blood dripping on to your knee; it's like warm syrup. You can't get it into your head it's your own blood."

Bob told Sam to slow down, and soon they made the turn on to the railroad line. Sam drove slowly along the ties, keeping one rail under the car and steering by it.

"I hope we don't meet the flyer," Sam said laughing.

"If we do it'll be it that meets us. We're on the up track," McIsaacs said.

They continued along the tracks for almost a mile, before swinging off west at a level crossing over a suburban residential street. They crossed the river and turned south, running now through the countryside, the county road lined with market gardens. Sammy stopped a couple of times as they crossed highways, both of them looking carefully for parked police cars before they whooshed across the intersections.

"There's not many cars out here tonight."

"No, not on Saturday. Sunday night is the night."

Sammy asked, "Do you remember that fat kid that Olive brought up to Scolley's that time?"

"What fat kid?"

"I think her name was Florence. She had a good voice. She had a real good voice."

"Oh yeah."

"How far is it to the Lakeshore?"

"About two more miles, maybe less."

"I can't help thinking about that stupid cop," said Sammy, in his good unaccented Polak English.

"No."

"He was real dumb."

"It's not smart to be a hero."

"What would he get, a hundred-'n-a-half a month?"

"Maybe not even that. How's a gas?" Bob asked.

"We got plenty."

"Take it easy after we get around the next curve. Cut the lights an' let 'er coast down to the highway."

"Supposing there's cops there?"

"If there is, turn on your lights an' give her everythin'."

"There won't be cops here yet."

"No."

"Jesus, I hope not. How many miles is it to Scolley's?"

"Eighteen from the city limits. Maybe fifteen, fourteen."

"We've come twelve now from the store."

"Maybe we're four miles west of the city limits."

Sammy doused the lights as soon as they reached the next curve in the road, and they rolled silently down the grade to the highway.

Bob pointed to a car heading along the highway. "Slow down and wait for that guy to pass. If the law is on the highway we'll be able to spot them in his lights."

Both youths peered through the windshield at the highway. The eastbound car flew along towards the city, its headlights throwing the trees and fences into relief.

"There's nobody there," said Sammy.

"No."

Sammy put on his headlights, started the motor, and they made the turn on to the highway with a squeak of tires. As the car began to purr along the straightaway the needle climbed around the speedometer. Sammy rested his torn hand in his lap.

"Let me tie up your hand, Sammy."

"Just a minute till we get around this bend." He slowed the car, and when they hit a straight stretch of road he said, "All right."

Bob tied a handkerchief around Sammy's hand, flattening the strip of skin and flesh over the knuckles before pulling the handkerchief tight. "Better?" he asked.

"Yeah."

"You'll be all right once we get to Scolley's."

"Yeah. I'm getting dizzy. Open a window, Bob."

They tore through a small town, well above even the highway speed limit, keeping to the centre of the business street. McIsaacs saw a couple of men turn and watch them from the sidewalk.

"About five more miles."

"Yeah it won't take us long."

"Mind the next railroad crossing, it's the CNR main line. There's a lot of freights this time a night."

"There's nothing coming."

The car bounced across the tracks and settled down again on the highway. Across a field with a small herd of horses bunched in a corner they could see a big house with all its lights on and some cars parked in the front yard.

"There's a party on there," Sammy said.

"Yeah."

They both retreated into their own thoughts as the big car gobbled up the pavement. They passed around a slow-moving truck, and passed two cars and a transport truck going the other way.

"They probably think we doubled back and are somewheres in the city," McIsaacs said.

"God, I hope so."

"Watch out!" Bob cried, his shout almost a scream.

Sammy pulled at the wheel and the car screamed sideways across the highway, just missing the other car that had pulled into the road from a driveway, hidden by a shed. The car's back wheels tore up the dirt shoulder, and dragged them into a tearing skid. When the car overturned the left-hand wheels, the last to leave the pavement, pulled the car around and it slithered along on its side. Bob clutched the back of the front seat with his left hand, and felt himself falling against Sammy, whose breath left him in a long whoosh.

There was a sound of tearing upholstery, and the left-hand windows flew in with a crash. The motor made a series of small explosions and then the car sheared off a telephone pole, throwing both boys against the dashboard and steering wheel. Bob thought he heard both headlight bulbs pop, one at a time, but the noise was off somewhere else. His cheek was numb, and his right arm was cold, except at the elbow, where it burned.

There was an interminable interval without sound, smell or sight, and then his senses returned to him with a rush and he could read the clock on the dashboard, hear a woman's frantic screams, and smell burning wood and rubber. Sammy began to scream about his eyes.

A big man, upside down, opened the right-hand door and pulled Sammy out. Then another man climbed inside the car, pulled Bob up from where he was wedged on the floor, and shoved him up to the big man.

"Watch my arm. I think it's broke," he said.

Sammy was laid out on the shoulder of the road, and there was blood over his face. The handkerchief was still wrapped around his hand. He swore repeatedly in a dull monotone. Two women stood several yards away, afraid to come any closer.

"Are ya all right?" the big man asked Bob.

"Except for my arm."

"How's your face?"

"I've broke some teeth off I think."

"Your friend's face is pretty badly cut."

The man made him lie on the ground. "My friend's gone to phone for an ambulance and the police. The house is over there. Do you think you can walk that far?"

"Sure. Hey, Sammy."

Sammy didn't answer, but kept on swearing.

"See if *he* can walk," McIsaacs said to the man.

The man bent over Sammy.

Bob pushed himself up with his left hand, turning his body until his knees rested on the ground before straightening up. He had a hard time getting his gun from his right-hand coat pocket with his left hand, but he managed it. He walked to where the man was bent over Sammy.

"How is he?" he asked.

"He's all right, I think, except for his face."

"Get up, Sammy."

"That you, Bob! Oh, Jesus, I can't see!"

"Help him up, you."

"Maybe it'd be better for him to stay here till the ambulance comes."

"Help him up, you big Hoosier, before I give it to you."

The big man swung around, then suddenly saw the gun pointed at him. He lifted Sammy to his feet.

"Help him over that fence."

"Hey, Bud, listen here—"

"Do what you're told, you big bastard!"

The two women stayed where they were, not understanding what was going on. The big man helped Sammy over the wire fence, and at Bob's urging climbed over behind him. McIsaacs swung himself over, falling on his knees from the elastic rebound of the wire, the gun still clutched in his hand.

"Where are we goin'?" the big man asked, his voice quavering now.

"Never mind that. Lead him over the field. Ain't there a deep ravine or valley around here somewheres?"

"It's across the highway."

"Oh shit! Never mind. Take him across the field."

The three men stumbled across the uneven ground, that seemed to bump up against their feet in the darkness. Sammy was whimpering with terror about his eyes. The big man would say, his voice cracking, "Watch out for the hole!" or "Step up, here's a ridge," as they half-ran through the furrowed field. Bob followed the other two, his right arm flaying against his hip and sending sickening stabs of pain up to his shoulder. The feeling, and pain, was coming back to the side of his face.

"There's another fence ahead," the man said.

"Is there a gate in it?"

"Yes, but it's at the other end, over to our right."

"Take us to the gate."

They ran through the grass along the fence. Bob could smell the ground, and hear the small noises from the town they had passed through back along the highway. His heart had been beating with a slow uneven beat at first but now it began to race. He looked back and could see a car's headlights shining on the two women. A truck was drawn up beside the wreck. It was no use heading for Scolley's now. The cops would guess where they'd been heading. Nothing to do now but cut around back to the highway and try to make it back to the city somehow.

When they reached the gate the big man opened it, carrying the open end of it a few feet to allow them to pass through.

"Okay, get that boy through," Bob ordered. The man led Sammy into the next field.

"Where do these fields end?"

"At the railway tracks."

"Is it far?"

"A couple of hundred yards."

"Okay, go on."

Sammy asked plaintively, "Where we going?"

"We've got to get away from the cops, Sam."

"I can't see, Bob. Why should I bother? It don't make a hell of a lot of difference keeping going when you can't see! I wish I could just see!"

"You've got blood in your eyes."

"His eyes is pretty badly cut, mister," the big man said.

"Who asked you, you big farmer! Just shut your mouth and help him."

The big man stopped. "What do you intend to do to me? That's what I'd like to know?"

"Get going. I won't do nothin' to you unless you give us a bum steer. Where's the tracks?"

"That's them up ahead, running along the bank."

"Let's hustle it up!"

They went through another gate and crossed the railroad tracks. Beyond the railroad was another field and then a winding river. They crossed the field in silence and waded through the cold water to the opposite bank. Bob's right hand floated behind him as the water lapped above his waist. When they were across Sammy sat down in the grass and refused to go any farther.

"Come on, Sammy, let's go," Bob implored him.

"No. It's no use, Bob—You go ahead—I can't *see*! I'd never be able to make it. What the hell's the use of trying when you can't see!"

"You'll see after a while. We'll make a doctor wash out your eyes."

"It's no use. I'm blind, I tell you! Jesus Christ, I'm blind!"

"Do you want to be hung? They'll hang us for sure."

"I don't care no more." He mumbled a string of oaths like a little boy who has just learned to swear.

Bob crouched in the grass, bent over Sammy. His wet shoes made squishing noises when he moved his feet to keep his balance. "Come on, Sammy, you don't want us both to be grabbed. Gimme a break. I don't want to run out on you."

The big man said, "I'll take care of him, mister."

"You hear that, Sammy?" Bob asked bitterly. "This guy says he'll take care of you."

"Yeah. You leave me, Bob."

"I can't, Sammy! I can't leave ya to be hung!"

He could hear a car speeding along the highway. It slowed, then stopped, somewhere beyond the railroad bridge.

"That might be the ambulance," the big man said.

"Or the Provincials. Come on, Sammy, before the law gets here!"

"No. You go ahead."

"I don't wanna run out."

"Oh, God, my eyes hurt! Jesus, Bob, don't try to be a hero like that stupid cop!"

"Do you want me to leave you here with this guy?"

"Sure. He sounds like good people," Sammy said.

"Jeez, I hate to."

"He'll be all right with me," the big man said.

"I'd better get goin'."

"Here, Bob, take this," Sammy said. He groped with his good hand in his pants pocket and brought out a small wad of sticky-wet bills which he handed to McIsaacs.

"Yeah. I'll need that. Don't tell 'em nuthin'. Maybe they won't—on account of—maybe Burns can spring you in a few years."

"Go on, get outa here! Don't go near Taffy's."

"No," Bob said in farewell.

He stumbled through the tall weeds of the river bank, and cut through a field of head-high dry cornstalks. Each time his hand banged against his leg it sent pain shocks up to his shoulder. His mouth was sore, his cheek thickened around his broken teeth. Every few steps he spat out some blood. The corn made a loud rustling as he pushed through it in a straight line, trampling the long dry stalks underfoot. When he realized the noise he was making he began running between the rows, his progress less noisy and easier.

He climbed through a snake fence, forcing himself between the rails and edging sideways with his broken arm lying along his hip. He crossed more fields heading towards the lakeshore, and while crossing a flat-cropped pasture noticed that the sole of one of his shoes was flapping with every step. This inconsequential thing infuriated him, and he cursed it between his labouring breaths.

At the next fence he stopped to catch his breath. The veins in his temples were pounding, and he had a cramp beneath his ribs. He rested his forehead against the fence, feeling the new-released perspiration coursing down his face and beneath his belt.

He forced himself over the fence somehow, and stumbled through the next field, making a forty-five degree turn in direction to avoid a house and barn that loomed up ahead. The revolver was heavy in his hand as he staggered along, arms hanging loose at his sides, his swollen mouth agape to gulp the air, his legs heavy and loose-jointed. His mind was beginning to wander from exhaustion, and only obstacles like fences and ditches that obstructed his lurching gait brought him back to partial consciousness.

His running slowed to a walk and then to a stagger. He crossed a golf course, the rolled fairways giving a silly spring to his step, and he found himself at last on the top of a low bank overlooking a thin strip of sandy beach. He slid down the slope to the sand, and lay there beneath a narrow overhang, gasping and coughing. He allowed his eyes to close and his aching body sank into the cold sand.

When he and his sisters were small, his mother used to take them to swim at Simcoe Beach during the summer. Mrs. McIsaacs preferred Simcoe, at the foot of Leslie Street, for, though it wasn't quite as "tony" as Kew Beach, it was a couple of steps up the social ladder from Cherry Beach, where most of Cabbagetown swam.

They would board an eastbound streetcar at Sackville and Queen, and ride across the Don to Carlaw Avenue, from where they would walk down Carlaw, across Eastern, and south into an industrial neighbourhood of paint, tar and patent-leather factories, then by means of a wide cinder path cross the vast empty expanse of sand and dwarf willow clumps to the shore of the lake. Occasionally, when his mother's rheumatic knee was bothering her, she would herd them aboard the five-cent jitney-bus, and they would ride in style past the plodders on the cinder path.

One fall Sunday morning his father had taken him and his older sister Elsie down Cherry Street and east along the concrete wall of the ship channel and turning basin, he and his sister leap-frogging over the cast-iron niggerheads that the ships tied up to. They had walked along the lakefront all the way to a channel opening into a small bay, and his father had called it Coatsworth Cut. Back from the lake the bay had disappeared into a wide marsh covered in bull-rushes and aquatic weeds.

"This is Ashbridge's Bay where I learned to fish as a boy," his father had said. "And many a meal of perch and mudcats I've caught in there too. In the winters, before the city was built up so thick around it, we used to ice-boat around the bay."

It was an aspect of his father's life never revealed to him before, and never mentioned again.

"See them ducks !" his father said, pointing to a pair that rose from the weed-choked water. "Them's mergansers, American mergansers. Fish-eaters. They c'n dive just like loons."

He had been awed into shamed silence by his father's newly-revealed knowledge, and ever afterwards when he saw his parent, battered lunch-pail under his arm, going off to work at the mean bone-wearying job he had for most of his life, he had wondered what law of nature had changed him from an outdoor boy who fished and ice-boated on the bay to a man doomed to spend most of his life indoors at a job that gave him nothing.

He must have dozed off! When he awoke he lay still, smelling the flotsam-smell of the shoreline, feeling the cool breeze against his burning cheek and the bared calves of his legs. His pain had gone, leaving him only a feverish thirst. As the events of the evening came back to him he shuddered. Now, instead of two penitentiary go-boys he and Sammy Spilluk were hunted murderers.

He scrambled to his feet, the sand gripping and filling his broken shoe sole, his head thick with fever, and his arm a swollen appendage that flapped painfully against his side. Behind him, across the fields, he could hear the sound of pursuit, sometimes muted but at other times loud with shouting.

He ran east along the shoreline, past the golf-course clubhouse, his breath wheezing in his chest. The gun in his hand was choked with sand, a useless burden that he carried in an unheeding hand. He ran across an elevated wooden jetty and jumped down to the sand again. He paused in the lee of an eroded cliff and pulled a pack of cigarettes from his jacket pocket, knowing before he opened it that his cigarettes would be a sodden mockery. "Oh Jesus, Mary, Joseph!"

He cut back inland when halted by a heavy barbed-wire fence that jutted out into the lake, and followed the fence along the side of the golf course. On the other side of the fence he could see the large cylindrical tanks and cat-crackers of an oil refinery, and a well-lighted office inside which a man sat reading a newspaper.

He came out of a small patch of trees and ran along a fairway, through a sand-trap, across the billiard-table smoothness of a green, and headed for a flag that beckoned to him three hundred yards away to the north.

Back towards the beach the beams of flashlights rose and fell across the golf course, and he knew they had followed his fresh footprints in the evening-damp sand. He looked back across his shoulder to try to see once more the figure of the man reading his paper in the refinery office, but the building was now hidden behind the trees. The only other human being left in his nightmare world.

He sobbed now, his mind beating to the stumbling cadence of his shuffling feet. Go on. Go on. Go on, you fool. Go on, you poor suffering fool. Go towards the lights. No, go against the lights. Go on, you moth. Go on, you moth-bitten bum. This is a field and somewhere ahead is a road. The roads cut the earth into squares of fields.

The fields cut all the roads into strips. If there were no fields the whole earth would be paved. The worst pain is really toothache, but mother used to say it was earache. Mother used to call, "BO-O-OB!" from the front door at nine o clock. Early to bed keeps boys good. All boys are good. All men are bad. Men are good and bad. Good bad men and bad good men. Good men kill bad men, and bad men kill good men. Bad men kill cops, and cops kill—No man can run when he can't run. No man can climb every fence. When a man's arm—

There were flashlight beams now ahead of him. He turned and stumbled to the barbed-wire fence and pulled himself up with his good hand, the heavy pistol hanging from his groping fingers by its trigger guard. The beam of a flashlight swung across him, then returned and held him in its naked obscene brightness. He shoved his broken arm between the strands of the fence, and holding himself to the wire with an aching biceps, swung his good hand around, a wrong finger finding the trigger of the revolver, and aimed it in the general direction of the source of light.

A hoarse voice shouted, "Drop it, McIsaacs, or we'll let you have it!"

He squeezed the trigger, and nothing happened.

Turning his head until his face pressed into the cool strands of the wire, he moaned softly, once, before the first copperjacketed slug mushroomed through his skull. His body twitched in a macabre dance as the other bullets struck it.

When the smoke and noise blew away, his body hung by its broken arm from the fence, looking like a boneless golliwog against the light-stabbed darkness.

**7**

During the winter of 1935 Ken
Tilling discovered he had become something that a short time before
had been an odious designation: a socialist. The spark had been set
one evening on a walk from the Bowery twenty-five-cent flophouse,
at the corner of Houston Street, where he was living at the time. As
with many momentous happenings in a human life, it had been a
commonplace conversation (with his flophouse companion, a professional safebreaker named "Legs" Fisher who had recently been
sprung from the Nevada State Penitentiary) which had changed his
mind. They had been talking about the young Jewish Communist
agitators who held forth in Union Square every night, and whom
Ken despised as he despised all true believers. Legs had said, "Maybe
it's different for you an' me, Ken, but for the ordinary working stiff
Communism seems his only hope."

Just that. Nothing that would ever make Bartlett's, change the
world, be quoted widely, or even be remembered by anyone else; yet
this simple sentence of a professional criminal was to remain with
him for the rest of his life.

His new political radicalism was a queer amalgam of Fabian
socialism, hobo bumology, the anarchist teachings of Bukharin, the
principles laid down in *The Communist Manifesto*, the libertarian
philosophy of the IWW, and the social reformism of the New Deal.

Once he had convinced himself that the system of society under
which he lived was responsible for everything from bedbugs to
whores and from hungry children to cross-eye and harelip (which
were still quite prevalent among his former classmates from Park and

Dufferin public schools), he became possessed of a witch-burning fervour, and his arguments with those who opposed them matched in bigotry the soul-saving sophisms of the evangelical Bible-thumper.

Bob McIsaacs had been quietly buried by his family. A month after the funeral Ken, true to his word to his dead acquaintance, delivered the envelope containing the two hundred dollars to the McIsaacs' house.

He sat in a broken chair in the carpetless front room as Mrs. McIsaacs asked him how Bob had looked the day he had called at Ken's house. He told her that Bob had been well, and that his big worry was the shame he had brought on her and his father with the notoriety he was getting.

"Bob was a good boy," said the woman. "He never would have got in trouble if it hadn't been for bad companions."

Ken nodded, but he was thinking that in her son's case it had been Bob McIsaacs himself who had been the bad companion.

"When he was a young boy we were going to send him through school, then college, to study for a priest," she said. "If it hadn't been for him getting scarlet fever when he was ten and missing a year's 'xaminations he would have gone too. He used to want to be a priest."

Ken nodded again in pretended agreement with the poor woman's delusion.

"Times are so bad these days it's a wonder more poor souls don't turn to stealing to try and get ahead. Bob would have been a good boy if he could have got a steady job."

Another sympathetic nod. Ken knew that her son had been a criminal because he had wanted to be one; because he liked the easy surface opulence of flashy clothes and money in his pocket; because he wanted the adventure, and the sense of power that was his when he stood behind a loaded pistol. Economic security would not have changed Bob McIsaacs.

"I don't think I oughta keep this money," Mrs. McIsaacs said. "It must belong to some poor devil."

"I'd keep it if I were you." Ken said to reassure her. "He wanted you to have it. I guess he figured you'd have a lot of expenses if he was—if he didn't come back. That's why he told me to give it to you a month after—I last heard of him."

"We *have* got a lot of bills to meet," she said.

"I'd keep it, Mrs. McIsaacs, if I were you."

"We'll see then," she said, staring at the money in her hand. "I'd offer you a cup of tea but I'm right out. Tonight's father's pay night."

"I had a cup just before leaving the house," Ken lied.

He never did discover whether the McIsaacs kept the money or not. A few weeks after his visit they moved away, and he never did see any member of the family again.

One summer evening Ken sat on his front steps talking to Jimmy Cluff. Dorothy was across the street gossiping with Mrs. Porter, Mrs. Wells, and a young woman named Gallagher who had recently moved into No. 9. A noisy group of boys were playing "Buck, Buck, How Many Fingers Up?" against the high board fence of the printing-ink factory.

It was a warm, clear, lazy evening, following the severe electrical storm of the early morning. Jimmy was telling Ken that he was thinking of chucking up his three-nights-a-week job at the foundry to work for his brother-in-law who had put a down payment on a small suburban market garden.

"I didn't know you knew anything about gardening," Ken said.

"I don't, except maybe I can tell a carrot from a radish, but from what Royce tells me you don't have to know nothing. It's the same as anythink else, Ken, they make it look tougher than it is to keep other people from horning in. There's a good living to be made out of it if a couple of guys work hard and watch themselves. It's like down at the foundry, the moulders have to know their jobs but outside of them what does anybody else have to know? Any dumb cluck like me can do the bull labour for thirty-seven-an'-a-half cents an hour. No job is that tough that a guy can't learn it."

Ken said, "It'll be better for Dorothy too. You'll be able to have a house out there."

"That's what I'm figuring. I want to get away from this part of town. Out there we'll be able to afford a coupla kids, and they'll have lotsa room to play around in—"

"I wonder what this bird wants?" Ken asked, pointing down the street as a fat policeman thumped towards them with a stolid tread.

The women across the street were also watching the oncoming cop, for they knew that his appearance meant a complaint, a summons or even an arrest.

When the policeman reached Ken and Jimmy he asked, "Is either of you two named Tilling?"

Ken said, "I'm Tilling."

"You'd better get ready to go downtown. Your mother's had an accident."

Ken felt the blood draining from his cheeks. "What kind of accident? Is she in the hospital?"

"You'd better get ready to come with me," the policeman said.

"I *am* ready. Where is she?"

The policeman shifted his bulk from one foot to the other.

"Come on, man, for God's sake tell me!" Ken shouted.

"She's in the morgue. At least they think it's your mother, Mabel Tilling. They want you to go down and indentify her."

Jimmy was questioning the policeman, but Ken didn't understand their words. "Do I walk down?" he heard himself ask.

Jimmy Cluff pressed a quarter into his hand, and he shoved it in his pocket and trotted down the street towards the corner.

By the time he reached Queen Street his head had cleared a little. Some small boys passed behind him as he stood at the streetcar stop, chattering and laughing together. Their happy laughter made him angry, for how could they laugh—how could there be any joy left in the world—at a time like this. He felt an insane urge to cuff their ears.

The streetcar ride downtown was a dream. He stared through the window at the people strolling past the second-hand store proprietors, who were standing in their doorways ready to pounce on a likely customer, and wondered why things still went on as they always had. Maybe it wasn't his mother at all, and in a few more minutes he too would be able to laugh again. A queer hysteria made him giggle to himself at the thought.

When he entered the large front doors of the morgue building on Lombard Street, he stood in the cool dim silence of the hallway wondering where to go or what to do. From an office to the side came the ticking of a large clock, and he crossed the hall and peered through the doorway into the room. Two men, one in shirtsleeves and the other wearing a business suit, sat reading sections of an evening paper.

The man who was fully dressed asked, "Are you the Tilling boy?"

Ken nodded.

Both men dropped their newspapers and led the way along the hallway to the back of the building. In the room they took him to were a series of small icebox doors, miniatures of the ones at the rear of a butcher shop. The man in shirtsleeves opened one of the doors and pulled out a stretcher on rollered tracks, on which was a body covered with a brown tarpaulin. A crazy thought struck Ken that the whole movie scene was wrong, that in all the other pictures he'd seen the body was always covered with a white sheet.

One of the men took Ken's arm and led him to the side of the pulled-out rack. The other man lifted the edge of the tarpaulin and showed Ken the head and one shoulder of his mother. He stared down at her in disbelief, wanting to tell her things were okay now, that he'd come to take her home. She wore her old blue dress, and her hair was tangled and wet. Her eyes were closed in a face that was waxy yet puffed, and her lower lip was stiffened over her City Welfare bottom false teeth.

"Do you know her, son?" one of the men asked.

Ken nodded.

"Is it your mother?"

"Yes. She doesn't look like this—She didn't always look like she does now," he said, apologizing for her, as he felt she'd want him to, and as she would for herself if she could.

"Sure. We understand, kid. Take it easy."

The man in the business suit took him by the arm and led him out of the room. From behind him Ken could hear the noise of the heavy icebox door being slammed.

In the front office Ken was seated in a chair, and offered a glass of water, which he declined with a shake of his head. He answered some routine questions, and then signed some papers.

"How was she—How did it happen?" he asked.

"She died of natural causes, as far as we know now," the man in the business suit said. "There'll be an autopsy in the morning. She was found early today in a lane off Bathurst Street out in the West End. Because she didn't have any identification and was so far from home we had a hard time finding out who she was. I'd say she'd been lying in the lane all night, because she was still soaking wet from the storm."

Ken answered more questions. He told the man they were on city relief, and answered yes when he was asked if he wanted her buried from the house. He signed more papers which were meaningless to him. The shirtsleeved man handed him a small change purse containing twenty cents, and he shoved it into a pocket. "Your mother is still wearing her wedding ring; I suppose you'll want her to be buried with it on?"

"Yes. She never took it off. It never left her finger from the day she was married," Ken said.

When the questions and the signing of papers were finished, both men said they were sorry. The man in the suit told him to go to the relief department the next morning and make arrangements for the funeral. He bid them goodbye, tugged open the heavy front door, and went into the deserted short downtown street.

The sidewalks and the almost empty buildings had the same smell they had always had. Nothing else in the world had changed, but behind him in the shabby red-brick building lay the body of a dead female drunk, found lying dead in a laneway—inside the building lay the woman who had bore him and worked for him through his childhood, and had made sacrifices for him—and mistakes, many mistakes, but had been his mother.

*He was a little boy again, coming down to breakfast one morning, and his mother was saying, "The thunder's turned the milk, so we'll have to wait for the milkman before we have our porridge. Don't worry, when I get my icebox the milk'll be fresh all the time. . . ." There was the day he came in crying, his head cut from a sweep of Charlie Plummer's shovel while they were building a snow fort. His mother had washed the cut and swabbed it with peroxide, and she'd said, "Never mind, Ken, when we move away from here next year you'll have a big yard to play in, and you'll be able to build all the forts you want, like the one we saw that time at the Idle Hour show with Victor McLaglen—"*

But of course they hadn't moved, and Mabel hadn't ever had an icebox, until the one they put her in when she was dead.

Before the funeral most of the neighbours dropped in to see Mabel Tilling in her coffin, which was supported on a pair of cloth-covered sawhorses in the emptied-out front room of her house on Timothy Place. Mrs. Gaffey and Mrs. Wells dropped in at every opportunity, bringing a pair of kitchen chairs into the front room where they acted as self-appointed greeters, sniffling into their handkerchiefs.

Mabel Tilling's body was swathed in white muslin, and her head was covered by a square of thick black silk, pulled down almost to the eyebrows to hide the post-mortem trepanning scar. The black silk head covering made Mabel look Spanish and much more youthful than she had done in life.

"They make them look so natural-like," Mrs. Gaffey remarked at times, almost envious of Mabel's distinction of having been taken first to the morgue.

Many of the children from Timothy Place and even from Sumach Street were drawn to the house by the black ribbon bow on the door, and by their childish curiosity. Ken would sometimes take them into the front room, and hold the smallest ones up so they could look into the coffin.

Mabel not only had recovered some of her lost beauty in death but her long-lost dignity as well. She lay propped up on the cheap satinette lining of the Welfare-purchased coffin, her gnarled and thickened hands clasped beneath her bosom, and her face set in a mask of waxed repose.

Some cut flowers bought by Mrs. Wells and the Porters stood in a pair of unmatching vases borrowed from the Cluffs and the Gaffeys, giving the tiny room the floral dignity that was expected.

None of his mother's old drinking friends visited the house to pay their respects, and Ken wondered whether deference, fear, decency or drunkenness kept them away. Some of the callers he hardly knew—men and women who had been his mother's friends years before. Two or three couples drove in from the rural section of the province where she had been born, but no relatives, even if some remained alive.

The milkman and the bread salesman came in together, crushing their caps in their hands and glancing briefly into the coffin. Both were ill at ease, and after standing beside the bier in silence they shook Ken's hand soberly and left the house.

The things the postman said were what surprised Ken most. It was the first time in more than fifteen years that Ken had ever seen him with his cap off, and though he had delivered mail to the house since Ken was a toddler neither Ken, nor anyone else on the street, had ever called him by name.

After gazing at Mabel the old man turned to Ken and said, "Maybe it's just as well she's out of it, son. She had a lot of trouble did your mother. I've seen her dozens of times in the past few years carrying on drunk, if you'll pardon the expression. But I seen her too, years ago when I come back from the war, going to work and taking you to the day nursery over on River Street. You'd be too young to remember much about them days. She was a good-looking woman then, always chipper in them days, laughing and with always a pleasant 'good morning' for me. I'll always remember her from then, not like she'd come to be lately. Don't take it too hard, son, but be happy that she's out of it all now."

Before the old man's unexpected eulogy broke him down, Ken pressed the postman's hand warmly, and turned his head away as the old fellow, mailbag over his shoulder, left the house. From then on it was the anonymous postman who came to Ken's mind whenever anyone mentioned "the decent common man."

Mabel Tilling left No. 5 Timothy Place for the last time supported on the shoulders of Jim Cluff, Mr. Wells, Mr. Porter, and her son and only child, Kenneth Tilling.

Her obituary, if one had been written, might have read, "Before the remains of the deceased left her home, a brief oration was given over the casket by the Rev. J. J. Bainbridge of St. Bartholomew's Anglican Church. Floral offerings consisted of two unostentatious wreaths, one donated by St. Bartholomew's and the other by the Roy G. Maybee Funeral Home. Other floral pieces accompanied the modest procession to the Fields of Hope Cemetery where she was laid to rest. These were supplied by Mr. and Mrs. George Wells, Mr. and Mrs. Bernard Porter and Mr. and Mrs. James Cluff, all of Timothy Place. A bouquet of lilies-of-the-valley was placed on the casket by her son Kenneth, and a large colourful wreath of greenery and wild flowers was placed in the hearse just before it pulled away by Mr. Michael Razinoff." (The "foreigner" who had moved into No. 4.)

On the long drive to the cemetery Ken sat back against the seat cushions of the undertaker's limousine, pressed into a corner by the ample forms of Mrs. Wells and Mrs. Gaffey, hearing them whisper together between eye-wipings and noseblowings. He turned once and looked through the rear window seeing Jim and Dorothy Cluff sharing the front seat of Dorothy's brother's Model T.

The cemetery service was brief. The Rev. Mr. Bainbridge spoke a few words about the inevitability of death, and about the better life that awaited everyone "on the other side." He spoke cautious words of praise about Mabel, whom he had never met, and ended the service with the appropriate prayer as laid down in *The Book of Common Prayer.*

Ken stood at the graveside, his head bowed as he watched the workmen throw shovelfuls of bright yellow clay into the grave. The minister walked over to Ken and placed a brotherly arm briefly around his shoulders before getting into his car. The undertaker's assistants, looking like a pair of unfunny burlesque comedians in their cutaway coats and derby hats, loaded their gear into the hearse and lighted cigarettes. As the few members of the cortege strolled toward the cars, Ken said his own brief private goodbye over the grave, then turned away quickly and hurried after them.

On the way back to Cabbagetown Mrs. Wells and Mrs. Gaffey relaxed from their period of mourning, and each rolled herself a cigarette from Ken's package of Ogden's Fine-Cut tobacco. By the time the undertaker's car turned down Sumach Street from Gerrard, Mrs. Wells was telling Mrs. Gaffey about some new-bought curtains that had shrunk with the first washing and had torn along the hemline.

Dorothy Cluff made a cold-meat and fried-potato supper for her husband, her brother and Ken, and they crowded around her tiny kitchen table in the back room upstairs to eat it. Ken told them he had until the twenty-eighth of the month to remain in the house, but then the Relief Department rent would stop. He would sell or give away his few bits of furniture, then get himself a furnished room somewhere.

"We'll have to find a place ourselves," Dorothy said. "Now that we've got to move anyways we might as well take Royce's offer to give him a hand out at the market garden."

"That's what I've bin tellin' you all along," Royce said.

"It'll be good to get away from the foundry, where I can take a breath of air without tasting soot for a week," Jimmy said.

"This is your golden opportunity," said Ken.

"We'll have a couple of kids too," vowed Jimmy. "That'll give the wife here something more to do than sit around the house and mope. Don't you think that's what she needs, Ken?"

Dorothy winked at Ken from where she stood behind her husband and brother.

After supper the Cluffs left with Royce to take a look at his new property. Ken went downstairs and carried the wilted bunches of flowers from the front room to the back door, where he threw them into the garbage can. Then he opened both the front room and kitchen windows and let the sickly-sweet smell blow out of the house. After moving his couch and dresser back to their accustomed places he climbed the stairs to his mother's front bedroom. There with a key he found in the bottom of a dresser drawer he opened his mother's old tin trunk, and sat down on the edge of her bed.

In the trunk tray were some lapsed insurance policies, old keys, three or four chinaware souvenir figures, snapshots of people he did not know or remember, some photographs of himself when he was younger, various booklets and newspaper clippings, an out-of-date city street guide, a Butterick pattern book with crumpled patterns inside, a pair of knitting needles, birth certificates, regimental cap badges from the last war, and a few small pieces of embroidery wrapped in newspaper.

One of the snapshots of himself showed him wearing a loud checked overcoat his mother had made him once from an old one of hers. He remembered it had been taken on the day of a Santa Claus parade. He had been so childishly angry at having to wear the overcoat that to pacify him his mother had taken him into a Childs' and bought him the most luxurious strawberry soda he had ever sipped through a straw.

Beneath the tray the trunk was half-empty, and now he remembered gazing into it years before when it was crammed with bed and table linen, which his mother must have sold or traded for wine. Beneath a woman's old sweater were some yellowing photographs in frames. One of them was a picture of his maternal grandfather, who had died before he was born. Ken compared the old man's looks with his own which he viewed in the dresser mirror. He said to himself, *The old boy looks like a staunch Hastings County Conservative. I wonder what he would say if he knew his grandson was a Red.*

There were other old and faded photographs, of school and church groups; and in an old Manila envelope he found his parents' marriage certificate, her engagement ring set with a tiny diamond, and several snapshots of his father.

He picked up the ring. How many times must she have fought against taking it down to a pawn shop? There had been hundreds of mornings, he knew, when she had been sick almost to death, and this ring would have brought her a few dollars at least. She must have removed it from her finger years before so she would not be tempted to pawn it while drunk.

He stared unseeing through the curtains covering the window, thinking of how the cheap engagement ring had remained to his mother a symbol of her young womanhood, and of the love she had carried for his father. As he turned his father's snapshots over in his hands he realized that this man had not deserved the love his mother had felt for him. He tore the snapshots into small pieces and dropped them on the floor.

Then he bent his head and cradled his elbows on his knees, crying as if his heart would break. He did not try to halt the tears, but let them drip from his chin to the pile of torn snapshots on the floor.

**8**

Myrla Patson entered her downtown room and groped her way to the centre of the floor. She stood in the near darkness and placed both hands above her head, moving them in concentric circles as she searched with her fingers for the bare electric bulb that hung somewhere above her head. When her fingers found it she ran her hand up its smooth contoured side until her fingers reached the switch, then she turned on the light.

Walking back to the door she closed it, shooting the heavy bolt into the hasp on the doorframe. She kicked off her shoes, and walked in her silk stockings back to the rumpled bed. After lifting the corner of the blanket and sheet from the floor where they had been kicked by her last trick of the evening, she sat down and removed her stockings, tossing them on to a chair. After gazing with critical concern at the red indentations her garters had made in her thighs she rubbed them briskly with her hands, feeling them tingle with the release of circulation. Then she scratched them languidly with her long red pointed nails.

Standing up she pulled her dress over her head and shook her long black hair from her face. The dress followed the parabola of the stockings to the greasy-backed easy chair. Pushing a hand between the bedspring and the mattress she removed a thin wad of paper money which she placed in her purse on the dresser. She lighted a cigarette, a Millbank, and tossed the wooden kitchen match into the useless fireplace that served as a handy receptacle for cigarette packages, gum wrappers and burnt matches.

She inhaled a long drag from her cigarette and blew the smoke against her reflection in the web-cracked mirror. She pinched the loose skin of her flattened belly, turning this way and that as she viewed herself in the glass, thinking that she must have lost ten or twelve pounds since she had quit her job at the Union Jack Cafe.

From the night almost a year before when Mike had first discovered her association with Tony she had come a long way, sideways and downwards. For a short while she had held on to the tiny apartment that Mike had provided for her, paying the rent now herself. Finally her new trade had forced her to move from that part of town to where she now lived, in the centre of the city, a stone's throw from Pembroke and Dundas Streets.

When she had made enough contacts with regulars who lived at times at the Royalcourt, she felt that splitting her earnings with Tony was a charity she no longer wanted to afford and, after threatening to tell everything to his fat little Italian wife and her family, they had broken off. Now she was in business for herself.

Her pickups now took place in beer parlours and restaurants, with a very few nocturnal forays into the streets when business was slack. Through an unspoken arrangement with her landlady, who pretended to be both deaf and blind as long as she was renting the room for three times its normal price, she was allowed to entertain her customers there.

On good weeks she made as high as fifty-sixty dollars, and seldom averaged less than forty. She had a closet full of cheap clothes, a perennial morning hangover, and had aborted herself twice during the past six months. In a savings bank in the Bay Street financial district was a nest egg of several hundred dollars, and she now believed that a girl with any kind of looks at all was crazy to work for ten or twelve dollars a week.

She generally slept during the mornings, went shopping or to the movies three afternoons a week, or sometimes, at first, had taken Derek to the beach, to the Islands or to the Sunnyside amusement park. Her mother had drawn away from her, despite the extra money she gave her each week, and Bertha had hinted several times that she would be more appreciated from a distance than by flaunting herself in front of the family's neighbours. For several months now she had visited her family, and Derek, only on Sunday afternoons.

She bent close to the mirror and inspected her face. There were a few hard lines beginning to show around her eyes, and some vertical lines along her upper lip. She pursed her mouth at the sight of them and walked over to the bed.

There was a light knock at the door, and Myrla asked, "Who is it?"

A female voice answered, "Dorothy."

"I'm working, honey," Myrla said. "Call on me tomorrow at noon."

"Sorry, dear. I didn't know," the voice said.

"'s okay. Tomorrow."

She heard a pair of slippered feet retreating down the hallway.

With five tricks tonight she was too tired to be bothered talking to her colleague from down the hallway. Anyhow she had heard Dorothy's story many times. How she used to be statuesque, not fat, an Icelandic immigrant's daughter from Winnipeg who had met a Danish sailor who was visiting his sister in the Manitoba city. How he had courted her, given her a cigar-band engagement ring and left her in a family way.

How the young, statuesque, betrayed Dorothy had gone to Saint John, New Brunswick, to wait for the return of Carl's ship, the *S.S. Norgenfeld*, only to learn a month later, when she was broke, that the ship had been chartered to carry cargoes of guano from Peru to Antwerp.

Her letters to her erstwhile lover had not been answered, and she had taken up with Scandinavian sailors in Saint John. Almost until the week her baby was born she had lived this way, her natural heaviness hiding the fact of her pregnancy from all but the soberest of tricks.

Her baby had been born in a Roman Catholic institution for she feared that somehow word would leak back to her Lutheran family if the baby was born in a Protestant hospital. She had left the baby with an order of Catholic nuns, and had gone back to the streets around the waterfront. In the spring when the shipping slackened off, she took a train to Montreal, where she was picked up by a man who put her in a house in Saint-Henri. With her natural light blonde hair and large fat figure she was a favourite of many men, especially West Indian Negroes who were crewmen on the CN "Lady" boats. After the shipping season ended on the St. Lawrence she thought of going back to Saint John or Halifax for the winter, but instead joined three French-Canadian girls who were accompanying a madam to open a house in the new gold-mining town of Geraldton in north-western Ontario.

Some months later she happened to see one of her young brothers on the street, and hardly taking the time to pack her things took the next bus to Long Lac where she boarded a Toronto train.

Now, becoming grossly fat, her former looks disappearing under dewlaps of flesh, she worked the cheaper restaurants along Dundas Street from Sherbourne to Yonge, and at times even played the Oriental trade in Chinatown's Elizabeth Street. Someday, she promised anyone who would listen, she would get married and move back West with her husband, preferably a white middle-aged widower.

Myrla, who knew Dorothy's story by heart by now, knew she never would.

Shucking herself of her bra and panties but leaving the light on, Myrla walked to the window, let up the shade, and stood there for a moment or two for the benefit of a skinny old man who waited in his darkened window across the narrow carriageway between the two big old houses for her every night. She smiled invitingly across the space dividing them, held up five fingers of her hand, then with a bawdy laugh strolled slowly to the centre of the room and turned off the light. She was too tired tonight to bother watching his dim form leave his window and climb into bed, and she threw herself down on her own bed, pulled the covers up to her chin, said a short prayer for Derek and her family, and almost immediately fell asleep.

The following afternoon, after having a lunch of hamburg and fried eggs in a White Turret lunchroom near George Street, Myrla strolled up to Allan Gardens and sat on a bench in the sun. She wondered why Dorothy hadn't called at her room, but put it down to the other woman's discovering that she'd been alone in her room the night before. Poor fat, thirtyish Dorothy with her self-delusions and her slow sinking into—what?—like a hippo sinking into mud. She shrugged off thoughts of the other woman, and closed her eyes. The sun felt warm and clean against her face, and she turned her head, opened her eyes again, and watched the clouds racing across the sky.

*It was a summer Sunday afternoon when she was very small, and she and Minnie Layton and Minnie's younger brother Archie had taken the radial car up to Scarboro Bluffs for a picnic. After they had eaten their sandwiches (she had called them "sangwidges" then, after the way her Scots mother pronounced the word) they had lain back in the grass and watched the puffy white clouds chasing each other across the blue of Lake Ontario beneath the bluffs. Archie had called them "cotton-wool balls," but his sister had told Myrla they were white sheep that were hurrying home to beat the rain. Later on the three of them went exploring in the eroded hollows of the bluffs until they found a patch of buttercups. Minnie told Myrla that if she held a buttercup under her chin and her skin turned yellow it was a sign she liked butter. They tried it out on each other and it was true, their skin turned yellow, and each admitted they liked butter very much—*

Two youths in their late teens sat down beside her on the bench and began making wisecracks for her benefit. One of them asked her if she had the time, and she gave him a cold no as an answer. The other asked her if she had the inclination. She stood up and walked away in the direction of Carlton Street.

When she neared the park gates she heard the brassy music of a band coming along past Sherbourne Street, and she looked east to where a short parade was approaching behind a line of flags—Canadian Ensigns, Union Jacks and some red flags with a crossed hammer and sickle in the corner. She took up a position near the gate and watched the parade approach her through the bars of the cast-iron fence.

Behind the line of flags was a shabby-looking band, that had now stopped playing, and whose members were carrying their instruments under their arms. Behind it came straggling files of shabby marchers, who carried signs reading WHAT WE WANT IS WORK, WARD TWO UNEMPLOYED COUNCIL, JOBS—NOT RELIEF, and other slogans.

She recognized one or two familiar Cabbagetown faces, but most of the marchers were strangers to her, foreign-looking men and women, who were singing in a babel of languages. Some of the women shouted to Myrla, inviting her to accompany them in their march to Queen's Park.

A few of the marchers were middle-aged workingmen, some wearing red berets and with their war medals pinned to their shirts. The tail end of the parade was made up largely of younger men, who did not sing but waved and blew kisses at her as they passed. In the last file of marchers was Ken Tilling, carrying a large banner that read, WAGES, NOT TWENTY CENT A DAY SLAVERY IN GOVT. CAMPS! Ken was staring resolutely ahead of him as he marched, and did not notice her.

When she first caught sight of him Myrla felt her knees grow weak, and she had to prevent herself from crying out his name. Then her feelings turned to a maternal pity for him, for he looked so—so decent and—dedicated, and so out of place. Her warm glow of affection for him changed to a vague feeling of humiliation, as one person feels when unknown to another he catches him in a shameful act.

She watched him disappear along the street before she turned and made her way back towards the centre of the park again. This time she was on the lookout for a two-dollar trick.

9

Ken stood leaning with his back against a tree, out of the sun, on the outskirts of the large crowd of marchers and demonstrators who were listening to the Communist orators such as Tim Buck speaking from the raised platform of the wooden bandstand in Queen's Park, behind the Ontario legislative building.

The Communist Party leaders exhorted the crowd to "action" and "proletarian solidarity" and other left-wing slogans of the day. They cried that it was inspiring to see so many downtrodden representatives of the city's unemployed taking part in the demonstration. They said this sort of peaceful "democratic" gathering was a foretaste of what the "union-busting reactionary drunken Premier, Mitch Hepburn" could expect in the future. One of them ended by crying, "Remember your Russian comrades' attack on the Petrograd Winter Palace!" which was met by a sustained cheer.

Ken glanced around him at the other marchers, all of whom had assembled here from other parts of the city and suburbs. Some of those from the West End were very well organized, their European and Jewish members wearing red berets, trade-union wedge caps, and arm bands. Most of the Anglo-Saxon groups from the East End and the suburbs wore their everyday clothes.

Several uniformed policemen stood beside a radio cruiser near the bandstand, while Ken spotted many plainclothes policemen who had infiltrated the crowd. A small troop of mounted city police stood on a nearby street, holding their mounts by their bridles.

When the speeches were over a band played "God Save The King," and followed it with the *Internationale*. The crowd, now enlarged with the addition of hundreds of idle spectators, stood at attention and removed its hats for at least one of the anthems, which one depending on their political beliefs.

A man jumped to the microphone, and over the loudspeakers cried to the crowd to "organize a spontaneous demonstration" to march to the main door of the Parliament Buildings behind him. As some of the outlying groups began drifting in the direction of the legislature, a uniformed police inspector grabbed the microphone from the speaker's hand, to be greeted with loud boos and hisses from the crowd. Ken saw the inspector speaking with the C.P. leaders, shaking his head.

A voice from behind him asked him for a match, and Ken turned to see a short shabby man standing at his elbow. The man wore a pair of steel-rimmed glasses, a badly-knotted necktie, and a shirt whose collar was clean but crumpled, as if it had been washed but never ironed. He wore a half-smiling expression as if savouring a secret joke.

Ken pulled some kitchen matches from his pocket and gave them to the little man.

"Quite a crowd," the man said, after lighting his handmade cigarette.

"It's not a bad turnout," Ken answered.

"Were you one of the marchers?"

"Yes." Ken pointed to his furled banner leaning against the tree.

"Where from?"

"Down in Ward Two. Cabbagetown."

"Oh yes. I saw your bunch marching in. What did you think of the speeches?"

"Not much. It's the same old stuff all the time."

"Didn't you like the heartening summing-up, about storming the Winter Palace?"

Ken shrugged. He wondered if the man was a fascist, a police *provocateur*, or what.

The little man seemed to sense what Ken was thinking. "I'm just a fellow worker the same as you. Are you a C.P. member?"

"No. I don't belong to any party."

"I thought you came with the marchers?"

"So I did."

"Do you mean that you marched up here with the Comrades without being forced to? Just on your own?"

"Certainly I did," answered Ken, becoming angry with the man. "Why?"

"Because I think all the unemployed should have joined in. They'll never do anything for us unless we stick together. This crowd doesn't represent one in a thousand of the people who are out of work in this town alone."

"I'm glad to see there was at least one sensible person in the march. You know though, don't you, that this thing isn't to help the unemployed at all? This is a recruiting drive for the Communist Party."

"I don't believe that."

"I'm not asking you to. I'm only pointing out some things *I* believe in, and you can agree or disagree as you see fit."

"You're within your rights there."

"Do you believe the Communists are out to better the lot of the unemployed?"

"Yes I do."

"Or do you think that the C.P. wants to represent the working class—I know they claim they do already—and sit in that stone building over there as the Soviet dictators of this province?"

"No!"

"Do you think they'd have any strength at all if it wasn't for the people out of work, and this world-wide depression?"

Ken didn't answer.

"Yet you're sympathetic to them."

"I'm sympathetic with all the parties of the Left. I'm a socialist."

"So am I, son," the little man said. "I'm against the C.P. because I know it's led by opportunists and failed workers who want power only. Power! The same thing Hepburn wants, and Mackenzie King wants, and Sir Joseph Flavelle and his capitalist cohorts want. And without unemployment and discontent they'll never get it. So why should they want to destroy their only basis for achieving power? Hey, tell me that!"

"I believe there's a lot of dedicated Communists," said Ken.

"I agree with you. Marx and Engels were dedicated social and political scientists, but they're dead. Jesus Christ believed in something great—'Do unto others as you would have them do unto you.'—perhaps the greatest sentence in any language, but He's dead too. Today's so-called Christians have slipped a long way from the teachings of Jesus."

A scuffle began in the crowd across the park, and several uniformed policemen headed in that direction. The mounted officers climbed into their stirrups.

Ken said, "I wonder what's happening over there?"

"It's probably somebody who doesn't agree with the Communist Party line," the little man said.

Things quieted down as the crowd broke up into small groups and became involved in loud and heated discussions. Other marchers stood around, in their berets and white shirts giving the park a picnic air.

"The Nazis do these things much better," the little man said. "They too organize workers' demonstrations, not out of a phoney love for the working class but to win their support. Caesar's bread-and-circuses moved to Nuremburg. The Commies are amateurs in comparison."

Ken was puzzled by the little man, and was trying to figure him out.

Another disturbance broke out on the far edge of the crowd, and many people began pushing their way in its direction. Ken said over his shoulder to the man, "I'm going over and see what it's all about," as he began walking away. He was eager to get into whatever it was.

"Let's go this way," the man said, pointing out that by skirting the crowd they could reach the fracas quicker than by pushing their way through the mob.

After they had gone about a hundred yards to the southeast section of the park they saw a group of about a hundred college students being chased towards the fence surrounding St. Michael's College, the slower runners being kicked and pummelled by several big European immigrant workmen.

"Look at that!" Ken shouted to his companion. "What the hell right have those goddam punks got to come here to make fun of us! I'd like to bash in every one of their well-fed faces! A bunch of fascist dogans from Rosedale! My mother always claimed you couldn't trust a mick!"

"Don't let it get you," said Ken's companion soothingly, taking his arm. "They're Catholic students but they're not fascists. They just don't understand, that's all. Don't show as much intolerance as those hunky comicals that are kicking them."

"Oh, to hell with that crap!" shouted Ken. "I don't like their kind. Maybe if *their* families were on the pogey, and their old man wasn't able to pay their way to college, they'd have more sense."

He left his companion and ran over to where small groups of students and demonstrators were spilling from the massed crowd. There were several individual fights going on. A tall thin young man wearing a St. Mike's blazer crossed Ken's path, grinning smugly to himself. Ken shouted, "Hey, you!" and the young man slowed down and looked around. Ken grabbed him by a lapel and punched him as hard as he could on the mouth. The student broke from his grasp, and ran as fast he could towards his fellows, a hand holding his face.

Somebody grabbed Ken by his shirt, and he found himself in the centre of a slashing punching kicking mob. He lashed out in all directions, while dodging the kicking feet. He noticed a mounted cop heading towards him, with a big foreign-looking demonstrator wearing a union cap holding on to the horse's martingale. The policeman was leaning over the horse's withers slashing at the man with his long riding crop. Ken ran into the anonymous safety of the crowd.

When his former companion found him again, the little man said, "Well, you got into it, didn't you? Do you feel any better now since striking your blow against reaction?"

"I feel great!" Ken said, and he did. An exultation seemed to possess him, as he remembered the crunch of his knuckles on the tall student's teeth. "Brother, if you knew how many bastards I've met in my life that I hit with that one punch!"

"It looks as if the demonstration's over, thanks to all you hot-heads. Let's get out of here."

They walked out of the park on to Queen's Park Crescent, and followed its eastern curve around the legislative building, past the provincial police garage, past the building that would later house the Forensic Psychiatric Clinic, past the Connaught Laboratories, where Drs. Banting and Best had discovered insulin, and where Ken had listened to the laboratory dogs barking on quiet Sunday mornings as he sat on a park bench outside, and strolled east along College Street.

They halted once, as the little man introduced himself to Ken as Noah Masterson. Ken said, "I'm Ken Tilling." They shook hands.

Masterson told the younger man that he had been in the radical movement long before the 1914-1918 war, in which he had served in the Canadian Army, in the 4th Mounted Rifles.

"When I was younger I was a boomer all through the States," he said. "I knew all the old timers, Eugene Debs, Robert Minor—before the Comicals got to him—Emma Goldman, Big Bill Hayworth, the whole lot of 'em."

"I was afraid you were a stool-pigeon just pumping me," Ken said, as both rolled cigarettes as they walked.

"Me! In 1919 I led a bunch of veterans in a jobless march right up to those very Parliament Buildings in the park, and even then the cops rode us down with their horses."

"What happened then?"

"The same thing as always happens, most of the veterans backed down. A few of us stuck it, and we went back again—and again. The papers played it up, and we got some backing from the brass hats, the old generals and colonels we'd fought under. They made the governments—city, provincial and federal—give us jobs. They asked me, because I was just young and crazy enough to be the leader, 'Do you represent Canada's jobless veterans?' I said, 'I represent about a hundred war veterans sitting out on the front steps.' They took down our names, and within two weeks every one of us had a job. A bunch of them got jobs as conductors and motor-men on the street railway, some of them began braking on the CNR, a few became postmen. I got a job as a city garbageman."

"Is that what you do now?"

"No, I guess you could call me an 'unemployable,' if that's the new word they're using today. I wasn't eligible for a city pension, but I went before the Board up at Christie Street Veterans Hospital and they increased my war pension ten per cent. I was gassed and got a Blighty in the back at Ypres (he pronounced it "Wipers") in 1916."

When they reached the dingy downtown street on which Masterson lived, he invited Ken up to his room for a cup of tea. They climbed through rising dust whorls up to the third floor of a decaying old house, and entered an attic room with an acutely slanting ceiling.

"It's lucky we're both short," Ken said, having to stoop to look out through the narrow window in the front of the room.

"Yes. Everything has its compensations they say. This was probably the housemaids' room when this crummy neighbourhood was genteel. Poor little skivvies were too damned hungry and low-paid to become too big or too tall for the low ceilings then. Generations are getting taller now; even with the low rations of the Depression the sons are taller than their fathers were."

Ken sat down on a chair while Masterson put a kettle to boil on a rusty gas plate.

"I see you do a lot of reading," said Ken, pointing to some upended orange crates packed with books.

"I read quite a lot; always did. Now I've got time to read things I used to put off when I was younger."

Ken went to the bookcases and read a few of the titles.

"You have some good books here, Mr. Masterson," he said.

"Never mind the Masterson; just call me Noah."

"I can't seem to get interested in the classics," Ken said.

"Neither could I at your age. When you're young there's too many women to love, too many places to see, too many better things to do. I used to think some of the Greek and Roman writers were of no interest to a guy who wanted to change the system. I used to think, 'What do those guys who lived a couple of thousand years ago know about today's problems?' Now I've read a few of them I see that they had to face the same things we do. There were even young fellows like I was—and like you are—who were trying to change *their* systems overnight."

Noah filled a small teapot with water. "Where did you say you lived, Ken?" he asked.

"Timothy Place, down in Cabbagetown."

"I know the district, but there's so many of those small streets and lanes around there that I don't know Timothy Place. Do you live with your people?"

"No, my father deserted my mother and me. My mother died three weeks ago. I'm moving into a room next week."

"I'm sorry about your mother, Ken. How old was she?"

"Forty-four."

"She was too young to die." He pulled two cracked mugs from a cupboard, took a pair of spoons from a drawer in the dresser, and a can of evaporated milk with two holes driven into its top, from the cupboard that had held the cups.

"Have you found a place to live yet, Ken?"

"Yes. The woman next door to us, a Mrs. Wells, is going to board me for a while."

"Good. You may as well stay down there where you know the people."

They talked about unemployment, the lack of differences between R. B. Bennett and Mackenzie King, compared Hitler to Mussolini. Noah poured their mugs of tea. "Condensed milk, or that stuff there, is no good in tea, but I can't keep fresh milk here."

Ken told Noah that he'd worked in the twenty-cent-a-day relief camps, and had actually helped build a sewage disposal plant at Trenton RCAF base for those wages. He told the older man that he too had ridden the rods—"not the rods really, but the tops or inside the boxcars; the rods can't be ridden much today, not on the modern freight cars. I've been all over the States, and down into Mexico, and out to Vancouver."

Noah nodded his gray balding head and smiled. "Good, good. Some day you'll drive your kids out past that sewage disposal plant at Trenton, and you'll point it out to them, and tell 'em you built it for twenty cents a day, and they won't believe you."

Ken laughed. "I'll never have a wife and kids if things keep on like they are now."

Noah shook his head. "I don't know what's going to happen to you kids," he said.

"What are you politically?" Ken asked him.

Noah leaned back in his chair and polished his glasses with a teatowel. "I guess I'm what can be called a tired radical now. At one time I was a member of the Socialist Labour Party."

"I met an ex-Wobbly, just like you, in the Rupert Street cells in Winnipeg," Ken said, interrupting.

"There's still a few of us old mossbacks around, but both those parties are dead. It was great while it lasted though." He tilted his head back and shook it in bewildered thought. "They were the only real native North-American radical movements," he said. "Later I joined the Socialist Party. I was an organizer in Pittsburgh for them, for a while, before 1914."

"How do you stand today?"

"I guess I'm still a socialist, though I haven't much use for that new CCF Party. Too many ex-preachers in the ranks, too many fruity professors. They want to change the working stiff's morals more than they want to fill his belly. They're against beer, against gambling, and for all I know maybe they're against screwing—all the pleasures, the free pleasures of the poor, the last one anyway, as Bernard Shaw says.

"I've no love for the Communist established church, or for its Trotskyite opponents either. Mr. Two-gash-willy and Mr. Bernstein are both a pain in the butt to me. They're Stalin and Trotsky's real names. The whole Communist movement is breaking up into evangelical sects: Trotskyites, Fieldites, Lovestoneites. They're getting harder to keep track of than the Protestants."

He laughed and struck his knee with his hand. "One of the signs this afternoon in the park read, 'Free Tom Mooney!' Why, son, if those labour-fakers in the park ever heard Tom Mooney speak they'd all throw a wingding. Free the Scottsboro Boys, free this, free that—bah!"

Ken smiled. "What radical party will end up on top?" he asked.

"Stalin's gang will, I think. They're the best organized, and they have the Soviet treasury behind them. As for me I haven't liked any

Soviet group since they shot down the sailors of Kronstadt in 1921."

Ken refused a second mug of tea, and they talked about books.

Noah said, "I don't care much for the new novels, especially the so-called proletarian school. This book here—" he took a small book from one of the shelves "—is the only one that'll live of all those written during our lifetime."

Ken read the words on the dust jacket. *Jurgen*, by James Branch Cabell. "I never heard of it before," he said.

"I'll loan it to you. Take it with you." Noah forced it into Ken's hands. "Now tell me what books you've read," he commanded.

Ken named some whose titles came to mind, as Noah nodded his head in approval. "You've done a lot of reading for a young fellow," the older man said. "Where do you get your books?"

"I borrow them from the public library at Gerrard and Broadview."

"Keep it up, you'll never regret it."

"I only read so much because I'm out of work and there's not much else to do."

"That doesn't matter. Suppose you'd been working steady and you'd been laid off last week, you'd be in exactly the same boat you're in today except you wouldn't have read the books you have."

"I'd sooner be working, and have read nothing but the figures on a pay envelope the last few years. Look at me, Noah. I left high school in 1929, the second form at tech., and since then every dollar I've earned could be changed into half-dollars and they wouldn't fill that teapot. Do you wonder that I'm bitter?"

Noah questioned him, and with a little prodding got Ken to talk about his mother's drinking, and about such friends as Billy Addington, Theodore East and Bob McIsaacs. He even told the older man about Myrla Patson.

Noah was amused by Ken's description of Theodore East. "Don't be too bitter about him," he said. "He's not a fascist any more than—

than those college kids in the park this afternoon. By the way, you're not anti-Catholic are you?"

Ken smiled. "No, I don't think so. My mother was though, in a sort of negative way. Where she came from they were all true-blue Orangemen and Conservative Protestants. Down in our neighbourhood we still call Catholics dogans or micks. We also call Jews sheeneys, and Central Europeans hunkies, Italians wops. They call us limeys, or more often bronchos. It doesn't mean much. Bob McIsaacs was a Catholic, and so are several guys I've chummed around with."

"I don't think you'll ever be a Communist, Ken," Noah said. "Or a practicing socialist either. You may believe that socialism will come to this country some day, but I think you're incapable of helping it much." He held up his hand to shush Ken's unspoken protest. "The trouble with you, Ken, is that you're a rebel, and for a negative reason. It may sound funny but real rebels never make good revolutionaries."

"How do I fit in then?"

"You don't. That's why you haven't joined a political party. You're a born critic, a born loner. You call yourself a Red, but you're only interested in throwing out the things that helped make your mother a drunk, or that friend of yours get scalded to death in the hot chocolate, or your old sweetheart become a whore. You're against poverty and the government's inability to do anything about it, and you hate the fascists because you think of them as an arm of capitalist reaction. You want to believe everything good about the Jews, and none of the bad, because you know the anti-Semites are wrong. You're an agnostic, and you have to be religious to follow any religion, political or otherwise."

"I'm an atheist."

"I doubt it, because that's a religion too. You're an agnostic if you're anything at all. Do you think that believing there is no God changes anything that bothers you? I don't know whether there's a

God or not, but don't be an atheist because a lot of your fellow radicals claim there's no God. Read Clarence Darrow and Bob Ingersoll. Read Bernard Shaw's long preface to *Androcles And The Lion* if you want to learn about religion. And after you've read them all, read G. K. Chesterton."

Ken said, "I'm a materialist. I believe man has to find his own way around this planet."

"So do I, but with the help of something, maybe what we call God."

"What the hell are you, a Christian socialist!" Ken shouted.

Noah laughed. "You're even more bitter than I thought. You've come to some pretty good conclusions for a man your age, about politics and economic theories. You did it with your own system of trial and error—by asking yourself, will it work, is it good for the most, will it help them who need it? Do the same with other things, like religion. Don't try to think with your emotions. Because you know that a great many religious people are phonies or bigoted fatheads, don't let it make you say, 'There is no God.' Think out your own answers."

When Ken left Noah's room he carried the older man's copy of *Jurgen* under his arm. He read it that evening, amused by it, but failing to see what made it so special in Noah Masterson's eyes. He felt sure, however, that the old man was wrong about it surviving his generation.

After he laid the borrowed book carefully on the floor beside his downstairs couch he marvelled that of the two people he had met in life so far who would probably exert an influence on him until he died, one had been a criminal, a professional safe-cracker, and the other an ex-garbageman and radical.

The main things he had learned from Noah were that a political equation could be mathematically correct but none the less wrong, and that tolerance was not something you gave to the ideas of an enemy but also to those of a friend.

He picked up the old dollar-ninety-eight alarm clock from the floor and read it in the light from the window. It was twenty-five past one. From above his head he heard Dorothy Cluff go to the bathroom, then heard her descending the stairs. She hesitated a moment before she opened the door to the middle room.

"Come in, Dot," he said.

She stood at the foot of his couch in her white cotton nightgown.

"Strip your nightie off and stand in the light from the window," he said.

"Oh—you!" she exclaimed in mock exasperation, but did as he asked her.

"Now come and get in with me, and we'll see if we can start your family off before you move out with your brother Royce."

She drew back. "Jim's going to be the father of our kids," she said gravely. "I wouldn't do nothing like that to him."

"That's why I love you," he said. "Hurry up and crawl in. I'm getting cold."

He sold his mother's furniture for twenty-two dollars to a second-hand dealer, and with part of the money paid a month's room and board to Mrs. Wells. When he moved next door, Jim and Dorothy Cluff moved out to the suburbs. "Come out and see us sometime, Ken," Dorothy said. "South of Bloor just west of the cemetery across the Humber bridge."

Myrla Patson had not seen big fat Dorothy, the Icelandic Brunhild of the CN Lady boats, since Dolly, as she had begun to call herself when she met Charley, had married him and moved to his adopted small city in Southwestern Ontario.

Charley Ching was neither white nor a widower, but a Chinese restaurant proprietor in his middle thirties who had met Dorothy one evening in a small sleazy hotel on Queen Street, opposite the law courts of Osgoode Hall. This particular hotel had a free-and-easy policy of co-educational, co-racial drinking and dancing, and quite a few of the girls who worked Chinatown picked up their tricks there.

With Charley it had been love at first sight with Dorothy, who would make three petite little Chinese girls, even if the country's laws at the time would have allowed him to import them. He proposed marriage to her *after* they'd made love in a Chinese rooming house on Chestnut Street, and she'd accepted before he changed his mind or the opium wore off. She stressed the *after* significance of his proposal to Myrla as a sign that it must be true love, as most tricks she'd met, white, black or yellow, had wanted only to bid her a large goodbye and get out of the room at such times.

"The on'y thing about him, Myrla, is he calls me Dolloty, so I've changed my name to Dolly, that he can say real good."

"So long as you're happy," Myrla said cynically, thinking that Dorothy would be back on Dundas Street within a month, with all the money out of the restaurant damper in her stocking top.

"Maybe you don't think I'm smart being married to a Chinaman—a Chinese," Dolly said. "Believe me, I think it's the smartest thing I ever done. He's a good guy, Myrla, really a good guy. He says I won't have to do no work at his place, and all he wants me to do is sit around and drink tea, eat chocolates, get my hair rinsed regular, and be good to him."

"Good luck."

"He drives a snappy new Durant, an' do you know what he calls me?"

"I can guess."

"His Lotus Leaf. Cute, eh?"

"It brings tears to my eyes."

Nearly a year had passed now, and Dorothy had not returned to the Toronto streets. Myrla had lost Dolly Ching's address long before, and she had changed rooming houses several times since Dorothy's marriage, though always staying in the same general neighbourhood. She had acquired a patina to her already stained brassiness, and she carried herself with a take-it-or-leave-it air that was almost a sneer.

She had had her hair bobbed short and bleached, so that hardly anyone who had known the younger Myrla Patson would have recognized her now. Her mother had made it plain one Sunday that she was no longer welcome around the house, but she still sent Bertha five dollars a week for Derek's board.

One morning she met her brother Donnie, who was now a telegraph messenger, and she had stopped him as he almost passed her on his bike, and had asked him about Derek and the family. Donnie had been shocked by the change in her, and kept repeating that he wouldn't have known her if she hadn't called to him. He finally told her that Derek was fine, and was getting pretty big. The baby had suffered from whooping cough during the winter but his grandma had cured him by boiling a pot of tar on the stove, and making him inhale the fumes. Derek had become quite a chatterbox now that he could speak pretty good.

George Patson was just about the same except he was real old-looking now, and his hands shook all the time. Her mother had to feed him with a spoon. The old man had sneaked out of the house a couple of times, and one day a policeman had brought him home from Riverdale Park, and said he'd found him wandering through the weeds along the river bank, and had been afraid he'd fall into the water.

Donnie told Myrla that her mother's hair had now turned quite gray. Bertha had been sewing doll dresses all summer for a toy company, and with the few dollars a month she earned, his own pay and Myrla's five dollars a week, they were managing to scrape along. Margaret had passed her high school entrance exams with honours, and she was going to go to Eastern High School of Commerce in September.

Myrla had to fight against the feeling of homesickness that Donnie brought her. She questioned her brother about Derek. "Do you think he'd know me now?" she asked.

"I don't know, Myrla. Gee, you're so thin and changed—your hair . . . I nearly didn't know you myself." He looked her up and down. "You must have a good job to dress like—"

"Does Derek ever say, 'Mama'?"

"He calls Ma, 'Ganny', and Dad, 'Gandad'."

"Doesn't he ever ask for me? Doesn't he ever ask about me at all?" she asked, gripping the handlebars of Donnie's bike.

Donnie saw how much it meant to her. "Oh sure he does. He looks at your picture, you know, the one you had taken in your uniform at the restaurant, and he says, 'That's Mama,' plain as day."

"Oh I'm glad!" Myrla exclaimed. "What else does he do?"

"He plays out in the yard. We've got a cat now, a big one we call Whitey, and he plays with the cat and pulls its tail—"

"The cat doesn't scratch him, does it?"

"Oh no. He's pretty tame. Decky sings too. We always call him Decky because that's what he calls himself. We couldn't get him to stop singing "Jingle Bells" after Christmas. He doesn't know all the words, but he sounds so cute."

Before they parted she made Donnie promise to have Margaret bring Derek to the corner of Sackville and Queen at half past eleven Sunday, when she knew her mother would be at church. Donnie had to swear on their mother's body to do as she asked before she'd let go of the handlebars.

Shortly after eleven o'clock Myrla was waiting beside the wine warehouse at Sackville and Queen. After what seemed hours she saw young Margaret leading Derek by the hand as they crossed Sydenham Street, and she had to hold herself from running up to meet them.

When they arrived at the corner, Margaret stared at Myrla's hair in shocked surprise. She pushed the baby in his mother's direction, unable to do anything but stare at the changes in her older sister's appearance. Myrla paid no attention to her, but devoured the baby with her eyes. He was so much bigger than when she had seen him last, and he'd looked so comical striding along on his sturdy little legs.

Stooping over she said, "Hello, darling."

"He thought I was taking him to the store for some candy," Margaret said.

"Why sure he is. Do you know me, sweetheart?"

"Look, Decky, that's your Mama," Margaret said, as he tried to hide behind her skirt.

"Isn't he lovely!" Myrla said, beginning to cry. "I don't know what I'll ever do without him." She leaned against the building and sobbed.

"Why don't you come up to the house and see Mama," Margaret said. "She'll be home from church just after twelve. She's not sore at you for not coming around."

"No, Maggie, I couldn't do that."

"Why don't you come back and live with us?"

Myrla shook her head.

"Go and give your pretty Mama a kiss, Decky," Margaret coaxed the little boy.

Myrla bent over quickly and kissed the top of his black curly head, then drew away, as Margaret stared at her in amazement. "I don't want him to get scared of me," she said. "After all babies forget people pretty quick."

"Don't you want to give him a real kiss?" Margaret asked her.

"No. Not now. I'll have to go now. Thanks, Maggie, for bringing him down to see me. Don't say anything about it to Ma." She pulled a ten-dollar bill from her purse and handed it to her sister. "Get something to wear to high school," she said. "I'm glad you passed with honours."

She looked east along Queen to where a streetcar was just leaving the Sumach Street stop. She gazed deep into the puzzled face of her little son until the hot tears filled her eyes. Then she swung around, waited on the curb until the streetcar came to a stop, and boarded it without looking back.

In September 1936 Ken Tilling began work as a clerk in another grocery warehouse, but a much bigger one than McDonald's Wholesale had been. The job had been secured for him by Noah Masterson who had served under the company's general manager during the war. The work proved much easier than his job at McDonald's and the pay was twice as much.

The foreman of his section of the warehouse was a young man, not much older than Ken, named Barney Hackett. When there were no trucks to load or unload, or orders to make up, he and Barney would keep busy bagging bulk goods. Ken would argue with Barney about the Spanish Civil War, which had begun in July.

"I don't see why you're so interested in the Spaniards, Tilling," Barney would say. "I say the Royal Navy should go down there and blast both sides off the face of the map."

"That's the trouble with people in this country," Ken would answer. "You'll wait until Hitler and the other fascists are right here outside your door, before you'll even bother finding out what it's all about."

"Quit worrying about things that don't concern you, Ken. Hell, they've been fighting in that part of the world for a thousand years."

Ken was almost pathologically interested in the war, and he read every word in the three Toronto papers dealing with the Civil War news. At times he was elated, but most of the time, as the rebel fascist troops advanced up from the south and from Morocco, taking Seville, advancing inexorably on Madrid, he became almost sick with worry. To him the Loyalist militia were his own people, the poor little guys from all over the world who always got the dirty end of the stick. The

Loyalists were fighting for the things he most believed in, while he was four thousand miles from the fighting, bagging raisins and beans.

One evening a newspaper photograph showed a Polish kid, wearing a wool turtleneck black sweater and baggy corduroy pants, sitting beside a road as a newly-formed battalion of the International Brigades, made up of French, Poles, anti-Nazi German refugees, Englishmen, marched past behind him. The kid was also wearing a bandolier of ammunition and had a rifle in his hand. They were heading for the University City sector of the Madrid defences, where General Mola was expected to make his big push, into the country's capital, and to the welcoming cheers of what this fascist general called his "fifth column" inside the city. Ken knew then that somehow, and he didn't care how, he had to join the Polish kid and his comrades.

The last battle between the workers and the fascist reactionaries had begun. It was time now to put aside the political theorizing of the Stracheys, Laskys and Shaws, the proletarian editorials of Mike Gold and the intellectual Commies of the *New Masses*, the pamphlets of Engels and Proudhon. Those who *really* believed in a better world were already manning the barricades blocking the entrance of the four columns of professionals, Moors and fascists advancing on Madrid.

At times he fretted and worried that the war in Spain would be lost before he could get there. "Look what those rats Baldwin and Anthony Eden are doing with their non-intervention farce!" he'd shout at Barney.

"I suppose you want them to give the war to your Red friends?"

"The Loyalists aren't Reds. They're just guys like you and me. Britain is actually helping Franco and Mola and his other fascist generals, just like Mussolini, and the German pocket battleships in the Mediterranean. Sometimes I wish I was a Mexican or a Jap or anything but British. Look at this picture of the Spanish fascist Duke of Alba conferring so friendly-like with the public school fairies in the British Foreign Office. As thick as thieves! Bastards all of them!"

"You'll blow a gasket, Tilling, if you don't forget those things."

In the evenings Ken attended all the rallies for the Spanish Loyalists he could get to attend. He gave as much as he could afford to the collections taken to buy medical supplies for the Loyalist people. The thing he noticed at all these meetings was that the Communists took the lead in their organization and in the work they did, and he would argue mightily with Noah Masterson over it.

"I don't care what you think of the Communists, or how you dislike their theories," he would say. "Maybe they are opportunists and dupes of the Russian government. But right now, when every member of every working class in the world should be behind the Spanish people, they're the only ones who are doing anything concrete to help them. I don't care what their motives are. To hell with the motives!"

"We'll see," Noah would say quietly. "We'll see."

On Saturday afternoons, when the warehouse was closed, Ken and Barney would go downtown to a show, sometimes to Shea's Hippodrome where they'd laugh themselves silly over Olson and Johnson, George Burns and Gracie Allen, Ed Wynn, Ken Murray, and many other comedy headliners, and where they'd both hear and see such bands as The Dorsey Brothers, Wayne King, Guy Lombardo, Kay Kyser, Shep Fields, or Fred Waring and His Pennsylvanians. Other times they'd go to the Roxy burlesque house and watch Sliding Billy Watson, Smith and Dale, Sally Rand, and an everchanging weekly show that featured companies straight from Minsky's. On Saturday evening, after eating a cheap supper at Bowles Lunch, they'd go to the Mutual Street Arena to watch the Toronto Maple Leafs play, or see a fight or wrestling card.

One late fall Saturday afternoon as Ken and Barney came out of the Roxy, Ken glanced across the street and saw a blonde Myrla Patson walking west from Bay Street. Even with her emaciated figure and blonde hair he knew he wasn't mistaken. There had been too many nights when he'd lain awake in boxcars and flophouses thinking of her not to remember the way she walked, the dimple in her right cheek when she smiled, the way she used to say, "Don't be so crude, Ken," when he'd make a small off-colour joke. She was the one girl he'd remember all his life.

He stopped and stared across the street at her.

"Who are you looking at?" Barney asked.

"That girl there. The one with the short bobbed blonde hair."

"Oh, Ken, why she's—"

"I know her," Ken said.

"Are you bragging?"

"I've got to speak to her," Ken said. "You go and eat. I'll see you later at the Arena." He hurried through the traffic to the other side of the street, leaving a bewildered Barney staring after him.

Turning up the collar of his overcoat against the heavy wet snow that was falling he followed her. She was hatless, but was wearing a sealskin coat and fur-topped overshoes to match. He caught up to her, and matching his step to hers said, "Hello, Myrla."

She was startled, and she turned her head away as soon as she saw who it was. Then she whispered a quick, "Hello," and tried to walk away from him. He kept up with her.

"Don't say it," she said, looking straight ahead.

"I've nothing to say."

"You don't need to come with me. I'm only going along the street a ways."

"I'll walk with you."

"I'd sooner you didn't."

"It's been a long time since we saw each other," he said, trying to make it sound as if nothing had changed between them.

She didn't answer, but walked along with her face averted from his.

"I've often wondered how you were getting along," he said. Her head was bent against the falling snow.

"Well now you know."

"I didn't mean it that way. I've known for a long time. What I meant was, I wondered where you were. I hardly see anybody I used to know a few years ago; it's been months since I saw Theodore East."

They crossed Elizabeth Street. He took her elbow but she shook his hand off.

"I guess you heard my mother died last year?"

"No. I'm sorry to hear it." she said without looking at him.

"How are your folks?"

"You tell me!"

"Why do you act like this, Myrla?" Then as he tried to make it sound casual he said, "You don't need to be stuck-up with me. I'm your old boyfriend, remember?"

"Please leave me alone."

"I'd like to talk to you. I didn't walk this far just to act smart or rub anything in. I know pretty near everything that's happened to you, or I can guess. I'm not going to try to save you, or lecture you."

"Then leave me alone."

"I can't, Myrla. You're not acting fair with me."

Her upper lip curled back in a sneer. He was tempted to turn and leave her, but he sensed she was ashamed and confused at meeting him again like this.

"After I came back from the States the first time, I tried to get in touch with you. I went down to the restaurant where you used to work, but they told me you didn't work there any more."

"*Annie doesn't live here any more*—It sounds like a sad little song," she said with a nasty little laugh.

He felt like shaking her. They walked along in silence before he said, "Do you still remember the first time I called for you at that house you worked in, in North Toronto? I was so crazy about you, and so ashamed of my shabby clothes, and so shy with you, that I tried to act rotten to cover up how I felt. You're acting rotten to me now because you think I'm only trying to be nice."

"I'm not ashamed of anything," she said. "Why are you trying to pick me up?"

"Because—oh goddamn it, because you're you and I'm me, and we're us!"

She stopped and faced him. "Whatever you want to say, say it," she said. "I can't stand around here in the cold and snow all day."

He saw the lines in her face and how it was coarse and hard, and not half as pretty as it had once been.

He shrugged. "All right, Myrla, if this is the way you want it. I've tried to be decent but I see now it's impossible. Go on, get going. Beat it!"

"I'm sorry, Ken. I'd like to talk to you too."

She brushed the wet snow from her face with the back of a gloved hand. He took her elbow and they walked along the street, past the law courts and across University Avenue. This time she didn't try to shake his hand loose. "Let's go to the women's room of the Rex Hotel. I don't come this far west very often, and nobody knows me there."

Inside the small women's beer parlour they sat down, and Ken ordered two draught beers. "Why did you pick this hotel?"

"I've already told you. I like it here."

"You're still a pretty woman, Myrla."

"Don't kid me, Ken. *You* haven't changed much. Still the handsome kid, but not so shy any more."

As they sipped their beers he told her what he'd been doing the last couple of years. She listened to him silently, smiling faintly once in a while. When he finished she said, "I'm glad things are going good for you. I suppose you've got a girl on the string?"

"No."

"Who're you kidding!"

He asked her again about her family. She hunched her shoulders.

"Don't try to act tough with me," he said. "What about your little boy?"

"Please, Ken, I'll talk about anything but that," she said quietly.

He ordered some more beer, and they drained their glasses.

After drinking a few beers she told him everything that had happened to her since they had last seen each other in the Union Jack Cafe.

"It's your life to live as you please," he said.

"Do you remember that time at the restaurant when you told me we were all beat? I've thought of it plenty of times since. I guess I was beat from the very beginning. Not because I couldn't get a job or anything like that, but because I beat myself. My mother knew what was coming. Years ago, before you even knew me, she knew I'd turn out bad."

Ken thought of Bob McIsaacs. "I don't know much about it, but I think that the real criminal and—well, like you, have a psychological quirk in your makeup. It's not your environment or poverty—" He let his point drift off into the dim light of the room.

Myrla laughed, and her laugh reminded him of the old Myrla, so that he picked up his glass and drank to hide the feelings it brought back to him.

"You always used big words," she said. "Sometimes I tried to remember them so I could look them up in the dictionary."

"It must have been the beer I've drunk that made me come up with that mouthful," he said, and they both laughed.

After a pause Myrla asked, "How is your architecture coming along?"

"Oh that. I'd almost forgotten about it. Sometimes I pick up the odd book from the library on the subject, that's all."

"You could take courses at night, couldn't you?"

"Yes, but I'd need to complete a high school education first, then something else. I have other things in mind."

Myrla stood up, doffed her coat, and draped it over the back of her chair. He noticed how thin she'd become and, combined with the deterioration of her facial beauty (for she had been beautiful not just pretty), her comedown both saddened and angered him.

"Listen, Myrla, never mind about me becoming an architect. Why don't *you* take stock of yourself. You're still a young woman. Get out of this life you're leading. For gawd's sake—"

"You said you wouldn't lecture me."

"I'm sorry."

"You told me once that we all had to find our own solution, remember? I've found mine. Why should I find a job at a few bucks a week when I can make twice as much in an evening?"

He said angrily, "You owe it to your kid."

"I owe it to my kid to make enough money to pay his board and buy him clothes, and later see that he gets a better break than you and I ever got."

They did not speak for some time. Ken drank his beer and ordered more, then toyed with the ash tray, spinning it around on the table.

Suddenly he straightened up and smiled at her. "I nearly forgot something," he said. He pulled some money from his pocket and peeled off a five-dollar bill, handing it to her.

"Do I look as if I need this?" she asked, smiling angrily.

"I owe you this. Remember when you sent me the five when I was out in California?"

Her smile changed from anger to friendliness. "Thanks, but don't leave yourself short."

He waved away her words.

"I'd forgot all about sending you the money that time."

"It came in pretty useful, Myrla. For a while I stayed at the Volunteers of America Mission on Fourth Street in L.A. I used to eat at a Jap restaurant over on Main. Breakfast twenty cents. They gave you a stack of hotcakes and syrup and butter. You helped to keep me fed."

"I'm glad," she said, smiling almost like she once had smiled at him.

After a short silence Ken said, "It's funny how so much can happen to a few ordinary people in six years. Billy Addington, Bob McIsaacs, my mother, have all gone. Mrs. Plummer has moved away, and the Gaffeys. Nobody could tell what would happen to us."

Myrla mentioned several girls she'd gone to school with. "One of them, Jenny Styles, used to live on Blevins Place, she died of an abortion that an old woman on St. David's Street used to do for twenty-five dollars. Maybe you remember the case? Maybe you knew Jenny?"

"No." He shook his head.

"Most of them got married. I remember one of them, her name was Beatrice Oliphant, she lived on Sydenham. Do you know what her ambition was? To move to a house north of the Danforth, with hardwood floors."

They both laughed, but each knew how important even hardwood floors could be to a teen-age girl inviting a new boy friend home. There hadn't been many hardwood floors in Cabbagetown.

"Did Beatrice realize her ambition?" Ken asked.

"I don't know. I haven't met any of them for years." And added, "Not that I'd want to."

"I guess that brings us back to you and me?"

"What is that creep East doing now?"

"I can't say. The last time I saw him he was still working for the government, as a clerk or something."

"That kind always seem to get along."

"Getting along is a career with them. When they see a small opportunity they grab it. They don't let it pass like people like us might."

Myrla said, "Ken, let's just sit here and talk about us."

"Great! What about us?"

"Well, about the things we talked about that first night at the Riverdale rink."

"I was crazy in those clays; I said everything wrong. I guess I was so much in love with you I didn't know *what* I was saying half the time."

"I remember you telling me that people were happy on Sunday mornings because that was the one day they were free."

"Did I say *that*?"

"I never forgot it. I used to wait for Sunday morning—but let's talk about—let's begin where we began that night."

"Okay. *May I have this skate with you?*"

They both burst into laughter.

So they talked about the weather, and about Christmas not being far off.

"Do you know something, Ken? We never had a song we could call 'our song' did we?"

"I think we did. 'Don't Blame Me.'"

She pursed her lips and shook her head.

"There's one song that came out about four years back that always reminds me of you. I heard it the other night, I think it was Ray Noble's orchestra playing it. I first heard Bing Crosby sing it on his Primo Cigar program. Remember, he used to sing for fifteen minutes every evening, just about suppertime, sponsored by Primo Cigars—"

"What's the name of it?" Myrla asked impatiently.

" 'I Don't Stand a Ghost of a Chance With You.' I guess it turned out to be true. It started, *I need your love so badly, for, oh, I love you madly. But I don't*—Something like that."

"Do you know what song always reminds me of you?"

"No."

"One called, 'My Silent Love.' The Street Singer, what was his name, Arthur Tracy? Well anyways he used to sing it."

"Everything's gone; it all blew away," Ken said. "After that night up at Riverdale I didn't hate my job at the soap works any more. All day I packed cartons of Flako, and thought ahead to six o'clock when I could rush home and clean up to come and see you."

Myrla bit her lip. "Ken, I once asked you to tell me about the movie stars in Hollywood. Did you see any?"

"Just a few. One night I stood in a crowd outside the Ambassador Hotel in Los Angeles and watched the guests going inside to a big party or something. I meant to remember all the stars' names so I could tell you, but I've forgotten most of them. I remember W. C. Fields and Johnny Weissmuller and Mary Astor and Norma Shearer—"

"Were the actresses the same as they are on the screen?"

"Just the same. They're little women, about your size."

"I'll bet they're beautiful," she said.

He told her about California, about Fresno and San Francisco, then about meeting Noah Masterson, and about wanting to go to the war in Spain. The beer had now gone to their heads, and they were both happy and loquacious. It was warm in the small dingy beer parlour, and soon they forgot who and what they were.

Ken smiled at Myrla across the table and caught her crying. She was smiling to herself and listening to him, but the tears were running down her cheeks. She brushed them off with her fingers.

"I'd better go now, Ken," she said.

"Where to? Can I take you anywhere?"

"No. Just don't follow me, please."

"No, I won't." There was nothing left but some old tattered memories and regrets.

Myrla pulled on her coat and her gloves. "It was always you who left me before," she said.

He nodded. "I'm sorry, Myrla, about—about everything."

"There's nothing to be sorry about," she said, regaining her street veneer. "I get along okay." She buttoned her coat, put her gloved hands in the pockets, and standing widelegged, looked down at him. "So-long, Ken, and thanks."

"Good luck, Myrla."

He watched her cross the floor to the doorway. She turned then and blew him a kiss. Then she was gone.

**12**

Noah Masterson took Ken to an exhibition of prints one evening in January. The older man spent quite a lot of time explaining what he should look for in them, but to Ken one was no different from another, though there were some he liked better, in the pictorial sense.

"I didn't think there was so much to learn about pictures," Ken said.

"There isn't that much. Interest in painting, in any art, is the most important thing. To enjoy them it's better not to have much knowledge about techniques or the various schools, or even about the artists themselves. In that last room you were drawn to the print of the girl in the orange blouse because your eye told you it was beautiful. As it turned out it's probably the best thing in the exhibition."

They spent some time in one of the gallery rooms hung with several line drawings. Ken found these more interesting than the colour prints.

"That's because you're interested in architectural symmetry."

Ken laughed. "I know no more about architecture than I do about painting," he said.

"But you're *interested* in it, see?"

"You mean I used to be."

Noah talked to him about line drawings, about George Grosz, whose early drawings were sometimes reproduced in the *Masses*. "That was the old *Masses* not the *New Masses*," he emphasized. "Paul Klee is another man whose drawings you should see. I thought he might be represented here, but he's not."

In another room they were standing in admiration before a print of a northern Canadian lake, when a small group of noisy people entered the room and took up a position a few feet behind them. One of them, a woman, began pontificating loudly and at length about "brush strokes" and "the obvious pyramiding of the subject matter." She called the painting, which Ken thought was very good, "academic and definitely old hat."

Another of the intruders said, "Barbara's criticism has changed since she left Jake Creighoff for Steve. If a painting doesn't contain a striker being beaten over the head by a cop it's no longer art but the opiate of the artist."

Ken glanced around at them.

"What do you say to that, Rogers?" asked an ugly young woman in a tweed suit.

"I don't listen to Tommy any more since he joined the lotus-eaters."

Ken turned and looked at the painting again. He didn't understand people such as those standing behind them. Neither their lives, their manner of speech, their—anything.

The voice of the ugly, tweedy young woman asked, "By the way, Rogers, now that they're asking for volunteers for Spain here, are you going?"

Ken swung around and stared at the man called Rogers. He was a gangling young man wearing a heavy plaid shirt beneath an expensive-looking tweed jacket.

"No, darling, I'm not. I can do far more important work for the Spanish *campesino* right here at home, and for the Party also. They need just as many volunteers on the propaganda front as they do in the trenches. Why don't you ask your *petit-bourgeois* friend, Theodore East, if he's going to enlist in the Spanish Foreign Legion and fight for Franco?"

Ken looked away from them, before they caught him staring. So these people, or some of them, were friends of Theodore East. He was almost tempted to turn around and tell them that East was no more middle class than he was, but a working stiff from Cabbagetown. As for the Communist called Rogers, he'd already met several of his ilk at the parties given to raise money for the Loyalist cause. Parlour Pinks was the phrase that fitted them best.

When the group had made its noisy centre-stage exit from the room, Ken said to Noah, "Did you ever hear such a bunch of phoney-balonies in your life?"

"It takes all kinds—" answered Noah, leading the way around the room.

"You must have been listening to them. What did you think of that woman's criticism of the northern landscape?"

"It's true if she believes it," Noah said. "Anybody can criticize a painting, or any other work of art for that matter, and it can be criticized from as many angles as there are angles of vision. I don't believe she really gave a hoot about what she was saying, as long as she could say it loud enough to impress others within the sound of her voice. When anybody who is not a painter, collector or professional art critic, begins talking about 'brush strokes' or any of that high-falutin' stuff, it's a safe bet they're showing off, and have probably read such things in a catalogue at one time or another."

After leaving the gallery and getting back to Noah's room the old man treated Ken to a long discourse on painting. He seemed to have a smattering of information about different techniques, and showed Ken how etchings were done, what was meant by tempera painting, and other things that Ken immediately forgot.

When the lesson was over Ken said, "You must have been an artist yourself, Noah?"

"No. At one time I tried a little painting, but discovered I had neither the talent nor the dedication for it."

Ken told him about George Patson having tried to become a painter until he'd lost his job and consequently his sanity.

"Wasn't it G. K. Chesterton who said that art could never drive a man to madness—or that an artist never went crazy? This is in spite of what has happened to hundreds of artists, including Van Gogh and Paul Klee, the one I mentioned to you in the gallery. But you've never read Chesterton, have you? You should. I believe he said that the businessman, the logician, the mathematician went insane, but never the artist. Perhaps he was right in some things and wrong in others, as we all are." He slapped his knee and laughed. "I know without you telling me that you don't happen to think that James Branch Cabell's *Jurgen* is the great book I think it is—"

"I didn't.—"

"Maybe I'm wrong about that but right about some other things. Anyhow, Chesterton was Catholicism's greatest lay preacher in English. Being a fellow Papist I appreciate him probably more than you will."

"I didn't know you were a Catholic," Ken said.

"Bell, book and candle."

"You'd have had a lot more arguments lately if I'd known that, especially about the Church in Spain."

"I'd have been glad to argue about it, or any other aspect of the Church. I don't follow that utterly stupid rule of the nitwit that religion should never be argued about. Chesterton argues about it very well, and for an Englishman quite well indeed, from the affirmative side."

"I must have angered you sometimes, talking about the Catholic Church?"

"Not at all. Your hatred was aimed at the clergy not the religion."

"What do *you* think of the clergy?"

"I've been a professional anticlericalist for years, thirty or more to be exact. I almost became an atheist once, when I belonged to the SLP, but reason won out over socialist faith. I'd have slipped back into religious belief again anyway. It's too easy to be an atheist; much easier than being an anticlerical. That's why Voltaire, who came out with just about as many profound truths as any man who ever lived, is still comparatively unknown to the masses, while somebody else, who said nothing very poorly, is made a saint. You can offend the intelligence of a congregation, and even offend God, but be very careful when offending a bishop."

A few days following his last conversation with Noah Masterson, Mrs. Wells handed him a letter when he arrived home from work one evening. He hurried up to his room to read it, wondering who it could be from, for he seldom received mail. Before opening it he held it to his nose, but there was no discernible scent coming from it. One thing sure, the envelope hadn't been bought at the five-and-ten.

He was surprised to find it was from Theodore East, a short note written on expensive stationery and an engraved wedding invitation. He read the wedding announcement first. It invited him to attend the wedding of Miss Eloise Burton to Mr. Theodore East, the ceremony to take place the following Saturday afternoon at three o'clock at a fashionable St. Clair Avenue Church of England.

He was totally unprepared for such news, and all he could do was shake his head as he sat on the edge of his bed. He had not seen Theodore in a long time, but had never dreamt that Theodore had a steady girl friend, never mind being engaged to get married. He hurriedly opened the short note accompanying the card.

Theodore wrote that he hoped Ken would come, and that he had once met his "betrothed" (he smiled at Theodore's use of the word) when he had been working on the Canadian National Exhibition midway. Ken vaguely remembered the girl who had been with Theodore that evening, with her middle-class makeup and the straight, brushed-across-the-head hair.

Theodore was sorry not to have seen Ken lately, and so forth. He was finished with politics, and intimated that he had had a falling out with the leadership of the National Canadian Youth, especially the leader, Jack Sharpe, though he didn't say what about. Theodore advised Ken to get out of politics—all politics. "Since being so close to things up at Queen's Park," he said, "I've found out the fallacy of trying to change anything that the establishment doesn't want changed. We'll never change the world, Ken. My advice to you is to stop worrying about the downtrodden, and help yourself."

Ken laughed, crumpled the note and the wedding card into a tight ball and placed them in his pocket. When he went down to supper, he put them in Mrs. Wells's kitchen stove.

So Theodore had made it! Out of the small group of youths and girls who often hung around together in Cabbagetown and up in Riverdale Park, the only one to end up a real winner was the con-fessed opportunist, Theodore East. He chuckled to himself, so that Mrs. Wells asked him what was the matter, shifting her gaze from his face to his unfinished shepherd's pie.

"Oh it's not the supper, Mrs. Wells," he said. "It's fine. I'm laughing at the letter I got today." To mollify his landlady's concern he attacked the shepherd's pie and green peas as if he hadn't eaten for a week.

On the morning of the Saturday when Theodore was to be married, Ken Tilling walked into the grocery warehouse, tossed his hat and coat onto the nail near Barney Hackett's small cubbyhole of an office and said to Barney, "Well, I worked it."

"Worked what?"

"It's a secret," Ken answered.

"You're crazy, Tilling. I've suspected it for a long time but now I'm sure. One time you're all et up about some girl called Myrla you don't see for years at a time, and another time you're mad at, or jealous of more likely, some guy from your gang who's marrying into dough. What is it this time?"

"I'm not supposed to tell anybody."

"Then don't come in here shouting it at the top of your lungs. Are you getting married too?"

"No."

"Is it something to do with that Commie outfit you hang around with?"

"The League Against War And Fascism? Well, in a way."

"What are you loonies going to do, picket the city hall?" asked Barney, laughing.

"I'm going to Spain."

"What!"

"You heard me."

"You mean as a soldier? To fight in that spic civil war?"

Ken nodded. "My application for a passport is in now," he said. "It should be back next week. Do me a favour, Barney, and keep it under your hat until it's definite, will you?"

"How long will it be before you leave?"

"Probably as soon as my passport arrives."

"Then you'll be quitting the grocery business, just when I was about to line you up for a store managership. After me wasting my time showing you how to use the pyramid and starter-gap method of piling can displays. After you've finally learned the difference between a prune and a cantaloupe." He laughed. "Well, I'll be a son of a gun!"

"You'll have to hire another man."

"That's the easiest thing in business today. Don't forget, Ken, we'll have to go out and have a few beers together the night before you leave."

Five days later Ken received a phone call at the warehouse, telling him that his passport was waiting for him at the office of the shipping company, and to pick it up in the morning. He was also told that he would be contacted by somebody at the bus depot the following afternoon at four, who would give him his bus ticket to New York, and instructions as to whom to contact there for his ship passage.

When he hung up the phone he found he was shivering with excitement. Despite what Noah thought, the Communist Party, or at least the Communist International functionaries who were handling the sending of young men to Spain from scores of different countries, were models of efficiency. He knew, from what he had heard about a couple of other Toronto boys who had already arrived in Spain, that the whole operation was run like a well-oiled clock.

He told Barney what the phone call had been about, and thanked him for not saying anything to the office about his going away.

"I'll go upstairs right now and tell them you're quitting, that you're leaving town or something. There won't be any trouble," Barney said. "It's too bad we can't go out for those beers though, Ken."

"I'd sure like to, Barney, but I'll be pretty busy tonight."

A short time later Barney returned to the warehouse floor and handed Ken his pay envelope. "There's ten guys got applications in for your job already, and you ain't even left yet," he said.

Ken put on his hat and coat.

"Well, here's the best, Ken," Barney said, sticking out his hand.

"Thanks for everything, Barney. You're the best foreman I ever had."

"You musta had some beauts." As they shook hands Barney said, "Don't forget to drop a guy a card or somp'n sometime. Let me hear about the senoritas."

When he arrived home Ken told Mr. and Mrs. Wells that he was leaving for Spain the following afternoon.

"My goodness, Ken, I can't believe it," Mrs. Wells said. "If you get a chance to visit England you take it. The crocuses'll be coming up down in Devon and Cornwall."

"Ken's not interested in crocuses," Mr. Wells said.

During the evening he went to Noah Masterson's room to bid the old man goodbye. Noah was almost as excited as Ken was. He stamped up and down the room saying, "I wish I was your age again. I just wish I was your age!"

Noah went downstairs and came up carrying a quarterfilled bottle of gin that he had begged borrowed or stolen from somebody on one of the lower floors. When he had poured two drinks of the fiery stuff he toasted Ken's departure.

"Keep your head down, and never volunteer for anything," he said. After they had downed their drinks Noah said, "What am I talking about anyway? You'll learn. Going on the bum was the best training any young fellow could have for soldiering."

Ken refused any more drinks, wanting to leave what was left for Noah. As the old man acquired a glow-on he told Ken many anecdotes about the First World War. From a bottom drawer of his dresser he took a greasy old envelope holding his war medals and showed them to Ken. "That one with the wide stripe down the middle is the only decent one," he said. "The D.C.M. Right after the war it was good for a two-dollar stem off my old officers, including one ex-chief-of-police of this town. The other two came up with the rations."

When Ken was leaving, Noah placed his hands on the young man's shoulders and said, "I know you're not going to Spain, Ken, strictly as a young man's adventure, though that's part of it. You're not going because Byron fought for Greece, or anything like that. Try to remember that you're fighting for guys like me, who can't go. I waited for something like this for thirty years, and now when it's come I'm too old and crippled to go." He shook Ken by the hand. "I had my war, though it wasn't the one I wanted."

When he let go of Ken's hand, Ken saw that his eyes were wet behind his steel-rimmed glasses. "Goodbye, son. I'll say some mick prayers for you once in a while."

Ken swung on his heel and hurried from Noah's room. As he ran down the stairs between the second and first floors he paused, took out his handkerchief, and blew his nose. He walked quickly down the street, afraid to look up at Noah's window.

The 500 volunteers for the Spanish Republicans' International Brigades climbed down from the buses that had brought them through the Pyrenees Mountains into Spain. A sign on the small town's station read *Figueras*, which most of them mispronounced. They were ordered to fall in, and formed a long unmilitary-looking column that climbed a long hill to where a large medieval fortress commanded the mountain pass through which they had entered Spain.

After crossing a drawbridge over a moat, and into the courtyard of the fortress, they received their second meal of the day, tin plates of chickpeas and hard dry bread, and tin mugs of red wine. They squatted on the courtyard ground and ate the food, then carried their empty plates and mugs back to the long wooden tables from which it had been served. Later, according to language groups, they were led down a long series of corridors into the heart of the fort itself, where each man took possession of an army cot.

"Look after Lou, will you, Comrade?" Ken Tilling was asked by his group leader, Danny. "I'm afraid those English boys we met in Perpignan demoralized him with their talk about the war this afternoon."

"They seemed pretty disenchanted with it," Ken said.

"Well, some of them had been wounded, of course, but they're probably right in what they say. I'm telling you this because you're not a Party member. It's going to be tough from now on. We're going to be asked to fight with poor equipment, and very little of that.

Remember we're not a professional army yet, though we might be some day. When you feel let-down, or that you've been lied to, as the Englishmen felt, look around you at your comrades. All of us who are here, and the thousands more yet to come, are all going to be in the same boat."

Ken nodded, and fell asleep almost as soon as he had thrown himself on his cot and pulled the woollen army blanket up to his chin.

He awoke very early in the morning, and after looking over at Lou, who was snoring peacefully in the next cot, he climbed the long corridors and walked out to the ramparts of the fort.

Below him the small town nestled against the foothills of the mountains, while to the east the flatlands stretched to the sea. From the direction of the French border a small blacked-out train ran on toy tracks towards the south, the light from the engine cab stabbing the darkness as the fireman opened the firebox door, while in the distance a full moon dappled the surface of the Mediterranean.

Ken sat down on the thick stone wall, and listened while from behind and below him in the fort came the sound of Italian voices singing their revolutionary song, *Bandiera Rosa*. He heard a door open, and looked down into the courtyard and saw two men crossing it, laughing, and talking together in French until they entered another doorway.

Still half bewildered by all that had happened to him over the past week and a half since leaving the bus depot in Toronto, he thought back on the long trip that had brought him from Canada to Spain.

It had been a wet snowy morning at the beginning of February when he had climbed the third-class gangplank of the Cunarder *Berengaria*. As the big ship groped her way down the Hudson there were the noises of free-running winches and the plop of heavy mooring lines being stowed. The vortex of steaming water left behind by the slow-moving ship smelled green and lonely in the cold morning air.

Ken stood up on the third-class outside deck and watched the almost ethereal skyline of New York slowly disappear into the murk and falling snow as the ship gathered speed and passed out of the inner harbour, past the Statue of Liberty and into the channel between Staten Island and the mainland shore. When he became chilled by the cold North Atlantic wind he turned from the rail and went below.

There was a knock at his cabin door, and when he opened it he found a big blond young man standing there, who introduced himself as Danny and told Ken that he was the temporary leader of the group of volunteers for Spain who were aboard. Inside the cabin Danny warned Ken to be careful of what he said to strangers, who might be U.S. government agents checking on the volunteers. He handed Ken a five-dollar bill (the third he had received since leaving Toronto) and told him it was to buy cigarettes or small incidentals on the voyage.

"Have you met your cabin mate yet?" Danny asked. "His name is Lou Kargan."

"I might have met him last night at the party they threw for us at the Italian anti-Fascist club," Ken said.

"You probably did. I'll see you in the dining room at lunchtime," Danny said, smiling and closing the cabin door behind him as he left.

He had taken to Danny right away, a little puzzled by his almost imperceptible accent, and didn't find out until later that Danny was a real honest-to-God Russian Communist, who had been studying automobile assembly line techniques as a U.S.-Soviet exchange engineer in Detroit.

Though the ten Spanish War volunteers did not sit together in the dining room, Ken was able to spot them, for they fitted none of the other categories filled by the off-season tourist passengers. During the afternoon the volunteers held the first of several shipboard meetings in Danny's cabin, and it was then that Ken learned seven of the ten were from Detroit, six of them undergrads from Wayne State

University, while the other four were Danny, himself, and two foreign-born Canadians from Sudbury.

Danny began the informal meeting by saying, "Well, Comrades, most of us know each other by now, but perhaps we haven't yet met the three Canadian comrades." He introduced Ken and the two Sudbury men to the Detroit contingent.

Ken's cabin mate, Lou Kargan, said, "I'm glad to know you, Comrade. I'm sorry I didn't meet you sooner but I've been up on deck feeding the fishes since we left the pier." Then he excused himself and rushed, presumably, back to the outer deck.

After lunch Ken took a walk around the small third-class upper deck with two of the others, Joe, a little Jewish boy with horn-rimmed glasses, and a tall handsome Anglo-Saxon student called Scollard. He learned that Joe was a member of the Young Communist League, while Scollard was a YPSL, or member of the Young People's Socialist League.

One of them asked Ken what his political affiliation was, and he told him that he was not a member of any party, but supposed that he could be classed now as a Communist Party sympathizer.

"Good!" Joe said. "Scollard here calls us Party members 'Red Rotarians', which is only a mark of his *petit-bourgeois* socialist background."

Ken spent much of his time during the six-day crossing to Cherbourg in the company of a young married woman from Ohio, who sat at his table in the dining room. She was disembarking at Southampton to go up to London to buy woollen goods for a department store in a small Ohio city. Her cabin contained four bunks, but she was the only occupant, so that she and Ken enjoyed a short affair aboard from the second evening out.

The name of his temporary mistress was Stella, and when she noticed that he and the other nine volunteers were always talking together, and having meetings in one another's cabins, her woman's curiosity was aroused. Ken told her they were members of an amateur hockey team who were going to Basle, Switzerland to play a series of games with European teams. This seemed to satisfy her.

On the last evening before the Cherbourg passengers disembarked by lighter, he and Stella had a quarrel during the third-class passengers' party. When they crossed to the lighter in the early morning for the trip to the pier and railroad station, Stella was not around to bid Ken goodbye. He was glad she wasn't. Ever since the afternoon when he had walked out of the Toronto Chinatown restaurant leaving Myrla Patson, all his affairs had been of short duration, and most had ended in a break-up that he himself had caused.

Danny told the volunteers that they had been booked at first to sail on the *Ile de France*, which had left New York a day ahead of the *Berengaria*, with more than a hundred volunteers aboard.

"I sure wanted to cross on a French Line boat," Lou Kargan said.

"We're lucky," one of the Detroit boys named McMasters said, "A guy I know crossed a month ago, on a Holland-American Line ship that took ten days."

"We have to use every line we can," Danny told them. "Don't forget there's comrades coming from South America and South Africa too, as well as from the U.S.A. and from all over Europe."

"I'm glad we didn't get a booking on a North German Lloyd Liner," said little Joe Greenspan.

"I don't think any of us would be welcome on *them*," Danny said.

One afternoon Ken lay on his bunk and listened to Lou Kargan and Scollard arguing about Detroit politics and the influence of the new C.I.O. When the subject came back to Spain, as it invariably did, Ken said, "I wonder if we'll be sent to the Madrid front?"

"Not right away, I hope," Lou said. "The closer I get to this war the more training I feel I'll need."

Joe Greenspan, who was sitting on Kargan's bunk said, "Maybe they haven't time to train us."

Scollard said, "I don't think they'll even send you into the front lines, Joe." He winked at the others.

"Why not?" Joe asked, indignantly.

"You're far too small. They'll find you a job somewhere behind the lines."

"Not me they won't. I'm going to volunteer to go straight to the front. Don't worry, I can handle a rifle. I spent a year in the Wayne ROTC."

To Ken it seemed that what Scollard said was true. Joe Greenspan looked like the typical little campus pacifist, with his undersized frame and his myopic eyes peering through his horn-rimmed glasses.

(Ken thought about that moment many times later, for little Joe Greenspan turned out to be braver than any of the others in their party, and was wounded four times before he'd been in Spain a year. On the other hand Bill Scollard, who was a perfect Hollywood casting for a hero, spent all his time in Spain working for the *Intendencia* in Albacete, the base town for the International Brigades, where Ken spied him months later walking around with a briefcase in his hand.)

Until Danny put a stop to it the kidding of little Joe went on almost until they went ashore in France.

Once, McMasters said, "Comrades, can you—in all seriousness now—picture Joe in a front line trench?"

"I'll be there, don't worry," Joe said. "Don't forget I'm a Jew. I owe those Nazi-Fascists plenty."

"I'm a Jew too," said Lou Kargan, "but I can't imagine *me* in a front-line trench. I lie awake nights wondering what was wrong with living the good life back in Hamtramck."

That switched the laughter from Joe to Lou. Then somebody asked Danny, "Do you think they'll keep us all together, Comrade?"

"They're forming the Abraham Lincoln Battalion now, and so I guess most of us are slated to join it."

The morning following the third-class *au revoir* party Ken woke up to find that the ship was no longer vibrating. When he had dressed he went up on deck and saw that the big ship was lying tied up on the outside of a sea wall, and two small lighters were warping themselves across the wall from her. Beyond the placid waters of the harbour shone the red, blue or orange rooftops of Cherbourg, pretty as a postcard.

Ken went below and woke up the rest of the party. After breakfast Danny gave each of them another five-dollar bill, with some of which they tipped the cabin and dining-room stewards. Then, carrying their luggage, they crossed the sea wall to the lighters and chug-chugged across the harbour to the town.

As a moustached customs inspector in the train shed checked Ken's bag, he flashed a smile at Ken, whispered, "*Bon chance!*" winked, and waved him on.

The small boat train snaked through the spring-green Normandy countryside, its shrill little whistle beep-beeping for the level crossings. Ken stared through the compartment window at the stonewalled fields and ancient farmhouses, unable to believe that little more than a week before he had been a Toronto warehouse clerk. They all bought sandwiches and beer on the station platform at Caen, and after they entered the outskirts of Paris Scollard said, "Look, you guys, you can see the Eiffel Tower."

They all pushed to the window and looked across the miles of low rooftops to the Meccano-like structure that hardly any of them had expected to see, at least not yet.

Ken, Joe Greenspan, McMasters and Lou Kargan took a cab from the Gare Saint-Lazare, and Joe, in his college French, told the driver to take them to the Place de Combat. They went out along the Boulevard La Fayette, and turned right down the Rue Louis Blanc, and so to the Paris headquarters of the Spanish Loyalist volunteers.

When all of their small party had arrived Danny called to them from the headquarters office doorway, and they filed in, were given a cursory medical examination, and signed up formally in the International Brigades.

Ken Tilling felt a strange sense of elation then, as he came out into the stone-flagged yard and saw the crowds of young men either chatting in small multilingual groups or standing silently against the whitewashed walls of the buildings.

In a few minutes Ken and Lou Kargan were given slips of paper and directed to a nearby pension where a concierge led them to a first-floor room, containing two big double beds covered with large eiderdown quilts. The room opened right on to a dirt courtyard surrounded by a circling three-storey building. Ken told Lou it looked like a brothel, for the upper balconies were being traversed by girls and women wearing bathrobes and carrying chamber pots.

Lou went outside to see for himself, and when he returned he said to Ken, "Have you seen the plumbing here yet? It's a hole in the floor with two raised stands for your feet."

"The beds are good though," Ken said, throwing himself on to one of them so that he almost sunk out of sight.

"That probably explains France's low birth rate," said Lou. "When you go to bed here you fall asleep right away."

After they had eaten a restaurant supper with tickets given to them at the Place de Combat, Joe Greenspan and Lou Kargan took a taxi to Belleville, to visit a Jewish family whose address Joe had. Ken and Bill Scollard played the mechanical soccer game in the restaurant for a while and then went for a stroll along a nearby canal, then back in the twilight along the Avenue Jean Jaures, where the street-walkers all propositioned the handsome Bill Scollard.

By the time Lou Kargan returned from his visit with Joe's friends it was quite late, and he and Ken turned in, each with a big soft double bed for himself.

In a few minutes Lou sat up and called to Ken from across the room.

"What?"

"I hope I didn't wake you up, Ken. I feel lousy tonight."

"Why?"

"I guess I'm scared, of going to war, of going over the top, all that kind of stuff. I'm afraid I'm not going to make a very good soldier."

"You'll be okay, Lou. Don't worry about it."

"No I won't. I'm going to be scared all the time. Do you ever feel—well, a little apprehensive about what we're going into?"

"Sure I do. Everybody does."

"Right now?"

"No, not right now. I just didn't happen to be thinking about it."

"I think of it all the time," Lou said.

(Though he didn't know it then, Lou Kargan of Hamtramck, Michigan was freed of all his fears and apprehensions in about two weeks time, February 27, 1937, when the Abraham Lincoln Battalion went over the top in a suicidal daylight attack against banked enemy machine guns in an olive grove that neither he nor Ken Tilling had ever heard of up to then—but it was a sector of the Jarama Front.)

The door was flung open suddenly, and Ken heard some men talking German. The light was switched on and he and Lou stared at the two young men outlined in the doorway. They were wearing khaki twill ski jackets, and each carried a pair of long skis on his shoulder.

When the new arrivals saw that the room was occupied they spoke together, then one of them backed away and looked again at the number of the room.

Lou spoke up then, in what Ken took to be Yiddish. The two skiers answered him in German, smiling shyly. Then as they saw that Lou understood most of what they were saying they poured out their story. Ken picked out words like *Amerikanisch* and *Osterreichisch*. They came inside, leaning their skis against the wall.

Lou said, "These comrades are Austrians, and they have slips directing them to this room. I guess one of these beds is theirs." He spoke to them again, at times having difficulty making them understand. He pointed to Ken and said, "*Mein Kamerad Canadian.*"

"*Genosse,*" they murmured, smiling at him.

"Hello, Comrades."

Lou pieced together their story. He told Ken they were two of a party of twelve university students from Vienna who had skied across the Alps into Switzerland, and had later skied again into France. They had lost four of their party, one of them a girl, who had been shot down by Austrian border guards. All of them had wanted to go to Spain, and those who were left were going there, to join the German anti-Nazi Ernst Thaelmann Battalion of the International Brigades.

"I don't feel as bad as I did a while ago," Lou said.

The next morning when the American group went to the restaurant for their *café au lait* and *croissants* Lou told the others about the young Austrians.

"I'm rooming with a Negro comrade from Cuba," Bill Scollard said. "He speaks good English. He used to be a professional ball player in a Negro league in the States."

It excited them all to discover that the International Brigades were really international.

After lunch Ken bought some postcards, mailing one to Mr. and Mrs. Wells, one to Noah Masterson and another to Theodore East and his wife, addressing it to Theodore's old Cabbagetown address.

Late that evening about five hundred volunteers, black, brown, yellow and white, from a score of different countries and at least four continents, piled into a special train at the Gare d'Orléans which would take them to the Spanish border. It was a corridor train, and Ken and Joe Greenspan were jammed into a compartment with three young expatriate Germans, two Irishmen, and a Rumanian, who one of the Germans told Joe was a gypsy. One of the Irishmen, whose name was Cox, claimed to have upset the Irish fascist General O'Duffy's motor car on a Dublin street.

Each time the train stopped during the night the Irishmen would jump off and come back clutching bottles of wine. When they were drunk, long before the train reached Lyons, they tried to join the Germans who were singing Communist marching songs. Cox cried that the Irish fascists were nothing but the bastard sons of the Black-and-Tans.

The train arrived in Perpignan, near the Spanish border, the next morning, and the volunteers were marched to a large dusty school-yard at the edge of the town, where they were fed large pieces of hard dry bread which they washed down with black chicory coffee.

Ken met some Englishmen on their way home from the war, and gave them his overcoat and his suitcase full of clothes.

"How is it down there?" he asked one of them.

"It's murder, Comrade," one of them said. "Just a bloody slaughter. We were with a partisan group on the Cordova Front. They attacked us with tanks and cavalry. They just cut us to pieces."

"What was the trouble?" Lou asked.

"We had nothing but our rifles and a few potato-masher grenades, Comrade."

"How about all the Russian equipment they're receiving?"

An Englishman with his leg in a cast said, "Don't listen to that stuff, Comrade. Most of it's French or Czechoslovakian. The rifles are Russian, but they're no good. They heat up and jam, don't they, Alf?"

"I'd have given anything for a good Lee-Enfield in my hands down there. Wait till I get home and confront Harry Pollitt, the British C.P. General Secretary. I'll tell him a thing or two."

In the afternoon the five hundred volunteers climbed into buses for the trip through the Pyrenees. The convoy carried them through the winter-brown vineyard and olive grove country of the French foothills, then along a narrow paved highway that wound through a high mountain pass. When they reached the Spanish border some indolent Catalonian *milicianos*, with P.O.U.M. shoulder flashes and oversized Luger automatics in wooden holsters, looked them over distastefully and waved them on.

Ken got to his feet and stretched, gazing to the east to where the shoreline was barely visible in the morning mists. The big news about the war on the radio the night before had been that the coastal city of Malaga had fallen to a Nationalist army, and that thousands of refugees were streaming north to Valencia.

Ken wondered if Madrid would hold, and if the Loyalist militia, plus the Internationals, would be able to stem the fascists, or even stave off total defeat. Sleeping below him in the depths of this fort were five hundred young men: the dedicated, the cynical, the adventurers, the party-disciplined, the disillusioned, the rebels, the brave ones and the cowards. They were a ragtag of Communists, socialists, trade-unionists, social-reformers, intellectual anarchists, liberals, and the just plain angry, from twenty countries, drawn together by a strange social osmosis, yet each man's reason as individual as he was himself. The Internationals had already proved themselves in the suburbs of Madrid, in University City and Casa Del Campo, these amateurs who sometimes defeated the Spanish regular army, the Moors, the Spanish Foreign Legion, the Carlists, the Falange, the Italian Blackshirt divisions, aided by the German Condor Legion of the Luftwaffe, and the Portuguese. None of them knew it then, but they were already doomed to defeat, not by Spanish fascism, or Hitler, but by the machinators in Whitehall, the Quai d'Orsay and on Washington's Capitol Hill.

Kenneth Tilling felt the breeze from the sea cool against his face. From the town below the fort came the sounds of morning: a slamming door, the crowing of cocks, a hoarse voice shouting at a mule that would not stand still.

The dawn can be seen to the east, but it really comes from the west. It comes across the watcher's shoulders and envelops him in its light as he watches for it. It starts as a narrow ribbon of lighter darkness, then squeezes together before it fans high into the sky. As the watcher looks for its birth it begins at his feet and lights him, so that he becomes a part of it. The dawn is in the crease of his trousers and in the new-appeared eyelets of his shoes. The dawn is in the new shapes around him, and in the lighted fields. The dawn is a widened earth—a populated earth. The dawn is not only the beginning of the day, but the ending of the night.

# About the Author

HUGH GARNER was born in Yorkshire, England, but he grew up in the Cabbagetown section of Toronto. On his sixteenth birthday he left technical school and started work at the *Toronto Star* the following day.

During the Depression he rode freight trains across Canada and the United States, working at every conceivable kind of job. With the outbreak of the Spanish Civil War, he joined the International Brigades. He returned to Canada after the war and worked at odd jobs until World War II when he joined the Navy and served on Atlantic convoy duty until 1945.

Writer and television personality, Garner authored several books including *Storm Below, Silence on the Shore, Author, Author!, Men and Women,* and *Hugh Garner's Best Stories* for which he won the Governor General's Award for Fiction in 1963.